PENGUIN CANADA

SMOKE

ELIZABETH RUTH is the author of the acclaimed first novel *Ten Good Seconds of Silence*. She lives in Toronto.

ALSO BY ELIZABETH RUTH

Ten Good Seconds of Silence

Bent On Writing:
Contemporary Queer Tales (ed.)

Smoke

ELIZABETH RUTH

PENGUIN
CANADA

PENGUIN CANADA

Published by the Penguin Group

Penguin Group (Canada), 90 Eglinton Avenue East, Suite 700, Toronto, Ontario, Canada
M4P 2Y3 (a division of Pearson Penguin Canada Inc.)

Penguin Group (USA) Inc., 375 Hudson Street, New York, New York 10014, U.S.A.
Penguin Books Ltd, 80 Strand, London WC2R 0RL, England
Penguin Ireland, 25 St Stephen's Green, Dublin 2, Ireland (a division of Penguin Books Ltd)
Penguin Group (Australia), 250 Camberwell Road, Camberwell, Victoria 3124, Australia
(a division of Pearson Australia Group Pty Ltd)
Penguin Books India Pvt Ltd, 11 Community Centre, Panchsheel Park,
New Delhi – 110 017, India
Penguin Group (NZ), cnr Airborne and Rosedale Roads, Albany, Auckland 1310,
New Zealand (a division of Pearson New Zealand Ltd)
Penguin Books (South Africa) (Pty) Ltd, 24 Sturdee Avenue, Rosebank,
Johannesburg 2196, South Africa

Penguin Books Ltd, Registered Offices: 80 Strand, London WC2R 0RL, England

First published 2005

1 2 3 4 5 6 7 8 9 10   (WEB)

Grateful acknowledgment is made for permission to reprint lyrics from the following songs:
The Green Door: Words and Music by Bob Davie and Marvin Moore. Copyright © 1956
by Alley Music Corp and trio Music Company. Copyright Renewed. International Copyright
Secured. All Rights Reserved. Used by Permission. **Folsom Prison Blues:** Written by
John R. Cash © 1956, 1984 Renewed. HOUSE OF CASH, INC.
(BMI)/Administered by BUG. All Rights Reserved. Used by Permission.

Manufactured in Canada.

LIBRARY AND ARCHIVES CANADA CATALOGUING IN PUBLICATION

Ruth, Elizabeth
Smoke / Elizabeth Ruth.

ISBN 0-14-301624-5

I. Title.

PS8585.U847S66   2005   C813'.6   C2005-900290-5

Visit the Penguin Group (Canada) website at **www.penguin.ca**

Dedicated to the memory of Mona and Milton P.
And to Shannon Olliffe with love

The story I do not tell is the only one that is a lie.

Dorothy Allison

May 1958

The boy jolts awake in his bed. He finds the bright flicker of fire and the blur of searing heat. Orange and blue flames surround his mattress like expatriates at a flag burning. He is the flag. He screams but his voice is as distant as a fox caught in one of his father's traps out in the backwoods. It's him sounding desperate, helpless. His mother's hands wave frantically about. "Oh my God, Thomas! Do something!" His father covers him with his own nightshirt to trap the flames, lifts him from hell, runs him down the hall, drops his burning body into the white enamel bathtub. Water, water, to sizzle, fizzle and stub him out. Extinguish him. But he is too burnt already, for water. The pungent smell of singeing hair and skin is overwhelming, the stink of near-death—a halfway place—and then the agony of consciousness. *Am I dying?* the boy thinks. His father is sharp and in charge: "Goddamnit, Isabel. Get Hank. Put out that fire. NOW!" Fear clogs his father's throat, making him gag while he speaks. "Son? Can you hear me? I'm taking you to the hospital." Then his father, usually bold and unflinching, vomits beside the bathtub. This is when the boy knows; this is when he understands that he won't survive. All sound and smell rescinds, voices fade and light is replaced by a blanket of merciful darkness....

HE OPENS ONE EYE to foggy vision and a shadow moves about the room. The smell is of bleached sheets. Stale chemicals. Burnt skin and hair. An acidic paste coats his dry mouth. His face is an open wound. He moans and a familiar voice interrupts. A man's voice, but not deep.

"Hang on, son. You're going to be all right."
Dad?

1

The body leans closer. Rubbing alcohol, stale blood. Aftershave. *No. Someone else.*
The touch is cool. It lingers on his arm. A soft, reassuring hand.

THE DOCTOR FEELS the fine bristles of the brush graze his palm. He sees that water in the basin at the side of the bed is peppered with bits of flesh. Skin floats to the surface and gathers around his wrist. "I know it hurts," he says. "But the morphine should help. Your swelling has come down and I need to prevent infection. Just hold still now." The boy parts his charcoal lips. His cheeks are red and glossy, leaking fluid. One side of his face is covered in blisters. "Looks like there might be some skin loss."

"Leave me alone."

The doctor leans back, pushes his glasses up on the bridge of his nose. "I'm afraid I can't do that. Listen, I want you to try and forget what I'm doing and just follow my voice." The boy nods gingerly. "All right then. Did I ever tell you about the Purple Gang? Not a very fearsome name for a gang, I know. But they made up for it with their strong-arm tactics." The doctor works fast to clean the wounds, moves his hands quickly over the boy's forehead and rests his fingers along the hairline. The skin here is white and when he touches it the boy doesn't react. Nerves have been damaged. "It all started at the Old Bishop School," he says. "A trade school in Michigan. There were four Bernstein brothers. None of them studied much, though folks said that Abe made good grades. He was the brains behind most of their operations. At first they committed petty crimes—terrorized the Jewish quarter where they lived by stealing from shops and rolling drunks. But unlike most youngsters, those boys grew bolder with time. They blackmailed locals and extorted protection money from friends of their father. They fought with rival gangs and before long they had other young toughs working for them and a junkyard in Albion, the Riverside Iron and Metal Company—a front for their headquarters. Abe, the oldest, was the quiet one of the lot, kept to himself most of the time. He just stood back counting the money while Joe, Raymond and Izzy were busy breaking bones."

"Don't." The boy flinches, shrinks from reach when the doctor adds pressure to his scrubbing and peeling.

"The world had gone topsy-turvy, son. When the prohibition went into effect, let me think ... January of 1920 if memory serves, it was a chance to earn big money. Gambling, handbooks—that's horse-betting parlours—and of course, the booze. A good man found himself going against his conscience to keep food on the table. A bad man didn't look so bad any more, and women— women behaved as they pretty much pleased—drank, smoked, acted free and loose. But it was those border-town brats, the Purple Gang, who controlled us all; ran booze across the river from Canada and sold it as far away as Chicago and Philadelphia. Rum-running. They were famous for hijacking; interrupting a load and leaving a string of dead bodies in its wake. Took good-quality Canadian whiskey and cut it, sometimes three ways. Imagine. Operations were set up all over the city, went on round the clock supplying the blind pigs—illegal saloons. Those brothers built themselves up from penniless Eastern Europeans to swashbuckling leaders of a hard-line American mob. Oh, they were fearless."

"Fearless." The boy shifts in bed, weighs his head down into the pillow.

"That's right." The doctor drops his shoulders, sees that with no escape the boy has finally opened himself to these words, is hanging on to them—clinging to them as if they are strong ropes that might pull him to safety. He speaks more confidently now. "Wasn't long before the whole country knew them by name and no underworld operation went on without the Purple Gang taking kickbacks. I tell you, they tore through the streets of Detroit like bandits answering to no one. I still remember the first time I saw them in the flesh." He holds his hands away from the boy's face. "You ever seen a fight?"

The boy tries to shake his head but can't. His green eyes water involuntarily.

"No. Well until you've seen a real fight up close you don't know how much pain a man can really withstand. Now listen 'cause this is something I've never told anyone. It was a Sunday like today. A hot and sticky night at the Motor City gym in an industrial area out on the Lower East Side. The place didn't look like much from the street, just a deserted old building waiting on condemnation. But the second you stepped through that shady entrance, paid the girl with the tight top and red lips for your ticket and walked down the hall into the main room, you were hit with more colour and sound than you'd ever seen or heard before. Picture it: a big rectangular space, an arena is what it was, and around the grey cement walls, close up to the ceiling, flags from all the countries of this world. Stars and Stripes, of course. Any other place you can think of too. And down to the bottom, at eye level, there were hand-printed signs for the fighters when they were training, in case they might want to give up. Quit. 'Wasted talent is the oldest story in boxing,' said one. 'Second place is the first loser,' said another.

"The crowd that night was mostly common folks blowing off steam in their workaday clothes, dirty boots, caps on their heads. A few in suits. I don't know where their wives were but something told me the girls they had giggling on their knees were standing in for the evening." The doctor winks and then, feeling awkward, clears his throat. "There were young fellas too, the Bernstein brothers like I mentioned, and others more your age. I didn't know the place had been bought by the Purple Gang or I wouldn't have been there. Anyway, it smelled of old sweat, cigarettes and wet leather, ladies' perfume and all-beef wieners in mustard. You could hear bottles clinking—soda pop I thought—but when bills were exchanged under the counter I saw that it was something stronger. Could hear different languages too. Let me think now; Ukrainian, Polish, Spanish and Eye-talian."

"You almost done?"

"Almost. It was mighty warm that evening, and just when I thought things would never get going the lights came on over the ring." The doctor whistles long and high. "What a beaut. Floor the colour of sky on a clear day, and the ropes on all four sides bright as carnival candy. Each of the four judges was sitting on his side of the ring. The referees were there, in their white shirts and black pants. One of them ducked under the ropes. That's when I saw it: Abe Bernstein walking right up to a judge. I would've known him anywhere with his hollow-eyed mug always splashed across the front page of the papers. Bernstein pulled a thick wad out of his pants, peeled off a few bills and slipped them into the judge's shirt pocket. He leaned over and whispered something."

"That hurts."

"Hurts?" Doc John ignores his own trembling hand, the boy's burns being so raw. He raises his voice. "Julian Fingers Fontana versus Ruthless Eddie, now *that* hurt. But the fight never happened, see. The next thing I knew the announcer called both boxers and their coaches into the ring. There was a heated discussion, which I couldn't hear, and someone pointed to front row centre, behind the trophy table. There sat the rest of the Purple Gang, Raymond naked-chested and wearing boxer's shorts and boots, Izzy wrapping Ray's wrists and Joe passing him gloves. My heart somersaulted, I tell you. I sank down in my seat. Ruthless Eddie didn't look ruthless any more and Fingers Fontana couldn't stand still. I swear, if it'd been me I don't know what I would've done. Fight a Purple? There was no way to win."

The boy fights the urge to yawn. He is unspeakably tired.

"Fingers Fontana and Ruthless Eddie had trained all year, were ready with their best techniques. Neither wanted to take a dive. Imagine fighting when you know there's no chance of it coming out fair. Imagine having no choice. Well Raymond stepped into the ring and the other Purples consulted each other. Joe approached and pointed at Fingers who turned whiter than a bedsheet. Fingers' coach nodded like a marionette, shoved a mouthguard into the fighter's mouth and pushed him forward. Ruthless Eddie was whisked out of the ring, more than a little relieved I suppose. When the second bell sounded Raymond beat it into the ring and Fingers was up against the ropes, in his own corner, faster than you could say Boo! Ray pounded on him like a hailstorm, like he was beating on some double-crossing thief. Upper cut, another upper cut, left hook, then right. Fingers had his gloves up in front of his face, couldn't manage to fight his way out. Didn't want to try. Finally there was an opening and instinct must've kicked in 'cause he jabbed Raymond in the forehead, snapped his neck right back. Fingers slipped out of the corner and went after the gang boss hard, like a hound smelling weakness, but Raymond hadn't taken as much punishment so he recovered fast and waled Fingers square in the nose. It broke on impact and bright red blood spurted all over his face and ran down his chest. Fingers grunted like an animal in a pen, charged at Raymond, forgetting who he was fighting I guess, and waled him in that spot under his rib cage. Right here." The doctor points sharply to his own torso and the boy opens his eyes as widely as he can manage. "This area can send a big lug of a man crashing to his knees in seconds."

"That what happened?"

"Yeah. Raymond dropped like he was praying for forgiveness and pretty soon the ref was calling six ... seven ... eight seconds on him. He staggered back up and the room went woolly. Half the place was cheering for Fingers and the other half was booing him. Folks didn't know how to react. Some beat it out of there. I froze when I saw the rest of the Purple Gang sit back in their chairs and open their jackets to let us have a good look at their hardware. Izzy crossed his legs, I remember that. He crossed them leisurely and lit a cigar. The ref went through the motions of collecting the judges' results, reading them and holding the fighters' arms over their heads by the wrists. He made the announcement, kind of singing it the way they do. 'And the winner is ... Frrrrom the red corner, Raaaaaaymond Bernstein!' Well, you can guess what happened next. Fingers shoved the ref, and his coach jumped into the ring to hold him back. All three remaining Purples hopped the ropes and stood behind Raymond. Other folks were standing on their chairs, shouting obscenities at the judges. And what did the Bernstein brothers do?

They straightened their jackets and adjusted their ties. Abe pulled out a sparkling .38 Special and pointed it at Fingers. He twisted the barrel in the air, like he was taking aim, and just as Fingers squeezed his eyes shut and sucked in what he thought was his last breath, Abe pulled the trigger. It fell on an empty chamber and when Fingers opened his eyes Abe and the whole Purple Gang roared. The worst part was seeing Fingers' face cave in. Before he'd been filled with heavy wet sand and now he was a dry, hollow man. He didn't care any more what happened to him; that was plain. The sight of him empty like that has stayed with me all this time."

"Not fair."

"No." Doc John sets his brush in the basin of tepid water. "Not much in this life is." He pats his hands dry on the front of his white coat, looks up to meet the boy's eyes. "But I suppose you already know that by now." He turns towards the basin to carry it out into the hall and the boy reaches for his arm, holds him by the wrist.

"Did they kill him?"

"Fingers Fontana? No. Not that night."

The boy releases his grip, closes his eyes and drifts off with thoughts of the Purple Gang. When he wakes hours later, in the black of night, he listens for the old man's voice but finds that it isn't there. Only the story remains.

PRIME, TIE
AND CURE

Despite the sweltering heat of September 1958, in homes and stores and church basements on the sandy soil, the village of Smoke is looking forward to its hundred and fiftieth birthday. The big parade, the bake sale, the dance in the town hall are one year away although Hazel Johnson has marked the celebration on her calendar and volunteered to organize the new flag selection committee. Alice Gray, the doctor's wife, is eager to prepare her Sunday schoolers for a rendition of "God Save the Queen" full of such patriotism—such spirit—that her United Empire Loyalist ancestors won't help but shiver in their graves. And everyone assumes, despite recent family tragedy, that Tom McFiddie, wealthiest grower in the region and president of the Tobacco Growers Association, will be the one to lead the parade up Main Street.

On Main Street, meat is bought at Williams' butcher, hair cut at one of three barbers and the bakery visited daily by most wives. Deposits and withdrawals are made at the Bank of Commerce across the street from the hardware store. There are churches of course. The United, a yellow brick structure, built over a century past, sits gleaming on top of Palmer's Hill. The large copper bell rings daily, reminding even the most reluctant churchgoers of the value of toil and labour for the soul. An Anglican stone building snuggles into the side of the white pine woods on the east end and a red brick Baptist church stands directly across the road. Catholics travel a few miles south to LaSalette to worship. Most speak about the importance of decorum, modesty and good citizenship all in one breath, but *genuine* faith exists only for those who, like Doc John, understand that a lie is sometimes the best way to preserve the truth.

In the early-morning hours an enchanting fog rises and settles over the river that trickles more than pours, joining countryside to village, over frog ponds, the mill, the abandoned cannery and the Old Coal Road. Some say the place got its name because of that fog, others say it's because the secret of transforming the landscape from one of the poorest in the country to one of the richest is hidden here. People in Smoke have primed and tied tobacco for decades, cured it in kilns and then stripped it, burning the mouldy and bruised leaves out behind their barns. The fumes off a rotting heap are not something soon forgotten and they blow clear across south-western Ontario.

On each tobacco farm there is one bunkhouse with a cot and hydro for the curer—a southerner who migrates north after the Carolina and Virginia harvests. He is hired for the season and paid by the kiln. French-Canadian boys come from Northern Ontario and Quebec, having heard that they too can make their fortunes if they get themselves hired on as primers for the short, intense season. While waiting to be placed for work, they sleep in a section of a barn or near the Tillsonburg unemployment office. Local teenagers socialize under the streetlight at Main and Dover in the early evening or smoke cigarettes at the foot of the cenotaph inside the park. Most attend church functions, as this is where social life is at a high. The rest of the time they work in the fields for long hours or behind serving counters at the greengrocer's or the dry goods store, all the while *tap tap tapping* their feet to Buddy Holly and Elvis Presley and quietly, religiously, yearning for a life less predictable.

Tom McFiddie's property boasts one hundred acres, thirty-five of them tobacco, and a large brick house. The kitchen often smells of rice pudding, which his wife, Isabel, makes from one of Mary Walpole's *London Free Press* recipes. His farm, over the years, has employed more workers than any other industry in the region. Tom knew tobacco was for him the first time he heard tell of it growing on Smoke soil, for growing tobacco is a gambler's trade, as sure as betting on the races. He enjoys this. He gambles on the weather, he gambles on market demand, he gambles on producing a good enough quality of leaf to bring sufficient money at auction. Every day on the farm is a gamble and if there's no hail, no frost and nobody passing out or quitting, then he can rightfully feel that he's done his job well and that this ravishing hell has been run as smoothly as it can be run.

This year his crop is worth close to forty thousand dollars and competition is fierce so he's keeping both eyes wide open to what's going on around him. The marketing board is being implemented; he needs to have premium bales and make sure he's able to hold his own. He's instructed the handers to pass the tiers a larger bunch of leaves, more than their usual three at a time, in order to put more into a kiln. Tom pays the curer per kiln and hopes to save money this way, but he knows it's not good practice. There's been grumbling about it from the tiers because tying larger bunches means the string breaks often and it's harder to hang the sticks. The shortcut is a risk and it's at their expense. No one says anything directly to Tom. Those tiers who do as they're told—wrap their blisters, ignore their swollen wrists, get over to Doc John's for a needle against the tobacco poisoning—are the ones who will last for the duration and be hired back next season.

Harvest lasts six or eight weeks and Tom begins every day at the first hint of sunrise when a burly brume rises off the field and dew drips from the leaves. He wears a black rain suit to keep from getting soaked. The rubber heats up with the sun and creates an unrelenting vapour, a second skin, which sits over top of his own. Harvest means bending backs in the hot sun until the kiln is full, working as long as ten hours, weather depending. Once a primer's down, Tom knows, it's better he not stand straight again until lunch. It's the straightening that kills the back. Harvest means one kiln hung each day, means crouching down low in the rows, no other way to do it, where the leaves block even a hint of a breeze and temperatures seem to reach one hundred and twenty degrees.

Priming is thirsty, back-breaking work, though Tom wouldn't dream of complaining, not even if he hated every leaf and every stack, which he doesn't. "Can't use a whiner for long," he's fond of telling his boys. "A whiner can always be replaced." In fact, there isn't anyone so valuable that he can't be replaced so you'd best earn your spot before someone else grabs it away. It sounds hard, mean. But it's true, he knows. The strained, sinewy, bone-weary truth of putting in a solid day, laying your head on a pillow at night and knowing you deserve that soft landing.

UPSTAIRS INSIDE THE HOUSE Tom's youngest son, Brian—Buster he's always been called—sits on the end of his bed dressed for his first day back at school, alive but not yet thankful. It's been four months since the accident took place, three months since he returned home—an eternity for any boy. The skin on his face and neck has hemmed and tucked and sealed up for good and his eyes have grown accustomed to the velvet fog, of seeing less than what is there. Doc John won't be coming for any more checkups, so that's that. Buster's lungs weren't damaged. He's in pain but he's as healed as he is ever going to be.

From the second-floor window Buster watches the table gang near the kilns hand and tie leaves, and without knowing he is doing so, he opens and closes his right hand automatically, matching their rhythm. His fingers think they feel the gummy tobacco. His palms sweat. When the primers hunch their way down solitary rows he feels his knees bend. The men outside work fast, running two days behind schedule due to a bad hailstorm, and Buster watches as they prime the seventh level up the plant—tips they're called because they sit up high, nearest to the sky. Tips are what give a cigarette its aroma and flavour. The sand leaves at the bottom are the part of the plant that makes a cigarette burn. His father's old horse, Darlene, moves slowly down the rows pulling the wooden boat while primers set leaves on it. At the end of each row Tom unhooks the boat, attaches it to his tractor and delivers it to the table gang.

The plants have matured to their fine ripe and bubbly green and been topped, and for the first harvest that Buster can remember he is not out in the fields priming with the others, with Percy Bozek,

Bob Bryson (when he isn't hungover), with another local fellow named Frank Wadley, and with his father and Hank. He glances out the window in his brother's direction and sees that Hank could easily be their father; both are filled out in the same thick way. Same height. Same brown hair and eyes. Same solid, uncomplicated step. Buster was always the better looking of the two brothers and he knew it, but now he watches with envy as Hank removes his cap and wipes his sweaty brow. Hank is a shiny, sleek hunting knife out of its sheath.

Before his accident, Buster assumed that he would one day take over the farm. Hank prefers working with livestock; chickens or pigs. He's often playing with the barn cats or helping the neighbours with birthing a foal. Hank wants to be needed, and tobacco goes on with or without them. This is precisely what Buster's always loved about growing it: the arrogance of the plant, its indifference. Even now he swells with pride at the thought of who they—the McFiddies—are in the world because of it. It's a small world, sure, but it's the only one that's ever mattered. "Watch the burners close!" his father shouts to his curer as he passes the kiln. "If the leaves dry too quick they'll be a poor grade. Won't sell at auction."

His father supervises everyone. Babysits more like. Buster turns from the window. He has grown weary of looking out at them day after agonizing day. His only relief since returning home from the hospital has been the doctor's ongoing visits to cheer him with wild stories, and the invisibility of night. After the sun sets and his bedroom darkens, he is no longer confronted by the high, clean ceiling—plaster perfect—or his family's eyes so obviously trying to hide pity.

He looks around his room. Beside his bed stands an end table and on it a glass of water and a pitcher, both in solid cobalt blue. Also a roll of clean gauze, a pair of small scissors for cutting it, ointment to prevent infection and a brown clay bell for when he'd needed assistance. Next to the bell is a brand-new battery-operated transistor radio. "Something to lift his spirits," Walter Johnson told

Isabel when he dropped it by the house for Buster's birthday. "Give the boy something to look forward to again." His dresser is filled with clean socks and underwear, corduroy overalls and blue jeans for outdoor work. His Sunday clothes are hanging on a hook next to it.

Walter also left a photograph showing himself—portly and balding—standing on the front steps of the hardware store in his checked shirt and baggy pants, the straps of his suspenders hanging down above his knees, with one arm around his daughter, Judy Beatrice—Jelly Bean—and the other around his wife, Hazel. Buster remembers taking it three years ago, on the day that Hazel appointed herself president of the first local chapter of the Barbara Ann Scott fan club. That day Hazel also presented Jelly Bean with a figure skating doll that she'd ordered from Toronto. Jelly Bean was unappreciative though. She shook that doll, upon receiving it, shook it so hard that it seemed if it had any brains at all they might rattle and come loose from its smiling plastic head. It still sits on the counter at the hardware store, Buster knows. A miniature figure complete with lace costume trimmed in marabou, cross-eyed. Gaze fixed inward.

The smell of smoke from the fire is everywhere—in his furniture, in his bedroom walls, a lingering acrid odour that cannot be scrubbed away or aired out through open windows no matter how hard his mother tries. It reminds him daily of the accident, his own carelessness, and of his father's distance. It leaches in through his pores, lines his soul with a putrid haze and resentment so combustible that the idea of working the land again, of doing any of the things he used to do, is impossible.

Above the dresser are deep shelves built into the wall. Hank's old catcher's mitt looks down upon him with its well-oiled skin. On the next shelf sits a series of electric trains. At one time they *click-clacked* in a circle on a steel track and the whistle blew. The trains were an inheritance from his late grandfather. Also there is an atlas and a globe of the world that his father picked up in Toronto when he stopped on their way to Wasaga Beach; the continent of Australia is facing outward. Buster sighs. Before the accident the farthest he'd ever thought to travel was to the end of the Old Coal Road. Now, Australia doesn't seem far enough.

He tries to think of himself as he was before that night, getting blotto with his friends then stumbling inside his house and up the stairs angry, falling into bed in his damp and stinky clothes. Before he lit that second cigarette and alone, under his sheets, dared the rest of the whiskey to warm the back of his throat. Just a few minutes and that's all it took for him to nod off, for the white stick dangling between his fingers to land on his pillowcase and for the bottle's remaining contents to spill. His hair, like dry-brush, caught fire and burned clean back to his scalp.

Since returning home from the hospital Buster has spent hours listening to his transistor radio, waiting for the infernal ache crawling across his skull to cease. He's tried to have faith that healing is possible but the leathery gullies and ravines that are his landslide face prove it is not so; some wishes don't come true. He's heard Elvis singing *Heartbreak Hotel* and tried his best to believe in a promise of liberation. But he can't. He glances down at the blue and yellow checked sleeves covering his arms and buttoned at both wrists. His collar is tightly buttoned also, making him feel like a boy with a noose around his neck. Ugly can be like that. Tight. Ugly is a scar, a bruise, a plum-coloured attitude erupting under the surface of skin. It's real and yet it's also the mind controlling the eyes, controlling the outcome and everything strong and alive burned into submission. Ugly is a miracle turned into a monster in a split second and now Buster knows it all too well—scars that don't heal with time, just get covered up and multiply, one terrible layer on top of another until living under them feels fundamental to a person, until it's like there's never been any other way. Ugly. He almost relishes the word; at the end of the day ugly is the one sure thing he has left.

The skin on his face had melted like liquid glass, dripped and hung off him in black streamers and hardened into dead lumps and pockets and seams which the nurses and Doc John removed. They'd laid cold cloths across his face, wrapped his head in tight white gauze, pressure garments to help the new skin heal. The blood soaked through in patches. His mother had cried upon seeing him. She took his hand in her own, touched it to her soft, wet cheek.

Doc John had surprised him by showing up, familiar white coat of authority. He'd spoken with Buster's attending physician and gained special permission to take over the job of scrubbing his raw skin with a soft brush—gently at first, barely any contact—but even what little pressure he applied was like someone dragging razor blades across Buster's forehead, across his chin. The doctor sat in the chair next to the bed and distracted him from the terrible pain with stories. They barely registered at first, though when they did Buster pretended to ignore them, simply rolled onto one side laying his cheek on the cotton pillowcase that he could barely feel under the damaged skin. He stared at objects in the hospital room and imagined himself as a cold, cool thing. Plastic. Metal. Glass.

Doc John saved the best parts of his tales for when he needed to touch Buster's most damaged skin, reserved the exciting, shoot-'em-up scenes for when the boy might want to cry out. He didn't. He never did. He just lay back on his pillows with his gritty eyes closed, listening and imagining it all in colour and with sound. The doctor also implied that fighting against all odds and the loyalty of brothers was worth any life sentence that might be received, but now that Buster is back at home and the doctor won't be passing by any more he is once more a helpless and pitiable victim. Deformed. Already his imagination is beginning to falter and it's becoming impossible for him to divine any other life than the one looming ominously ahead. The throb in his temples is growing louder, his mouth drier no matter how much water he sips.

After he got home school chums called on the telephone but Buster refused their calls. What could he say? He hoped to never see them again, or rather he hoped to never have them look on him. He wanted to be relegated to a place in their minds normally reserved for the forgotten, or the dead. Donny hadn't bothered calling even once, let alone showing up, and this was a surprise. Buster didn't know what to make of it so he cavalierly brushed it off whenever his mother made mention of it. He also dismissed his brother's stilted attempts at conversation. Ignored the sweet trays that churchwomen dropped off at the house. He hadn't even permitted his mother to show Jelly Bean upstairs when she dared to visit. He was sure she stood in the front hall armed with a basket of blueberry muffins, vanilla custard or the last of the hickory nuts gathered the winter before, because she'd been sent against her will. The only person Buster found tolerable was Doc John, for *he* understood the gravity of what had happened without saying so. He didn't look through Buster full of regret or sorrow.

The familiar fields are alien to him now, and the countless sluggish green worms, stray cats and occasional thieves who live in the margins feel more like kin. He longs for the times before the accident, those warm summer nights when he'd lie back in the dirt in his blue jeans and T-shirt, surrounded by the musky scent of his own sweat, able to hear a rustle from half a mile off. He loved the farm, every rotten inch of it. And now he's stuck here. Those tall stalks outside his window are nothing but bars on a jail cell. For months he's pored over newspaper pictures of the brand-new Corvette and the Ford Thunderbird and imagined flying down Main Street in either of these. Driving out of the village past Springford, past Tillsonburg, singing a daring new rock 'n' roll song or a robust baritone calypso with his sandy blond hair blowing in the wind, the wind smoothing out his face again.

Before the accident he'd thought only about batting home runs at the ball diamond, playing practical jokes with the other boys and getting lucky enough to brag, like Hank, about reaching his hand under some girl's brassiere. The world beyond Smoke is all Buster thinks about now, escaping to a place where no one knows him, where he could start over. He loathes the thought of returning to school where he might become the butt of the very jokes he so often propagated. He hates the fields outside his window where his father's fortune was made; green for the time being but with a certain, arid fate. There is nothing now that he doesn't despise.

Through his window Buster glimpses his brother crossing the field. The early-morning sun falls on Hank's features like a warm shroud, calling attention to his strong jaw and clear eyes. Hank moves swiftly and then breaks out into a slow jog and Buster remembers when the Lions service club first built the swimming pool inside the park. It was the only pool in the county. He was seven years old at the time. The sunny afternoon of the grand opening Doc John, Walter Johnson and his father held and cut the ceremonial ribbon and Hank took him down to the big swings and the teeter-totter. They picked wild raspberries. Hank was proud to have a little brother. When their faces were crimson with delight and their bellies full they ran back to join the others, peeled from their high-cut runners and socks and shirts and shorts and cannon-balled into the deep end. Buster can barely stand to think of that day now, with Hank lean and muscular and himself carefree, perched upon his brother's shoulders like a prince.

He moves to stand before the mirror. Looking is the hardest thing he's ever done and though he's been looking frequently he instinctively turns away from the image. He tries to raise courage inside himself where there is only a thin lining left and is filled with that terrible smell that makes him gag whenever memory of the accident presses through. He still feels the singeing from when he crumpled like paper into ashes and everything truly fragile. Still feels sheets of flesh peeling back and up into black puffs, his life puckering and curling back like the lid on a tin can. His life. He stares into the mercury glass and slowly lifts his eyelids, blinking and blinking again as if his lids are heavy velvet curtains raising and lowering to make way for a new player onto a surreal stage. Please, let there be someone else behind this faded and drawn material, he thinks. But it's him every time.

His fingertips scan his melted forehead, nose, cheeks, lips, chin. The corner of his left eyelid is sealed to the top of his cheek. One nostril deformed. The top rim of one ear is partially gone. As the sun from outside shines brightly in upon him like a mean spotlight, he takes another peek. It isn't so bad. There's still some of the old him lurking under all that tough leather. Yes, his scalp hasn't suffered the damage that his face has and so his hair has grown back in, and part of his nose is more or less as it was. About a quarter of an inch changed; still, there it is all the same, his old nose. Both eyebrows and his forehead remain intact. Then, all at once, trying to turn disaster to his advantage becomes too much of a burden and a grotesque chill reaches up from inside and rattles through him as if he's an old, abandoned house. For the first time since being burned he begins to cry for no reason other than the loss, the criminal loss, and it shames him.

He reaches over to lock the door, then undoes his shirt and finds his naked chest. He unfastens his blue jeans and allows them to fall and gather around his ankles. And then he searches his entire body for beauty in smaller and smaller increments. Even less than beauty he is desperate for humanity. He reaches down between his legs and yanks and tugs violently, his eyes never moving from the mirror as a sickening kind of lust grows in his hand. It's a reminder of what living feels like and he needs to remember, if only for a few short seconds. In front of this new and odious image he is frantic and compulsive. Why me? he thinks when he comes. Why did this have to happen to me?

Through the glass patio door in the McFiddie kitchen there is a view of most of the farm. Looking at it, Isabel is filled with the same sense of pride she gets whenever the house is clean and organized, and in winter, when the snow is shovelled all the way up the drive. Satisfaction sits on her round face, a fullness that only comes at harvest when it's curing time. She grabs the handle on the door, pushes it open, and steps out of her warm kitchen into the large back patio. Tom built the rose arbours and picnic table years before, when they moved into the house—Hank just a toddler and Buster not even an idea. Opaque light rises through the clouds, a pale sheet of mother-of-pearl. She closes her eyes and allows the faint breeze and cool morning mist to absorb into her skin. The hardest weeks of the year are almost behind them. There's been no frost yet, money is expected, and her first trimester and the danger that accompanies it have passed. Buster is strong again. Isabel opens her eyes expectantly, ready for whatever challenges fall might bring.

The stripping barn is full of a sweet, ripening scent. Every day the hanger and the curer remove tobacco from the kilns, pile the leaves onto a farm wagon and take them over to the barn where they are stored until harvest is over. This year, because they're running behind, stripping is happening simultaneously. The tobacco is removed from sticks and sorted according to colour. Then it's baled. Sorting is Isabel's favourite activity to do and to watch; she loves to be reminded of the plant's variant hues, the difference between one leaf and the next, and to find each its proper home.

Six red kilns with green roofs are lined up behind the stripping barn; five are full and another is getting started on. She will avoid the kilns and the barn as she moves into the next stage of her pregnancy. Smells become excessively powerful and the humidity causes her ankles and hands to swell. She has grown more cautious with each passing day, determined to carry a healthy new baby to term. Doors and shutters in the kilns will be opened and closed according to the stage of curing; what the tobacco needs. Everything on the farm, everything in their lives, is subsumed to what Tom's crop needs. Isabel feels a twinge of jealousy. How silly, she chastises herself. How ridiculous to be envious of the land. Still, this place, she knows, monopolizes her husband's touch.

Looking out across the property, she sees the vast emerald and lime field. Tom is always there with the rest of them. Every day. Supervising. Or, if there's a free moment, bent over priming until his fingers chafe and callus, tanning to a dark brown crisp, pulling the meaty tobacco worms off his clothes, each hour as long as a single lifetime. Hank's the same; never a peep. Works when it's working time, drinks when she or Tom or the boat driver carries water out into the field. Eats her feasts of sausage and steak, hamburg, potato salad, corn, and heads back to work again with whatever needs to be done—topping, suckering, priming, stripping, sorting, wrapping the bales in brown paper and string. It's better on a farm to have as many hands as possible, and until Buster's accident Isabel was content to be grateful for her small clan of men.

Buster should be out there. He was made for the land. He was swift, confident. Alive. His stated ambition was to become the best curer around so that his father wouldn't have to hire a fellow from the South any more. It would be him Tom wanted. Now it appears that he's given up trying to impress his father. It's as though he wants nothing to do with the farm, or even the family. Isabel noticed this right away after the accident, when she tried to offer comfort in the hospital and he craned his neck away from her. He'll be the one to leave me, she's been thinking, with all her childhood fears of desertion in tow. Of any of them, it will be Buster. She fights the urge to cry as it occurs to her that he already seems gone.

A chair scrapes across the kitchen floor and Isabel turns to discover her youngest son slumped over his empty place setting, waiting on breakfast. She watches him through the glass door a moment and his downward eyes and sunken shoulders remind her of herself when she was still in England. An orphan's posture. A child without entitlement. The glimmer in nobody's eye. She wants to rush and grab him up in her arms, squeeze until he knows that he is indeed one of the wonders of her world. At the same time she feels a sharp, sadistic desire to slap him hard across his scarred face. Be thankful you're alive, she wants to shout. Stop feeling sorry for yourself! Self-pity only digs a deeper grave. Instead of doing either, Isabel opens the door, leaving it cracked a foot for fresh, cool air, and steps back inside the house.

The kitchen is warm from having cooked and served breakfast to six primers, the curer and her family—with the exception of Buster—not an hour earlier. A clear moustache of perspiration soon dots her upper lip.

"Remind me to cut this," she says, mussing Buster's messy mop as she passes him on her way across the kitchen. She grabs a full-length apron from the countertop, wraps it around her thickening waist and moves to stand before the refrigerator.

"I like it long!" Buster snaps, lifting his head and hiding his face behind a wavy curtain. "Suits the new me." His voice is low, barely audible, and fades on the word "new."

Isabel opens the refrigerator door and lifts out a bowl with two fresh brown eggs, retrieves a matchbox from out of her apron pocket and strikes it to light the gas stove.

The sound of the match striking the sandpaper strip at the side of the wooden box causes Buster to shudder. He clenches both fists and grits his teeth. For a moment he is unable to think. He slumps lower down into his chair while his mother returns to the stove and cracks speckled eggs, one after the other, into the cast-iron frying pan. They sizzle and bubble. She scrambles them with a fork.

"You all right?"

Buster folds his arms across his chest like two metal bars. He doesn't want to go to school. He knows he will be gossiped about. Not that he hasn't been already. But he knows that when he reappears at school and on Main Street tongues will cluck louder and heads will shake more sympathetically after he's passed. There is no privacy in a village, only the quiet pretence of not noticing and not knowing. He stands and storms off through the house.

"Brian Ernest McFiddie!" Isabel turns and is standing with an aluminum spatula in one hand and the other poised sternly on her hip. "I was talking to you." She knows she sounds trite, insensitive, but nothing she says or does makes any difference—it's as if he's angry with her, blames her for the accident. She calls out again. "Buster?" But he's ignoring her and there's nothing she or anyone else can say to ease the pain of this transition, so she does the only thing she can think to do, the womanly thing. She scoops the eggs onto a plate beside the home fries and bacon she'd already set aside for him, grabs cutlery from a drawer, pours a small glass of orange juice and follows her son into the living room balancing his breakfast on a Melmac TV tray. "I know it'll be awkward," she tries in a gentler tone. "But it'll be harder the longer you wait. Really. You'll feel better after you get it over with."

"No I won't." Buster spits his words like nails, each one pronounced more sharply than the previous. "You know I won't. How can I—look at me. I'm a freak!"

"Don't talk like that, I won't have it. Your whole future is ahead."

"I'm not going, so just drop it."

"Yes you *are*."

"Hank didn't finish high school. Neither did you or Dad. What's the big deal?"

"He can work with me." Tom's voice booms from the patio door. Then *stomp, stomp, stomp*—he moves through the kitchen and into the living room. "I've got plenty that needs doing. Enough to keep him busy." A lit cigarette dangles from between Tom's lips and Isabel shoots him a cross look. She's been making an effort not to smoke in the house since the accident, at least not in front of Buster, and she hoped that her husband would have the presence of mind to do the same.

"Someone in this family's got to get an education."

"He should be alongside Hank until harvest is over. He can start school a week late like he's done other years."

"Thomas, he needs to get back to his friends."

"Maybe he wants to help his old man for a change."

"Will you two stop talking about me like I'm not here! And I don't need your help. I'll find myself a *real* job." Buster says this although the instant the breath leaves his lungs he knows it isn't true. He can't imagine anyone hiring him the way he now looks. His stomach turns at the smell of his father's cigarette and he watches smoke file towards the ceiling in an unbroken line.

"Fine." Tom is hurt. "If that's the way you want it. But until you've found something better it'll be school like your mother wants or here on the farm with me. Choice is yours." He tucks his undershirt into his work pants with confidence.

Buster meets his father's unwavering brown eyes and looks for any sign that he'll relent. He sees a man who's never lost at anything, a self-made man. Now, as much as his father believes in the entrepreneurial spirit, he also believes that the only sure way to beat the accident is for Buster to put it behind him, get back out there and act as if nothing serious has happened. This, of course, is infuriating. Something *has* happened and no passing of days and nights is going to fix it.

"Things will be back to normal in no time," adds his mother.

"Normal!" Buster hollers. "Normal? I have no face to recognize. There's no such thing as normal any more!" There is no hope for the future either. He has begun to think that in a place like Smoke there never was. He's listened to Buddy Holly on the transistor radio for months singing *That'll Be the Day*. He's drifted into a half-sleep thinking how the farm was originally made by blazing trees. Fire had eaten back the tree line and stolen ground as cunningly as it stole his life out from under him while he slept. The accident feels inevitable, even when he wishes it away. It feels inevitable and somehow, his destiny. "I'm a crip, Mom. I'm not even me any more, though no one around here seems to notice." He watches grey ash fall from the tip of his father's cigarette onto the carpet.

Tom turns his back to the boy, begins flipping through the newspaper on the coffee table. "Guess it's settled then. Now eat up; I'm driving."

Buster's shoulders droop, he reaches for the plate and silverware his mother is still holding and stabs at his eggs with a vengeance. When he looks up, a mangled scowl upon his face, he's in time to catch his father and mother exchange worried glances.

TOM'S RED DODGE rattles and hums backwards along the drive with its wide fender flashing in the bright sun like a toothy smile. The name McFiddie is stencilled on the side in thick black letters. As Tom heads down the road he feels the dry pinch of his chapped skin and unwashed hair dangling in his eyes from beneath his cap. His mouth waters at the scent of a freshly cured kiln and fills him like a good meal. A Mennonite family in their horse-drawn carriage *click-clack, click-clack,* passes and waves. The man, holding the reins, tips his large wide-brimmed hat and the young woman, with a small child in her lap, smiles from under her black bonnet. Buster keeps his head low, eyes on the rubber floor mat. The windows in the Dodge are rolled down and his father speeds much faster towards Norwich, it seems, than he's ever done before. Fast, fast, carrying him backwards into an old life that will no longer fit.

The wind whips across Buster's ruddy face and directly into his lungs as if a giant bellows has exhaled. His eyes tear from the force of it and just as soon dry—salt and trepidation crystallizing. It's been so long since he's been off his own property that everything holds new fascination—a fascination tempered by anxiety. An insect hits the centre of the truck's windshield and its plump body spatters green and red. The Dodge's springs creak as they bounce over every pothole, over loose stones spinning backwards under the tires. Buster sits impassive and seething while his father lurches into a higher gear.

He can't help feeling anger; his father dutifully arranged for the business of cold cloths and changing bandages during his recovery, but he wouldn't talk with him about it. Sometimes Tom wouldn't even bring himself to look at Buster straight on. And whenever Doc John visited the house his father retired to the humid barn and sat on a bale of tobacco listening to a ginger or a tabby cat scratching at the door—no comfort to Buster, who has begun to sense that even the world of fathers and sons is off limits to him now. He shuts his eyes tightly and tries to conjure his once fine features, his tanned skin and dirty blond hair, scruffy and hanging in his green eyes. And then he remembers something the doctor told him. "Living leaves its fingerprints on each of us, son. Now yours are on the outside is all." More than providing comfort, these words made Buster realize that his boyhood was gone for good, shed as remarkably as a snake sheds its skin.

Tom leans forward and twists the knob on the AM radio, jacks up the volume so that Elvis is belting it out as they turn a sharp corner veering north onto Highway 59. There is a field of tall corn, a dozen Holsteins grazing in a pasture next to a red barn. The last of the goldenrod sway like a sea of earth tones. Morning sun warms the land and the day-song of crickets and birds accompanies Buster's rushing pulse. The whole country moves and rings and coils up inside him with the smell of corn, pig and sweet, bitter tobacco leaf, one smell and sound leaking into the next. It's peaceful. He concentrates on the radio—*Don't be cruel* ... Tom pulls to an abrupt stop forty feet from the school's entrance, shifts his truck into neutral. "Anybody gives you trouble, Buster, you let me know." He gestures to the door with a prominent chin. "Now, show 'em what we're made of."

Buster opens his mouth to protest, but making a public appearance is unavoidable and is as much for his family's sake—more so—than for his own. In the face of war, unemployment, even scandalous local affairs, the villagers always look ahead with a resounding "Never mind!" Stony-faced and tight-lipped is the only respectable way to carry on. He understands first-hand the courage this stoicism requires. He is different in a place that doesn't accommodate difference easily. Hell, even *he* doesn't. Maybe there are other villages, he tells himself, other towns and cities far away where someone like him, with his appearance the way it now is, might feel less exposed. Though if such places exist he doesn't know where. No, odd is odd. Different is different, anywhere. Even among gangsters like those in Doc John's stories. Even in sprawling, electric places like Detroit or Chicago or New York. Why should Smoke be any better? He cranks the door handle and slides out of the truck without raising his eyes. He slams the door as hard as he can and watches his father drive away, leaving him standing there to face his new life with fear and dread coursing through his body like wildfire, the gritty taste of soil sticking to his tongue.

Norwich High sits mightily on the outskirts between villages. Its yellow brick walls are two storeys high and as unyielding as Buster remembers. Open windows sparkle and wink in mocking delight. He covers his face with one hand, using it as a visor, and squints. Others arrive—three, four, five to a cluster. Hank, years before, walked to school with him, and in a rare instance Buster wishes his big brother was alongside. He faces the school like David facing Goliath, shrinks back into his mottled skin until he's certain he is surrounded by scars on all sides, and darts across the street to hide behind a large oak tree.

He watches with gigantic eyes as his best old buddy in the world, Donny Bryson, drives up in a big car with whitewall tires. It's so big, Buster thinks, it probably doesn't fit inside Mr. Bryson's garage. And then Donny skids that robin's egg blue Chevy Bel Air to a careless stop in the school parking lot and slips out the open window instead of using the door, like a flaxen-haired James Dean. How did Donny have money for it? He must've bought it second-hand, Buster thinks. Fixed it up. It hadn't occurred to Buster that while his life turned inside out, someone else's might have altered. Donny has also grown an inch or more, his chest filled out barrel-like. He even has muscles.

The most popular girls stand nearby in a small circle, comparing new clothes, a wristwatch, who is wearing a girdle. Buster knows their names: Sandra, Diane, Karen, Susan. They giggle and titter by the front entrance, craning their pale thin necks like Canada geese while Ivan Rombout and Donny slug each other, pull off their black leather jackets, sling them over their shoulders and puff up, peacocks showing off plumes.

Jelly Bean trails the others. She slips out of the school bus and runs to catch up to the older girls in her shiny navy and white saddle shoes that pinch. She is younger than her classmates by one year, and was advanced to grade ten because she is clever. She might have spotted Buster across the street before he ducked back out of view. He isn't sure. "Just keep moving," he whispers under his breath. "No one's asking you to be friendly."

Nobody asks Jelly Bean Johnson for anything. Not to a dance or to the movies or even for a walk home after school. It's her air of desperation, always trying too hard to fit in, coupled with her clumsiness, which causes people to avoid her. Her skinned knees and plum bruises mark her for an absence of grace. She's even been known, on occasion, to trip over her own two feet. Rumour has it that once she was taken, at her mother's insistence, to visit Doc John about an inner ear problem, perhaps find an organic explanation for why she was so often off balance. But it turned out that there was nothing physically wrong with her and ever since her mother accepts no excuses for what she sees as her daughter's careless and lazy habits. Hazel attributes the problem to Walter. To his kind. Not that she considers herself prejudiced. Certainly not. She simply reasons that it's the uncivilized side of the family making itself present. And she says so every chance she gets.

In an effort to compensate for her shortcomings, Jelly Bean walks, before bed each night, with the new King James Bible (in white leather) balanced on her head. She studies hard at school and rarely speaks out of turn. She keeps her clothing pressed and neat and in the winter she ceaselessly practises those ice figures Barbara Ann Scott has made famous. Though she is unlikely to ever make a nation proud, Jelly Bean would settle for the village or even her mother. The excruciating combination of her pursuit of excellence in all regards and her chronic inability to achieve it keeps her isolated from the others. She wears prim outfits the other girls envy, and her hair is bleached to an unnatural white-blond, always pinned back tightly with a bow or rolled into ringlets. She is beautiful by conventional standards, but only when standing still. The rest of the time she seems at odds with her appearance, trapped inside bumbling flesh.

It was Ivan's twin sister, Susan, who, after losing a relay race because Jelly Bean dropped the baton, publicly declared the girl to be clumsy. "She's as uncoordinated as a gimp," was how Susan put it, in true Rombout fashion, and Jelly Bean has been living up to expectations ever since. Unlike Susan, whose perpetually combative nature and leggy soldier's stride clear her a path wherever she goes, Jelly Bean moves with captive longing, insinuates her way into the tight network of girls and stands around the tattered edges of social circles with whoever will have her, biting her nails and hunching her shoulders as if she has something of which to be ashamed.

The boys take each other beyond the bounds of the schoolyard at lunch for a punch and jab and are done with it. No big messy emotional deal. Ivan might start a fist fight or tease a younger fellow until he finds himself stuttering; those are the prices to be paid for hanging out with the big boys. It's all good for building character, at least that's what Buster's father and the grown men like to say. The boys with cars head into a starless night for a chicken run out on the Wolftrack to see who will flinch and veer off first. Sometimes there are accidents near the curve before Ball's Falls. Still, all of this is nothing compared with what a girl will do to another girl. Susan, as hardened as her brother, has formed a catty little gang, a frightening horde of backward glances and grimy sneers that linger for days and weeks and even years.

Buster watches Jelly Bean walk over to Susan and the others and sighs with relief when she doesn't stop to say hello to him. Then, as if sensing his eyes on her, she turns, finds him and waves. "Hey look everybody. Look who's back. Hi Buster!" He drops his hand from his brow and ducks back flat against the tree. He stands with both arms tightly at his sides and a lump the size of a cherry jawbreaker lodged in his throat. There is whispering but nobody moves. Nobody knows what to say or how to behave. The moment holds a raw and creeping stillness that somehow tells them all to keep back. It's his one chance, Buster knows, his only moment to cross that invisible line the fire has drawn and reintroduce himself, but he can't find the courage. The familiar faces stare with blank, unmarked expressions as if the sight of one so disfigured has erased their sense of themselves. It's a look he will soon come to expect, and even take for granted. He steps up halfway to meet Donny and Ivan.

"C'mon," says Donny fidgeting with his hands. "We should make good."

"Act normal," whispers Ivan.

Buster reaches out for the secret shake and Donny hesitates, then gives the double wink, the right eye and the left. Buster tries to reciprocate but his left eyelid simply will not move. The scar has grown dense, closing the outer edge of his lid to the top of his cheek. He grimaces with the effort and this draws lingering attention to his face. Donny shuffles his feet and Ivan stares. Again Buster tries, using all the muscles in one side of his face, to force his eye into that old position and render everything right again. But it won't cooperate, and when he realizes this he drops Donny's hand.

"No big deal," Donny says, wiping his sweaty palm on his jeans. "Let's just go in." He turns, hoping his revulsion is concealed and that Buster will simply follow him back towards the others. Buster doesn't budge. He expected the others to react as he might have if the accident had happened to someone else. He expected nervous laughter. Pointing. Staring. Name-calling like "Matches McFiddie," "Buster the Combuster" or something simple and mean like "The Face." But they're being phony and this shows how profoundly different things are. Even the handshake is changed. "You coming?" Donny calls out from the bottom of the school steps.

Buster shakes his head. His face is a terrible new truth, an errant tale. Run away, run away, the morning breeze seems to whisper in his ears. Or else fall now, and know the sudden weight of exile. Ivan turns and, as if on cue, the others turn away also. Buster doesn't see or hear anything except his own hideousness and fear until everyone has scuffled safely up the school stairs and is far away inside. They're afraid of me, he thinks. They don't know me any more. He is strangely relieved.

Soon large windows open from inside the school and the distant echo of chatter and excitement carry out. It's the sound of lunch boxes, lockers, new seats being selected, rubber bands shooting through the air and the singing of the anthem, followed by laughter. So much laughter rippling, pealing, stabbing at the day until Buster knows for certain that there's no way he's walking in there now. No one is going to treat him with kid gloves ever again. Jelly Bean has a big mouth, he thinks. Why can't she mind her own business? And Ivan is a jerk. It was Ivan who'd made the dare and led the charge to taunt him into drinking to the point of blotto in the root cellar that fateful night, and now in Ivan's face Buster can see exactly how far he's fallen. But *Donny*. Donny is the one Buster is disappointed in and disappointment is far worse than any anger or resentment he carries. Donny stayed away all these months pretending there hadn't even been an accident—no sense of loyalty whatsoever—and now he's tiptoeing around, all nicey-nice. He used to be a real pal, Buster thinks. Now he's nothing but a fake. Him and his fancy car!

Buster's about to turn and head into the woods when Jelly Bean's slim figure and silky blond ponytail appear once more, this time in a second-floor window. Her poodle skirt and sweater are both lime green, and from where she's standing behind a clean pane of glass she resembles one of the mints her mother gives out in a large glass jar on the counter at the hardware store. Fresh and shiny and too flawless to be real. Then he notices that her normally scrawny frame has filled out since he last saw her. She is beautiful, he thinks.

Jelly Bean lifts her hand tentatively, opens it wider, and Buster sees in it a stop sign, a warning. He turns without acknowledging her for a second time, and heads off. Chuck you, he thinks. Chuck you Donny and Ivan, all of you. Chuck this whole stinkin' place! He stomps and kicks at tall grass along the side of the road for a good twenty minutes, trying to shake the sense of mutation that engulfs him. On every kiln, on every farm he passes he finds family names staring back, and in those unavoidable letters a reminder of what a prison life can be.

He winds alongside the park and the river where nothing has changed, where familiarity should offer comfort. He grows angrier because familiarity feels like a luxury he can no longer afford, and comfort is merely luck or self-deception. The pine and maple and oak that have stood, more or less, in the same posture for decades appear to be lording it over him, their branches like skeletal arms waving *ha ha ha!* Buster kneels at the riverbank and tosses stones at carp sleeping near the surface, tries to ping a couple in the head but misses. He could be a hotshot too, he thinks. The way Ivan and Donny are. The way Hank is and he used to be. He looks down at the surface of the river and finds the sky, the most reliable of all heaven's creations, churning and cackling like a blue-faced witch.

Ivan and Donny are boys who make trouble together. "Those darned boys," his mother would say, half disapproving and half creamy-dreamy impressed. It could be Ivan telling crude stories about his twin sister, Susan, or setting George Walker's watering troughs over-end until the hogs were snorting so fiercely that you'd swear a slaughter was on. It could be Donny hiding his sister's cat, convincing her that the mangy thing was killed by a rabid bull or smashed flat by a car. Buster used to be one of them, a prankster known more for his shenanigans than any true accomplishment. *Now look at me,* he thinks. His friends are still making mischief together while he's sick with envy that thickens in the pit of his stomach like sourdough bread. He didn't know he had it in him to be this angry but here he is, stomping through the countryside ready for a fight.

Well, as Hank would say if he'd been at school to witness what happened, "Ivan's a wise guy and Donny's a stinking bastard who sold you out." Yes sir, he's had long enough to mull it over and it's been confirmed; Ivan is the same Ivan he's always been—indifferent, callous—but Donny, it turns out, is a good-for-nothing traitor and first chance Buster gets he's gonna let him have it.

At an early age tobacco had pressed him and Ivan together, pressing so hard at times that it felt like a collision. Ivan's father and his own were often at odds—most recently because Tom is pushing hard to negotiate the new tobacco marketing board just when Len has found his rhythm on the land and made contacts. Len Rombout is the sole member of his family in the region, having moved with his wife from Leamington when Ivan and Susan were still too young for school. Len's money is new money so he's insecure and flashes it around whenever he has the chance. Occasionally Buster has found himself continuing his father's battle though today he wonders why he should bother. But Donny is a different matter. Donny is a friend Buster *chose*. He too was born and bred in Smoke though the Brysons live in a rented house on Dover Street. Bob Bryson works as a primer during harvest most years, and the rest of the time finds odd jobs—this and that. Brick laying, equipment repairs, electrical; whatever he can drum up between his drinking binges. And though Donny's father isn't wealthy or a grower, it's never mattered one iota to Buster. He and Donny have swapped comic books, laughed at the same movies. Mooned Ivan and Hank. When younger they played Cowboys and Indians and jumped off the top of Buster's garage, pretending it was a sacred mountain. They dug elaborate snow tunnels in the winter and waged war on other boys. They spent time, the two of them, fishing. Buster and Donny versus the whole world is as old a game as boys themselves. Sure all three fellas hung out together, smoked their first cigarettes in the old tree fort, drank, looked at girlie magazines and raced their bicycles, but when they went their separate ways it was understood that Ivan was on his own again and Donny was to follow Buster. In fact Donny would eat shit off Buster's shoes if Buster told him to. At least that's what Buster used to believe. His dad's a shiftless drunk, he tells himself now. Can't count on a Bryson to stand upright. What did I expect?

Buster still remembers as clear as day when he and Hank talked Donny into snooping on Susan Rombout. Early one morning they rode into the village on their bicycles, met up with Donny and pedalled up the hill to the Rombouts' farm. They stood a tall wooden ladder against the side of the house so Hank, taking his turn, could climb up to Susan's bedroom and watch her dress. Ivan turned up out of nowhere in a blind rage, shoved Buster away from his watchman's station at the bottom of the ladder, swore at Donny. He kicked the ladder out from under Hank's legs causing Hank to fall so fast that he couldn't see Susan's horrified face in the window before he came crashing down on top of Donny. Buster was doubled over, holding his gut. It *was* pretty funny come to think of it. A big tickle. But it's just another example of how Donny can be talked into anything no matter how lame. Yes, he's a toady of the very first order. Hank's arm got broke in two places that day and Susan didn't speak to any of them for a long time, but guess who stuck up for Donny when Ivan threatened to break both his legs if he ever stepped within a two-mile radius of his sister again? Who shouted down Ivan when he called Donny a lard ass? Buster that's who. And who popped Ivan square in the kisser? Hank. So, where in Sam Hill is Donny now, the one time he, Buster McFiddie, needs someone to watch *his* back? Nowhere, that's where.

The highway is visible through the trees and silent except for the occasional car or truck speeding past and then it sounds as if a zipper is being ripped open leaving a seam of road exposed. Buster wishes it would open wider, all the way, and swallow him whole. He stops and looks ahead to a sign in the distance: "Welcome to Smoke. Population 507."

He marches and marches, pressing up against the edges of his small world until morning bleeds into afternoon under the stern sunshine. The countryside is loud, an endless cacophony that starts his headache back. The gravel under his boots crunches like popped corn. Crows squabble over treetops, dragonflies with pretty blue bodies buzz around like small motorized fans and the trees in the nearby forest whisper, shout and dance maniacally in the breeze. Heading towards Arthur's Corners where the Old Coal Road will meet Highway 59, Buster thinks that maybe he'll carry on to Little Lake and never return. He could walk it, no question. His legs still work just fine. Or maybe he'll continue south and eventually reach Delhi. Smoke doesn't miss him. Why not keep going?

Getting to Windsor, where Doc John said he crossed when he left Michigan, would take days walking Highway 3, but he's got time. Maybe the doctor *was* dragged along on a rum-running vessel to treat the injured, Buster thinks, or held at gunpoint and made to smuggle booze in his black bag. Maybe he really *had*, as he said, witnessed some poor sop's body being dumped off the Ambassador Bridge? Naah. But what would it feel like to step across a border like that, Buster wonders. Right away, he knows. It would feel like being on the edge of time, in a no man's land, with no way back. He knows that because, well, he's there already isn't he? Homeless in a way.

He trudges up and down the other side of Palmer's Hill. The land here feels strange beneath his boots, the personalities of each farm palpable through the shape and contour of dirt underfoot, the holes in the road, bumps in the earth, through the colour of the fields. Each farmer's aspiration is as evident to Buster as the pig shit fuming off George Walker's place. George's troughs, fifty yards away, are lined in rows of loud grunting and groaning. The hogs sound like a town hall meeting of seniors snarling local politics through their pipes. Rombout's place comes upon him next and their "Private Property" sign stuck up at the entrance to the drive makes him even more defiant. A dirty-white flatbed is parked beside the house. Buster follows closely by the ditch at the side of the road and runs his outstretched hand through the feathery weeds growing there. He grabs a handful and pulls several stalks up and out of the earth.

His black boots begin to weigh him down like anchors dragging a sinking ship. He's been walking for hours, the longest he's walked in six months, and he is exhausted. Blisters form on his heels like small bleeding flames. The low voices of cows in the pastures soothe his aching head and he is sleepy from heat and dehydration. He pushes himself, and notices how the road underfoot feels harder and the air unusually arid for fall. The earth warms as the sun moves directly overhead and rich nutrients rise up through a blurry haze of gravel. He also realizes as he walks that he longs for school, misses his friends and science experiments, making things bubble and blow up. He misses high jump and jogging around the track. He even misses history class where the past has always felt much duller than the present. He doesn't miss home.

Finally, he reaches Arthur's Corners and is faced with a decision: north or south? All their lives divide here into sandy soil and rich clay loam. He hesitates and stares directly up at the sky, shutting his eyes to the blinding light. What would've happened to him if no one had ever grown tobacco? If his father hadn't. His retinas sting and his patchwork skin pulls taut like a canvas sack. This place doesn't belong to me any more than I belong to it, he thinks. I belong to the fire now. He takes a step forward and then stops. How will strangers react to his face? A hot fist clenches in his gut. There is no leaving, nowhere to turn, so he swivels and stomps back along the Old Coal Road exactly as he came.

By the time Buster wanders onto Doc John's porch on Main Street his new blue and yellow shirt is unbuttoned to the third hole, though he doesn't remember undoing it, the waist is hanging out one side of his blue jeans, his sleeves are rolled up above his elbows, his hands are damp and dirty and he is parched.

The Grays live smack in the village centre, in a sparkling white wood frame house with a wrap-around porch. Number 237 Main Street. Company walks up the drive and enters through a screen door at the side leading directly into Alice's kitchen, though patients always ring for Doc John at the front door off the veranda where the gold nameplate reads "John Gray, M.D." Alice is working inside the house on lesson plans for her Sunday schoolers and writing up minutes from the last Violet Rebekah's meeting while she waits for Hazel Johnson to arrive. Together they will begin a quilt for the sesquicentennial. In the past, Alice has assisted with her husband's paperwork, booked medical appointments and answered the telephone. The calls are still coming in from all over the region, although she's been whispering into the receiver of late: "No new patients right now. Try Doc Baker instead."

The doctor and his wife are two of Smoke's most upstanding citizens. They are vocal in meetings about zoning bylaws and personal hygiene. They give ten percent of their annual earnings to the United Church. Most folks have rarely seen Doc John, regardless of the occasion, dressed in anything less formal than a starched shirt, tie, vest and pressed pants. His white coat. Alice, the daughter of a strict United Church minister, is an ardent believer in the evil of drink. "Not to be confused with other spirits," she sometimes reminds her Sunday schoolers. Together, the Grays are a formal and tactful couple who never raise their voices in public, rarely disagree in private. They are childless, despite almost twenty-five years of marriage. Doc John is growing slower and feebler than a man his age should (sixty-three according to his birth certificate) and Alice, younger by ten years, worries about his flagging energy.

Buster raises his hand to acknowledge the doctor and cuts across the lawn. He mounts the front steps and hurries to drag a chair over so the old man won't struggle on his behalf. He sits, stretching his legs out before him like two felled logs.

Doc John is wearing a thin blue wool cardigan and a white dress shirt with suspenders. His pants are black with wide hip pockets. His bushy eyebrows rest high and tilt on his forehead like two downy caterpillars unable to crawl away. His hair, in the unforgiving afternoon sun, is also white and a hint of pink scalp peeks through. His face is the colour of sunlessness. He removes his old wire-frame glasses and when he speaks his jowls shake like a rooster's comb.

"Morning," he says, as if he's been expecting company. The side door slaps open and shut and Alice appears with a tall glass of milk.

"I thought that was you coming across my yard, Buster McFiddie," she smiles. "Thought you might be thirsty too." Buster stands to greet her. Her thick dark hair, streaked with grey, is cut straight across and pulled back behind her ears. She is wearing a short-sleeve pin-dotted dress. Nothing in her posture suggests that she is forcing her enthusiasm. She doesn't even flinch at the sight of him. He is more than grateful. "So you're up and about again?"

"Uh-huh." Buster offers his chair.

"Thank you, no." She waves him back down. "Hazel's on her way. Be here any minute as a matter of fact. We're quilting and trying to decide what quantities of material to order."

Doc John pokes Buster in the ribs. "These women been planning already."

"Planning?"

"For the sesquicentennial."

"Yes, and we're busy, busy, busy. We Rebekahs have become quite determined to raise a goodly amount of money for new playground equipment. Buster, can you keep a secret?" Alice winks at her husband.

"Sure."

"Hazel and I are also ordering firecrackers!" Alice's voice rises at least two notches. She rocks onto the toes of her shoes and back down again. "Not the usual sort. There's going to be a large display in all colours of the rainbow. That'll be something different won't it?"

"Fireworks," Buster repeats.

Alice holds up her finger as if it's an exclamation point and continues enthusiastically. "I know we do them time to time, but this will be some show. We'll also have darts, animal tricks, clowns, the Miss Tobacco Queen competition of course—you name it. We're going to draw a real crowd. Hazel says it'll be exotic as all get-out. Now remember, the fireworks are to be a surprise."

Buster forces a smile. Everyone he's ever met in attendance, and an overblown hundred-and-fifty-year-old party raises nothing but dread in the pit of his stomach. "As long as you don't skimp on your cream pies," he says, changing the subject.

"Oh, I won't," Alice beams. "And in the meantime don't you be a stranger around here." She reaches for Doc John's empty cup, gives him a squeeze on one shoulder. "I hope you're not going to be filling this boy with any more of those ridiculous stories, John." She faces Buster once more, smiles, and walks off into the house leaving the side door to creak and slap shut behind her.

"The sesquicentennial." Buster is sour and incredulous. "It's a whole year off."

"Well, don't let her hear you talking like that. I'm told you can never plan *too* far ahead." Doc John chuckles but a choking sensation grips him. He coughs. His stomach begins to burn, a low hot cloud that sometimes comes over him, and he coughs harder until he can't stop. The discomfort that he's been suffering on and off for years has recently grown worse, dramatically worse an hour or so after he eats. It's impossible to ignore. He leans forward in his rocking chair, grips the chrome-and-cushion arms tightly and waits for the pain and nausea to pass. Buster offers his drink but the doctor pushes the glass away and tries to catch his breath.

"John?" Alice calls out through the kitchen window. "Everything all right?"

He waves her off and gestures for the boy to thump his back, which Buster does a couple of times, and despite its doing nothing to quell the pain Alice ducks back and disappears into the house. Inside, she uncrosses her fingers from behind her back. A simple gesture, like so many of her superstitions, to buy more time.

The doctor breathes more freely and resumes his conversation. "The first time I saw fireworks it was July fourth. I was down at the riverfront with all the other spectators." Buster leans into his chair, takes a gulp of cold milk. "Jefferson Avenue was bumper to bumper. They had these barges in the middle of the Detroit River and thousands of people lined up along both shores to watch." He gestures widely with his hands as if to recreate the marvel. "Never heard anything so loud in all my life. Must've gone on for half an hour, popping them into the air and watching them fall like red, white and blue bombs. Your father and I are going to rig something like it here. You gonna stick around?"

"Suppose so," Buster says. "Where else would I go?" He thinks about Doc John's tales. Distant cities. Living incognito. "Can't even get along at school these days," he adds, searching the old man's face for an argument.

"Why's that?"

Buster shrugs and looks at the floorboards. "Guess I'm not much for people any more."

"I see," says Doc John. And he does. He knows what it is to hide. Once you start there is no stopping. "Many ways to learn besides school. Don't worry; you're just out of practice. Listen, you know about the Oakland Sugar House Gang, right?"

"The who?"

"Oh, see now to understand the Purples you've got to know about the Sugar House Gang. They taught the Bernstein brothers everything." Doc John takes a deep breath and feels the pain in his abdomen wane. With Buster healed he hasn't been telling his stories, and he realizes he misses them, misses the relief of sharing them. "Let me think ... It was Joe Bernstein who came out of the Sugar

House bunch. Of all the Bernsteins he was the most dangerous. Joe dabbled in businesses on the up and up too—had a barbershop once. He used his criminal career to save and bankroll a legitimate business. But it was when he was younger, at the Bishop school, that he met a bookie named Solly Levine who introduced him to Charles Leiter, head of the Sugar House Gang, and the man who would become his best teacher yet."

"Funny names," says Buster, pulling his chair in closer.

"Nothing funny about them. Detroit was a mixed bag. You had your Irish, your Eye-talians and your Jews like the Bernstein brothers, and they were all fighting to carve out territory. Even the boys who weren't organized added excitement. Like this blind-pig owner named Slappy so-and-so, who stood in the doorway of his establishment guarding it with a four-foot-long boa constrictor wrapped around his shoulders and a couple of hungry German shepherd dogs at his side."

"Coolsville."

"It was. Unless it was you caught in the crossfire. But as far as questionable opportunities presenting themselves you couldn't find a better place. Blind pigs, gambling, rum-running, opium dens." Doc John clears his throat and lowers his voice. "Ladies of the night."

"Is that how the Sugar House Gang made their money?"

"No, no," the doctor wags his finger. "They used a regular business to front for the rum-running. It was all about the liquor. See, the Oakland Sugar House produced cane sugar, sold it for corn syrup. Every underworld racket specialized. The Jaworski Gang in Hamtramck were known for their high-profile bank robberies. The Legs Laman bunch made a name kidnapping other gangsters for ransom. The Westside Mob squeezed money from bookmaking operations, encouraging donations for what they called betting services." The doctor sits back in his chair, plunks his feet up on the banister.

"Now when Joe Bernstein was introduced to Charlie Leiter it was like hitting the jackpot, only Joe didn't know it yet. The old man's fastest and most vicious days were over and in Joe he saw the possibilities of youth again. He took the boy under wing. Taught him simple things like how to improve his pickpocketing technique. Next, Charlie's lessons turned to the weapons and such. Joe learned how to cut the whiskey—pure chemistry—and how to cross on the river with the illegal cargo without getting caught. Joe learned how to get rich in a city dazzled by the almighty dollar, and he, in turn, passed all this education on to his brothers. With their old-timer connection, the Purple Gang was destined to become the most powerful in Detroit."

"Wow!"

"And you remember Ruthless Eddie?"

"Sure. The boxer."

"Right. He was soon as loyal to the Bernstein brothers as they were to Charlie Leiter. After the fight with Fingers Fontana, Eddie was out of work, you might say. Tainted. He had no money, few friends—no one wanted to risk an association. Some said the sweet science was ruined but I think folks exaggerate. Anyhow, Ruthless Eddie didn't want to wind up like Fingers Fontana right? Face down in a gutter with a bullet to the back of the head. So he did what any smart man would do—cozied up to the enemy."

"I can't believe it. Not after what Raymond did to him."

"Well he did. I know. It happened one rainy night at the bathhouse on Oakland Avenue. A shvitz, the Purples called it. A local fellow who'd also gone to the Old Bishop School owned the place so the gang wasn't likely to be ambushed by a rival there. The shvitz was a dark brick brownstone where you walked down a few steps and entered through a narrow basement door. The night of Ruthless Eddie's conversion, let's say, the boys dropped their clothes in a change room on a bench and each one grabbed a towel. They filed into the hottest of all the rooms, the Russian bath. The place was teeming stone walls and floor, hotter than Hades.

"There they were half-naked, defenceless, no hardware, and totally unawares when up sat two of the three other men in the room, cousins of the River Gang boss Pete Licavoli, pulling weapons out from under their towels. Had them fastened to their thighs with electrician's tape, if you can imagine. One cousin leapt towards Joe with a hunting knife. Joe managed to spot him coming at the last instant, out of the corner of his eye. He made a fast roll down to the bench below, righted himself and grabbed the knife. After a brief struggle, he managed to stab Johnny Licavoli in the heart. His chest parted like the Red Sea. Blood everywhere. Heat. Steam. He was useless. But the second Licavoli cousin had gone after Raymond with a gun and because Raymond had both his eyes closed, something he would never do again, not even when it was time to sleep, he didn't mark the danger that was coming. *That's* when Ruthless Eddie made his move."

The doctor lifts his shoulders and stretches his neck. "See, Eddie was the third one in the room. He'd been watching and trying to decide whether he was better off to stay or make a fast exit when the attacker went after Ray. Acting on fighter's instinct, he leapt from his place on the bench and grabbed the murderer's wrist before he had a chance to do any real damage. Eddie's physical strength was indisputable and the Licavoli chap couldn't resist. Eddie squeezed the thug's arm until his hand opened and the gun, hot as a branding iron, dropped onto the floor. Then Ruthless Eddie, taking every bit of rage he had bottled up inside him since that lousy night at the boxing ring, turned muscle into grace and gangster mayhem. He broke the fellow's arm in two parts and tossed him at Raymond Bernstein's feet. 'He's all yours,' said Eddie, barely realizing what he'd done."

"Why would he help Raymond?"

"He was helping himself, Buster. That's what I'm trying to tell you. Ruthless Eddie heard opportunity calling and he answered it quick. Paid off, too. Next thing he knew he was Raymond Bernstein's personal bodyguard."

"Unreal. Are you sure?"

"Sure as a shadow." Doc John leans back in his chair, drops his feet and casts one warm brown eye towards the kitchen window to judge if his wife might be listening.

"So what happened after that?"

"Oh, that, son, is a story for another time."

"Aaw, you can't leave me hanging. Let's hear the rest."

Doc John chuckles, rises from his chair, knees cracking. He stretches his arms above his head to yawn and waves Buster inside.

"C'mon. I've got something here might interest you."

BUSTER FOLLOWS HIM inside the large office with its high ceilings, where it smells of rubbing alcohol and lemon oil. Pushed up against one wall sits a Mission oak desk and a captain's chair. On the desk is a calendar with the date, September eighth, circled and next to it a rotary dial telephone, a stethoscope, a blood pressure belt, a jar of tongue depressors, a small pad of paper and a ballpoint pen. Standing at attention beside the desk is a hat tree. Across the room is a scale with weights, a wooden examination table, a locked cabinet with glass doors. Through them he notices amber, cobalt and clear glass bottles, tins filled with cotton batting, gauze strips and rubbing alcohol. Beside the cabinet there is a new refrigerator cooling vials marked with insulin and penicillin and two trays with sterilized instruments and syringes. The walls on either side of the entrance have built-in bookshelves holding medical texts, journal clippings, a copy of Charles Darwin's *On the Origin of Species,* a cherished Frank Merriwell book and row upon row of paperback novels. There is a small window above the desk but the room is otherwise lit by three lamps, each fixed to the wall inside a triangular sconce. All told, the old furnishings give the comforting impression that Buster is in practised hands.

Even though he is up to date on the latest medical discoveries and treatments, everyone understands that Doc John is a traditionalist. It's one reason they respect him. He is even rumoured to have declined work in Brantford, in the Big Hospital. And, as Buster knows all too well, he favours house calls.

One door inside the office leads into the living room of the home and the other, smaller, into a tiny washroom where patients disrobe in private or pass urine into jars for tests, leaving them on the counter of the vanity to be collected modestly. Doc John keeps a fresh change of clothes for himself hanging on the hook on the back of the door, and he shaves and sponge-bathes there rather than upstairs where he might disturb his wife in the early hours of the morning. Only once a week does he fill the claw-foot tub on the second floor and climb in for a full soak. Buster has been here before, many times. Just last year his mother dragged him and Hank in for mandatory polio vaccinations. No need to worry about telling their father about the expense, Isabel had said at the time; the vaccines were free from the government. Today, however, is the first time Buster has been invited inside to talk man to man, and for a split second he forgets about his appearance.

"Have a seat." Doc John gestures to a formidable oxblood leather chair. He lifts the top of his desk and fishes inside to find a small silver key in one corner. He moves to unlock the medicine cabinet and Buster can't tear his eyes from the bottle of whiskey there—Old Log Cabin, with a dusty label and a top that looks as if it's never been opened. It might as well be gasoline and matches at which he is staring for his poor sooty heart pumps like thunder inside his chest and he feels unusually warm. Hot. He pulls his checked shirt away from his body. By now Doc John is hunched over with his hands on his bony knees for balance, searching the shelves. "This old body," he complains with a cobweb tickle in his throat. "Can't seem to make it do what I want any more." He moves objects around on the top shelf, the middle, tries to reach under to the bottom but clutches at his stomach when the gnawing pain returns.

"Are you all right?" Buster approaches, kneels on the floor. "Here, let me help."

Doc John sucks in his breath and tries to straighten. His energy has dissipated in recent months and the pain in his abdomen has become more frequent. His voice creaks like an unhinged door. His hands fumble and drop things. Used to be he'd chase Alice around the kitchen while she giggled and swatted him away. Used to be he'd try to catch her and pin her to him for a lingering kiss, but now he can feel that his running and kissing days are almost over. "Just a stitch," he says. "It should be there. Right where I left it." He points with an arthritic finger while his other hand holds his ribs, more feebly than Buster has noticed before. Buster's been so accustomed to looking at everything and everyone from a patient's point of view that he finds it awkward to discover the family doctor to be merely human after all. He crouches lower.

"I see an inkwell. That what you want?"

"No, no, what else is there?"

"Um, a watch fob." Buster holds up the long chain. Doc John shakes his head. "The only other thing is this box."

"That's it. Give it to me." Doc John stands, moves to his chair, his breathing laboured, and Buster notices that he wears lifts in his shoes. He follows the old man across the room carrying the small dusty box, hands it over and watches as the doctor opens the lid and places his hand on top of a blue felt cloth, closing his eyes and sighing as though an old friend has finally turned up. "I've had this since I was not much older than you, if memory serves. Kept it all this time for sentimental reasons. I don't mind passing it on if you'll take good care of it. Nothing foolish, hear?" Buster nods, not knowing to what he is agreeing and yet already caught up in another of the doctor's stories. When the old man reaches his hand under the cloth, Buster's eyes follow.

"There are times when living ... when a person starts wishing things could be different. If only this or that hadn't happened, right? He gets angry and tries to bully his way through each day hurting the people who care most, sounding off at every turn. A man can turn bitter like cider vinegar, if he lets himself." Buster averts his eyes. "A person might think he has no real friends to speak of," the doctor continues. "No future in sight, though he'd be wrong. He'd be wrong to think like that. What he needs most is to keep busy until things change again. Oh sure, I know what a boy needs. I'm not *that* old. Cars. Girls. Adventure, I know." And with that, he pulls a .38 Special out from inside the box and hands it to the boy with no thought for what he might be providing other than entertainment. "Maybe you'd like it?"

Buster reaches out, trembling as if a live wire is twitching in his hand. It's thrilling to be this close to power, the power to destroy. Now it's within *his* control. He clutches the pistol tightly and feels a shift in attitude. For some it would be a new crop, or maybe a paintbrush or even a warm body to curl into. For him this old gun holds all the potential he thought had been destroyed in the fire.

"Wait a minute. I almost forgot." Doc John retrieves the pistol, opens the chamber and removes all six bullets, placing them inside his desk. Then he turns and relinquishes the gun for good. "Go on," he says. "What am I gonna do with it now except watch it collect dust? Mind, no need to mention this to anyone. This is not a toy. She's a thing of beauty, hardware like this. Deserves respect. Every time you hold her I want you to repeat after me. I know who I am. I know who I am."

"What?" Buster shifts his weight from foot to foot. What good is pretending to shoot?

"C'mon, let me hear you."

"Um," he clears his throat.

"C'mon."

"I know who I am?"

"No, not like you're asking permission. Like this." Doc John raises his narrow shoulders high and expands his chest. "From the gut. Like you mean it. Like you *really* know." Buster imitates the doctor's posture. "Good. Better." Doc John relaxes. "At least once in his life every man asks himself, Who am I? It's not always easy to answer, son. Now, you hang on to this and maybe it'll help you like it did me." The boy turns the pistol in his hand. He's never seen one this old in his father's case.

"Where'd you get it?"

Doc John stands, moves to the small bathroom, ducks inside and returns with a white fedora, a black ribbon around its base. "A friend gave it to me. Long time ago."

"Raymond Bernstein?" Buster can hardly contain his excitement. "Ruthless Eddie?"

"I knew some people who knew them." Doc John plunks the hat on top of Buster's head. "This'll help keep the sun off your face."

"Were you friends with the Purples?" Buster asks. "Or a rival? Were you *really* there? You can tell me. I won't squeal, I swear. C'mon, tell me everything!"

Everything?

Doc John shudders at this. Everything is a maelstrom he can't afford. The hair on the back of his neck stands on end. "You'd best get going," he says. "School's waiting."

Buster reaches for the box and places his new gift inside as delicately as if he's lifting an infant from a crib. "I'll take good care of her, sir. I swear."

"You do that," the doctor whispers. "You do that."

BUSTER TAKES THE BACK ROADS, stops to lie down in a cornfield with the gun box on his bony chest and examines the gun in the bright sunshine. It's blinding to look at it out of doors. Clouds roll overhead and he imagines all the times it's actually been fired. Who might've pulled the trigger? Who was injured, even killed? He will find out soon enough, but today the edges of his village move with pigs and cattle and there is no urgency for answers.

From a distance the long, narrow troughs of the Walker farm hold swine as big as calves. Sturdy enough to be ridden, Buster knows from experience. Hank often volunteered to train a few to compete in the fall fair. The best ribbon would go to the smartest, the pig that could count, the pig that could sing along. *"Su Su Suey!"* everybody would scream over the fence, and *"Suey!"* the prized pig would snort in return. Young men no different from Buster before he was burned, boys like Ivan and Donny, sneak from their homes and slip into these pastures on balmy nights. They move up behind cattle, creeping like snails barefoot and holding their breath. Then in unison, from years of practice, they shove into the side of a targeted animal as hard as possible and laugh as the dingbat cow falls over, humiliated. A boy like Ivan wanders into the field with other thoughts too, thoughts he doesn't share with his comrades. He'll encounter a calf who reaches about waist high, grab it from behind, fists full of flank, lift the tail, force himself inside and ride the animal until he finds release.

Buster lifts the pistol, aims it at the sun and pulls the trigger. *Click*. He hears it fall on an empty chamber. Squinting and partially shaded by his hat, he studies its design with the same intensity that some of his schoolmates will soon be showing for their new assignments. If the anatomy of a weapon were assigned as a topic for a school essay instead of that bloody and not-so-distant battle at Dieppe, he might become an A-plus student. He knows the violence of local games as expertly as any Rhodes scholar knows his books. He understands that sulphur and saltpetre are the primary elements in gunpowder. He's hunted partridge and pheasant for sport and wild turkey for Thanksgiving with his father and his brother. He knows the difference between the casing and the bullet as sure as he knows his family name, and how the hammer, when retracted and released, pops rather than bangs as most people expect. Once the pin sends the casing and the bullet rotating out of the chamber and through the barrel, the spin, the curve and twist, is what makes firing most powerful, like the spin of a well-thrown football. Lounging about, Buster realizes that, even knowing these things and even knowing pain at its worst, there is still so much he doesn't know. Like, how to return to school with his head held high, and what ever happened to Raymond Bernstein?

He remains hidden in the corn, dreaming and scheming and sheltered under a big blue sky, until late into the afternoon. He stares up at the clouds with the unloaded gun tucked into the waist of his blue jeans and it doesn't matter that he has no bullets. The simple fact of holding a gun, an all-powerful appendage that he can produce at will, is enough protection. The hat fits snugly on his head causing his temples to pulse, and it shades his eyes and makes him feel taller and broader and capable of real damage. Deep in those stalks on the edge of the village, distance is as far and wide as he needs it to be, and possibility endless.

Eventually he sits up and stretches, looks around for a good spot and buries the box in the middle of the field. He heads home with the pistol hidden in his jeans and budding intrigue beating close to his wounded heart.

The next morning, Buster walks the two miles to school. He arrives before any of the others and props himself up on the cement steps in front of the large doors, one leg crossed over the other knee. He's wearing his most comfortable pair of blue jeans, roomier than he remembers, a short-sleeved white T-shirt, his jean jacket and his good black leather boots, already spit-polished. Before long, Ivan and Donny come his way. Ivan spies him first.

"Look," Ivan says, lighting a cigarette.

Donny glances at Buster sitting by himself. "I hadn't figured on him coming back. Not this soon, anyway." He thinks about the time he's had riding in a flashy car, talking trash in the park with Ivan and having girls pay him attention. He isn't sure he wants to give it up just yet.

"He's asking for trouble," says Ivan, blowing large smoke rings into the air. They hover and separate and dissolve like ghostly outlines.

"He's all right." Donny swats the dirt from his jeans and steps away from the car. "I'm going over to say hello."

"Suit yourself." The stub of Ivan's cigarette dangles precariously between his lips.

Donny mounts the wide cement staircase to where Buster is sitting at the top, his knobbly knees bent and his spindly arms folded across them like twine tied too tight on a paper package. He notices that his friend's face is stretched, engraved and staring up at him crooked, carved out and two-tone. He feels his stomach turn.

"Hi Buster."

"Don. What finally brings you around? Slumming it?"

"Just wanted to say hey."

"Hey." Buster chews a stick of bubble gum.

Donny shifts his weight to one side. Tries to appear casual. "So ... how's it going?"

"It's changed," Buster says flatly.

Donny drops his head. Kicks at the school wall. "Sorry about him." He turns his back to Ivan, who is staring. "He's a goof."

"And now you're like him?"

"Um, no. Not really."

"Yeah that's what I thought." Buster gestures sharply to Ivan with his chin. "Why don't you just go on back where you came from. No one's asking for your company here." He spits on the steps at Donny's feet, a big clear gob.

Donny lowers his voice. "C'mon, I know it's rough but—"

"You don't know squat," Buster snaps. "Now, get lost. You're good at that."

Donny feels the space between them stretch out thinner and thinner like a rubber band. "Listen, why don't you come check out my new wheels? She's a '51 but she lays rubber in all three gears. I worked tobacco for Mr. Rombout to pay for her."

As soon as Buster saw Donny hanging there at school with Ivan like the weakest link in a chain of command, he knew for sure that he'd be washing his hands of his closest friend for good. When he speaks again there's no irony in his voice, no prankster's smile leaking from his otherwise serious expression. "What for?" he says. "I can see it fine from here and you know what? It looks kinda yellow."

Donny drops his arms to his sides. "Have it your way." He takes a step back. "If this is how you get your kicks now, fine by me." He lowers his voice further. "I meant to come by, you know."

"But didn't," Buster corrects. "Cry me a river."

Donny is silent. What defence can he offer? Each morning after learning of Buster's accident he'd told himself *that* was the day. That was the day he'd force himself to pass by McFiddie's and try not to gawk at Buster's freakish mug or ask stupid questions, but he'd always find a million excuses to be anywhere else. Thing was, and he knows it in the cowardly marrow of his bones as sure as he's Donny Bryson, it isn't Buster's mangled face he's been avoiding. He wishes to dispose of that night in the root cellar, fix it, make it disappear. He regrets ever going along with Ivan, urging Buster to drink more. Sorry has gradually spread through him, head to toe, like thick syrup he is now stuck in. But he isn't going to stand around and let Buster rub it in. "Nothing personal," he says. "I've been busy is all." Of course there's nothing more personal to Buster than his friend's betrayal and they both know it.

Donny feels genuine regret, sure he does. He feels the muddied embarrassment of one who hasn't tried hard enough. But who can blame him for getting on with things? Deep down, he's pretty sure Buster would've done the same. They've outgrown each other, that's all. Or the accident sparked a meanness between them that neither knew existed before, and now as Donny looks across at Buster on the stairs with an expression that shouts How dare you change everything, Buster looks back with something close to hate. The fire was a test. A test in how much one fellow can change before he can't see himself in the other any more.

"You're nothing but a two-faced traitor," says Buster. "And traitors should be shot."

"You want to be like this, go ahead." Donny is visibly shaken. "Don't say I didn't try." He turns back towards Ivan, though he knows better than to think this will be the last of it. Buster is stubborn but no true friendship ever ends. It simply cracks open like a gull's egg on a rock face and the worst part, the things that are never meant to be spoken out loud and shouldn't be, fly from lips like premature birds flung out of their nests. "Goof," Donny hisses over his shoulder.

"Told you," Ivan says, dropping the remainder of his lit butt on the grass when Donny returns. "He's bad news now. Just like his dad. Mr. McFiddie's robbing the village blind with this new marketing board, you know."

"What?" Donny is distracted.

"The tobacco marketing board."

"Oh." He never pays any real attention to adult debates. Now he tries to remember what he overheard his own father say. "Maybe regulation is a good thing."

"So you're for it then?"

"For it. Huh? I'm just saying." Donny turns to face Ivan. "If they dump the barn-buying and the favours that go along with it, things could be fair."

"Well, my dad won't be able to make ends meet at an anonymous auction." Ivan spits on the ground. "What are you now, a Commie?"

"Yeah right Ivan," Donny says, whipping his comic book out from his back pocket and swatting Ivan with it. "I'm a Commie, and you're the Crypt Keeper."

The only thing Donny knows for certain from hanging around tobacco farms over the years is that growing and priming is about as hard a thing as can be done and Buster's dad is one of the best. Donny also knows that men who want work, or need it, find it on the McFiddie farm, no questions asked. Even his own sauced-up father has stumbled into those fields for pay from time to time. He isn't going to run down Mr. McFiddie no matter how he and Buster are getting along.

"My dad says the board's been in the works for years."

"Your dad couldn't find real work if it fell on him." Ivan punches Donny in the shoulder.

"Shut your pie hole." Donny punches him back. At least his father doesn't put on airs the way Ivan's does. At least Bob Bryson is a waste of skin who knows it.

Donny also holds a soft spot for Buster's ma. She's always been kind to him, kinder than kind. Once, when he spent the night, she stayed up talking with him in the basement. Told him her memories of London. He remembers it well because after she'd leaned over on the pull-out and brushed his bangs away from his face, she'd kissed him goodnight as she always did with her own boys and her robe gaped, exposing her breasts. Donny hasn't been able to hear mention of England since that night without pining for Isabel

McFiddie. He sneaks peeks at her sideways, as if he alone is seeing her shadow dance, as if in some private way she belongs to him or with one glance could evoke belonging. He searches his clothes after they've run into one another, hoping to spot a renegade strand of her hair. He keeps the red curls until they form a bunch in his pants pocket or until they vanish after one good churn in his mother's wringer washer.

The school bell rings and the boys watch the last bus pull up and some of the girls funnel towards the entrance. Ivan, fuelled by his conversation with Donny, starts up taunting as soon as he reaches the top. "Well well, look what's here." He brushes against Buster forcefully, knocking him out of the way. "It moves," he says, shaking spasmodically. "It's alive."

"Cool it," says Donny. "Why do you always have to stir trouble?"

Buster rests his attentive gaze on Ivan, cracks his white knuckles without taking his eyes off the boy. "Got a problem?"

"I'm looking at you aren't I?"

"Rumble!" someone yells as the bell falls silent and a chant breaks out, rippling backwards into the crowd. Other kids come running from across the yard. "Fight! Fight! Fight!"

Ivan whips off his leather jacket, passes it to his twin sister for safekeeping, and rolls up his sleeves. He isn't thinking any more than he ever does. He is impulse without control or conscience.

"Don't do it," whispers Donny.

"Eat my shorts," says Ivan, already working himself into a lather. "He thinks he's too good for us now. If you aren't going to fix him I will."

Buster stands taller, sees Jelly Bean push her way through the crowd, chewing on her thumbnail and climbing to the top of the stairs. "Leave him alone," her voice squeaks. "Leave him alone, Ivan Rombout!"

Ivan grabs Jelly Bean by both arms and pushes her sharply in Buster's direction. "I dare you to kiss him then. Go on. Kiss your new boyfriend."

Jelly Bean blushes and fights back tears. She loses her balance but regains it at the last instant. Several of the other girls titter nervously but Susan looks away. Her brother picks on those who are weaker. No one knows it more intimately than she.

"Look," says Ivan, pointing. "He's got a girl defending him."

Buster steps back against the wall humiliated. His hands are shaking and his mouth is dry. Then as if realizing he has options, he reaches deeply into the waist of his blue jeans and retrieves the sleek, shiny .38 Special. He could be the laughingstock or he could be in charge again. He holds the gun out in front of himself, pointed directly into the crowd. Everybody gasps. Ivan looks at Donny and squints. "You never said he was cracked." Ivan retreats down the stairs, causing the other kids to trip backwards. "The accident's made him crazy."

Buster ignores the comment, thinks of the characters in Doc John's stories. What would Raymond Bernstein do? He twirls the gun with his pointer finger. He recognizes that Ivan is afraid of him and he enjoys this. "I think you chumps owe the lady an apology," he says loudly enough that everyone can hear. "Now, who wants to go first?" He approaches Donny, who instinctively covers his face with his hands and ducks when the barrel of the gun is pointed at his temples. "Okay then." Buster sounds agreeable yet sinister. "Okay, guess I'll just have to help you along." He cocks his head to one side, swaggers closer to Donny and leans in.

"But I didn't do anyth—"

"Say it!"

"Sorry," Donny whimpers. "Sorry, Buster."

"Not me you moron. Apologize to *her*." He gestures to Jelly Bean.

"I'm sssorry Judy. I tttake it bbback."

"Your goose is cooked Donny Bryson!" snaps Jelly Bean. "You too, Ivan. Wait till I tell my dad." She is sure her insides are glowing hot pink. No one has ever defended her in public before.

Ivan takes the opportunity to bolt, pushing through the crowd and running into the nearest patch of brush like a newly branded steer. So that's what he looks like defeated, Susan thinks. Donny, gripped by the sense that he is unable to prevent this turn of events, freezes in place, paler than usual. Jelly Bean stares with wide-open eyes, unable to believe what she is seeing.

Buster jumps on the ledge at the top of the stairs and stands before them all. He is shocked by his own behaviour. It's as if someone else has taken over. He didn't know, until pushed, what kind of violence he is capable of. This new knowledge frightens him. And gives him a charge. He stuffs the gun back under his belt and fastens his jean jacket one cool button at a time. You've got to fight to be somebody in this cruddy place, he thinks, with a satis-fied air of reclamation. Maybe ugly is my fate, but the rest is up to me. "Allow me to introduce myself!" he shouts, as the others huddle together like a frightened flock. Then he simply reassembles his clothing and without another word, walks away.

As HE WAITS to wash up outside the upstairs bathroom later that evening, Tom comes charging down the hall. "That was Len Rombout on the phone. You been threatening Ivan with a gun?" Tom whips off his hat in a flourish, tosses it on a small table. His brown hair is sun-bleached and his nose peeling. There are dark moons seducing his tired eyes. Judging by his tone of voice he isn't really asking a question.

"Whoa, he can't even shoot," says Hank, emerging with vestiges of dried toothpaste stuck in the corners of his mouth.

"Wanna try me?"

"All right, everybody. Calm down." Isabel appears in her dressing gown, belting her robe around her protruding belly. "Where in the world did you get hold of a gun, Buster?" She waddles towards him.

"I told you they'd laugh. I told you they'd think I was a freak. They did too." He lowers his voice. "At least now they'll keep it to themselves."

"Jesus Christ. How many times have you heard me say it? Never point a rifle at a human being!" Tom's face is flushed.

"It wasn't loaded, Dad." And it wasn't a rifle, he thinks.

"I don't care. What in hell's the matter with you?"

"What's the matter with me? What's the matter?" Buster's voice rises until it's a harsh explosion in his father's face. "I'm a crip, that's what! Your son is an ugly crip! Admit it!"

Tom wants to hit Buster, knock that tone and that expression of disrespect from here to Kingdom Come but he can't will himself to maintain eye contact, can't stand the sight of his own flesh and blood—his boy—destroyed in an accident he should have somehow prevented. "Len doesn't need another excuse to ride my tail these days," he shouts instead. "And I don't want to hear any more about guns at school! You hear me?"

"Jeez," says Hank. "You mean you *did* try and shoot Ivan?"

Isabel moves to place an arm around Buster. "Of course he didn't. He just wanted to be left alone, isn't that right?" Buster smells cigarette smoke on her clothing, shakes her off. God! His mother mauling him at his age! Raymond Bernstein would never have put up with this kind of treatment.

"Let's see it," Tom demands.

"What?"

"The gun. Hand it over." Tom turns towards Buster's room. Hank and Isabel follow closely. "Where did you get it? It better not be one of mine."

"Wait. Okay I'll show you." Buster charges in ahead of them, shutting and locking the door. He is once more surprised by the distinctive charcoal scent hiding in the walls. His mother applied a fresh coat of paint after the accident but it's made little difference. "Give me a minute," he calls out.

He opens and closes his dresser drawers, making noises to suggest that he is retrieving the weapon from a secret location. Then he pulls down his pyjama bottoms, scrunches his face to look even more prune-like, bites his flimsy slit of a lip to hold the screams in and rips the .38 Special from his left thigh where it's been fastened with his father's electrical tape since he changed clothes after school. He catches the pain in his throat halfway up and swallows it, pulls up his pyjama bottoms and throws the crumpled, hairy tape across the room. It sticks to the floor on the other side of his bed, out of sight. When he opens the door and hands the gun to his father, handle first, his head is already beginning to pound.

"Well I'll be," Tom says. "I haven't seen one of these for at least twenty years." He opens the chamber to confirm there are no bullets. "Where in hell did you get it?"

"Um, Doc—"

"*Wow*," Hank interrupts. "You actually tried to murder Ivan Rombout with that."

"Stop it you two. He did not." Isabel grabs the gun away from Tom before Hank has a chance. "He wanted to make himself understood." She exchanges a wordless conversation with her husband. "We *all* understand now, don't we?"

"Too bad he didn't go after Len," Tom mumbles, and when Isabel pinches him he adds, "No guns at school Buster. I mean it. Keep it in the basement with my hunting rifles or I'll confiscate it."

"Yes sir."

"Now where did you say you got it?"

Buster averts his eyes. He doesn't want to get Doc John in trouble. Besides, what right does his father have to interrogate him when he's barely spoken a complete sentence to him since the accident? "That's my business."

"*Your* business? Anything that goes on under my roof is my business, mister."

"It happened at school, Dad," says Hank.

Buster smirks and Tom grabs him by the collar of his pyjama top.

"All right." Isabel steps in between them. "All right you two, that's enough."

"You want to deal with this?" says Tom. "Fine. He's all yours. I'm turning in." He stomps off, and slams his bedroom door. On the other side, he sinks his weight against the wooden frame and stares at the unmade bed where his wife was reading one of her dime-store novels only minutes before. The book is face down on her pillow, its smooth pages spread like paper wings. He closes his eyes to it and to the room. For the first time the full implications of Buster's deformity reach him. No son of mine, he thinks. No son of mine should have to defend himself. That's my job.

In the hall, Buster drops his shoulders an inch as Hank leans in and whispers in his ear. "Can I borrow it sometime? I've got a few scores of my own to settle."

"Scoot," Isabel swats him. "I want to talk to your brother alone."

With the others out of earshot, she hands the pistol back to Buster and he feels a certain remedy with the weapon, as mighty as any two pounds of steel can be, sitting in his sweaty palm. His breath uncoils, his posture straightens. He lifts his eyes to meet his mother's. For an instant he misses her—the way things used to be between them. She leans against the wall for support, her joints loose and hollow, getting ready for the coming baby.

"Your father's right. I don't like guns in the house. I don't like them at all in fact. Someone could easily be hurt. You included. I thought you'd know better."

"I know, Mom. I'll be more careful."

"You must never threaten anyone again. Promise me?"

"Uh-huh."

"And wherever you got it you'll take it right back."

"Yes ma'am."

The disapproval on Isabel's face fades and she appears once more gentle, proud. She knows she should stay angry about something this serious for longer but can't help herself. Buster was, until this recent pregnancy, her baby, her last great accomplishment, and she's never been able to feel anything other than impressed by him for long. Now she can't bear to make his life any harder than it already is. "Promise me," she repeats. Buster nods, sensing her tacit approval, and doesn't try to stop her from ruffling his hair. Her fingers banish his migraine. "That's my little man," she says, turning to follow her husband to bed. From behind, except for the waddle, she hardly looks pregnant at all.

In his bedroom Buster finds his hat. Plunks it on his head. He will return to school with the gun. He can't help what he understands through the jump in his blood and the itch in his bones; this place feels smaller now and is shrinking daily. It's a world in which he is forever marked as damaged goods. He glances in the mirror above his dresser, holding the gun at the side of his head with the barrel pointed at the ceiling. He looks as though he's modelled himself on an outlaw.

"That's better," he tells his reflection.

One unusually warm November morning, Alice pulls aside the Barkcloth curtains and wonders what in the world is keeping Hazel this time, and there's John bundled into two sweaters, sitting in a floral-cushioned chair on the veranda rocking and voraciously reading *The Tillsonburg Observer. The Detroit Free Press* and *The American Journal of Medicine,* which he sends for from time to time, are piled in disarray beside his chair. His walking cane leans up against the porch banister. At his feet sits a black leather clarinet case and an open letter from the College of Physicians and Surgeons. The College is checking up on his books, as is usual. He stands, stretches and sits back down and Alice drops back behind the curtain unnoticed. From inside the house she listens for his movements the way a new mother listens for her baby's breathing, and hearing him slurp tea that she made from a bag, goes back to clearing the kitchen table.

Marriage is a strange, almost feverish condition, she thinks. You wake up one morning and ask yourself, Who is this man I'm married to? It's the way a new hat sits on his head or the fact that he knows the geography of cities to which he's never been, or maybe it's the faint birthmark you one day discover on the back of his neck. How could you have missed it all this time? Why has he never pointed it out before? Who is it really, lying next to you in bed? No one can say for sure. Time goes on and before you know it, it's twenty-five years later and you've stopped asking. You just accept. You accept more than you're willing to admit.

Hazel steps onto the veranda. "Getting some fresh air?"

"You caught me." He waves with the paper. Alice slides the side door open and sticks her head outside. She motions to Hazel.

"C'mon, I'll make us a fresh pot."

Once inside Hazel takes the chair closest to the window where there's a slight draft. At her age, on the flip side of time, she's been feeling warm wherever she goes. "I saw the McFiddie boy on his way to school."

"Looks dreadful doesn't he?" Alice shakes her head, runs water at the sink. "My word! He's lucky to be alive. John won't say it but I know." Alice sets the kettle on the stove burner, turns it on high.

"I think Judy was sweet on him. Completely out of the question now of course." Alice's eyes widen with interest. A faint sadness. "Don't look at me like that, Alice Gray. Don't you even start. You know exactly what I mean. He's *changed*." Hazel whispers this last part.

"I know he needs our sympathy. I'm sure Buster's still a good boy."

Hazel gives one of her dismissive snorts, the sort that remind Alice of George Walker's hogs. "Good isn't good enough. I want my daughter to have what's best. Better than I have, at any rate. You'd feel the same if you were a mother." She pulls out her needle and thread and begins sewing on the quilt.

Alice knows that Hazel's husband, Walter, is a Mohawk, that his parents lived beside the canning factory and the railway station in the east end of Smoke, supervising seasonal workers for decades until it closed and then returning to the Six Nations at the forks of the Grand. Everyone knows history. But only Hazel refuses to accept it. "What do you mean, better?"

"You know full well that I was two months along when Walter and I married. I never should have gone with him in the first place, but then the war was on and so many of our men were overseas. I guess I didn't want to be alone." She pauses, looking for Alice's reaction, and when Alice nods uncritically she continues. "So, am I the only one who's wondered what life would be like if she'd taken up with someone else?"

"What are you saying? You without Walter? And me, with someone other than John?" Alice takes a seat at the table opposite and waves her hand in the air. She laughs. "Maybe I should have. I mean, John can fix broken bones, heal abscesses and infections. I've even seen him tend a broken heart or two over time, but ask him to unplug my sink or rewire a lamp and you might as well be talking to the wall. No interest whatsoever in the practical side of life." She shakes her head lovingly. "He's got a mind for medical things alone."

"Well Walter isn't much for book learning and I'm *still* waiting for electricity in my canning room. I have a brand-new washing machine, like yours. Newfangled dryer even. I've got the best electric iron—saves hours of work. Just about every convenience a woman could want is mine, and on top of it I've got a husband who thinks he's whistling Dixie. But the things I *need?* Electricity in my canning room? No. My kitchen sink unplugged? No. The handle on the upstairs toilet replaced? No." Hazel lowers her voice, drops her eyes. "Someone more ... well someone more like me?" There is a long pause then. "From where I'm sitting, Alice, your life looks simply perfect."

Alice is embarrassed by her friend's declaration and by her own lack of honesty. There were indeed times when she reflected that she might have done well to have married differently, perhaps George Walker who'd made his feelings plain once, a long time ago before John ever took up residence in Smoke. Or the plumber from Zenda township who'd come courting before that. Who didn't have doubts? "Nothing is perfect, Hazel. You ought to know that by now. Besides, I've never been sick a day in my life. Some useless insurance policy my marriage turned out to be."

Hazel smiles at this. "But still. You couldn't ask for more."

"No babies," Alice hears herself blurt, shocked by the force of her own words. "That's been *my* cross to bear."

Hazel is still and silent at last, the womanly score now even between them. "Of course. I'm sorry. Sometimes I can be so insensitive. John's injury, I forgot."

Alice begins to sew tight stitches along the edge of a large blue square. She recites the facts as neatly as if she's had them folded in her breast pocket all this time and is just now taking them out.

"Three ribs snapped when the other vehicle slammed them head-on. He was only sixteen months you know? His lungs are still weak from the puncture. Can't run for falling short of breath. Even the stairs are hard for him now. I worry."

"I've noticed he's using his cane more often."

"Yes. Any support lessens the strain." Alice's voice bends towards shyness. "The rest couldn't be helped though."

Both women work steadily, until the kettle calls out, and with every stitch pulled Alice remembers. She remembers how a year into her marriage talk of the Dionne Quintuplets was all over the radio, frustrating for a newlywed couple trying unsuccessfully to conceive. She'd felt like a failure, a barren bride. The greasy aroma of fried pork chops permeated the air after dinner. The doors in the house were shut and she'd double-checked the pilot light on the stove. She climbed into her old spool bed beside John and soon he rolled over on top of her, began kissing her softly, more urgently. They were tentative, apprehensive from so long trying and being disappointed but soon John moved inside her, unravelling that inner quake she'd been craving. After, he fell off to one side and took a deep, mournful breath. He pulled her to him and held her reverently as if to say, You are my wife. Alice felt the itchy sensation she sometimes gets in her right palm whenever something bad is about to happen. She lifted herself up onto her elbows.

"What is it? Was that all right?" She was stinging with a slight stain of rejection.

"It's me," he admitted. "I can't." His voice cracked. "I'm unable to give you children."

"Nonsense John." Alice reached for his hand.

"I mean it. I'm physically unable." He pulled back. "There was an accident."

Alice remembers being stunned hearing about it for the first time. What a story that was! How his reckless father had been driving too fast again, how the other car was bigger and its driver intoxicated. How no one had died, thank goodness for small blessings. But little John's lower body had been trapped between the dashboard and seat. He didn't meet her eyes while he told it. She didn't believe one word.

"It's true," he said, sensing her scepticism. He ran his tongue along his top row of teeth deciding how much to confess, how much was too much. "I'm not the man you think I am."

Alice felt the damp cotton of her nightdress clinging to her rib cage. Her fingertips had turned blue with cold. You can't live with someone for a year and not notice that he's hiding something. She'd simply never found a way to ask what she hadn't wanted to know. After all, she was the only child of a minister, sheltered from life's greatest intimacies but wise enough to understand that sometimes living with a question was easier, less complicated, than living with the answer.

The conversation hung in the air over their bed like a nightmare unhatched. Then came a joyless minute when a gulf stream rushed in between them, and finally the flood. "Do you mean we can *never* have children? And you *knew*. You knew this all along and still you allowed me to marry you?"

"I wasn't sure how to tell you. I thought maybe you'd—"

"Get away from me! Don't touch me. How *could* you? How could you deceive me? You tricked me!" Alice sat up, flicked the light on. She was sobbing, hyperventilating, she wasn't sure if she was angrier because of what he'd told her or because she had been an accomplice to the deception. And what about babies? "I've been blaming myself all this time. I've been thinking it was my fault."

"It's nobody's fault." He tried to reassure her but when she spoke again it was from a place so deep even she hadn't known it existed, a bottomless place.

"How dare you! How dare you come into my life and do this."

He wanted to tell her that nothing needed to change, that they could stay together and be happy, the two of them, but in looking at her face—the mistrust flaring behind her eyes—he immediately regretted everything.

"If you want me to go ..."

"Get out! Get out of my house and don't you ever come back. I hate you!" Alice threw a feather pillow at him and the cherrywood picture frame from their wedding that was sitting on her bedside stand. It smashed to pieces on the floor.

Doc John tossed off the covers and climbed out of bed nauseous, with the weight of truths still unspoken resting on his shoulders. He stood with the broken frame at his feet, his eyes bleary from lack of sleep and his pyjamas long for his short legs. His heart breaking. He shook, trembled before Alice, before the life he had taken care to build, before its imminent collapse and the fear of what his frightened, angry young bride might do now. "I'm sorry," he said, in a tone as pure as it was on the day he'd proposed.

She wanted to hate him, Alice remembers that still. She had every right. She wanted to rob him of something precious too, though all she could bring herself to do was dent his pride. Humiliate. The truth was that she hadn't known what to say or do. She'd never met anyone like John, with or without his stories and surprises, and she didn't know, in that moment alone in the dark of their bedroom, if the shiver crawling up and down her spine was because there would be no children or because there would be no John. She wanted him. Was that possible? Her mind chased the rapid beat of her heart and with every passing minute she blamed herself for not storming out. Unable to pull away, she understood that whatever was coming, God help her, was now also her burden to carry. She remembers screaming that he was a criminal. Evil. A weak-blooded man. She said that she wished they'd never met, but she hadn't really meant those things, they just sparked out between her lips to burn him. Good. She wanted him hurt. She discovered that life was not going to unfold exactly as she'd always assumed, that her husband's past was a space largely unrecognizable to her and her future shaped by voids that might never be filled. The rest of the night passed like an endless white scream and she felt nothing but a cold knot wind up tighter and tighter inside.

Alice hadn't realized what she was getting herself into by marrying a man she'd only known a short while. She saw what everyone else did—a dapper older fellow in a crisp, well-pressed suit with polished buttons. A professional man. A person from away who adored her. A physician no less. The whole extended family approved, said he was a fine catch. "You know he don't gamble," her one aunt chimed in. "He's no big drinker," the other said. And there was the doctor himself. "I love you better than any man, Alice Armstrong. More than any man will. Won't you please marry me?" That was how he'd put it. Plain and simple. Squashing yellow tulips in her mother's garden on bended knee while looking up at her with big brown eyes that shone as promising as two gold nuggets. It had all seemed so easy. So certain. Questions don't occur when there's pushing from behind. Pushing on all sides, pushing that says how wonderful. How *natural*.

They had met on the train heading to Port Dover. She was on her way to see Guy Lombardo at the Paradise with her aunts and there he sat across from her, observant. Looking for work, he said. He was new to Canada. He kept his eyes cast down, read a medical textbook for much of the trip, she remembers, though she cannot recall its title, and then he fell asleep with his head gently knocking against the windowpane. Alice watched him. His clothes were boughten not homemade. His hands, much like her father's, looked as if they'd never known physical work and seeing them folded in his lap, every part of her cried out with the threat of a premature ending. Stay, she thought. Whoever you are. Stay.

John insisted on helping her and her aunts onto the platform, escorting them to the waiting bus and darting back to his seat on the train. And so a month later Alice was more than happy to make his acquaintance a second time when he turned up in the village to start a new practice. She'd been holding herself back for someone special—it didn't have to be a wild or wicked person as it did for other women. Someone a little different was all. Above average. Someone to hold her interest. And the community did need a physician. With all the driving and travel to surrounding parts, a local doctor's day was long and strenuous and folks had already gone through many young fellows. Only Elgin Baker, in Tillsonburg, was reliable and he couldn't possibly care for them all.

Alice raises her eyes from her handiwork to find that Hazel is also deep in thought so she resumes sewing. She made up her mind that night in their bedroom that she would never speak of John's past again, that as long as he didn't force the conversation upon her she could stay with him and be content. After all, he possessed the sweetest disposition of any man she'd met, including her soft-hearted father, may he rest in peace. John didn't cultivate a temper the way other men did. From the beginning he'd been quiet and slow to furnish an opinion and his air of contemplation had made him appear all the more wise. What most endeared Alice to him though was his steady confidence and his sense of propriety; he was a gentleman through and through—a gentle man—and every one of her girlfriends was secretly green with envy.

John had tried to do penance; Alice remembers that best. He'd spoken of forgiveness and even of adoption, written achingly beautiful and tortured letters and left them under her pillow. She still has every one, folded neatly in its envelope and piled in the corner of her fine linen drawer. All the things that never were, held safe from public scrutiny. The smell of lavender from the sachet she keeps fresh brings those times to mind each morning. How the house was full of cut flowers. How her husband's attention was lavished upon her night and day, unencumbered by distractions. He'd given fully and without hesitation. And with much soul-searching she had forgiven him. Eventually she'd welcomed him back into her bed.

For a long time, Alice asked herself questions she couldn't bear to utter out loud. If he was half the man she'd thought and yet she wanted him, what kind of woman did that make her? She watched her friends Hazel Johnson and Laura Claxton start their families, pushing prams up to town, and Isabel McFiddie act as if there were no greater station in the world than that of motherhood. Alice watched her husband out of the corner of her eye too, and noticed things about him she hadn't noticed before. How modest he was, even in slumber. The way, when they lay together as man and wife, he touched her tenderly and yet never wanted to have tenderness directed at him. How his eyelids fluttered while he slept and left her wondering what other untold confessions tossed and turned beneath them, looking for a chance to escape. She drifted off, always keeping her thoughts to herself. She now knew there was something more, something other than what they'd openly discussed, but she wouldn't admit it to herself until much later, and never to another living soul. Alice hadn't been any more able or willing to face the answers back then, so she'd simply permitted time to pass and come to accept John as he was, accept that people are often less than what we expect and more than what we imagine, and despite all of this there can be more good life lived in one square foot than in all the miles leading away from home.

Did she now wish, as Hazel had intimated, that she'd chosen differently though? Travelled abroad or married a man more like George Walker? A man who worked with his hands until they were cracked and blistered? A man with a deep voice and a loud, commanding personality? A man who could give her children? No, not really. Not once she got over having been deceived. The disclosure had changed her too, not only altered the way she saw her husband but permanently altered her sense of herself as a Christian, as a woman, and as a wife. How could it not? She'd learned that two people could become tangled together in unexpected ways. She'd discovered that good people do questionable things, and that the details of those things can be held at bay. She made up her mind, all right. She would carry on with John. At least with him the worst of it was probably over. She would be his and he would be hers, and whatever had happened before all of that she didn't want to know.

She could have pressed the issue of children and they would have adopted; John had had Elgin Baker look into it once. But Alice discovered, much to her own surprise, that she did not crave the full-time responsibility of children. Growing up she had babysat often. It was the security of love, not diapers and minding, she'd really been after. Family was more than blood and babies. Cracking the door to his previous life open, even a sliver, John had changed their pattern of relating to one another. He had breached morality by marrying her under false pretences and after her anger had subsided, and trust rebuilt, the door was still ajar. Alice slipped in and out of common decency and found herself. The terrible revelation that John was fallible, that he could be dishonest and disappointingly human, carved out a space for her to be mortal also. By the second year of their marriage she was reborn, loosened into womanhood in a way that her strict religious upbringing had discouraged. She came to feel a greater intimacy with John, discovered the earthbound nature of her own irascible existence. Sacrosanct. Gritty. Sublime. She opened herself. She even flirted with impropriety, sometimes initiating their encounters. If John could be more than one person inside their marriage, so could she.

Alice amply fulfilled what instincts to nurture she did have, through teaching Sunday school and by assisting John with his work, occasionally helping him deliver a baby. Yes, she reconciled to the fact that she'd wanted him more than she'd wanted any other life, including one with children of her own. It was true. Was that a sin? She sometimes wonders still. Am I pitied in the company of my women friends? But of course not, she tells herself. We must all, in our own ways, choose our happiness.

She could have left him, gone to live with one of her aunts in Delhi or with her parents in Ingersoll, or kept the house and learned to drive the car. John wouldn't have fought her. She'd also been young enough and pretty enough to have married again but something stopped her from leaving and it wasn't compassion for John's plight, her own stunned grief, or even her strong belief in the sanctity of her marriage vows. No, if she is to be truly honest with herself and with God she has to admit that she knew what it was as soon as it had crawled under her skin and made a home of her heart that day on the train. The possibility of real passion, simple and sure. The kind that shakes your insides like a favourite verse from the bible. First Corinthians chapter thirteen, if she was to pick one, the verse her father read on her wedding day. *Faith, hope and love; these three. But the greatest of these is love.* My word! Alice thinks. It still tingles her fingertips and explodes her taste buds remembering. Passion that only comes around once in a lifetime, if you're lucky.

So, despite his grim disclosure there was a keening love that defied loss, a pooling, swampy kind of love that sucked her down and through it like an undertow, and she hadn't wanted to rise to the surface, not even after learning there was more she didn't know, not even now, not ever.

Alice rises to attend the kettle and pours the boiling water into a Brown Betty, adds two RediTea bags, sets the lid on top and fits the cozy on for it to steep. She notices that John's chair has stopped rocking and moves swiftly to the window, peering outside. He is sitting on the edge of the chair, spine straight, assembling his clarinet. He slips the delicate cane reed between his lips to moisten it, lifts the longest tenon-and-socket joint from the case and screws the bell onto its bottom. She watches him add the top joint, force the barrel on, then the mouthpiece, slip the ligature over it and take the reed from his tongue and slide it into place. Alice grins when he fusses to line up the sharp tip of the reed with the edge of the mouthpiece. "Hazel," she says as sternly as if she's reading to her Sunday school class. "When a man gets his best trousers stained in your mother's favourite tulip bed crushing the poor little darlings and smiling up at you with the shiniest, most hopeful grin you've ever seen and all you can think is Yes, yes, yes I will! it *must* be Heaven sent."

Hazel nods. "Marriage is in sickness and in health." She measures and cuts another square for the quilt.

"Right." Alice's tone is easily back to business. "And in many ways it's the luck of the draw."

BILLS COME DUE

Isabel sits in the kitchen with her legs spread widely apart to make room for her overripe belly. A mentholated filter-tip burns in an ashtray beside her. The radio is playing. With the boys out of the house there is time to work on bills. She lifts a pile of papers and allows them to slip through her fingers. "Seed, fertilizer, a rented tractor that's only half paid for. I don't know, Tom. We've even got small equipment outstanding."

"Crop's sorted and baled," Tom says without looking up from his coffee. "Ready for auction. We'll manage. Always do."

"If we're lucky, after the mortgage there'll be a little left over for Christmas."

"Let me see." Tom reaches for an invoice, reads. "Hail and frost insurance." He sets his mug down and selects another invoice. "Wear and tear on the Dodge." He straightens and pushes the pile away. "It all adds up. We'll cut corners for a while but I'll figure something out. Every member of this family still gets a new pair of shoes at Christmas. That's the way it's always been and that's the way it'll stay."

Isabel smiles warmly. The day Tom no longer concerns himself with providing will be the day she'll know he is no longer in love with her. She feels a slackening inside. Desire. Devotion. She's heard it said that tobacco produces lust in its growers. Maybe the same is true for a grower's wife? The chewing and sucking and the air of indulgence that accompanies the divine herb could be stimulating. Tobacco has medicinal qualities; perhaps it's also an aphrodisiac. Just last night she woke in the wee hours and climbed awkwardly on top of him with the same urgent fancy. C'mon man, she'd thought. Plow *this* field. But he was too exhausted then and she can still hear depletion in his voice. She watches him lift his mug to his lips, sees the dirt caked under his ragged nails and wishes that it were her scent, instead, lingering on his fingertips. She lifts the cigarette, takes her first long drag of the day, and exhales, enjoying the sweet flavour coating her tongue. "You talked about buying one of those new priming machines. Have you given it any more thought?"

"Like to. It would speed things up. Supposed to make priming easier for the men."

"I'm not convinced it's a good idea. Len Rombout says it might damage the leaves."

"Len. And you're listening to him now? He was the last grower to install the new curing system." Tom isn't going to be out-primed or out-smarted by Len Rombout—or anyone else for that matter. "There's nothing anyone can do to stop progress, Isabel. Progress has a way of making room for itself. Fighting it only shows your ignorance."

"That so?" She sets her cigarette in the ashtray.

"Yes it is."

"Well I'll just wait and see what you bring in at auction, then. Now, would you like me to fix you something to eat?"

"Naw, I'll wait on dinner for the boys."

"They might be out all day. Hank's gone to Tillsonburg for a matinee at the Strand and Buster's at school." Isabel reaches over and draws Tom's free hand across her abdomen. "Feel the kick?"

He leans in and moves his face closer to her belly, listening while he feels for the baby. "Sounds like the ocean."

"Which one?"

"Pacific."

"Not the Atlantic?"

"Naw, too cold."

"You've never even dipped a toe into the Pacific, Tom McFiddie. How would you know the difference?"

"All right then, sounds like the Michigan Central coming over from Buffalo, *kshook-kshook-kshook*."

Isabel laughs at this. It's true. Sometimes at night her newest guppy swims inside keeping her awake and she's had the very same thought of a rapid train speeding much too fast towards home. "Think he's coming soon?"

Tom's thoughts leap forward to auction—he visualizes loading bales onto the truck and driving them to the warehouse, watching the tobacco marketing representatives walk up and down the aisles and indicate in their catalogues what they'll instruct company buyers to bid on. He sees the Dutch clock winding backwards to a reasonable price. Hears the buzzer as a buyer locks in. "I guessed wrong with Buster."

"It's too early but my back's aching already, if that's any sign."

Tom reaches around and kneads her lower back with his fisted knuckles. "How's that?"

"Hmm." Isabel closes her eyes and relaxes her shoulders, allowing the song on the radio to run through her like warm water. *Volaré*. Smoke from her burning cigarette spirals upward and spreads into the faint, carnal shape of a suggestion. All of a sudden she needs to bear down, be made still or readied. She spreads her legs another inch so that Tom might breathe in her musky scent. When she hears a moan catch deep in his throat her lips curl in satisfaction. "You sure you're not hungry?" she repeats, looking down over two milky boulders and the mountain of baby she's making.

Tom adores Isabel, always has, since that first time seeing her sitting on the bench at the railway station with her small blue suitcase in her lap. He'd stopped by the canning factory next door and on his way back to the truck noticed her alone, waiting for her new family to retrieve her. He understood that she was a Home Girl on first glance; it was her wandering, aimless expression that told him, a look in desperate search of a place to land. The corners of her mouth curved upward in relief and defiance. Her pallid, malnourished complexion spoke of abandonment. He'd wanted to bring her home himself, have his mother feed her, help her to grow. It wasn't until many years later, after she turned sixteen and her adoptive family dismissed her, that he fell in a romantic way, hard and soupy, so that his torso went rigid but all his limbs went to rubber when she was near. It was her full hips and her big laugh and mostly it was her absolute refusal to be defeated that sunk him for good.

She'd been standing outside the greengrocer that overcast afternoon, frantically nursing a cigarette. "Hello," he said, on his way into the store.

"Humph." She was indignant, dismissive.

"Isabel?" He stopped.

"They put me out. After all these years, they actually put me out."

He'd known others, most of them boys, who were never fully adopted into their new families but instead raised alongside the natural children, treated as free labour and dismissed when the law required that they be paid. He reached for her arm but stopped when he was met with sharp, cutting eyes. He did not find the tears he expected, but one cold, clear pearl of rage rolling down her cheek. Isabel dropped her cigarette and crushed it with the heel of her shoe. "Time to make my own family," she said, walking off. He'd watched her leave that day and thought, Isabel will never be alone again. Isabel belongs with me.

He's bound to her. She charms, intoxicates. She overflows with affection in an earthy, sensuous way he'd never found in other women. Her cotton dresses don't hang with straight lines and flat fronts as they are meant to. Her red hair rarely stays pinned into place. No matter how plain or how controlled the attempt at self-presentation, Isabel appears to tumble out of her clothing as defiantly as a daredevil tumbles over Niagara Falls.

He is most powerfully drawn to her in spring when it's planting time, as if the ten thousand tobacco seeds found in just one ounce are a measure of his potency, and spreading those seeds across sterilized beds is like making love to a virgin all over again. He glances through the glass door towards that other territory he does so love to tame. Powdery flakes melt as soon as they hit the ground. He listens for footsteps in the garden. "Boys might be back early."

Isabel spreads her legs even wider now—as widely as they will stretch, and lifts her grey wool skirt an inch. "Better hurry then." She smiles, pulling him closer, and struggles down onto her back on the floor so that he might be more convinced.

After this Tom pays no mind to the possibility of interruptions. He turns and drops to his knees where he nuzzles his face in between his wife's thick thighs and inhales. He quivers as he runs his tongue along her damp underpants. "I forgot what a good cook you are," he says, pushing aside the cotton material and lapping at her like a thirsty dog.

THE BABY COMES in the night with a sharp wind wailing and rattling through closed windows like the threat of life itself. Tom leaps from bed as soon as Isabel, already dressed and in her slippers with the belt of her robe hanging undone at her sides, pokes him hard and says, "Something's wrong." He storms down the hall and dials Doc John's number. It rings and rings and seems to ring forever. Tom hangs up right before Alice reaches the end of the hall and lifts the receiver. He bangs on Hank's bedroom door but Hank isn't there. Furious and panicked, Tom steps into Buster's room without knocking. "Get up. Your mother needs the doctor."

Buster sits up in bed, bleary-eyed. He doesn't bother dressing, merely throws his winter coat over his pyjamas and slips into his boots, barefoot. He charges downstairs to the basement where he expects his brother has once more fallen asleep on the pull-out. He flicks the basement lights on and off fast. "Mom's gonna blow," he reports. But Hank is nowhere to be found so Buster flees out to the driveway and hops in the truck. He tears out fast along the dark country roads towards Main Street.

The sky is lifting like consciousness, waking and fading to white. There is no one else on the road, as if the world itself has closed its eyes to him. Breathing inside the cab of the truck is like inhaling thin needles of ice. He sees his cloudy breath, and the frozen steering wheel causes his bare hands to turn numb. Snow falls heavily.

Perfect for packing, he thinks. When he knocks at the front door he hears the hollow *rap-rap* of his white knuckles on the wood frame and his own fast breath in the night. He rings the bell and knocks louder. Still no answer. He's at the patients' entrance, he realizes, and darts around the side and thumps on the screen door with his fist, making a terrible racket.

Doc John's sleepy face appears on the other side of the door like a watery ghost. He is sinewy in his robe and pyjamas. "What is it, son?"

"It's Mom," Buster says, jumping up and down in place for warmth. "She's having the baby."

"Alice!" Doc John hollers over his shoulder. "There's a problem at McFiddie's. Maybe you should come." He pulls his robe more tightly around his body, folds his arms across his chest in a gesture that appears oddly self-conscious, as if he's been stumbled in upon while reading a dirty magazine. He stands up taller, stiffens. "Wait in the truck."

THEY AREN'T WITH ISABEL five minutes before Doc John announces that there is no time to drive her to the hospital in Tillsonburg. Alice scuttles Tom out of the bedroom. "We'll call you in when it's time," she says. "Say a prayer." And she closes the door.

Tom and Buster sit in the hall, leaning up against the wall rubbing their temples and yawning in that transparent way men do when they want to appear casual, unflappable. Tom cleans his fingernails with a pocket knife. "Thanks for your help tonight."

Buster notices that his father's thumb and pointer finger are stained yellow from nicotine. "Sure," he says. His mother's cries and moans sound disturbingly like the swine on the Walker farm, like his own from the night of the fire. He covers his ears to muffle her agonized voice and to block out the worst migraine he's had in months.

"She wanted another baby," Tom says shaking his head and forgetting that he's speaking to his son. "Out of the blue, just like that. One day she's happy with the family she's got and the next she announces it's time for another child."

"Yeah," says Buster, dropping his hands to his sides. "To replace the one she lost."

Tom snaps to, regards Buster. "What? Oh ... Where in hell's your brother, anyway?"

When eerie silence is replaced with heavy breathing at ten, eight, six, three and one minute intervals, Buster begins to imagine that he could unscrew his head like the cap on a bottle and leave it in another room for the night. Unsure of what to do with his hands, he settles them in his lap, one resting up against the hidden gun. He won't move a muscle, he tells himself. Not until the new baby's cry comes through that door healthy and strong and until he hears his mother's voice calm once more.

Twenty minutes later the bedroom door opens and Doc John emerges covered in bright red blood. Buster is first to his feet, feels his chest contract and his brain balloon.

"Is she all right?"

"Yes." Doc John holds the bucket half-full of afterbirth. It's covered with a blood-soaked towel and smells faintly of tin and battery acid. He looks like an old-time accoucheur standing there before them—a male midwife. He pats Buster on the back, leaving bloody fingerprints while Alice hands the new baby to Tom.

"Congratulations," she says. "You have a daughter." Tom takes the tiny shrivelled pink bundle in his arms; he's a father three times over now. Another reason to be grateful. His heart begins to race. One more mouth to feed.

Buster moves closer to examine his sister. "She's hairy," he says. He tickles under her chin, feels how smooth and clear her skin is. On her head swirls a storm of thick ginger hair. He judges that with her big round eyes she favours their mother and he wonders if her eyes will eventually turn green like his own.

"Can she see me?"

"Their eyes take a while to adjust," says Doc John. "And she's come early. But I'm sure she can make out who you are."

The baby gazes up at Buster with round wet pools that appear ancient. She is old and new at once. He wants to dismiss her, wants to ignore her out of being for all that she represents, but then something wonderful and devastating occurs to him: she is the first person since his accident who hasn't looked on him with fear or disgust. To his sister he is normal. He loves her instantly.

Later, when the others leave, Tom places the trusty bassinet beside his groggy wife and takes her hand. He knows that the premature delivery has unhinged her. He understands the insecurity that sleeps beneath her brave face. She can sometimes slip and fall, like any other woman. This insight, Tom suspects, is the reason Isabel fell in love with him. She secures her grip and when he kisses her she cries. Baby Elizabeth—Lizzie she is called—begins the first hour of her life soaked by her mother's tears.

Buster can't sleep. In his room he folds his good pair of trousers, removes lint from the shoulders of his only suit jacket and slips into it. He practises knotting his tie before the mirror. He understands intuitively that his mother and the baby were lucky to survive the delivery, though he wanted no more siblings, no successors to remind him of his deposition. Exhausted, he finally sets the fedora on his dresser, hangs up his clothes, slips the gun beneath his pillow and falls into the deepest sleep he's had in months.

The next morning Buster finds Alice pacing back and forth across the kitchen floor with Lizzie squalling in her arms. Hank is seated at the table, unshaven. He stinks of cigarettes and stale beer.

"Where's Mom?" asks Buster.

"Shush." Hank squints and covers his ears.

"She's to stay in bed," whispers Alice. "Allow her a chance to heal. Your father's asked me to help out for a couple of days until she's on her feet again."

Buster moves to sit beside his brother. He scrapes his chair along the floor. "Where've you been, Hank?"

"Out."

"No kidding. I looked for you. You're lucky nothing went wrong."

Hank clasps his hands over his ears as Lizzie lets go another loud, high-pitched wail and Alice steps out of the room. "Cut the gas will you, my head hurts."

"Were you with a girl?"

"Mind your own business. Or I'll see that you mind it."

"Don't have a cow."

A moment later Hank lifts his head. "Susan Rombout. Tell Dad and you're dead."

"Susan? You better give her up, Hank."

"What would you know about it?"

"You don't stand a chance. Susan told Gert from the beauty parlour and Gert told it to Mrs. Johnson who blabbed it to Jelly Bean who told the whole class: Susan would just as soon join the Baptists in not singing or card-playing, or even join a convent and become a bride to Jesus Christ himself before settling down with any boy from Smoke. She has ambitions. I'm telling you Hank, she's holding out for better options."

84

"What could be better than this?" Hank pounds on his chest like he's King Kong.

Buster laughs, his brother the ape-man.

Hank wishes that he'd stopped after his second beer last night but Susan said she had to be up early in the morning and that put a quick end to their date. So he dropped her off at her house and carried on back to the hotel where he spent the rest of the night slinging one drink after another, feeling sorry for himself. He doesn't understand what happened; she'd agreed to a proper date, she'd laughed at his jokes and seemed to enjoy his company. She even permitted him to hold her hand. But when he kissed her and whispered in her ear she sat upright and went rigid like a belt pulled taut at both ends. "Girls!" he mutters.

"Up half the night screaming," Alice returns with Lizzie. She sways and rocks the new baby. "Shush Lizzie. Shush."

Unable to withstand his sister's shrieking any longer, Hank stands and leaves the room.

"Mrs. Gray?" Buster raps his knuckles on the table. "Is Doc John always calm in a pinch?"

"Pretty much. He's had a lot of practice."

"He tells a good story too."

Alice paces back and forth across the kitchen floor. She watches Buster lift an apple from the fruit bowl, toss it into the air and catch it. She heard about the gun incident twice at church, and Hazel says that Buster is the talk of the party line. Alice wonders whether John is having a questionable influence on the boy. "I know my husband's entertaining," she says. "A showman in every sense of the word. But don't you think you should be spending time with your friends?"

Buster shines the apple on his shirt, bites into it and speaks through a juicy mouthful. "My other friends are dopes."

Alice is shocked to hear Buster speak disparagingly about anyone. Then she notices his face when he grins at her; relaxed and easy. She's found this same expression upon her own face many times over the years when she's glanced in a mirror. She recognizes it as a particular kind of happiness. This is when she knows she shares John. He has given Buster the ability to laugh at himself, to accept fate. He did the same for her a long time ago. There are people who change us, she thinks. Make men where there once stood boys. Make poets where there once stood brutes. They give us back ourselves and they don't even know they've done it. Or maybe they do. "Just remember," she says. "John's a humbug. Full of hot air. Don't pay him any mind."

A MAN IN A SIMPLE BLACK COAT and hat sits in a car outside the dairy bar in Tillsonburg. Two young mothers appear from around the corner, pushing prams up the sidewalk at a brisk pace. They're on their way to see the first mounted scout regiment ride through town. The man conceals his face beneath the brim of his hat when they pass. Then he rolls his window down an inch and permits the cool biting air to wash over him. Sweat on his brow evaporates. Be calm, he tells himself. Be steady. If he acts as though he's meant to be here no one will suspect otherwise. He knows this from experience.

The air smells of possibility. He opens his door, the car still idling, and makes crisp, snowy footprints on the road. He approaches the front door of the dairy bar casually. There is no one inside but the young boy who works there. The man finds the boy's face in the reflection of a shiny chrome drink mixer and assesses that he is not the type given to rash behaviour or quick reflexes. The boy lumbers, drying sundae dishes with a tea towel, inspecting each glass for spots and then setting each back on the glittering blue and white countertop. A radio sits on top of a mint green Frigidaire. The boy appears to be singing. When he turns his back the man opens the door, steps inside and quickly crosses the room.

The dairy bar smells of fresh cold milk, chocolate syrup, butterscotch and cherry topping. He moves in behind the counter unnoticed and points two fingers stiffly into the boy's back. "Drop to the floor," he says in a voice deeper than his own. "Do it fast. And don't turn around until you've counted to a thousand." The boy does as instructed. He is shaking and has already wet himself. The man presses on the register's keys until the drawer springs open. He empties the cash into his wide coat pockets and walks out.

Five minutes later he is safely hidden in a dense brush on the outskirts of town. He counts the money and places the bills in the trunk of the car with the rest of his dwindling stash.

On the last day of school before winter break, Buster sits two rows ahead and one over from Jelly Bean. She has a clear view of him slouched in his seat with both legs stuck out in front and he can feel her watching, her eyes boring hot on the back of his neck. His arms are folded across his chest, hands tucked under his armpits. He might appear to be asleep if it wasn't for the fact that he is, every now and then, counting on his fingers. There's a pattern and Jelly Bean has noticed it: One two three. Pause. One two three four. Five and he switches to count on the other hand. She observes, intently chewing on her thumbnail as if she is a small burrowing creature. She hears Susan whispering to Karen and Sandra. They are talking about her. She squirms as Susan pokes her in the shoulder blade with a compass needle.

"Psst? Psst, monster-lover? Does he set your heart on fire?"

Susan tosses a wad of bubble gum onto Jelly Bean's desktop. It sticks. Jelly Bean ignores it, though the smell of fruity sweetness reaches her and makes her nose itch. "Kiss him and I'll let you eat lunch with us."

"Amscray," Jelly Bean hisses. "Leave me alone." She turns and tosses the gum back. It lands on the floor at Susan's feet. She returns to her work and again is poked in the back with the compass tip. "Ouch!" Susan breaks the skin.

"I hear you're going to try and win Miss Tobacco Queen this year."

"I am not."

"Your mother says you are. You don't even know how to hand or tie leaves."

Mr. Kichler, a podgy stump of a man rooted to the front of the classroom with the Canadian map pulled down over the blackboard, stares a warning at the girls. "Windsor," he says, pointing to the southern tip of the province of Ontario with his yardstick. "What can any of you tell me about this city?"

Jelly Bean scrambles to write in her notebook, her heart racing. She can hear her mother's voice echoing through her brain. "Nothing like your father. Not a trace of Indian in you." Jelly Bean does not want to enter the beauty contest. She would rather go colour blind. How will she wheedle out of it?

Buster doesn't move to write. In fact, he's been taking no notes whatsoever. He busies his mind counting the months until the end of school. He counts the days of the week, the number of provinces, tries to name all forty-eight American states, forgetting that Hawaii and Alaska have just voted to join. He even counts the number of days that he spent in bed at the hospital.

"Windsor," Mr. Kichler repeats, walking down the aisle and towering over him. "Who can tell us the claim to fame of Windsor?"

Behind Mr. Kichler is a wall of windows and through them the back field covered in snow. Buster sits silently, remembering the facts as he's heard them. "Speakeasies," he answers without thinking. "The river was lined with hidden parlours and illegal booze."

The room erupts into a collective fit of laughter and Mr. Kichler stomps his right foot on the floor to restore order. "We are not talking about the Prohibition era. We are talking about the present day." Donny and Ivan stare at their desktops. Susan stifles a giggle and Karen and Sandra bite their lips. Jelly Bean feels beads of sweat forming on her brow, under her arms. She can't stand to see Buster on display like this. "Now I'll ask you one more time," repeats Mr. Kichler. "What is the city's claim to fame?"

"It's the southernmost city in Canada," blurts Jelly Bean. She slumps back in her seat, embarrassed to have spoken out of turn.

"Very good." Mr. Kichler nods in her direction.

"Very good," mimics Susan under her breath.

"Windsor has a salt mine," adds Buster. "And a cool bridge."

"Do you recall the name of this bridge, Mr. McFiddie?"

"The Ambassador Bridge, *Mr. Kichler*." He meets his teacher's muddy eyes. Of course he remembers; that bridge was where Mo Axler, Bernstein's ace machine-gunner, blew off some fellow's hands for thieving. Doc John said Mo left the poor bastard tied upside-down to the rail so he'd bleed to death like kosher beef. You never steal from your own pot, the doctor warned. Of course he remembers. What's wrong with everybody this morning?

"I'm glad you've been listening. For a minute I thought you took after your brother. Hank never was particularly good in school."

Buster's fingers tighten into two fists and turn from pinkish to dead white knots. They dig into his rib cage. "No I don't take after anyone," he says. "In case you haven't noticed."

Mr. Kichler takes a couple of nervous steps backwards down the aisle and his right foot lands on the chewing gum. It sticks to the toe of his shoe. He lifts his foot, which only stretches the pink mass from the floor to wherever he next steps. He pretends it isn't there. Susan and Ivan stifle laughs and Jelly Bean averts her eyes, embarrassed for her teacher but also secretly pleased with herself. Buster turns in his seat and mouths two words to her. "Good one."

Mr. Kichler returns to the front of the room exasperated, where he continues to scuff his shoe on the floor as though no one has noticed the gum. He turns to the class. "Newfoundland joined Canada in which year?" Hands fly up.

Buster knows the answer of course; 1949. But why in hell would he grant a moron like Mr. Kichler the satisfaction of a truce? The only reconciliation he will ever concede will be with himself. He stands, gathers his books and charges out of the classroom, knocking the wreath from the door. The other students pretend not to notice.

Jelly Bean is filled with envy watching him depart. She's always been partial to Buster. She's watched him on his bicycle, tearing through the village with the other boys when they were younger. She's seen him win snowball fights, sat beside him in Sunday school. Now, since his accident, she is even more drawn to him. All year she's been stared at by the other boys, once Ivan even grabbed her when no one else was looking, but Buster hasn't seemed to notice the changes in her body; he's been preoccupied with his own. She is sure she understands how he must be feeling; the scrutiny, no escape from prying eyes. More than this, she longs to know what it is to break things and not have others even blink with surprise, and Buster knows. She longs to exist outside the bounds of good manners, where for once she might not catch herself sideways passing a windowpane, not feel the need to fix her hair or straighten her skirt or say just the right thing. She wants to be left beyond the need for approval, beyond approval's reach, but girls relentlessly trying to be beautiful can never escape their own vanity. She has little choice in the matter; she is vain to the point of paralysis most of the time, vain until it hurts.

Buster isn't looking to be found when she races up to him at the far end of the hall beside a row of lockers. His is open and he's packing books into a fishing bag. He slips into his winter coat, slams the door shut and swings his bag over one shoulder.

"You following me?"

"Where you going?" She's out of breath.

"You're always gawking. Hovering like the bloody horizon. I'm not here for your amusement." He feels like a cad for treating her dismissively; she's always been friendly, never once been rude or mean, and she's the only girl who bothers to talk to him any more. Still, he can't hold back these minor explosions.

Jelly Bean stares. She wants to reach out and touch the distorted skin on his face, know what human feels like after all, *real* human, for her own features so fine and clear and uncomplicated leave only a bland, unremarkable sensation on her fingertips. Like painting white on white, she thinks. "I'm sorry. It's … um … well, people are always looking at me too. Trying to fix me. As far back as I can think people have tried to make improvements. They comment like they own me. Nobody owns you."

Buster stops what he's doing, raises his eyes to meet hers. Yes it is tiresome, gruesome, always being stared at and the thought that she knows it slides a light, buoyant feeling under his boots. "That's right. I'm my own man."

Jelly Bean sees the opening in his face, the splinter and tease of connection behind his eyes. He isn't indifferent to her, merely withholding. She is encouraged. "Do you think how you feel is more important than how you look?"

"Don't get weird," he says, spinning the dial on his combination lock.

Jelly Bean places the toe of one saddle shoe over top of the other. "It's just sometimes I can't tell the difference any more." She says this as an afterthought.

"I've got stuff to do."

She straightens. "What kind of stuff?"

"See you around." He waves over his shoulder.

"I know anyway!" Jelly Bean calls out. "I overheard."

Buster stops midway down the hall with the senior art class mural behind him. A painting of a spruce tree is decorated in red ribbons. He turns to face her. "What did you hear?"

"That you held up the dairy bar. That you're the bandit." She bites her fingernail.

"What are you talking about?"

"He took two hundred dollars—everything in the register. It was you, right?"

"Have you lost your marbles?" Buster approaches fast. "You're making it up. It's a lie!"

"No, it's true, I swear." Her eyes are as big and dumb as a cow's. "Everyone says so."

"Everyone. Who's everyone? Who's been talking?" He grabs her by one arm, fingers denting flesh. "Who's been talking about me?"

"Ivan. Susan. My parents. Let me go!" She tries to pull away. "Mother said—" But before she can shake loose Buster has released her and is off again, bounding down the hall.

He is out the front doors of the school and down the steps, across the yard and along the side of Highway 59 in a flash. He runs as fast and as hard as he can in the snow, until his lungs pinch and then he slows, bends over and catches his breath. Being reminded that he's an outcast by someone as ham-fisted as Jelly Bean Johnson is as painful as when he first saw his cauterized face after the accident. Ugliness seems to enlarge. Ugly was a foreign country before and now it is home. He's filled with shame and walks the rest of the way with that terrible ratty curtain descended over him again, a feeling he hasn't had in months. He reaches for the gun and grips it tightly through his jeans. Maybe he should find a bullet and be done with the whole mess altogether? Imagine *that,* he thinks. Jelly Bean could stumble on me all red and bloody in the middle of a snowy field. That should satisfy her curiosity. His head is heavy, simmering and weighted down as if concrete has been poured over top. People are talking behind his back. He feels as he has on many other occasions, picking tobacco in the hot, hot sun. Sweaty and parched with tight, sore muscles, only now it's every muscle.

Minutes later he knocks on the Grays' door and peers frantically over Alice's shoulder.

"Is Doc John around?"

"He's been feeling punk, Buster. He's napping. Can I help you with something?"

"I need him. When'll he be up again?" He steps back. "Never mind, I'll just wait."

"C'mon then." Alice opens the screen door and ushers him inside. "I can see you're determined. There's no point having you stand out and catch cold." She hugs herself for warmth. "Whew, it's blustery."

Buster removes his boots and coat and Alice motions for him to sit at the table. The kitchen in the afternoon light is bright and spacious, a serene room filled with quiet domesticity. The window above the sink is fogged and condensation drips along the inside. There are plates hung on the walls—most with English patterns like his mother's good dishes, which never get used. A tall corner cupboard is decorated with a glass chicken collection—covered dishes in milky white, yellow, iridescent blue and gold, all the same mould. He fiddles with the Christmas tablecloth and notices that the red and green pattern makes row after row of miniature bells with bows. It isn't customary to pry but today he doesn't care.

"Is Doc John very sick?"

"Just a cold. Knock on wood." Alice raps her knuckles on the table as a preventative measure. "He hasn't been able to shake it yet I'm afraid."

"He should call on Doctor Baker."

Alice moves to the counter, her right hand beginning to itch. "I was preparing frozen strawberries. John likes them after his nap." She pours half a cup of white sugar over the berries and mixes them together, keeping her back to the boy all the while. She scoops some into a bowl, grabs a dessert spoon from a drawer, turns and moves to the table. "Here you go." She hands the spoon and dish to Buster and sits.

"Do folks really think I'm the bandit?" he blurts.

"Well now," she says, with a voice as steady as her eyes. "Is that what this is all about? Oh I suppose I ought to let John speak with you, but yes Buster. I have heard some talk."

"I can't believe it." He shovels two heaping spoonfuls of strawberries into his mouth. "It's not me."

"Of course it's not." She pats his hand. "You wouldn't do such a terrible thing." But there is never absolute certainty. "Have you spoken with your parents about this? After you finish here you should go home. See John when it's all sorted out." She looks at the clock on the wall and at the windowsill where she saves a jar of lard so that John might oil the cork on his clarinet. She fishes up her sleeve for a hankie but doesn't use it. "People talk, Buster. You know that. Soon enough they'll be on to something else."

Buster feels refuge drain down his spine. He knows that in Smoke if you have no known past one is fast provided through gossip. Whispers. Stories to fill the disquieting gaps. Is this what they say when your *future* goes up in flames? He takes a couple more spoonfuls to be polite, stands, his tongue cold and stiff and unable to form words. He forces out a sound that resembles a "thank you" and steps into his boots, grabs his coat and pulls the screen door shut tightly, his heart sinking into his scrawny chest. They all think he's a criminal now. He wonders if it's because he pulled a gun on Ivan or if it's just because of how he looks. All at once he realizes what it really means to be an outsider, a person who is feared, even despised. A person set apart. How did the Purple Gang manage it? Didn't Raymond Bernstein ever miss being regular? A migraine presses up behind his eyes. He wants to tear his gnarled face off as though removing a tight-fitting rubber mask.

BUSTER TRIPS OVER LIZZIE'S PLAYPEN as he sprints into his own kitchen twenty minutes later. The house smells of roast pork and buttery mashed potatoes. He slips from his coat and tosses it across the counter, bounds through the living room, faster around the corner and up the staircase—taking two, three steps at a time. He races into his parents' bedroom without knocking and finds his mother nursing Lizzie in the rocking chair. Isabel lifts a finger to her lips. "Shush, I just got her down." She covers the baby's head with a white receiving blanket and adjusts the collar of her housecoat.

"You know what folks are saying?" Buster pants, rage tearing up his insides. His hands dig deeper into his jeans pockets.

"Saying about what? What's got into you?"

"They think *I* robbed the dairy bar in Tillsonburg. And it's all on account of this." He hits himself in the face with closed fists.

Isabel stops rocking. "What?" She struggles to her feet with Lizzie in one arm, pushing herself up with the other. She moves gingerly so as not to tear her stitches. "I can't believe anyone would think you … I'm sorry, Brian." They face each other and she wonders when he ever grew to be taller than her. "Some people have too much time on their hands, I guess. Just ignore them."

"That's your answer? Ignore it! How exactly am I supposed to do that?"

"Keep your voice down."

"Mom, are you blind? I'm deformed!" Buster is hollering now. "People will believe anything about me." Hot tears stream down his cheeks like trails of clear molten lava. "I've been trying, stuck like this. I can't take it any more. I don't want this, it's not me."

Isabel holds Lizzie closer, as if she's cradling a younger Buster. As if he'd never grown up and away from her. "There, there," Isabel rocks. She is struck by the humiliated, abandoned tarnish about her son. Has it been there all along? How has she not noticed it? "I thought you were getting on with things. You never want my help. I thought you were okay now."

"Okay? I don't exist any more. Cripes, can't you see? If there's even a chance I can be normal again. Even the slightest chance, *that's* what I want." But as he hears himself speak he knows he's never going back, back to normal. There is only forward now, a tide of different, different, different rolling over into a hardened, leathery reality to match his face. Even if, by some miracle, he could look like his old self again, everyone he knows would still see the scars. He flops down on the edge of his parents' bed crying, shoulders curled in defeat.

Isabel finds the will to raise her lifeboat eyes. "You'll always be handsome to me," she says, moving closer to him. "You will."

And there it is; that familiar and infuriating glaze Buster has wanted to stamp out. The tight bind that strangles him, coy gestures and a trivial, flirtatious tone that protects his mother from too much hurting. He recognizes it without understanding it for it has always been there, even more so since his accident, like a sieve through which she filters his corrosive troubles. He can't stand it one minute more. "A lot of good that does me."

Isabel feels him pull away but doesn't know how to prevent it. Yes she has a way of turning a blind eye and why not? She knows what a cold isolation being left out is, to sit knees to chest in the chilled stone windowsill of an orphanage waiting for someone—anyone— to pass by the room, point, and say that she is the child they want.

It never happened. And yet week after week she'd tried her best to win over prospective new parents by smiling prettily. Looking industrious. She had begged and she had cried for acceptance, giving away what little dignity and pride she had, and when that didn't change a thing she'd cultivated defences. She would wait for no one's approval or permission again. She sees what she pleases, usually the best version, because there has been too much ugliness already. When will Buster learn to do the same?

"I wish we could get along again," she says. "Remember?" She means the easy manner they once knew, the jokes they shared intuitively, inside jokes that Hank and Tom didn't pick up on. And the special way that only Buster allowed her to behave in his presence— binding. Possessing. Until the premature birth of her daughter, a miniature version of herself, no other person in Isabel's life permitted her to feel as rooted as her youngest son. He used to understand his place in the order of things. Smoke and the farm were his birthrights. He had been for the land without being against her and never once questioned the meaning of home. That's all changed though, and she's left scrambling for a way to get it back. She long admired Buster's inherent satisfaction, something she herself has never been safe or secure enough to know. "Lizzie reminds me of you," she adds. "Here, you hold her."

"Just tell me you'll put a stop to the rumour. *Please.*"

"All right," she agrees. "I'll see what I can do." She reaches for his hand, a gruffer version of her own, but he yanks it away, turns his face.

He doesn't remember what it feels like to be her boy any more. To be the son his mother or father wants. He is something new altogether now, an unnamed creature caught between fleeting worlds. Maybe he *is* an outlaw. A cold ache fills him up, chilling even his teeth; it's neither deadness arriving at last nor a new life force leaching in, but another fuel. He can't rattle on like this for even one more day. His body is a coffer. Home is a cage. He can't wait any longer to find out what will happen to him.

Buster rolls an extra pair of blue jeans and a T-shirt and stuffs them into his fishing bag with wool socks, a toothbrush, his gun and the latest copy of *Sports Cars Illustrated,* which he found in the rumpus room. He packs a scarf into the pocket of his winter coat and slips from the house in his black boots while Hank watches *Maverick* on television and his parents smoke cigarettes and play honeymoon bridge at the kitchen table. Lizzie stops crying the instant the front door opens.

Buster hurries. He isn't going to be the crippled son of the tobacco king any more. He's not hanging around to find out what else people will say behind his back, what they will make of him. There's never been a disfigurement of his kind in Smoke. Sure, men lost limbs using machinery or working at the cannery, occasionally the hanger sprained an ankle or broke an arm falling off the top tier of a kiln, and of course there were amputees after both wars. But no one's ever been so changed and lived to walk among them. Not that he knows. They're all busy looking ahead but the future can change for the worse, can't they see? Who you *are* can change. You can even disappear.

The dirt roads look shorter already. They snake through the village and off across its borders into faraway places, places he can reach. Reckless places like the ones Doc John has been describing for months. His father once told him that the dust kicking up from a Smoke country road could never be washed out of his eyes, that it would stay with him until they closed for good. Buster intends to prove him wrong. He'll be like Ray Bernstein, he thinks. Or one of the other Purples. Might as well since people already think it of him. He'll roam and land wherever he wants. Best of all, he'll be just like any boy again, answering only to himself. Quick-witted, with no one counting on him and no one to disappoint. Why not? He has nothing left to lose.

He jogs to the road and walks a good distance in case someone should see him, and then when he's sure that he's out of sight, doubles back across his father's field and slips westward into the woods. Trees break the cold wind and silence falls around him like a shroud of ash. He can see two, maybe three feet ahead under the moonlight, but knows the path well. His father hid eggs there every Easter when he and Hank were boys. And he and Donny, and sometimes Ivan, had waged battles with sticks and pellet guns, scoured these parts for hidden treasures. Once they found a brown jug filled with pennies half-buried in a tree stump. They'd staked out the area every day for a week, hiding in the brush hoping to catch a glimpse of the fellow who hid it there. No one was found and eventually they divvied up the fortune, two dollars and seventy-five cents a piece. He and Donny each bought Marvel Comics. Ivan bought a slingshot.

The woods is a different place for a boy alone at night in winter. Sound is muffled and yet amplified—the creaking of icy branches, the sleepy movement of cardinals and owls, dry breath. Trees take on ominous shapes in the dark, large deformed monsters. Giants of the underworld. The plan is to hitchhike to Windsor and then cross the border to Detroit. He'll find work on the shady side of the law—surely Detroit still has gangs, and his scarred appearance should qualify him. He's already got a gun.

The woods come out onto another farmer's field. He marches across it and decides to make the long trek over to Tillsonburg. Most locals use shortcuts, he knows, and avoid the main stretch at night. The speed limit slows them and police cars are hard to spot. He's bound to run into someone he knows on the roads. At Tillsonburg he finds the bright yellow light of Highway 19. He crosses both lanes and when he sees a car approach, stands by the side of the road and sticks out his arm to thumb a ride. A Ford passes without slowing, then two more cars in succession—no one he recognizes. He waits another hour and by now is wearing his scarf. He begins to walk south. Finally, an old Studebaker pulls up alongside and slows. Its driver reaches across the seat to open the passenger-side door. This is his chariot, this is his way out. He starts towards it, places his fingers on the handle and opens the door. "Thanks for stopping," he says. "I've been out here a while."

"Going as far as Windsor," says the driver. "Hop in." Then seeing Buster's face clearly for the first time the driver startles, puts his foot to the gas pedal. He lurches away, leaving Buster to jump back and be doused in car exhaust. The Studebaker swerves across the centre of the lane and back again when its driver reaches to pull the passenger door shut.

"Thanks for nothing." Buster waves his fists in the air. "Lousy son of a bitch!"

The Studebaker vanishes and night creeps down to earth like loose ink. Everything grows heavy and black except the few feet on either side of a streetlight. Buster steps out of its glare and back into invisibility. He doesn't look up again for close to an hour, when it begins to snow. He doesn't bother to stick out his thumb when passed by an Oldsmobile carrying two hundred dollars in stolen bills in its trunk. He simply crosses the street once again and slips onto a farm, resigned to his fate. The driver of the Olds watches him and notes his path through his rear-view mirror.

The river is frozen. Fresh snow decorates the field beyond Buster's window like wedding confetti. The window is covered in frost. He wakes to the sound of his parents down the hall. To firm and fleshy bodies merging, and the frantic stutter of the headboard against the wall as passion explodes. They do it all the time. It's disgusting. His heart aches with fear of unrequited longing and then bitterness takes over, blunts the senses. He sits up, yawns and falls backwards into warm covers. He slips his legs over the side of the bed, bare feet touching the chilly floor, and stands to stretch. He crosses the room, opens a dresser drawer and reaches a hand into the elastic waist of his pyjama bottoms where he lifts the pistol from his underwear, sets it inside the drawer under a stack of clean, folded T-shirts and makes his way out of the room and down the hall towards the shower before Hank, as usual, has a chance to use up all the hot water. After, he will dress and sneak downstairs and out the patio door, past the old oak, before either of his parents rise in time to stop him.

He approaches the Grays' veranda mustering the courage to knock on the door when it opens and Doc John steps out sporting new leather gloves. The old man takes one look at the boy—sees his boots unlaced, their tongues hanging long and dry, his coat partially open, and he knows. He knows that Buster knows something. But what? Before he has a chance to offer a greeting, Buster is upon him.

"Why didn't you tell me?"

Doc John closes the door to his office. His palms are damp. "Tell you?"

"About the rumours. You should have warned me."

"Oh, that." The doctor takes a deep breath, feels the acid in his stomach settle. "I don't pay attention to gossip."

"I thought you were my friend."

The old man digs his walking stick into the floor of the veranda, turns its handle like a corkscrew. The comment pinches. There is nothing worse than being lonely and lonely in its purest, most distilled form is what he hears in Buster's voice—a desolate, last-ditch effort to cling on to the rest of the world for dear life. Alice warned him the boy is troubled. He makes his way down the steps.

"I am your friend."

"Then help me."

He examines the boy's face and recognizes its fierce quality. Buster has been bargaining for a different life with a God he is no longer sure he believes in. Made a pact for the future in the hope of exchanging common happiness for his imperfect self. Cocoons are woven by creatures less delicate than monarchs and swallowtails, the doctor thinks. A human being can change so dramatically the world has no time to catch up. Buster was once a vibrant, active child. One who looked incapable of failure or misery. And now here he stands, defeated, the boy he delivered and caught with his own two hands. Doc John considers Buster, as he does all the children he's delivered, in some small part as his own. How can he bear to watch Buster in this kind of pain and do nothing to relieve his suffering? Anguish is no less debilitating than physical injury. And like all physicians, he'd taken an oath—*I will keep them from harm and injustice. I will come for the benefit of the sick.* He wants to offer reassurance—shake hands, slap Buster's back, for he knows that in a closed system even an outcast must remain inexorably part of the fabric. "You're right," he finally concedes. "I should've warned you before you heard it from someone else. But you think that would've made any difference? Knowing something doesn't always change it."

Buster shrugs and in his eyes there pools a familiar fragility. Doc John rests his arm around the boy's shoulders and guides him along Main Street. They walk, barely advancing, with the doctor leaning on the boy for support. Most of the houses they pass are garishly lit. Red and green and gold lights. Homemade wreaths. Bejewelled trees visible through front windows. Doc John fiddles inside his left glove, feels the thick gold band loosen around his crooked finger.

He hadn't worn a wedding ring when he and Alice married, but upon their tenth anniversary she'd presented him with one and he hasn't removed it since. "I ever tell you about the time Mo Axler cleaned me out," he says, "right down to my last penny?"

Buster wipes his cold, runny nose on the sleeve of his coat, shakes his head.

"Well he did. Waged everything I had and you know what? I lost it all and more. How's that for knowing something?"

"What was the bet? I mean what were you so sure about?"

"I was sure about a girl."

"A girl!"

"Not just any girl, *Mo's* daughter. She was fine fine fine, with sheer silk stockings, a yellow chiffon dress and the scent of lavender dabbed behind her ears." Doc John pokes Buster in the ribs. "Mo Axler was a man with connections so you can imagine that I had to be darn sure of myself taking *him* on."

"What'd he do?"

"Hold on now. Don't rush me, son. It started when I rented office space on the cheap. I had a small practice. Back then you could only acquire liquor legally if it was prescribed by a physician and the lineup at my door for prescriptions was impressive. It wasn't long before I realized I was treating every lush and half the gangs in the state, along with their families. At the end of one day this girl came around for a checkup. She was maybe twenty, a real looker. And sent by her father. I had no idea who she was, Mo being Ray Bernstein's right-hand man. If I'd known that … well. She came back each week at the same time, before close, always claiming to have a condition that needed tending right away. A fever, I think it was the first time, but I couldn't detect one. A sore throat the next. Bad nerves. Of course it hit me that she wasn't only turning up for my medical opinion so I wrote her the prescriptions. She kept coming back though, and soon we got to going for walks."

"What was she like?"

"Let's see ..." They pass before the bank and Doc John glimpses his reflection in the decorated window. "She was about my height. Dark eyes, dark hair cut short. It was wispy in the style of the day; kiss curl. Any room we entered and she was the centre of attention. She cottoned to hooch as much as her daddy did, I guess, because in the middle of the night she'd sometimes sneak away in fancy clothes and meet me on Lakeshore Road near Woodland, by the big Ford House. Sometimes over at Belle Isle where there weren't many folks about at that hour. We'd make our way to the blind pigs, one on every corner back then. This one night we crossed the river and tried the Canadian roadhouses for a change.

"I shouldn't have gone but I couldn't help myself. She was like a bad habit I couldn't lose. More addictive than any guzzle. Anyway, we hit the Chateau LaSalle first and the Sunnyside after that, both places built close to the water—easy for bootleggers crossing the river to unload. We didn't get involved in all that funny business though, just rolled the dice and ate our fill of pickerel and perch and frogs legs, and we drank. There was always a spotter at the roadhouses anyhow, a quick-witted fellow whose job it was to position himself in a window on the top floor and watch out for us." Doc John feigns smaller, lighter steps, losing years in the telling, almost tiptoeing as if he were a sneak. "So there we were, prowling in the early hours at the most popular gig around—the Edgewater Thomas Inn—owned and run by Bertha Thomas. Bertha was a tough-talking hostess, the kind of woman who was full of personality, as we used to say. Meaning she could stand up to any man and did. She was fond of my girl; they became fast friends.

"The Edgewater had a gingerbread entrance. I remember that. Mahogany-panelled walls. It had a buzzer bar, connected to other taverns with an alarm system that warned of police raids. Upstairs you'd push open a storeroom wall and there we'd be, taking in a razzmatazz jazz band or doing the Charleston, the room cloudy with Omar cigarette smoke and piled high with men in floppy tweed caps. But there was a secret passage running behind the dance hall, and it led to a private meeting room for Bertha and her suppliers. The shelves throughout the place were rigged to roll away, if need be, hiding liquor in the walls or sending it sliding down a chute into a wine cellar. Bertha could replace those shelves with soda faster than you could swallow what was left in your mouth. Lots of things—and people—went undercover at the Edgewater."

"Did you kiss her?"

"Bertha? No."

"Your girl I mean."

"You sure are single-minded." The doctor chuckles, clears his throat. "She wasn't made for the life and wanted out, see. Said so. And as we stood in some back room under the cool blue lights I started imagining that we could make a go of it somewhere else, together. 'You want to come away with me?' I asked her. 'Would you leave if I arrange it?' She grabbed my hand and pinned me to her. 'What I want is to try something different tonight.' The bulb was on the blink so only the flicker of her eyes reached me. We stood like that, face to face for a long while, her body pressing up flat to mine so that I couldn't hardly tell us apart. I knew what she wanted but something dangerous curdled up inside me like bad milk so I shoved her harder than I meant to."

"You hit a woman!"

"I didn't hit her. I said I shoved her … away from me…. She teetered back against the wall. I ran over to help her up of course."

"Course. Did she slap you? Threaten to call for her father?"

"It wasn't like that. It was … different. *I* was different then."

"How so?"

"You know how you were before the fire?"

"Normal."

The doctor shakes his head. "Ugly word. Let's say regular. Commonplace. You were Buster but not the same fellow as now, right? Now you're … you're …"

"A suspect."

Doc John swats the boy. "An exception. And I was an exception too. I was … not exactly the proper fellow you see standing here before you today. I guess you could say I was a lost soul. But my girl was used to living in the shadows and finding the very heart of a person there. And, she was all for breaking rules. She would've liked you just fine." The doctor holds one gloved hand out before him as though he can feel now what he felt long ago. "I offered her my hand and she took it and on her way to her feet she said, 'Not what you expected huh?' No words scratched out because it was true—I hadn't expected her to be so bold. I liked her plenty but us being who we were then, I never would've made a move like that. What if I'd misread her interest? What if someone saw?" He drops his hand to his side. "Nothing's ever what we expect it to be, son—it bears remembering time to time. Nothing ever is." He turns to face the boy. "After that I didn't resist any more; she smoothed out the skirt of her dress, slipped her hand around the back of my neck and planted one on me."

"I knew it! I knew you kissed her. Did Axler spot you there?"

"No, not there." Doc John adjusts his hat. "It was more than an hour later when we made our way downstairs. The Edgewater was rowdy as ever with customers still turning up. I paid Bertha and we said our goodbyes. Outside the air was thick with factory pollution. The river winked at us like it had black diamonds for eyes. We walked towards it down the alley, holding hands. *That's* when. Axler and a couple of goons were on their way inside."

"Uh-oh."

"Right. Axler's face was solid marble, lost all its expression, and his eyes turned to slits of dirty ice. 'What the hell are you doing here!' he shouted at my girl. 'You look like a tramp. And who's this …?' He looked me up and down, thought there was something familiar but couldn't place it. I let go of her hand then. 'My friend,' she stammered, as if she could introduce me like that and everything would be all right. Axler laughed. Laughed like he'd never heard anything so ridiculous. His little girl, out with the likes of me."

"But you're a swell guy."

"Hmm. Axler didn't exactly see it that way."

"If she liked you—"

"She did. And like I said, I was fond of her too."

"Then why not stick up for yourself?"

Doc John grips his cane more tightly, feels how unyielding the wood is. "Sometimes you fight and other times you give people what they expect. I've always known which is which."

"He must've clobbered you? He must have let you have it."

"Wanted to, oh I could mark it in his eyes. You know how it was with those Purples. But nobody acted before getting the signal from a Bernstein and none of them were there, so Axler raved on. 'Think you can run around putting your dirty paws all over my daughter, do you?' He stepped so close that I could smell the stink of bourbon twist up between us like a mad dog. 'She don't know what she wants unless I tell her. Got that?' Then he turned and grabbed her by one arm, slapped her hard across the face. His ring split her lip. 'You want to act like a whore?' he shouted in her face. 'Let's see what you're worth!' He ripped the front of her dress, exposing her undergarments. I thought he was going to kill her."

"What did you do?"

"Almost swallowed my tongue. I was in a cold sweat but Axler's men were watching me. I emptied my pockets and started to scribble a promissory note in the amount of my entire bank account. 'Here,' I said. 'This is all I've got and it's yours, every penny. Just let her go.' Axler grabbed the paper and stuffed it in his pocket. 'She's not going anywhere.'"

"Did you at least kiss her goodbye?"

"Kiss her again. Are you even listening?" Doc John gives a silent, wheezy laugh, like a car turning over. "Heck I didn't get close enough to touch her. Axler spat in my face and dragged her away, kicking and screaming. Last I saw she was down the alley being shoved, head first, into the passenger side of her father's sedan."

"You're making this up. The real Mo Axler would've shot you on the spot."

Doc John's eyes gaze into the distance blank and horrified, at something only he can see. "The next thing I knew the two Purple Gang strongmen turned on me. One thug reached into the trunk of his car and I heard a loud *crack!* The splintering sound of wood smashing pavement. I spun around, dropped my keys. Reached down to pick them up. Before there was time to think both men came at me with baseball bats, their faces friendly—their voices spitting mean. One restrained me while the other slammed my ribs. 'I know what you need,' he said. 'Let me have a go.' Their laughter and jeering cut the air like a buzz saw." Doc John shakes his head as if to fling off the memory. "Bertha must've heard the commotion because she flicked the tavern porch lights on and off, and both goons let go and turned to see who was watching. That's when I bolted. I ran as if hell had caught fire in my pants."

"What about the girl?"

"I don't know." Doc John straightens his glasses. He notices his young friend watching him, wet lips parted in anticipation. He wants to know more, the whole story, and for the first time in years Doc John wants to share it. He aches to share it before it's too late. Before he's gone and the past is gone with him. "There's something I haven't told—" Buster's eyes are curious. Too curious. Possibly the eyes of a squealer.

"Uh-huh?"

That gang was amoral, the doctor thinks. They were deviant. They were also proof of another way to live—a tainted, off-colour menace that was recognized. Michigan and those early years represent a time in his life he's tried to forget and can't, because you can't live long enough to forget when you were first introduced to yourself. But that's a story he must hold on to until the very end.

"It's nothing," he says.

"C'mon. What've you got to hide, Doc?"

"Sometimes I glimpse her, that's all. When I close my eyes."

"You do?"

"Sure. It's like that with some folks; they never fully leave you. But I wouldn't want to meet up with her again. Going backwards can feel worse than moving on and seeing that girl again face to face would surely be the death of me."

"You never saw her again?"

"That's right. You never know when the last time you'll see someone will be. We come into the world a howl but we often depart as seamless as vapour. So I ran, and I kept right on running until she was a distant smudge in my mind's eye. You don't approve by the way you're looking at me, I can tell. But survival's a racket, same as any other, and running got me here didn't it? *Here*. Nothing to be ashamed of in that."

Buster nods, tries his best to accept the prospect of his own surrender and his failure to run away. When he speaks again he can barely push the words out.

"I still dream about my accident."

"That right?" The doctor is surprised. He'd thought that by now it would have played over and over in the boy's mind and lost its potency.

"Yeah, only sometimes I get out safe. When I wake I'm myself again, without the scars. Then I remember what really happened."

"There's no mercy in a memory is there?"

"Hmmm."

"I know. By the time I stopped at my Model T that night, scrambled with the keys and jumped inside, I'd emptied my bladder and it was running down my legs, soaking the seat."

"Did you know the thugs?"

"Course I did. I dug a bullet out of the one fellow's chest not long before, as a matter of fact. Saved his ungrateful life."

"So who was it, Ruthless Eddie? Another lackey?"

Doc John raises a gloved finger to his lips, pinches his fingers and turns them as if locking his mouth and throwing away the key.

"Ah ah ah, never tell, son. The man who leaks no secret—"

"Is a man of honour. I know. You've told me a million times. But are you *sure* you're not making this one up?"

"What do you think? Exceptions are dangerous."

"I guess. But I still don't follow. It makes no sense. If the girl liked you, I mean? Was she like her dad said, a renter, is that it? A Bedroom Betty?"

"No, no. She was a lady of the first order."

"Like Mrs. Gray."

Doc John peers over his shoulder. "Yes, like Mrs. Gray." He adjusts his coat. "Here's my point: forget about the rumours. Forget thinking your problem is other people. Problems like yours and mine are best solved here." He thumps his chest over top of his heart with one gloved hand. "And here." Now he taps on his temples with one finger.

"Easy for you to say," Buster scoffs. "It all worked out for you."

"Are you kidding? I've never been able to show my face again."

"Really? You've *never* gone back?"

"It was a long time ago."

Buster thinks about all of this, about how everything can change in a split second, about how it's the things we don't plan that lead us farther away from our old lives than we ever thought possible. He tugs on the old man's sleeve.

"Tell me the truth, Doc. Will I ever be normal again?"

"The truth?" The doctor faces him. "Truth is merely wounded fact, son. Wounded fact."

HAZEL JOHNSON WAVES FRANTICALLY from inside the hardware store and Doc John and Buster step onto the porch. The bell over the door chimes and the radio is playing a tidal wave of a Latin riff when the doctor enters. "Is there a problem?"

Hazel is now behind the counter waving a letter in the air. A scrapbook is open and she's ready to place the letter next to a newspaper clipping. "You won't believe it." She is unable to contain herself. "Walter! Judy. This'll be the best parade ever. Just wait until I tell Alice. Oh, I almost forgot in all the excitement."

"What's going on?" Buster pretends to do a drum roll on his thighs.

Hazel doesn't meet his eyes. His face reminds her of those dried apple dolls she makes to sell at church bazaars. "This letter right here is from none other than our own Barbara Ann Scott."

"The skater?"

"One and only. I wrote her months ago. Judy, you remember?"

Jelly Bean sits on a stool at the end of the counter doodling on a pad of paper, imagining angels without wings and outlining the store window she will paint later on. She notices Buster and swings one leg over the other. "Uh-huh."

"Well, who would have thought that a famous star like Barbara Ann would take the time to respond to fan letters but here you have it." Hazel thrusts the letter up before Doc John's face. "Isn't her penmanship simply exquisite? Mine wasn't any letter, you know? I wrote specifically to invite her to our sesquicentennial."

"You did what?" Jelly Bean uncrosses her legs. "Mother, you invited her *here*?" She glances towards her father, to where the Barbara Ann Scott doll is staring back at her from its countertop pedestal with those ever-so-maddening white teeth and that fluffy white muff. Eyes perpetually locked in the wrong direction.

"She took us from Ottawa to the Olympics," Hazel says before Walter has a chance to respond. "She won gold at the European, World *and* Olympic championships all within six weeks. She's done more for this country than that monarch over there." Hazel points to a colourized photograph of a young Queen Elizabeth II hanging on the back wall by the staircase leading up to their apartment. "And you." She waves a thick finger at Jelly Bean. "You'd do well to follow her example, Judy. Perhaps you'd improve your physical education grade. Or even win at Miss Tobacco Queen this year."

Jelly Bean's stomach turns, her tongue flops from side to side inside her mouth like a scaly fish. She hates her perfect blond hair, her perfect white skin and her blue eyes. She is so tightly wound up in her ribbons and bows that she feels she might, at any moment, unravel and sit like a pile of string at her mother's feet. "Who cares about the contest," she snaps. "Who cares about gym class or figure skating. I hate winter and I hate the ice." Once she gets going she can't stop. "Barbara Ann can jolly well find herself another town to visit! Daddy, tell her. I paint. Tell her, will you please?"

"Those figure skates were mighty expensive young lady." Hazel turns her back to Walter and faces the doctor once more. "I knew it was a long shot. I mean, I never in a million years thought she'd say yes—well all right, maybe a little." She thrusts the open letter onto the counter. "Read for yourself. She wants to come. She will judge the contest and meet the president of her fan club. Me! *And* she's asked whether we need someone to lead our parade."

"Dad's leading the parade," says Buster, walking past Jelly Bean and peering over her shoulder to see what she's drawn. He delves into the jar on the counter for a hard candy, pops one in his mouth. Peppermint.

Walter taps his fingers on the counter. "There's been talk about that."

"What kind of talk?" Doc John removes his gloves, sets them beside the register. He's aware of Buster listening intently.

"Town council's still divided on the tobacco board. Len's leading the charge."

Just then Len Rombout enters the store, sending the bell over the door tinkling once more and a gust of cold weather rushing in.

"Gooday all."

They turn. Doc John is the first to offer a greeting.

"Gooday."

Len balances a lit cigarette between his teeth. "I could use a new stepladder."

"Help yourself." Walter points to the back of the store. "I'm just sharpening these blades." He lifts one of his daughter's new white figure skates. Jelly Bean massages her ankle and slips her drawing pad under a pile of magazines on the counter.

"Tom should be the one to lead the parade," the doctor says.

"But if it doesn't work out." Hazel waves the letter. "There's always Barbara Ann."

Len approaches the counter with a small stepladder under one arm. Smoke from his cigarette hovers around his ear. "McFiddie's been bringing in outsiders all year, might as well have someone else for the parade. I bet there's plenty who'd agree with me."

Doc John watches Buster's face sink at the thought of his father's displacement. "Nobody in this room," he says.

Len tosses a new bill onto the counter and walks out with his purchase. Jelly Bean waits for Buster's response, and when he follows outside on Doc John's heels she and her parents move to the doorway.

"Tom's a good man Len, and you know it. He's promoting the tobacco industry, and tobacco has kept this village in clothes for years. If Tom McFiddie thinks the marketing board is a good idea, I trust it is."

"That so? I could get a bunch of signatures that say otherwise." Len ducks his head from around the small ladder, drops it into the back of his flatbed. He has no time for a debate today. He spits the butt of his cigarette into a snowbank and lets it flicker and drown. Then he points at Buster. "Everyone knows what you've been up to young man."

Buster steps forward. "Oh yeah? What do they know?"

Doc John lifts his walking stick, points it into the air between Len and the boy. "See here. People won't stand for you stirring up trouble, Len."

Len slaps the cane away, steps back and opens the truck door, slides inside and turns the ignition. He rolls down the cloudy window, his breath visible. "You'll be caught one of these days," he says, looking right at Buster. "That'll teach you *and* your father." Then he sets his gaze on Doc John. "Stick to medicine old man." He tears off, leaving them both to get splashed by his tires.

"Did you hear what he said about me?" Buster is fuming. "I should've creamed him!"

"I dare say he would've deserved it." The doctor wheezes as though he's been sucking on gravel. His stomach is on fire again and he shifts in his clothes so that he might loosen the bandages wrapped around his rib cage. "You better hope your father doesn't hear about this."

"I bet Dad won't even care."

"Oh he'll care, all right." Doc John slips his small hands into his gloves. "Len's got an axe to grind, but you shouldn't be taking that tone with him."

"What do you expect me to do, just let him run us down like that? In front of the others? In front of Jelly Bean? You're the one who's always talking loyalty."

The doctor is off in a huff, walking home, his breathing laboured and his cane slicing into the snow at an even pace. The clean sound is of a clock—*tick-tock, tick-tock*—winding down.

"I'm sorry Doc. I am." Buster rushes to catch up. "You're right; I shouldn't get so frosted."

"Well are you angry because Len's after your father or are you just plain mad at everyone? Whose side are you on, son?"

"Yours," says Buster. "I mean Dad's. You're right. It's just family honour and all that. I swear, from now on I resolve to shoot straighter."

The doctor smirks, and then can't help laughing out loud. "Easy now. There's no need to get carried away."

On the afternoon of Christmas Eve Buster swaggers up Main Street in his hat. You all think I'm the bandit? Fine, might as well act like one. See if I don't command respect this way. He approaches the makeshift skating rink around the back of Johnson's store and stands in the snowbank along the lip of ice. He is bundled under so many layers that his face is barely visible. Walter, one floor up, aims his stereo out through his kitchen window and into the yard. It blares Giselle McKenzie and then the McGuire Sisters while the kids lace up.

Jelly Bean practises her figures on the small rink. She is wearing a new red plaid coat and a white scarf wrapped tightly around her skinny throat. Her ankles practically touch the ice as she cuts wobbly figures in her new skates. Hazel presides over the event, yelling down for encouragement. "Work on your axel dear, that's the hardest. Think of Barbara Ann. She's a ballerina on ice!"

Susan flies past. "Think *you're* Canada's sweetheart? Watch this." She glides a few feet, stops and picks the ice with the toe of her skates. This causes her to spin one and a half rotations, like a real professional. Hank, who is running along the road, reaches the Johnsons' in time to witness her spin. She makes him dizzy. He rushes to do up his own skates and weaves in and around the girls, gliding along the ice with the aim of making a big impression.

"Show off!" Buster hollers at his brother.

Hank whips a snowball and Buster dodges it. Then Buster imitates Susan by spinning on the balls of his feet, exaggerating his gestures and taking a dramatic bow in the snow. Jelly Bean, seeing this, giggles and pushes off towards him. She totters on the edge of the rink farthest away from the house where her mother might not see.

"Wanna join us?"

"Naw, not interested," he lies.

"Maybe you can't skate any better than me." She examines his hat and there's a long silence. Cloudy breath hangs in the air. "You look like a gangster in that."

"Good."

"Since when are you a gangster, Buster?"

Buster stands taller, his boots sinking a couple of inches. "Since I say so."

Jelly Bean's wet lashes flutter like a nervous moth.

"I heard Susan say there's going to be a New Year's Eve party."

"Sounds lame."

"Yeah," she agrees, trying not to be hurt. "I guess I could always go with someone else…." Hank speeds past and Jelly Bean smiles at him. Blood threshes inside Buster's veins like his father's field machine. Before he can calm himself Jelly Bean has pushed off and stumbled away, the blush on her cheeks suggesting more than cold weather. She waves a bright white mitten and he waves back, speechless.

Jelly Bean repeats the same figures over and over, trying to hold precisely to her line, and as she does so her fists, inside her mittens, are clenched. I've had it, she thinks. Being good and proper is boring. She pretends the blades on her feet are brushes and that the ice is a large grey canvas on which anything might be drawn. Barbara Ann began at the age of nine, her mother has told her. *She* practised seven hours each day. Big deal. What might I have already drawn or painted, Jelly Bean wonders, using all that ice time? What unique beauty is waiting for me?

Buster watches her teeter and skate. Watches Walter and Hazel join the others on the farthest edge soon after, and all the girls passing each other in wide rings of silent competition. He observes Gloria and Susan holding hands to steady one another and Hank speeding after them, strong as a wolf. He doesn't spot Ivan and Donny advancing up the drive until they're upon him and then he makes no attempt at a handshake.

"Hey." Donny's black hair pokes out from under his cap. Ivan stares at Buster's hat and Buster can tell he's impressed.

"So, I hear folks think *I'm* the bandit."

Donny and Ivan regard one another sheepishly.

"We heard something about that," says Ivan.

"I bet you did." Buster runs his fingers along the brim of his hat. "I bet you had something to do with it too."

Donny slugs Ivan. "Told you it wasn't true."

"Maybe it is and maybe it isn't," Buster grins. "Think what you like…." He kicks at the ice. "So, you fellas expect to bag any good loot this year?"

"Naah," says Ivan. "Just the same old clothes and junk."

"My mom found me another *Tales from the Crypt*," says Donny. "I saw it in the closet where she keeps the unwrapped presents."

"Which one is it?"

"Number twenty-seven. It starts with Four Way Split."

"Cool. That's got to be one of the last."

"Yeah, it's boss. Roy Dixon gets sentenced to the gas chamber and then he's on a scaffold. He thinks it's all a dream. Come by sometime. I'll loan it to you."

"Maybe I will." Buster kicks the snow, one boot and the other.

"Listen," Ivan finally says. "I'm having a bash on New Year's Eve. Everyone's coming."

"No parents," adds Donny.

"Yeah? I dunno. Maybe."

"Maybe maybe maybe," mimics Ivan. "You're the maybe man now."

Buster clenches his jaw, feeling provoked. Something in Ivan's taunting seizes him and sends him back to that night in the root cellar, the night of his accident.

"Bet you can't outdrink me," Ivan had dared, waving a bottle of Gibson's, and Buster knew he'd have to drink more than half the bottle without stopping if he was to beat Ivan's record. He dropped his lit cigarette into an empty cola can and grabbed the whiskey.

"No sweat."

"Ready?" Donny raised one hand and brought it down fast, as though to signal the start of a drag race. "Go!"

Buster remembers lifting that bottle to his lips and tasting the old flavour as it pressed against his teeth and clawed down his throat to rest, like a dirty mound, in his stomach. He remembers coughing and gagging at first, and the others laughing at him. Ivan pretended to take tiny sips from an imaginary bottle. "You drink like my sister," he said. That was when Buster held the bottle with both hands, closed his eyes and swallowed in bigger gulps. He hated losing to Ivan more than to anyone, for they were evenly matched in many arenas. Both their fathers were growers, natural born leaders, though Tom McFiddie inspired respect whereas Len Rombout demanded it. He and Ivan had tied scores for their school's broad jump record and tried to impress girls. He wasn't going to be satisfied unless he saw Ivan knocked down a peg or two.

"Don't quit now," said Donny. "Keep going."

Ivan moved to the corner of the root cellar where he kicked over a copy of his latest girlie magazine. The brunette on the cover was topless, her full, round breasts and dark nipples partially obscured by a soft lens. "She's all yours if you win."

Buster forced his throat open and tilted the bottle higher. He remembers gagging again and sputtering and finally wiping his mouth on his bare arm.

"You did it!" said Donny, examining the bottle closely. "Holy smokes; you outdrank Ivan by almost two inches."

"Hold your horses." Ivan kicked the magazine out of reach. "Let's see if he keeps it down."

Buster had done worse to defeat Ivan. Swallowed live minnows, stood barefoot in the snow until he couldn't feel the ground or his toes. But defeat, he was about to learn, is its own cruel master. The whiskey churned and threatened to rise and sure enough, before he knew what had hit him he was dropping forward on his knees, grabbing his gut and hurling the digested remnants of his dinner and the whiskey all over the root cellar floor.

"So what do you say," Donny asks, interrupting the memory. "You coming or not?"

Buster rubs his hands together. He considers his options: he could stay home with his parents and Lizzie on New Year's Eve and feel sorry for himself or he could endure the party and feel sorry for himself, but at least that way Ivan would have to eat his words.

"Okay wise guy," he says. "I'll see you there." He slides across the ice and waves to the boys over his shoulder. He waits to drag his brother away from Susan who is all over Hank—laughing, complimenting him on his athletic ability, grabbing on to his arm for support. It takes a few moments to convince Hank that it's time to leave, though once he does they hurry home together and Buster feels a strange unrelenting flutter in his chest. The flutter of a fragile new opening, even hope setting in. He is to be reckoned with. With the fedora sitting on his head and a fine weapon tucked away he is unstoppable again. Free for the moment, at least. What would a Purple do next?

2

The McFiddies pile into Tom's truck in their best clothes and head over to the Grays' as they do every Christmas Day. Isabel and Lizzie sit in the cab with Tom while Buster and Hank sit behind in the open box, their chins tucked into their scarves for warmth. Buster is wearing a new shirt, his good pants, his winter coat and of course the white fedora. He stuck a red bow from one of his gifts on the side like a paper boutonniere. He intends to give the bow to Jelly Bean and is holding it, and his hat, on with one hand.

"Susan was pretty friendly yesterday," he says.

Hank aims his face into the cold, dry air. "Yeah."

"Are you gonna take her out again?"

"I dunno." He looks at Buster. "What's it to you, anyway? And what's with that goofy hat?" Now Buster grips the side of the truck for balance as his father turns a corner.

"It's not goofy."

"Whatever you say … I can't believe we're stuck hanging with old sawbones today."

"Don't talk about Doc John like that. Besides, you got something more important to do?"

"As a matter of fact."

Tom pulls into the driveway and parks behind Doc John's Oldsmobile. Isabel bundles Lizzie into her blanket. "I hope those boys behave themselves," she says. "And promise me *you* won't get carried away. You know how Alice is." Tom rolls his eyes. Despite his distant Quaker blood, a taste for the occasional beer courses through his veins like a diluting tonic. He cranks the door handle, is out of the truck first.

Buster jumps out of the back and carries a bag of baby paraphernalia into the house without waiting to be asked. Hank carts in the remaining gifts and a box of their mother's baking while Isabel stands on the veranda with Lizzie asleep in her arms. The house looks and sounds too quiet, she thinks. Not alive. Something is definitely wrong though she can't put her finger on it. There are no candy-coloured lights strung up along the awnings this year, and five wilted poinsettia plants line the wrap-around porch. The flicker of a television set is coming through the window like a dying ember. Isabel shivers. She's developed a sixth sense over the years, a special sensitivity to loss, and she is certain these are warnings. But of what? When Alice waves to her from the kitchen door Isabel joins the others.

Buster slips off his coat inside the door and uses the heel of one boot to pry off the other. He hears Walter downstairs with Hazel, getting a tour of the canning room. He leaves his hat on and surveys the living room. The drapes and carpet are both a dusty floral pattern and match the couch. Three oil paintings hang in wide wooden frames, pastoral scenes. Two miniature watercolours sit in tiny easels on the white plaster mantel along with a clock, a pair of white candlesticks decorated with an ivy design and, at the far end, a large orange carnival glass dish filled with hard ribbon candy. Walter's French horn case leans against the side of a wooden television cabinet that is sitting along the far wall beside a tree. Pine needles are already beginning to dry and scatter on the floor. The fresh smell fills the room. Candy canes dangle from branches like red-and-white question marks.

Buster expects to see Ivan and Susan planted in front of the television trading insults, but Lorraine called Alice earlier in the day with her regrets. Bob Bryson is in the rocking chair in one corner of the room. His wife is unable to attend, according to him, as she's taken Donny's younger sister and gone to care for her aging parents in Port Dover. Donny is a few feet away from his father, leaning up against the mantel where a pyramid of black cut-glass rocks are piled inside like a stack of coal. Beneath them the electric element flickers red and orange. Jelly Bean sits on the rose-coloured divan, flipping through a copy of the latest *Reader's Digest*. Her face blooms like a flower for a bee as soon as she sees Buster enter the room. She bites her lip to keep from spilling out unnecessary greetings.

Buster tips his hat in Doc John's direction and moves to join Jelly Bean on the couch. She is wearing a baby blue sweater set. Her blond hair is pulled off her face with a navy and white headband and dark roots are beginning to show. When Tom enters the living room Doc John interrupts his discussion with Bob. He reaches down to lower the footstool of his brand-new recliner and struggles to stand and shake Tom's hand.

"How's business?"

"Oh, can't complain, Doc." Tom shakes firmly.

"Good. Now what can I offer you?"

"We've got ginger ale," Alice calls out from the kitchen. "Apple cider and, my, I see someone's brought beer." Isabel stops undressing Lizzie from her many layers and shoots her husband a sharp look.

"I'll have one of those," says Bob.

"Sounds good. I'll have one too." Tom slaps Doc John on the back. "Might even take up a pipe one of these days."

Isabel moves to stand beside the divan with a fussy Lizzie in her arms.

"Is she colicky, Mrs. McFiddie?"

"No Judy, she's making up for missed meals. In fact here we go again. Excuse me." Isabel carries the baby into the next room. Despite what people say about breastfeeding being wrong, even immoral, Isabel feels something special doing it. She knows she provokes talk but she doesn't care. She wishes that she'd done the same with her boys all those years ago and wonders whether Buster wouldn't still be more connected to her now if she had. She closes the door partway, settles on a chair and lifts her blouse. She undoes her brassiere so that the infant is able to burrow her face in and attach to a nipple. When Isabel looks up she finds Donny watching through the slim opening to the room. She notices the expression on the boy's face, how his brow furrows with displaced concentration. She smiles to herself but stops short of lifting her blouse an inch higher, and with it the boy's expectations.

"Cut it out, spy-boy," Hank says, elbowing him.

"Huh. Oh."

"You going to Ivan's bash?"

"Yeah, I'm going."

"Jelly Bean, what about you?"

"Shush. I might, but I don't want Mother to hear."

Walter and Hazel enter the living room from the kitchen and Walter plucks a candy cane from the tree, tosses it to his daughter.

"Now, isn't that lovely," Hazel says, pointing to the electric fireplace. "It's absolutely lovely isn't it, Walter? I think I'd like one for myself. It isn't even real. I mean *that's* a benefit."

"Here we go." Alice carries in a full tray. "I've made tea for those who want something warm. Judy?" She motions for Jelly Bean to assist with the pouring and passing out of beverages. "Thank you, dear."

Alice pours while Jelly Bean steadies each cup and saucer with both hands. Buster notices her chewed cuticles and ragged nails. Bob nurses his beer and inspects the chair and Donny leans back against the mantel, cranes his neck a bit farther and reaches his hand into the candy dish. Reaching, reaching, but still clasping at nothing. Isabel covers herself and returns to the living room.

"Come see this gadget." Tom snaps his fingers to grab his wife's attention and Donny moves so she can pass. "Take a seat. There you go, now flip the button on the armrest." Isabel does as instructed and allows the vibrations to purr beneath her. Donny plucks a long red hair from the headrest and discreetly slips it into his pants pocket.

"Amazing," says Isabel leaning as far back as she can. "All this new technology."

Hank steps forward. "Can I try?"

"Let your mother have a turn."

"No it's all right Thomas." Isabel rises once again and moves out of the way. "I've got my hands full." She kisses Lizzie on the forehead. "Give it a crack Hank."

Hank sits and adjusts the switch to its highest level. His whole body tingles and vibrates. He imagines Susan on his lap, her smooth arms looped around his neck. "Whoa, this is all right. Buster, you oughta try it."

Buster shakes his head, grabs a ginger ale from the tray on the coffee table and leans back to watch the mute television in the corner. A man on the screen waves his hands dramatically about in the air, making what look to Buster like mad gestures. The audience swoons and is apparently moved beyond earthly reach. One woman contorts and twitches when the preacher reaches his hand out and places it atop her head. "Whatever he's curing her of," Buster says, "looks like he's given her a holy seizure to replace it."

"John, must we have that thing on today?"

"Oral Roberts. Best actor I ever seen. Better even than Billy Graham."

"Well I think he's a scoundrel. He makes a mockery of religion."

"I don't know." Walter takes his turn in the chair, cranking out the footstool and resting both legs upon it. "Some people are pretty fond of him aren't they?" He gives his wife a nudge.

"He's got a way about him," Hazel defends, her face the colour of the upholstery.

"Sure does. A way of paying *his* mortgage with *our* donations."

"I'm mad for *Hit Parade*," says Jelly Bean. "I watch it every chance I get." She pours herself a cup of tea, spills some into the saucer and dips the end of the candy cane into the hot liquid, slurping because she knows it will irritate her mother. "What about you, Buster? What programs do you like?"

"I don't watch it much."

"But if you had to say?"

He hates to be forced to participate in conversations. Since the accident, every time he turns around someone is trying to induce him to speak. With little privacy, one-word answers and vagaries are all that provide him space. *"Gunsmoke."* He eyeballs Donny and casually pats his thigh. "Have Gun Will Travel."

Donny blinks nervously, shifts his weight from one foot to the other.

"So violent," says Hazel, with a snort. "All that shooting. It's positively disgraceful."

Tom reaches for a handful of walnuts from a dish on the end table. "The damnedest thing happened; a few months back Buster turned up with this old .38 Special. Most beautiful thing I've ever laid eyes on. Next to my wife of course. It had to be twenty, maybe thirty-odd years, wouldn't you say Buster? You should've seen it Doc." The doctor nods and so do Walter and Bob. "Makes me think of the gun collection my father had when I was a boy."

"Now there's a prime example," says Hazel, as Alice returns from the kitchen with a dish of Isabel's maple fudge and shortbread, which she sets on the coffee table. "Your father was a good man, Tom, though with his temper, an argument against owning guns if ever there was one." Tom pops another handful of nuts in his mouth and thinks how every hunting season his father shot the biggest deer the region had ever seen, record still unbroken.

"At least he kept the gun case locked," he mumbles.

"Buster, where on earth did you get hold of such a thing?"

The doctor peers up from behind his glasses, perched low on his nose, and gives his head the slightest shake.

"Found it in the field, Mrs. Gray. Tripped over it walking home one day."

"I found an arrowhead out there once," says Hank.

"Neat," says Jelly Bean. "My dad's got a whole pile of them, don't you, Dad?"

"Arrowheads, guns. My word," interrupts Hazel. "For crying out loud it's the Christmas season. Let's talk about something cheery."

"That reminds me," says Walter. "I hear there's been a strange sighting just outside of town. Some kind of makeshift camp set up in the woods near Zenda."

"That dairy bar thief," says Bob. "He's a crafty fellow all right."

"So close to here?" Hazel is alarmed. "That's just terrible. Walter I told you; we need better security at the store. These days it seems there's a desperado around every corner."

"Perish the thought," says Alice.

"Well, did they catch him?"

"Not yet. He drove off like the devil. Someone thought he saw an early model Oldsmobile but none was found."

"Doc John's the only one I know with a car like that," says Buster. "I suppose next folks'll be saying it's you who's the bandit." There is a tense silence until Doc John laughs, his voice rising a notch or two higher than usual.

"Heavens," says Alice. "That old heap. Wouldn't get him very far."

"No fooling. And with these legs I'd be caught and behind bars already." Doc John taps one foot and pushes his glasses up onto the bridge of his nose. His top shirt button has come undone revealing a fine collarbone. Slim wrists poke out the cuffs of his impeccable jacket. He moves to switch off the television. "Enough talk." He glances in his wife's direction to gauge her reaction. "I've got a better idea." He motions to Buster. "Fetch my clarinet, will you? It's just inside the office there."

Buster takes another swig of his ginger ale before rising. He's never entered the doctor's office from inside the house before. He fumbles for a wall lamp, his eyes taking a few moments to adjust. Curtains are pulled across the window so that barely a hint of sun leaks through the material. "To your right," he hears the doctor call out. He feels his way along the wallpaper with his palm, and coming to a sconce, turns the button and sets off a golden glow over half of the room. He scopes around for the clarinet case and without forethought eases his way over to Doc John's desk, turning to make sure that no one is watching. Gently, with his head beginning to pulse, he lifts the lid. "Where'd you say you left it?"

"On the floor, over by the bookcase."

Buster fishes inside the desk for bullets, finds them under a folded cotton handkerchief but has no time to grab one before Jelly Bean appears behind him. "Need any help?" He drops the handkerchief and turns to face her. Her cheeks are round and healthy, her neck vulnerable and exposed. The tiny blue buttons on her sweater set look as if they could, at any moment, pop free.

"No, I've got it covered." There's a spiderweb shadow of lashes visible on her cheek and he wants to brush it away. His eyes are drawn down along her body where she swells out to meet him. They both blink embarrassment and Buster steps away from the desk, bumping into the hat tree. He catches it before it topples over.

"Close call." Jelly Bean approaches. "Happens to me all the time." She peeks inside the desk. "Hey, what are all these?" Piled inside, in disarray, is a mound of old newspapers.

"I don't know." Buster moves to stand beside her and begins to root through the papers. Newsprint stains his fingertips. He smells the faint, sweet cinnamon odour of her breath and her perfumed shampoo. He wants to run his fingers through her hair but instead reaches for the paper bow stuck to his hat. He drops his arm before she notices, and returns to the newspapers.

Halfway down the pile is a cover photo showing three men in double-breasted black-and-white pin-striped suits, spats and expensive-looking fedoras, all being led into a courthouse in hand-cuffs. Their backs are to the camera but one man looks as though he turned to the photographer the instant before the flashbulb went off. His image is grainy and featureless except for caustic, marauding eyes that seem to have escaped time. "Wonder who he is?" says Jelly Bean.

The headline has been cut away but the name of the paper is unmistakable—*Detroit Free Press*—and the date, 1931. Buster flips to the next in the stack. A much younger man, from an earlier era this time. A bookish character in a physician's coat with two shady-looking types standing on either side of him and a child of about ten years in his lap. The girl has long, unruly hair and a wrinkled dress. Her legs hang indelicately apart and her legs and feet are bare. Buster stares at the child's hands—one around what he presumes to be her father's neck, and the other holding on to a black medical bag.

"What are you two doing in there?"

"Nothing." Buster slips the paper back into the pile where he found it and quietly drops the lid of the desk. He wipes his hands on his pants, turns and scans the floor, then grabs up the black leather case with two shiny buckles on either end. He and Jelly Bean hurry out of the office without another word.

Alice helps Minister Duff and his wife off with their coats. Laura and Hubert Claxton arrive, and Walter moves to the television where he bends to retrieve his French horn case. Tom goes out to the truck for his trumpet and Buster hands the clarinet case to Doc John. His mother rises to put Lizzie, who is by now half asleep, down in the spare room upstairs.

Doc John balances the clarinet case on his knees, unsnaps it and lifts out the longest joint. He begins to assemble the instrument by moistening a reed between his lips while he screws together the bell, top joint and barrel, adds the mouthpiece and ligature and takes his time lining up all four manufacturer's stamps so that his breath can pass along the body of the instrument making the best possible sound. Then he slides the reed along the flat surface of the mouthpiece, convex side up, and fastens the screws. He slips the tip of the clarinet into his mouth, feels the sharp slivers of the reed. It tastes of a sweet, woody flavour and mildly of the beer he's been nursing. He knows it's his current favourite reed by its thickness and texture. He gestures to Bob and Walter. "Now what say we have some good clean fun?" His fingers fly across the keys but he doesn't breathe into the instrument. "We could use another clarinet player … Hank? Buster?" Both brothers shake their heads.

"Donny?"

"Sorry Doc."

"Judy?"

"Doc John," she drawls. "You shouldn't tease. You know I never learned. They don't let girls play in the band."

THE SUN SINKS like a hidden treasure and Main Street is silent and still. Only the crunching of feet on snow makes any sound. It's as if the whole village has been swathed in cotton batting. It's snowing again, big flakes that make Jelly Bean think of doilies and paper stars falling from the sky. She opens her mouth to catch a flake on her tongue and it melts instantly. She and Buster walk farther along, the air so pure it can't be felt entering their lungs. Houses are outlined with brightly coloured lights and there is faint laughter and the distant clatter of dishes being scraped. One family has left a window ajar and inside, on the radio, Bing Crosby and Rosemary Clooney sing *I'm Dreaming of a White Christmas.*

"How old do you think Doc John is?"

"Gee, I don't know."

"Did he seem nervous tonight?"

"What do you mean? Nervous about what?"

"I'd wager he's seventy. Maybe seventy-five."

"Nah-ah," Jelly Bean shakes her head. "Not that old. Just frail." She turns at the corner by the bank and they descend into the blue-black darkness of the park.

"He talks about Detroit all the time. He must have family there."

Jelly Bean nods this time. "He posts a letter each month. I've seen him do it myself."

"Really? Why do you suppose no one visits?"

"Your guess is as good as mine."

Buster kicks at a piece of ice with the toe of his boot. "I don't know why he would move here in the first place. Smoke is dullsville."

"Where would you rather be?"

"Anywhere."

Buster walks farther along the path until they come upon the creek. He wonders what would happen if he were to grab her and kiss her, or stand close and breathe in her scent. Would she pull back? He steps onto the ice. "Look, I'm Jesus walking on water."

Jelly Bean giggles. "Don't let my mother catch you talking like that."

"Or Mrs. Gray." Buster stomps his boot heel. "Not even a crack, see? C'mon."

"But I'm wearing my good shoes."

"So."

Jelly Bean steps delicately onto the ice, trying her best to appear graceful. Her shoes, without treads, are slippery and her feet slide out from under her. Buster reaches out to catch her but she's down before he gets the chance to break her fall. Her coat spreads out all around like a broken parasol. He laughs and she looks up at him as if she might swat his pant leg or cry, hasn't decided which. "That's not very gallant of you!"

He extends an arm and pulls her up. "Could've happened to anyone."

"Sure but it always happens to me." She wipes the snow off the back of her coat and waits for him to deliver a cruel punchline. He doesn't. "How can Mother honestly expect *me* to win Miss Tobacco Queen?"

"You're a shoo-in."

"Think so?" She's surprised he would say this.

"Sure. You're a guaranteed wow." Buster's tough, guarded veneer is gone for the moment. He removes the red bow from his hat. "Here," he says, holding it out with a nervous hand. "Merry Christmas."

"For me?" She hugs him and he pulls back stiffly.

"It's nothing."

"Oh, thank you. It's beautiful." She sticks the gift to the lapel of her new coat and runs to catch up. "Was it on one of *your* gifts? Or did you buy it? Why'd you pick this colour?"

"What is this, *The $64,000 Question*?" He's finally managed to hand over the boutonniere and here she is blathering on about nothing. He should know better than to be open with her now—she might like to talk with him when they're alone, even try and snag him into going to some bash. She might sincerely believe that she's his friend, but that's only her wanting to feel like a do-gooder.

Jelly Bean tucks her face into the collar of her coat, scolding herself for being such a busybody like her mother. "I'm planning to leave here," she says, changing the subject.

"Oh yeah? Where to?"

"Toronto. For art school. Someday."

"You're just saying that. You're not going anywhere. You'll stay here your whole life like everybody else."

Jelly Bean's eyes narrow. She wants to throw the paper boutonniere in his rubbery face, compel him to take back his words. But she doubts herself. What *is* she saying? That she could succeed on her own, in a great big city? That she could paint pictures someone would ever want to hang? She bites her lip. Who is she anyway? Jelly Bean, her mother's nickname for her. Something small and inconsequential that can be swallowed in one bite. Still, she can't help imagining other students as interested in form and shape as she is, teachers with their paint-stained hands and the wide spectrum of brilliant colour. "I will not," she insists. "What do you know about me, anyway? I've even got a job lined up so I can save. I'm going to help your mother during harvest."

"At the farm?" His chest is a cave.

"Why? Don't you think I can do it? I count cash at the store every Saturday I'll have you know. I make deposits. I do exactly what Daddy says; wear my long brown skirt with the deep pockets, hide the cash in one of the pockets and his knife in the other in case there's trouble hanging around the park. And don't think I wouldn't use it either." She corrects her posture while she speaks. "I march straight into the bank like I'm supposed to. Nobody ever bothers me. Heck Buster, I can handle practically anything!"

He is impressed. The way she looks he never would have guessed she had it in her to carry a knife. He wonders if she's carrying one now and if she really knows how to use it, but he's even more absorbed by the thought of having her close in the summer. Harvest with its impossibly long days seals a bond between workers. If she were there she would become a part of that. "Sure, sure, I just mean, you've never worked harvest before, that's all."

"Uh-huh, I learn fast. I'll cook, and the rest of the time I'll work with the table gang."

"That's great. I mean it's great that you'll be helping out."

"Yeah. Then I'll have money for art school." She marches ahead. "And a real future."

He remembers that at Sunday school once, when they were young, she'd shown him how to mix blue and yellow water paints together to produce the colour green—a lesson he still recalls each time he looks out at his father's field. He remembers asking about the image she'd painted. "It's a dead bird," she'd said, rather dismayed that he couldn't tell. And when he called the painting goofy and asked what she'd want to go and paint some ugly dead thing for, she'd been adamant. "It's not ugly to me, Buster."

"Judy?" he catches up to her. "You know Ivan's New Year's bash?"

She turns. He's never used her given name before.

"Uh-huh."

"Well I was thinking … if you still want to go?"

"With you?"

"Never mind. It was a dumb idea."

Blood moves beneath her skin in swift currents. She's been flirting with the idea of Buster, with what it might be like to know him better, but agreeing to this would be real. What would people say? What would her mother say? She touches her fingertips to the petals of her paper flower and smiles.

On Boxing Day Jelly Bean wakes and reaches for the boutonniere she tucked beneath her pillow the night before. She lifts it to her face as if she might inhale a sweet scent. The bow is flattened so she pulls its petals open. It's a colour she cherishes; the most vibrant in her set of water paints, the colour of her new winter coat and as shiny as laughter. Passionate as an exotic dance from a faraway land. Its bright crimson with a hint of orange mixed in is a woman's colour and it makes her feel grown.

Hazel pokes her head into the room and the sharp smell of ammonia wafts in. "Up and at 'em, lazy bones. Time to do your hair." Jelly Bean shoves the paper flower under the covers. "What's that?" Hazel's eyes land on the boutonniere.

"Nothing."

"Doesn't look like nothing, Judy. Let me see."

Jelly Bean lifts the covers and watches her mother's spine fix into a straighter position. Hazel's brow stiffens and a small blue vein beneath her left eye pulses. There are clearly things going on that she knows nothing about. Her mouth opens but she is dumbstruck and Jelly Bean knows that her mother's voice, when it pushes through the shock, will be filled with disapproval. "Buster gave it to me." She slips it protectively under her pillow once more.

"I knew it. I knew we shouldn't have allowed you to go traipsing off alone. If I've told you once I've told you a thousand times, boys only want one thing and you my dear are not open for business. Besides, that young man may be trouble. In any case he's not for you. Not any more. And it's unkind of you to get his hopes up."

Jelly Bean is silent. She knows better than to argue with her mother on this or any other matter. When she wants something badly enough she's always gone to her father, made her case plainly and with reason, and he then took on negotiating with her mother,

133

or sometimes went over her mother's head, as he did last year when he drove her to Brantford to visit the reserve. But Jelly Bean can't ask her father about boys.

"I like him, Mother."

"Well, I like bread pudding but you don't catch me falling silly and sideways for it, do you? Certain things just aren't good for us and we all have to accept the fact." Hazel is now standing in Jelly Bean's closet inspecting her clothes. "Wear this today." She turns, holding up a prim pleated skirt and blouse that Jelly Bean hasn't worn in over a year. "Mauve goes with your complexion."

"I'm not wearing that. I hate that outfit."

"There are so many other boys, Judy. Don't make a big fuss over nothing. What about Ivan Rombout, his father's successful. Or even Donny Bryson? What about *Hank* McFiddie? Now there's a young man with prospects, and he's good looking to boot."

"He's not Buster."

"This is nonsense." Hazel drops the skirt and blouse at the end of the bed. "Buster is out of the question. I forbid it and that's that. Hurry up; I've got a million things to do this morning. Now. Before the peroxide sits too long and wastes."

"Leave me alone." Jelly Bean kicks the clothes onto the floor. "Stop telling me what to do. And I'm not bleaching my hair, so there!" She is sick and tired of being dictated to, primped and curled. She'll bloody well make friends with whomever she pleases. "I like him, Mother," she repeats, clearly and without confrontation this time, so that it sounds as if it's an already established fact. "I like him and I'm going to keep seeing him." This is when she knows for certain that it's true. She throws off the bedclothes and reaches for her bathrobe. The floor is cold on her bare feet. Her ankles are stiff from skating and her hip a bit sore from her fall on the river. She finds her slippers by the side of the bed. She knows what her mother wants for her, and she wants none of it. She hates her mother. She hates her hair and clothes and she even hates herself.

Hazel cracks the bedroom window an inch and icy air fills the room. She darts around the side of the bed, pulling up the covers and fluffing the pillow. She reaches for the red bow, finds it, crumples it in her palm.

"Hey that's mine. You've got no right!"

"I won't have my daughter parading around with that boy and that's all there is to it. You are going to finish high school young lady, and then you will attend business college in London as planned. Don't even think about going to your father. Someone has to take over at the hardware store one day. And I know all about Ivan Rombout's party. You aren't going. End of discussion."

JELLY BEAN SITS ON THE TOILET seat while her mother pulls a metal comb through her long, thick hair. The prongs of the comb scrape her scalp and the peroxide burns and makes her head itch. The smell coats the inside of her nose and her lungs. She refuses to breathe it in; holds her breath for as long as she can, exhales and immediately inhales again, the way children passing cemeteries do. The bleach is evil and she must somehow hold that evil at bay.

"We just did this two weeks ago. It stinks."

"Grooming takes organization and preparation, my dear. Your roots are showing. You don't want that, do you?"

There's never been any question of being a natural brunette. Jelly Bean has been sitting on this very spot having her hair bleached and dyed ever since she can remember. The smell is sickening and leaves a brackish chemical aftertaste in her mouth. Her hair is losing its softness; it's beginning to dry and frizz and feel like straw to the touch.

Hazel finishes combing the bleach through, rinses the comb in the sink and wraps her daughter's hair in clear plastic to hold the heat and help the peroxide do its job. "There," she says, drying her hands on a towel. "Almost done. Sit like that for twenty minutes and I'll be back to rinse you." She removes her wristwatch, sets it on the counter by the sink and leaves.

Jelly Bean turns to the mirror. Her hair is swept up off her face, and without the blond curls tumbling all around, her face is plain and strong and open. Her jaw is solid. Her eyes look wider, she thinks, and behind them lies an unmistakable longing to be praised without relentlessly being improved upon. Fussed over without condescension. It seems the harder she tries to pass for perfect the less she feels herself to be so. The more she determines not to be clumsy, the more she trips or bumps into furniture. When she strips her hair of colour, the less alive she feels. She is beginning to suspect that the pedestal her mother insists upon for her is pointless after all. A pedestal can't save a girl from herself. She leans in. Yes, her eyes look wider today, and bluer, and they are hiding much. Golly, she thinks, smiling. I look like Daddy.

Jelly Bean rises from her place on the sofa in the den and yawns.

"I think I'll turn in early."

"Already?" asks Walter. "I thought we'd pop corn and listen to Times Square."

"Night," says Hazel, without looking up from her knitting.

In her bedroom, Jelly Bean slides past her bible without a thought for placing it on her head, opens the closet and lifts out the outfit she's already pressed and hung. The skirt is cherry blossom pink and the knit sweater matches. She changes into both and into a new pair of tights she purchased especially for tonight. She pins a pale pink barrette into her hair, fastens clip-on earrings and pinches her cheeks to give them colour. Her saddle shoes are on the closet floor and she slips them on. Delicately, so that not even a whistle from the cold wind outside will alarm her parents, she lifts her bedroom window. An icy gust. Gooseflesh. She crawls out onto the slanted tar roof as though she is crawling out of a coffin and then she closes the window. Her breath appears before her face in tiny white puffs and fades. Her fingers and toes are already numb. Quickly, she brings her knees in tight to her body and balances herself so that her weight is evenly distributed between her feet and rear end and so she won't snag her leg on a nail or a splinter of wood and put a tear in her tights. She inches down the steep slope.

The roof comes out onto a flat area, the ceiling above the store's stock room. She is nervous about getting caught, nervous about slipping and falling though she knows that once she's successfully manoeuvred across the stock-room ceiling there will be but a small jump down to the ground where she will scoot around the back of the store and retrieve the coat and scarf she's hidden. She goes down with a thud, landing on her rear. Has anyone heard? Is she injured? No. She rises, wipes the back of her dress where there is now a wet spot, and finds her coat. Shivering, she covers herself, wraps the scarf around her neck and half of her face, and runs.

BUSTER IS WAITING behind the Bank of Commerce just as he said he would be. He walked the two miles into the village from the farm and he is now jumping up and down to retain warmth. Because of nerve damage from the fire his face isn't able to feel the cold as it should and Doc John has warned him to be careful of extreme temperatures. He's to monitor his skin in winter especially, and not catch frostbite. Now he cups his hands around his mouth and breathes into them for warmth, rubs them together. He's been waiting three quarters of an hour. Maybe she changed her mind and isn't coming after all? And then there she is, speeding through the clear black night like a red plaid beacon. She stops in front of him, out of breath.

"Sorry I'm late. I couldn't get away."

They hurry along Main Street, past the streetlight, and turn near Doc John's house where the giant maple tree stands. This road, unpaved and covered in snow, will guide them a mile up a small incline, and at the top of Palmer's Hill they'll find the United church where his parents were married and where Mrs. Gray taught them both Sunday school. Beyond that sits the Rombouts' property. Buster walked this route many times when he was younger, with Donny if they fetched Ivan for exploring or hanging out in the tree fort, or later, the root cellar.

As they approach the house figures cross the living room through the big front window. A truck is parked in the driveway but the town car is gone. Ivan's parents have driven to Niagara Falls to celebrate their wedding anniversary. He steps up to the front door, hesitates. Bill Haley and the Comets blast on the radio inside, and behind the loud crest of music there is an excited wave of chatter. "Sounds like the whole school's in there," he says.

Jelly Bean has never been to a party that wasn't chaperoned. "C'mon." She grabs him by his hand and pulls him inside.

Buster does as she does. He taps his boots on the welcome mat. He nods at faces he recognizes. He does not stop to think about where they are for he knows if he does he'll turn around and go straight back to the farm as fast as possible. He follows Jelly Bean into the living room where the song ends abruptly and they face the crowd. Conversations wane. People turn. Thirty or more pairs of eyes stare. There is jostling, elbowing. Sandra and Diane pinch each other. Jelly Bean drops Buster's hand and removes her mittens. Now it's her turn to be self-conscious. She slips out of her coat, unwraps the scarf from around her neck and stuffs it and her mittens into her coat pockets.

Buster is immediately buried by his surroundings. Walls ripple and claw as though they are about to collapse. The ceiling presses down. Beer mugs hang above the bar like unspoken fears. A mounted buck's head brags of long brown antlers. The panicked pressure builds in Buster's chest, whirs in his ears, and he can't breathe until gradually music registers again and he hears Donny's voice. "Buster? Jelly Bean? Over here!" Donny waves from the far end of the room where he's leaning against a wood-panelled wall.

"Been here long?" Buster shakes off his coat.

"About an hour."

"Where's Ivan?"

"Upstairs." Donny makes a rude gesture with both hands to show what he means.

Jelly Bean blushes. She knows that some girls make out. The ones with older boyfriends drive to Little Lake and park so they won't be found, or in the summer they go to Courtland for a drive-in movie. Back-seat bingo, she's heard it called, though she has only her imagination to help fill in the details. Her mother says a lady should keep her legs closed at all times or else she'll wind up with a belly full of regrets, so Jelly Bean can't help but conjure a picture of a girl in an upstairs bedroom, her legs tightly crossed and her belly growing ever bigger as Ivan tries to persuade them apart. Jelly Bean has never permitted any boy to kiss or touch her in places that are forbidden, not that anyone's tried, though she knows she would if Buster wanted to. All at once she feels her cheeks burning. What if Buster wants to go upstairs with her? She doesn't know how to interact in social situations—what to say to engage idle chit-chat, or even how to flirt. She isn't good at superficialities; she certainly won't know how to manage something more intimate.

"The place is cookin'," Buster says, surveying the room.

"Yeah." Donny taps his foot to the music. "This one's snappy." He sets his cup down on the counter of the bar beside his cigarettes and matches and is gone.

Jelly Bean notices that Donny's cup is half-full; its rich brown liquid inviting. She tasted alcohol only once before, when she was clearing the table after one of her mother's dinner parties. Her parents had retired to another room and left her to the dishes and she noticed that her father's wine glass hadn't been touched. She lifted the dark red potion to her lips and allowed it to paint the back of her throat. The taste was bitter and dry, and the strength of the flavour didn't fully hit her until she swallowed. She coughed and sputtered and chased it with water. The wine sickened her but she was drawn to it precisely because she wasn't supposed to have it. She lifted the bottle from the centre of the table and drank what was left, swallowing in gulps as if it were grape juice. Washing up that night she was slow and methodical, used both her hands to transfer the plates and cups and good serving dish from the soapy suds in the sink to the clean rinsing water, to the dish rack, without letting anything slip. She was tipsy, she remembers, and enjoyed the warm, fuzzy sensation. Now she lifts Donny's cup and drinks from it. Then she sets the cup back and fumbles to light a cigarette, nervously dropping the matchbox onto the bar top. She manages to open the box and lift out a small stick, but she can't seem to inhale *and* light the cigarette at the same time. Buster is watching her.

"Strike the cruddy thing and get it over with."

"Here. You do it." She passes him the cigarette and match.

His fingers, stiff from the damp night air, are reluctant and tremble when he lifts the stick, flicks its red-capped tip. The sound is grating. A flash sparks up before his eyes. He slams them shut but it's still there, full force, coming at him from all sides. He hears wood scraping wood and a jagged, raggedy-hot explosion. He shakes his head to knock off the smell of sulphur and skin, a bright red light, like blood, still lingering after all this time.

"Buster?"

His head throbs. He opens his eyes. The match remains unlit. His chest twists into a tight ball of elastic bands. A Purple could do it, he chastises himself. Ray Bernstein would be able to stare directly into the face of danger and not even blink. He pulls another stick from the box and once more tries to light it, this time with every bit of determination he can muster, but he accidentally snaps the match in two and, frustrated, tosses the wooden box into the air. Small weapons spill out on the bar top and the carpet like deadly pick-up sticks. He tosses the cigarette across the bar, away with all good intentions, and stuffs his trembling and bloodless hands deep into his pockets. The smell of stale tobacco surrounds him. He doesn't move, not even a shudder. Not even a shudder. "I can't," he finally admits. He feels like a deflated rubber tire. Anger rises in his bones. "Anyway, girls don't smoke."

Jelly Bean reaches for a match and another cigarette from Donny's package, and easily lights one now. She lifts the thin stick to her lips, takes her first drag. Inhales. It's a nutty flavour. Smoke fills her throat and she washes the tobacco down with a gulp of whiskey. It's stronger than wine. The taste is heady and sweet but mostly antiseptic. It tastes as she imagines bleach might. "Girls shouldn't do a lot of things," she says. "We shouldn't sneak out of the house. We shouldn't date boys our mothers don't approve of." She is already feeling disreputable simply by being at the party. She raises her eyes and bends her head back and there hanging above them is a tiny green sprig with small white berries. "We shouldn't kiss under the mistletoe."

Buster looks up and falls silent.

A moment later Susan appears wearing a white dress, white sweater, and white stockings which she adjusts as she enters the living room. "I didn't know you two were coming." The way she says this it's understood that she means she hadn't known Buster and Jelly Bean would be coming *together*. Jelly Bean balances on the edges of her saddle shoes, glances at Buster nervously. She's in Susan's territory and there's no telling what Susan might say or do next. The only wise course of action is to be friendly and placate her.

"I'm not trying out for Miss Tobacco Queen," she says.

"You're not?"

"Nope. Mother will be signing girls up though, if you're interested. Hey, great party. Don't your parents mind?"

Susan turns her back to the dance floor and to her brother who appears there. When she looks at Jelly Bean her eyes are dead colourless beads. "They don't know," she says. "They never know what Ivan's up to."

HANK STEPS INTO THE HOUSE as a cuckoo clock on the foyer wall sings eleven times. He tosses his coat across the banister. He is going to make his big move tonight, buoyed by Susan's recent flirtatiousness. No more pussy-footing around. A new year is upon them and he's made his resolution. He's just been over to George Walker's place talking to George about the possibility of part-time work. George is raising two hundred and fifty hogs this year, carrying most of the work himself. He could use help with fixing up the rail fence, filling troughs and shovelling out the pens.

"Hey lard ass." Hank finds his brother in the living room. "What're you doing so far from home?" He gives Buster a playful shove.

"Keepin' an eye on you."

Hank looks beyond Buster and Jelly Bean to Susan who stands like a silent white cloud. Like a bride, he thinks. He smiles at her.

Susan has never seen Hank this cleaned up, including the night he took her out. She notices his hands and decides that he must have scrubbed them raw for there isn't a hint of dirt caked under his nails. She smiles back.

Donny returns out of breath and pours himself a fresh drink. "Guess what, Buster? The kid working the counter at the dairy bar on the day it was hit up is over there."

"Really?"

"Uh-huh. He says one minute he was alone and the next he knew had a gun at his back."

"Did he see anything?"

"Don't think so. No one did on account of the scouts riding through town. Folks are getting pretty frosted."

"I bet they'll never catch him."

"Oh he'll be spotted one day." Donny watches for Buster's reaction. "Everyone's on the lookout now."

Jelly Bean holds her own cup out for a refill and uses the conversation as an excuse to move closer to Buster. "Just thinking about it makes me nervous."

Buster grins like a wide-smiling huckster. A Purple would get away with it, he knows. A Purple would be high off the challenge, already casing around for the next hold-up, ready to make a grab for every last penny. Yeah, if this local bandit has an ounce of the true criminal in him, he'll be back. Maybe he never left. Buster imagines gambling debts, cross-border boozing and the terrifying reality of men with nothing left to lose. In his mind he hears a twelve-gauge Winchester pump-gun firing fast and an expensive grey sedan with revolving licence plates squealing away from local police. He smells fear on the victims—especially that. He can practically taste revenge. He watches his brother take Susan in his arms on the dance floor. "Don't worry," he says, gently nudging Jelly Bean. "You're safe with me."

At a quarter of midnight Doc John stands inside the small water closet off to one side of his office. The door is closed and locked behind him, the key on the side of the enamel sink basin, although he knows no one is likely to walk in for there is only him and Alice in the house and she is upstairs turning the bed down. He can hear her slippers shuffling across the floor above like soft, reassuring whispers. He faces the door, stares into a small round mirror hanging on the back by a single nail. Only his face is visible, distorted by the warped mercury glass. A sharp burning pain attacks him and he doubles over, catches his breath. He coughs, this time coughing blood into the sink. It streaks down the white enamel and into the drain as red as any ambulance siren. He runs the tap to wash the blood away, swirls the water around the sink and remembers how the Detroit River circled and swirled in small currents, how it was a dark green, near brown body of water on the day he left, wet but not glassy, cold but not nearly so cold that he would have frozen falling in. He walked across the Ambassador Bridge with its thick metal beams underfoot, his suitcase in hand, a medical diploma and someone else's birth certificate and identity papers taken for his own, including the altered name and dates. It was July 20, 1932.

The bridge arched like a steely rainbow, wire and the beginnings of rust stretching from one world to the next, joining two places that time and history divided arbitrarily; a river with a French name mispronounced that had once been the pride of Chief Tecumseh. Most people on either side forgot they ever knew. He smelled the water mossy and sour and looked down at its still, sinister flow. So many had jumped or fallen or were disposed of there; or such was the lore. Even the fish were in danger of drowning. The air carried more than its scent of carp and worms and automotive plants that day. It was foul with the odour of shift work and kick-backs and mob rule.

Night turned to dawn and time evaporated into one precious hope. The city of music and motors fell back and disappeared into a steel curve while its twin of salt mines and roses came more clearly into focus. Grey smoke trailed from one side of the river to the other, blowing its poisons across to Canada and leading the way forward above barges and fish and garbage floating below. Smoke billowed black and sooty, mingled with fresh air and a whispering sunrise that was getting ready to shout. Detroit slumbered while Windsor sat flickering ahead, ready to rise to the occasion. At least that's how he felt at the time. That's how he remembers it.

It took less than half an hour to cross, even with fear getting in his way like a wall of fists. One foot at a time, he told himself. One foot and then another, like a soldier marching into unknown territory. He walked with a stride that might easily have belonged to another man, the one who'd gripped his left arm, struggled to speak, and collapsed across the table in that dingy back room on the Lower East Side. Their features were similar, their colouring and height close enough. The man was his mentor, his father. How then had he done it? He'd moved fast. Not stopped to consider the consequences. Stolen papers and clothes, and in a matter of minutes abandoned a fledgling practice and the rest of the family without leaving a trace. What gave him the strength? Ah, but it wasn't strength, he knows. It was necessity—the selfish human drive that keeps us all alive. Self-preservation. He'd been dreaming his own departure for too many years, flirting with the fantasy but never really believing it would come true, and then suddenly, in an instant, opportunity opened a door. He'd thought of the gallant ones with lives cut short, those who were swallowed whole by the lure and devastation of war or of a gang—or by their own gaping desires. It wasn't going to be him. He was fed up with an existence he hadn't chosen, one he never would have chosen, and so when his father collapsed on the examination table, murdered for his refusal to continue to treat the mob, and with no one else around to witness it, a real possibility to escape into a new life finally presented itself and he leapt. Dodge expectation, he told himself on his last day in Michigan. And maybe, just maybe, you'll have a chance to flame.

At the halfway point where borders were indistinguishable he stopped, leaned over the side of the bridge, felt the breeze caress the short hair on his newly shaven neck and took one last look at the shore, so familiar. East to Belle Isle and beyond to Grosse Pointe Park where his unknowing mother, now a widow, lay sleeping in a four-poster bed. His lungs twisted into airless knots inside his chest. There would be no more lines drawn from there to here or beyond. Never again. He wouldn't enjoy the comfort of being known from beginning to end. Crossing meant fragments and scatterlings, meant being flung into the atmosphere like a dandelion spore for the rest of his days. Crossing deprived him of background, of history, and he would not be free to speak of his family or friends or even of his childhood home. He'd never call; hear his mother's voice, although in time he would come to write. His life was dividing into drawers as he walked, or pockets, of which he alone would ever know the full contents. Did I choose this, he thought, looking directly ahead in the distance at the customs booth. Or did this choose me?

The Union Jack with its red, white and blue, and crosses plain and simple, flapped overhead like a soothing round of applause. One more step and he'd be on the other side, the Canadian side, safe. He stood very still and listened until no more cars passed. Confident that traffic had lulled, he quickly undressed and dressed once more in his new suit and tie. He tossed his old clothes over the side, underwear and all, and watched them tumble and fall—the royal blue material of his coat puffing open like a parachute or a bell, gliding and swaying, tolling mute on the wind and sinking under with all the other bodies buried there. Through squinted eyes he observed what felt like a ghost of himself contort and float off down the river. A shadow, a ghost, a blue shell meant for someone else. He was destined, he knew then, to remain as elusive as a cloud of smoke. Hidden. Camouflaged for the balance of his life inside shades of grey.

The rest of the way across he held himself noticeably erect. He wore the white fedora as he approached the border guards with a pulse so violent that it pumped through his cells like a neighbourhood bully, though he passed, as many outlaws have and will, by saying less than intended and looking as if he knew exactly where he was going. His dead father's pistol was strapped to his leg like a last resort.

Crossing a border as one person and arriving on the other side as another wasn't as hard as he expected. Even the ache faded with time. The rootless ache of a sapling pulled up and out of the earth. Motherless. Fatherless. What will become of me, he had wondered so long ago. Who will know me any more? Luckily, time had answered those questions, age and experience had arranged for replacements. Alice had become family. Medicine his only constant. Smoke was a second chance.

Now, all these years later, he holds a thick roll of gauze in his hands. His wristwatch indicates that it's almost midnight, a New Year, and the moon pours across the village as he winds the white bandages around his chest as if he is a living mummy. Around and around, under his arms, behind and across his back, again around the front, flattening his body into streamlined position. Secured down with a pin. Each morning while he dresses he goes through this same liberating routine. He runs the tap, drinks a glass of water to relieve his stomach, and unwinds by humming along to the guttural, back-of-the-throat voice coming through the transistor radio on the other side of the door. *It's Ooon-ly Make Beee-lieve!*

Doc John stares into the small glass hanging on the water closet door and notices how each new day has sunk more wrinkles deeper into his face, the old crater. He reaches up and runs his bulbous fingertips across the sprig of whiskers poking out his chin. He is sure the human body is an atlas of the future, at least a compass point-ing in the direction of unconquered territory. Already tuberculosis, polio, diabetes are better under medical control. Yet what of rarer conditions, those that also plague the mind and spirit? He can imagine all manner of illness wiped out with new medications. Limbs and organs eventually replaced. Skin harvested and grown back, and because he can think these things he is sure they will be possible in time. He believes in progress as strongly now as when he'd been a much different person. More so. For initially, under his father's instruction, he practised medicine in order to heal—correct, comprehend humanity—but now he knows he's also become a doctor so that he might better understand himself.

His heart *thud thuds,* his lungs lurch with each breath and his abdomen swells and burns the more he thinks about the past. What if he'd been born in another time, another place? The idea quickly leaves him. A passport is all he's ever needed to be happy—his coats and shirts and shoes, his hair and his handshake—passports. He regards his warped reflection and remembers something Alice said when he told her he was looking into a new surgery for Buster, a procedure that could remove some of the scars. "Only God," she said with an uncharacteristic measure of doubt in her voice. "Only our maker can unmake us."

He rinses the sink once more and makes sure no blood stains the basin. He pats his hands dry on a towel and walks out of his small washroom, grabbing his coat and hat from the hat tree beside his desk, unlocking the door and looking out through his office onto the front veranda. Off across Main Street and into the village the river runs chilled under its icy layers and reminds him how precious this life, how short. He breathes deeply knowing that this winter is to be his last—the end is already stinging in the moist air. There is new urgency now as the pain in his abdomen is sharper than yesterday and his lungs struggle to accommodate each new breath. He looks up at the awnings. For the first time since they bought the house, he wasn't well enough to hang lights. The church bells ring on Palmer's Hill and he stares out at the blackness. His neighbours, many of them his patients, sleep in houses all around. So many characters, he thinks. Even in one small village. More than will ever be counted.

SEED, PLANT
AND PRAY

The Lions Club holds a spring fling to raise money for the sesqui-centennial. Large clusters of balloons tied with baling string are hung at the entrance to the town hall. Green and pink bristol board cut into a row of miniature tobacco plants is taped across the door. As a member of the United Church Women's Association, Hazel Johnson has volunteered to manage food for the event and to round up contestants and register them for Miss Tobacco Queen, 1959. She cannot locate Jelly Bean anywhere.

Hazel is wearing a brown polyester pantsuit with an elastic waist and matching sleeveless top—pale orange with a darker orange collar. Her only makeup is a pinkish-orange lipstick—nearly fluorescent. "We've got twelve dishes coming," she announces when she finds Alice by the food table. "I don't know about Isabel's ambrosia though. Apparently she insisted, but it's always runny as the river."

Alice sets their finished quilt down along with a stack of raffle tickets and an empty fish bowl. She is dressed in a peach knee-length dress with white buttons and matching shoes. "Mind your language," she says as Tom breezes past.

Both women cut across the hall to where Walter is stationed in the corner with his record player and a stack of LPs and some 45s. An ashtray sits on the table, his lit cigarette burning. He steps around the front of the table, plugs the cord of his player into the wall socket and sets the arm and needle down on the black vinyl disc. *Wake up, little Susie* ... He lifts the cigarette to his lips.

"Evening, Alice."

"Evening."

"I wanted him to come in costume," Hazel says. "To get the spirit of the thing going. I suggested the Lone Ranger but he refused."

"Should've asked me to come as Tonto, dear. Jay Silverheels is from Six Nations too."

Hazel bristles. She quickly turns her attention to the far end of the room, scrunches her face like a sock monkey's and marches off across the hall and through the swinging double doors of the kitchen.

Walter replaces his cigarette in the ashtray, leans across the table and cups his mouth.

"I do love getting under her skin."

"You shouldn't tease," Alice wags her pointer finger. "She means well." Secretly, though, Alice is glad for Walter's good and open nature. Hazel's sanctimonious air is the one thing about her friend that she has a hard time tolerating. Alice rummages through the stack of records, tapping the toe of her shoe. "I don't know any of these singers. I must be getting old."

"This band's playing now." Walter holds up an album cover. "The Everly Brothers." He waits for the song to end and then sets another of their records on the turntable. He drops the arm and needle of the player on the disc and it makes a scratching, static sound before the instruments play. Alice stares out at the empty dance floor as the melody drifts over her—*All I have to do is dreeeam* ... Oh what on earth is keeping John? She scratches her right palm and resolves that if he doesn't show up within ten minutes she'll slip back to the house and check on him.

Soon others begin arriving and milling about the food tables. Gladys and Herb Peacock, the Claxtons, Tom's hired man Simon. Hank arrives in a buckskin jacket and coonskin hat. Alice moves to greet Gladys and Herb as if it's a wedding reception and she is the mother of the bride. She feels a bit racy in heels. She ordered the shoes from Brantford after finding a screen star wearing them in one of Hazel's gossip magazines.

George Walker arrives in his usual blue overalls, carrying a large bowl for cherry punch. He stops to admire the food—sugar cookies decorated with orange and yellow sprinkles, date squares, chocolate cake and cream pies. Len Rombout and his wife, Lorraine, tag behind with Susan carting a dish of orange and marshmallow Jell-O salad. Susan places the dish on the table and moves to join the other girls over by the corner where they're lining up to bob for apples. She'll sneak a cigarette first chance she gets. Hazel attends to filling George's bowl with water and mixing the instant punch crystals. The scent of a freshly baked yellow cake wafts through the hall. George barrels towards Alice at the music stand.

"Why that smell must be your fault. Not a woman for miles can fix a dessert as good as yours." He leans in and kisses her on the cheek and then shakes hands with Walter. George smells of a strong Castile soap masking pig shit.

"I hate to disappoint you George, but that's nothing more than a Betty Crocker mix." Alice smiles, guessing that the men won't know who Betty Crocker is. George and Walter exchange a look and then, catching on, George pretends he's been pierced by an arrow.

Hank approaches and soon he and George are thick into conversation.

"My boar cost two hundred dollars last year," says George. "Came from a litter of twelve. Made a hundred pounds of gain on three hundred and twenty-five pounds of feed."

Hank whistles. "You got a bargain there."

"Sure did," nods George. "You know, I been raising purebred Hampshires since high school, but ever since I tried my first production-tested boar, a Minnesota No.1, I seen a profit. Drove down to Indiana for him. Best decision I ever made. Changing keeps 'em all strong."

"Too many boars are really scrubs," agrees Hank.

"I could still use your help. Any time. Gotta ear-notch them now. And those rail-fence cribs really need fixing."

Ivan enters the hall with sisters Gail and Doreen Manning hanging off his arms like dogs on leashes. The girls are led across the dance floor together, each assuming that she is the lovelier. Isabel follows closely, carting Lizzie in one arm and a full bowl of ambrosia in the other. Seeing her, Tom strides across the room, lifts his daughter gently and swings her high into the air. She giggles and kicks her legs about. Just as Hazel pokes her head out of the kitchen, Isabel removes her jade green coat with the fur collar to reveal a tight red dress with flashy gold sequins sewn on for trim. Isabel McFiddie doesn't even know how to sew for goodness sake, Hazel thinks. But that won't stop a woman like her, no it certainly won't. Not even a twister would stop her from parading around like a Jezebel!

Hank glances around the room searching for a dance partner. Maybe he can make Susan jealous. The Manning girls are spoken for and besides he took Doreen to see a flick in Tillsonburg once, years ago, because she'd practically asked him to, and she smelled like his mother's perfume, and wasn't much fun. She talked too much, *yammer yammer* all through sundaes at the dairy bar and then *yak yak yak* all the way to the movie where she pushed his hand away three times in a row in the dark of the theatre. He knew she was teasing though, so he kept up the pressure and eventually she relented. Anyway, it doesn't matter; it's Susan he is set on—her brash indifference and powerful guard, and those long, long legs that she sometimes shows off in skimpy shorts during summer.

"Give her up," Buster keeps telling him. "You're out of contention." This drives Hank to threaten his younger brother physically, but now as he scans the hall for Susan, doubt seeps in through his every pore. Sometimes she is friendly with him and other times she is formal and dismissive, even on their one date. He's been waiting for her to make up her mind, and for what? Maybe Buster is right. Maybe Susan isn't worth the trouble after all.

Hank makes his way over to the food table and pops a coconut macaroon in his mouth. He notices Jelly Bean leaning against the wall all pale and white and fuzzy in a periwinkle dress and white angora sweater. She is the same height as Susan, although he has to admit that Jelly Bean *is* better stacked. She has none of Susan's grace or boldness though and that's what he goes in for. Finally, Susan steps out onto the dance floor to do the hop with Donny and the others, and Hank is sure all over again. *Mine.* He appears at Jelly Bean's side with a paper cup full of punch.

"What are you waiting for?"

She shrugs, accepts the cup. "Where's your brother?"

"Dunno. Maybe not coming. How about a dance with me?"

Jelly Bean casts a glance towards the entrance. Still nobody. Then, out of the corner of one eye she finds her mother holding up a bright pink Miss Tobacco Queen chest banner with black lettering. Hazel waves it with both hands, shooing her daughter onto the dance floor. Jelly Bean clenches her jaw. She feels indecent, tainted. She wants to refuse to dance with Hank but turns back to face the older boy whom she catches staring at her chest, and the next thing she knows she's agreed, and is tripping over his feet.

"I'm not a very good dancer," she explains.

"You aren't kidding. Don't worry though, I'm a great teacher." Hank leads her over to where Susan is with Donny, and Jelly Bean steps on his foot again. A crimson veil floods across her face and down her neck.

"See? I can't dance any better than I can skate!" She breaks off and bustles across the floor—"excuse me, pardon me"—bumping into people as she goes. She runs to the ladies room and locks herself in. It's there, moments later, that Isabel knocks to the sound of muffled tears.

"Judy is that you in there? What in heaven's name is the matter?"

Jelly Bean sniffles and wipes her nose. "I'm fine. Really. I'm not much of a dancer that's all."

"I see." A smirk spreads across Isabel's round face. "Come out here a minute so I can have a better look at you."

Jelly Bean wipes her wet face on a hand towel and reluctantly unlatches the door. Music fills her eardrums. She stares at Mrs. McFiddie's red high-heeled shoes. "I don't want to be Miss Tobacco Queen. I don't want to be Barbara Ann either." Her voice is so tiny that she isn't sure she's made it work. "I want to be—" Jelly Bean stops mid-sentence.

"Go on," Isabel coaxes.

"I want to be someone more like me." Jelly Bean hangs her head. There, it's out. "But mother prefers Barbara Ann."

Isabel lifts the girl's chin and examines her size two dress and the pain in her cobalt eyes. It's the pain of waiting for a better life to materialize—she recognizes it all too well. "You know?" Isabel continues, closing the door. "If you lost this sweater, say accidentally left it somewhere. And if your hair was straighter …" Isabel moves to run water at the sink and dabs it onto Jelly Bean's peroxide curls until they loosen. "Yes, more like that. If you stood up taller, well under the dim lights in the hall you'll look quite charming, and a bit like Natalie in *Rebel Without a Cause*."

"You think so?" Jelly Bean turns to face the mirror with the same enthusiasm she feels each time she marks a blank canvas with colour. Even if it isn't true, it helps to pretend.

"Absolutely. In fact, I bet no one except your mother will even know the difference." Jelly Bean giggles at the thought. Moments later, she crosses the dance hall without her fuzzy angora sweater, without her hair in tight ringlets, her head held high. She grins confidently and in a loud exuberant voice Isabel says to Tom and to anyone else within earshot, "Why, look how lovely Jelly Bean Johnson is tonight!"

Doc John's trim and tidy figure appears in the entrance. He catches Alice's eye and they regard one another for a split second as only people who've lived together many years can do, when all at once the pain attacks him sharper than ever before, and he catches the stab as it shoots across his stomach. He fights the urge to double over, waves to his wife and stuffs his handkerchief back into his breast pocket. He straightens and hurries over to where the music beckons. "Busy place," he says, holding one arm snug to his ribs for pressure.

"It's the younger folks," Alice beams. "They're turning out in droves."

"No Buster, though?"

"Not yet." Alice takes John's free hand. It's cold and clammy. She notices his colouring is off. "All squared up at home?"

"Mmm. I was on the phone to that hospital in Toronto again."

John's devotion to Buster during the preceding months has put doubts in Alice's mind as to whether he will honour his word and scale back on his practice. He needs to. She has only to search his face and light on the years of caring for others circling his sunken eyes, eroding his memory even. And his mouth, often having been the bearer of bad news, has begun to stumble on words in general conversation. Worse, he still insists on driving to faraway appointments to treat patients, ten miles an hour, creeping along when neither his eyes nor his twisted, arthritic fingers work as they are supposed to any more. She worries herself sick. "I'm determined to have you all to myself while there's still time left," she says, jostling him. "Remember we agreed on fall."

John turns his attention to the dance floor, to Hank and Donny and the other young men. He watches them keenly, with clinical detachment. It's as if he is engaged in research, taking notes on human behaviour. A man moves with a different centre of gravity than a woman, he thinks. A man lopes like bison, swaggers like an orangutan, his arms held out from his sides, his shoulders low and if he's a working man, loose. He leads with his shoulders and his legs, never with his hips, and those hips must not swish from side to side but remain tucked up neatly under his torso like the folds of an unused envelope. He checks his own posture.

All of a sudden the tinkering madness of a classical piano fills the hall—*Funny Face*—and there comes a collective moan from the younger folks, most of whom move off the dance floor. Alice folds her arms across her chest and taps the toe of her new shoes, impatiently, in an exaggerated manner. She wants to dance to this one but will not break with convention by asking. John releases her hand and extends his arm. "Would you do me the honour?" He slips her arm through his and immediately her shoulders drop and her breath, like hair pinned too long into place, falls out freely. She's always been, it seems to her now, keys on a piano when dancing with John. Her feet know exactly what pattern to form on the floor by his slightest suggestion. Her hands drape across his shoulders with natural grace. He presses his palm lightly into the small of her back and brings her forward or moves her back without hesitation, their outstretched arms forming a wide bow of space between them. He asks and she answers. A perfect match.

Alice twirls and laughs, looking more girlish than she feels, until Hazel's fixed gaze surprises and she realizes others are watching.

"John, no one is dancing." She slows to a stop.

"They will." He pulls her closer, twirls her once more with uncharacteristic bravado.

Before long Gladys and Herb Peacock have joined them and George Walker with Isabel. The crowd is a comfort to Alice who never enjoys drawing unnecessary attention to herself. Their two ordinary figures mingling with the others return her and John, she believes, to a safe and proper anonymity. The song slows and when Walter replaces the record with something faster, George Walker sidles up and Doc John suggests that the couples switch partners. "Here we go," he says, whirling Isabel across the floor. She steps closer, presses her belly into his belt buckle and smiles like a lioness. He is careful not to flinch. "I'm glad we've got this opportunity. I want to talk to you about Buster."

"What is it? Is there a problem?"

"No. Nothing to worry about."

"He's been acting peculiar," says Isabel. "He hardly acknowledges me or his father. Even poor Hank's on his bad side now. Sometimes I think he'd like to believe he's some kind of, oh, some kind of ..."

"Gangster?"

"So you have noticed?"

"The hat," nods the doctor. "I gave it to him."

"I didn't know that. Well you've been good to him. To all of us."

"To an old man like me the future is nearer to hand than I would like to believe but for a boy Buster's age, well, in his condition, it must seem like a mirage. He's trying out new things is all; his appearance. Even his attitude. In a roundabout way I think he's trying to find his way back to us." The doctor clears his throat. "I've given it a good deal of thought, Isabel, and I have a proposition for you. As you know, Alice and I haven't any children of our own. Buster has become like one of the family. Now, you're all adjusting as best as can be expected and that takes some time, but if you'd consider ... Turns out there's a way to remove some of his scars. It's a costly surgery, and that's no small concern, but if you and Tom agreed, I'd like to help out."

Isabel lifts her eyes. "You know how we feel about charity."

"Think of it as a gift. It'd do me a world of good too; I'd like to know I've made a difference."

"You already have, John." Isabel's breathy voice causes the fine hair on the back of his neck to stand. She is moved by his level of concern for Buster and presses her cheek up close to his, noticing how soft his skin is. "Surgery sounds dangerous."

"This hospital in Toronto specializes. They have a physician there known for his success with treatment of burns. He would lift skin from one part of Buster's body, his backside say, and then graft it over the scars. It would take time, and involve more pain. I know this is a lot to take in at once. I hope you'll think about it. On my recommendation I'm sure we could have Buster accepted within the year. I'd be willing to accompany him."

"He'd be gone for long?"

"A couple of months I would guess."

"Oh, that long ... Would he look normal again?"

"He'd likely require more than one operation." Doc John raises his voice above the percussive rattle of the music. "He will always be different, Isabel, but he might fit in better, yes." George slips in beside them with Alice in his arms.

"I can barely keep up with your wife. She's plain wore me out already."

"Must be my new shoes," Alice teases, kicking up one leg. She and George wait for Isabel and Doc John to finish their conversation as the song comes to an end.

"You'll talk to Tom then?"

Losing Buster once to the accident was a cavernous loss Isabel still hasn't learned to accept, but losing him a second time to distance or the surgeon's knife seems unfathomable. She wants to cling more tightly to all of her children, not let them out of her sight for a minute. "Yes," she says, knowing that despite herself she must. Then she winks, turns on her heels and is gone.

George parts from Alice and she and Doc John move off towards the food table where Hazel is standing. "Dang that Isabel McFiddie!" she whispers. "Sometimes that woman makes my blood boil. Fawning over these men like they're found puppies. Honestly! It's embarrassing."

"Don't let it get your goat," says Alice. "I'm sure they were only speaking about Buster."

"Is that all. I doubt it. Isabel may have been rescued to Canada but that street orphan will never get the gutter washed out." Hazel tilts her head in the doctor's direction and raises her voice. "What is it? The look on your face, you've got something scandalous to say."

"Me?" He knows from both sides and the middle how Hazel's world pivots on the axis of this or that, how in her mind they're all fighting the weight of social expectation and losing. He hates to admit it but her gate-keeping rankles. Every conversation he has with her feels bloated with pressure to mould and march the world of either/or into battle in straight, narrow rows. Lately it has caused him distress, even aggravated his condition. He is tired of it. Of monitoring himself and feeling as if in the flicker of an instant he could change for the worse in the eyes of those who know him best. It's all fine, this easy, clean line running along the edge of morality, if you can keep up. If you fit. But what if you don't? Or worse, what if you don't want to? No, what defines people most, he is sure, beyond personality, biology or belief in God, is the great wide world looking on with a punishing gaze—people like Hazel Johnson wagging her spindly finger, warning them all against stepping too far across any line. "All I know," he says, "is one way or another I hope the boy finds a way to settle down again. Be a real shame otherwise."

Alice takes hold of her husband's hand, this time for her own comfort. She's seen this frustrated expression upon his face before. It reminds her of the short end of a wishbone, candles not blown out on a birthday cake, a wish, a wish, as silly and desperate as any of her superstitions. He wants something more urgent, she can see. More certain. He would call it good science though all she can think is, miracle. "Yes," she says, entwining their fingers. "And the rest of us could help with that."

DOC JOHN FINDS BUSTER inside the hall's entrance.

"There you are."

Buster undoes his jean jacket. "I saw you dancing with Mom."

"Not bad for an old man, eh?"

"Not bad." Buster exaggerates his distorted smile. "I decided to come in costume. What do you think?"

"What do you think of *mine*?" Doc John pretends to fasten his tie. "I came as a real gentleman." He smiles and pulls at the collar of his shirt. "It's mighty warm though. I was just going out for some air."

They stand on the front steps of the community hall where the doctor does something Buster can't remember having ever seen him do: he pulls a package of cigarettes from his breast pocket, reaches into his pants for a lighter and lights one. He inhales deeply.

"You smoke?"

"Rarely." The doctor exhales, coughs. "A patient left these in my office the other day." He fidgets with the slim white stick. "Everybody's got a weakness." He turns, meets Buster's eyes. "What do you suppose yours is, son?"

"What do you mean?"

"I mean, when you catch yourself fretting. What do you do about it?"

"I find you."

The old man looks at his feet. "Right." He takes another drag and extinguishes the cigarette on the brick wall, tosses it onto the grass. "You're standing here with me when you could be in there with your friends."

"I don't need them."

"I see." The doctor taps the toe of his shoe. "You think a friend is someone you come by easy, is that it? Or a cobweb you brush aside when he gets irritating? Let me tell you something; it's not easy being them either, standing on the sidelines watching you destroy your life. I should know."

Buster turns sharply. "I didn't destroy my life. The fire did."

"No son, the fire destroyed your face. The rest you've been doing by yourself. Well, not entirely; you've had help from an old man who meddles too much."

"What are you talking about? Without you I'd be nowhere."

"You'd be in there," the doctor points. "You'd be inside getting along with the others."

"Inside. Big deal."

"Judy Johnson's in there."

Buster runs his fingertips along the black ribbon of his fedora. "So what." He folds his arms across his chest.

"All right, all right. There's nothing to do but tell you another story, because you won't listen to reason. Because you're starting to sound like Solly Levine and look where he wound up."

"Where?"

"Hold on, first there was a trial. Here, help me down." The doctor rests his weight on Buster's arm while moving to sit on the stairs. The dark green lawn spreads out before them like a stage and the late April moon, through a navy veil of sky, lights his features. "See, the Collingwood Manor Massacre trial was the beginning of the end for the Purples. That's when Solly was interrogated by police. He became the state's star witness, with near a dozen detectives guarding him. When he was hauled into court he was

163

sure he'd be killed right there on the witness stand. He slumped down, as pale as chicken liver if you ask me."

"The massacre arrests made front page news. I saw the paper in your office."

"You did?" Doc John wags his finger in Buster's face. "Shouldn't snoop, son. It might get you into trouble."

"I wasn't. I was just curious."

"Well, the Purples never could shake that story. Solly claimed that Bernstein and the others executed the killings and let him go. His testimony paved the way for others to come clean and before they knew what happened, Irving Milberg, Harry Keywell and Ray Bernstein himself were convicted of murder. All three sentenced to life without parole."

"It's hard to believe Ray finally got caught."

"It was 1932 and the first time he faced a jury on a murder charge. When the verdicts were read the courtroom erupted like a volcano. Wives and sisters screaming and crying. One girl fainted. Colleagues thumped their fists on tables. It was the usual brouhaha where the Purple Gang was concerned. Court officers restored order by waving their batons in the air and threatening the observers with arrest. The judge banged his gavel. Only the jury was silent. They'd said everything they had to say. Solly was escorted out of the room, and on the twentieth of July, he went into hiding."

"He got off easy."

"Nobody deserves a break, is that it? Not Solly, not Donny or Hank." The doctor gestures inside the hall. "Not your father. Listen, you're all caught up in make-believe and it's interfering with your getting on with things—look at you." He points to the fedora. "I gave you that hat for fun, not so you'd start inventing excuses to avoid everyone. And by the way, the problem for Solly wasn't that he was a rat like Mo Axler, it was that his stories were inconsistent. Too many discrepancies. Oh sure the police helped him along, lighting cigars behind his ears for encouragement—that made him squeal pretty fast. But after the trial, Solly recanted. He claimed he'd named the wrong names."

"The Purples must've got to him. He was afraid."

"Could be." Doc John nods. "We'll never know for sure. But in the end he told reporters that he wanted to return home and clear his conscience."

"So he was a good guy after all."

"Good. Bad." Doc John puckers his lips, makes his head sway from side to side. "I'll say this much for Solly Levine: honest Detroiters thought he showed courage standing up against the rest and they were right. Courage isn't gleaned from guns or might, Buster—it's having the stomach to go against the grain. That's all. When that case reopened Solly was nowhere to be found. To this day not another soul can say whether he escaped successfully."

"I bet he did. I bet he's doing all right."

"That's downright positive-minded. Better watch it or you might start enjoying yourself again." Doc John tries to stand with the boy's help. "You think you've got it all figured out. You'll be like them, like a Purple, and your worries will be whipped." He brushes off his pants. "Now I'm sorry if I sound like I'm coming down hard. I don't mean to. But what makes the Purple Gang so special compared with, say, the Boiler Gang in Philly or Chicago's Northside crew—or even this local fellow we've got holding up folks around here? Nothing. A man's just a man, whether his name's Al Capone or Pete Licavoli or even Raymond Bernstein. He's still got to fashion a life for himself and face the consequences."

"Sure but—"

"No, hear; if you want something worthwhile to mull over think about Solly Levine testifying against the Purples. Think about what it's like living every day with a gun in your mouth. How any minute could be your last, and how you can't trust your closest friends or family. Don't forget those Purples were convicted, son. They were cold-blooded killers who ended up with life in the slammer. Not a fact to let escape." Doc John turns, places his hand on the door handle. "One more thing."

"Yeah?" Buster follows inside.

"Even a louse like Ray Bernstein was good to his mother."

IN ZENDA TOWNSHIP, the widow Bozek is about to get the shock of her life as the bandit admits himself into her bedroom by climbing onto the roof of her porch and lifting the window. She is napping in bed and hears nothing of the intrusion at first. The man moves like a shadow across her carpet, his shoes leaving dark wet indents. The room smells of eucalyptus vapo rub and infection. He holds his breath and rummages deftly through a jewellery box on the old woman's dresser. He finds an emerald-and-diamond pendant necklace, a large antique cameo set in onyx and an 18-karat gold diamond engagement ring. The diamond is tear-shaped. He smiles; with this catch he can coast comfortably for a few months. As he slips out of the window and down to the ground once more, Mrs. Bozek stirs. Moments later the chilly wind wakes her; she rises, notices her ransacked dresser, and calls her son, Percy, to report the invasion.

In May the farm is ripe with sour manure and sweat, the smell of ambition. Barn cats parade around with their tails held high and flower beds, circling the house, are just as determined—bulbs poking up through the earth like bald babies pushing their way through a dark and grainy canal. Pussy willows flaunt their height along the side of the road. The land heaves and sighs, moist, damp and dewy. Life is on its way.

Last month Tom took advantage of the first warm sunny days to prepare the greenhouse—added a rich, decayed vegetation collected from local swamp lands, muck, and then steamed the whole greenhouse clean of bacteria which might've still been lurking in the soil. Now he watches the calendar with anxious, greedy eyes. His last crop sold well under the new tobacco marketing board management though he knows better than to feel secure. For a grower, any sense of security is a false one.

The farm will soon become a bustling place again, bustling with local men—Hungarian, Belgian, Dutch and German—and those rough boys from away who hang around the unemployment office in Tillsonburg like pack animals. Unlike Len Rombout, Tom hires them until they drink and flirt with the girls and then he lets them go. They aren't from around Smoke so don't carry the same loyalty to the land. This year there will also be the regular crew—and Simon Vandemaele who will tie. If only Buster would pull himself up by his bootstraps. If only he'd start participating again, they could be fast.

The rectangular glass enclosure is one hundred and fifty feet long and twenty-four feet wide, providing enough plants for thirty-five acres of tobacco. A walkway down the centre divides two twelve-foot-wide beds. Tom crawls through them on his hands and knees when checking the soil—all that expectant earth. Steam is supplied by his boilers, a few of them older than he is, older than his father was when he died, and it's delivered by hose to inverted steel pans. In order to kill disease, Tom raises the temperature up to one hundred and eighty degrees and has it penetrating six inches deep into the soil. After he steamed this year, he worked the muck and levelled it by raking. Most recently, he seeded. These are jobs he prefers to do alone. Preparing a greenhouse is the first task in establishing a new growing season, starting the cycle of work all over again, and it always sends a charge throughout his body, the same sensation he felt on his honeymoon with everything before him stretching out new and promising.

"Here, I've made these fresh." Isabel enters the greenhouse with a late-afternoon snack.

Tom sets the hose down and moves to accept a brownie. Water sloshes out onto the bed. "Hank's gone to grab me a rake," he says. "Where's Buster?"

"Reading."

"Again? Jesus! If he can read comics he can rake muck."

"Go easy. It's not his fault he's lost heart, Thomas."

Tom's face pinches into a grimace. "Whose fault is it, mine?" The more Isabel coddles the boy the more defensive he becomes. He can't imagine life without tobacco, or understand how one of his own has turned away from it, from him, showing no signs of returning. A day without dirt streaming through his thick fingers is incomprehensible. He is happiest when in command of a rogue army of workers, turning over the land, making money, and he wants this for his children. He bites into the spongy chocolate treat and tastes buttery icing. "Buster's got to get back to the land," he says with a full mouth. "Before the land won't let him back." Then he shoves the rest of the brownie into his mouth.

Isabel cocks her head to one side—chin up as if to proffer a challenge. "Let's give it a little more time."

"How much time? I need help now." Tom bends to retrieve the hose, walks with it a few feet down the centre of the greenhouse and speaks over his shoulder. "You wanted him back at school before he was ready and I went along with it." Tom licks his fingers of chocolate crumbs. "If it was up to you Buster wouldn't lift another finger around here. He's been living high off the hog for too long. I'm keeping him out of school this week and maybe the rest of the season. He can help with pulling and planting. It's time for him to earn his keep."

"All right." Isabel knows that the surest way to get what she wants is to look trouble squarely in the face and flirt with it, disarm it. In this way she has spun the muddiest of situations into rosy and pink as well as her husband turns dust to dollars. She meets his eyes with a softer gaze. "There's something I should tell you though. Doc John says there's a new procedure. An operation to cover Buster's scars. It's called plastic surgery. Now don't look as though you've just been introduced to a Russian spy. I've given it a good hard think. I told him we'd consider it."

"Without talking to me first?" Tom feels anger boiling inside his chest. First Buster hangs on the doctor's every word and now his wife too. He throws up his hands. "What about what *I* want?"

"If Buster can be fixed why wouldn't we help him?"

"He can't be fixed, Isabel. He is what he is. And this plastic surgery sounds iffy."

"I thought you'd like the idea; you're always talking progress."

Tom is speechless. He does plan for all their futures, assuming there will be a future. He wakes each day confident that whatever happens there will be a way to deal with it, and he'll be ready to charge in. But he wasn't when Buster needed him most, not soon enough. He was in the stripping barn looking over equipment when he happened to glance up and discover flames through Buster's window. Everything slowed to a grinding clarity. The wood counter needed a new coat of paint, bits of twine were scattered on the floor. A dried-out tobacco leaf was crumpled in one corner. The barn smelled stale and fresh at once, and there was a nice breeze passing through the open doors. All of this registered while he ran, his muscled legs propelling him forward with the strength of ten men, head down as though dodging grenades, and yet in some profoundly deep and unspoken place inside of himself he expected that Isabel would have beat him to the scene. Isabel had always arrived first with Band-Aids and kisses for their children, with praise and encouragement. But he arrived first, and even so, even after his best effort, it was the doctor whom Buster credits with saving his life.

"Where were you that night?" Tom asks.

"What?"

"The night of the accident. What were you doing before?"

"I don't know. I ... I was tidying up downstairs, I guess. Why?"

It's been a longstanding, unspoken agreement between them—one that Tom is only now beginning to fully recognize—that he will have Isabel and she will have the children. It's a deal that was forged in subtle ways, incidents too small and too fleeting to have been noticed at the time, though now he remembers those moments. Isabel acting exasperated or impatient and through such displays reinscribing in them all the notion that he is merely a man, a father, and therefore not naturally suited to the work of raising a human being. Stick to weeds, she seems to say. He hasn't always noticed, or minded, for though it irks him some to dwell on the special status mothering affords, the greater part of him believes in it, agrees with her assessment, and is relieved by its convenience. Isabel has always left him free of changing the diapers he has no interest in changing, and far apart from the drudgery that makes up a mother's world. He's colluded in the arrangement, just as his own father did, and now that his son holds more respect for another man he is paying the price.

"If you'd been upstairs sooner maybe—"

"Maybe what? He wouldn't have been burned? C'mon Thomas. Be honest at least. Tell the truth. You think I can't sense it? It's plain as the scars on his face—you're ashamed of him and now you blame me."

"I do not. I'm sick of always being the ogre, that's all."

Each time Isabel takes Buster's side, Tom feels her betrayal. It's a hambone's sentiment, he knows. But he also knows that he can never truly win his wife's undivided attention, for she's chosen her children—an unconquerable need for biological family, for the bonds of blood—at every turn.

"Buster thinks you've replaced him, you know?"

"I beg your pardon?"

"With Lizzie. The way you are with her. That you even wanted her in the first place."

"That's ridiculous!"

"Is it? Two children, Isabel. That's what you always said. Any more and they wouldn't get the attention they deserved. But then right after the fire you were pregnant again."

Isabel is silent, tugs her red hair behind one ear.

Tom clenches his jaw, feels a familiar frustration surge. With Lizzie Isabel is fast to grab the crying child away, soothe tears and reinforce that it's in mother's arms alone that comfort can be found. Will the pattern repeat again? Will Lizzie come to believe, as the boys have, that he is too busy, too otherwise preoccupied? But goddamnit, this isn't fair. It's his labour that pays the bills. It's his long hours in the fields that make it possible for Isabel to wear those dresses she prizes and for the boys to have fishing rods and baseball gloves and medical attention. Isn't he here beside all of them, joining in, holding up the foundation they take for granted? Yes. He is as available to his family as Isabel is, in his own way. He might be the invisible man around here but he's the father, not Doc John, and he refuses to be denied this respect any longer. Resentment dislodges in his throat and arches up like a broken bone. "The boys have always been yours," he says. "I'm lucky if I get to talk to them without you interfering. I've about had enough. If there's to be anything like an operation I'll be the one making that decision."

171

The next thing Buster knows he is sitting on a board in the barn beside Hank, pulling half-foot-long seedlings and laying them in a box to be transferred into the ground. This is soft work. Women's work. His father stands over him, dusting off the front of his overalls.

"Think you can manage?"

"Course."

"Good. I want your brother out planting for the afternoon. Let's go Hank."

Buster knows tobacco saves their father, wraps his hopes and luxuries in fancy ribbons or finely rolled paper and delivers them as far away as Europe for a large profit. He knows that it's tobacco permitting them all their big cars and modern conveniences. Nobody, not even Doc John, speaks a word against the stuff. Buster feels differently now, though he'll never say so. He understands the inherent danger in one thin wisp, the lurking menace of a foggy cloud, how it can reach out and grab you, pull you down into oblivion without warning. Anything can be ignited. A match. The old gas stove in his mother's kitchen, even his own incendiary heart that goes on *pounding, pounding,* longing to impress Jelly Bean even when there's no real possibility of it any more. The sting and stab of his migraines, the land he is used to tending, that black earth with its green and pink weeds, will always surround him like a wet wool blanket, reminding him of that.

He holds a young seedling up in front of his face to examine it. His father did market gardening before tobacco: strawberries, raspberries, watermelon and cabbage—all cash crops. Buster sets the seedling in its box. His father was one of the first sand land farmers to turn to tobacco. He's heard the story so many times that he sometimes feels as if he was there himself to witness it, though that would've been impossible for he hadn't yet been born. His father grew his first Burley in 1936—had to harvest it as the whole stock and leaf. By 1937 the first three kilns on their farm were built and flue-cured tobacco grown. Dad really made something of himself, Buster thinks. He must be a fast learner. Maybe that's how he stays ahead of the game now.

Buster raises his eyes to a dark figure standing in the barn doorway, blocking the sun. Jelly Bean is outlined by a sharp white light. She curves into the day like an hourglass. He stares at her full and changing body.

"Hey, what are *you* doing here?"

"Mother thinks it'll be good practice for when I help out later," she lies.

"So, you're gonna work harvest after all."

"I told you I was. Beats babysitting. Besides, art school's expensive."

Art school? He hardly thinks of her as a painter. Since New Year's Eve, despite himself, he thinks of her as his girl. "Right. Art school. You told me." He passes her a box and she accepts it, sets it down at her feet.

"Uh-huh." Her tone is impatient. She's hurt that he didn't remember, though she'd only mentioned it once. Still, of anyone, she expects Buster to understand what it's like to want to break free. "I'm going to apply next year," she adds. Her brassiere straps dig into her shoulders. Sweat rolls down her sides and she wonders whether Barbara Ann ever bears perspiration marks under her arms. The pictures in her mother's scrapbooks never show any. "Toronto's swell I figure. It's where Mother gets her catalogues. There are big department stores and street trolleys and there's the Royal York Hotel looking over Lake Ontario. I could see it all. I could arrange for lessons."

"But you already draw."

"Oh I just fiddle around. Real students learn from live models, paint on proper canvases. Imagine all the things we'll never know, being cooped up here."

"You like painting that much?"

She nods. "It's the scariest, most exciting thing in the world. That second before I drop the ink onto the emptiness and begin to fill it in with colour."

Buster shifts in his seat. "Why?" He doesn't understand.

"I never know if the picture in my mind can be matched. I don't want to be disappointed."

"Oh." He shudders. Is he one of her blank pages?

He plucks a seedling from its earthy bed and lays it in the box to demonstrate how it's done. Before the accident the land was his to feed and breed and claim. His to grab up and scatter through his fingers. His to smell. Taste even. Tobacco knew him inside and out, and even now, with everything else changed, it still lives in his lungs, in his bones, like a pleasurable poison. It rules him as Doc John's best stories do—all day, unshakable. But what if he wants out of it?

He'd once thought of this place as his empire, the best place there was. He wanted to become a curer himself—a king on this throne made of grass and weeds. He's a grower's son; it was natural that he would become a grower himself someday. Now he can barely stand the thought of planting these seedlings, never mind priming or curing them. *Cure.* A word he no longer believes in. Cured tobacco is nothing but a dried out, turned to yellow, wrinkled form. A scar. He looks at Jelly Bean.

How do you love something imperfect?

This single question lies alongside each row in the field. Sits in the creeping worry lines that guard his mother's protective eyes. In his father's impatient toe tapping. In every story Doc John recounts. The question presses through him with a force that he senses could squash him one day soon if he doesn't find an answer. He has to know because, if nothing else, he, Buster McFiddie, is sweet on a clumsy pest of a girl. There's no denying it any longer. And she's sweet on him, she must be. She's here, isn't she? Turned up of her own free will. Her hair and eyes colour all that is desire, and as he stares at her he is drawn in as if she's inhaled him.

"Does Toronto have a mob?" he asks.

"Dunno." She taps her foot and gazes across at him with big blue eyes like two open windows. He continues pulling, feels the firm stems in his hand.

"Doc John saved me the night of the accident, you know? I wouldn't have made it otherwise. He visited when I was in the hospital. He's awful secretive though. Never talks about his life before, in Michigan." Buster's face is shiny, the fedora yellowing around the brim. "Ever notice he won't give a straight answer? What do you make of that?"

Jelly Bean shrugs. "Old people are funny."

"Yeah but he wasn't always old. It's just he's been around for a long time and still he's kind of ... kind of like a stranger."

Jelly Bean laughs. "Silly, there's no such thing as a stranger here." She lifts a seedling and places it delicately in the box at her feet. She admires its bright green colour, wonders if she shouldn't try her hand at oil paints for a change. "Hey, you're so interested in other people's lives all of a sudden, maybe you want to help *me* with something?"

"What's that?"

"Mother wants to advertise for the sesquicentennial. She's asked me to create a few posters. I thought I'd travel to Tillsonburg and Simcoe with them." Her voice is quicksilver and shoots straight through Buster's most vulnerable parts. He lets her glimpse his waxy face full-on in the relentless light.

"I could ask Dad to borrow his truck one weekend."

"That'd be swell." She squints a near-perfect smile.

On the last Saturday of May Buster waits for Hank to return with the Dodge but he doesn't. So it's afternoon by the time Buster gives up waiting, grabs his fishing bag and a roll of electrician's tape and walks into the village to ask Doc John to borrow his Olds.

"What do you need it for, son?"

"Errands. Out of town."

Doc John fiddles with his glasses. "What kind of errands?"

"I'm taking Jelly Bean around with posters for the anniversary. No big deal."

"That's wonderful." Alice stands on her tiptoes, poking her head over her husband's shoulder. "I mean any early publicity can only help with fundraising."

"Hi Mrs. Gray. How are you today?" Buster tips his hat.

"Oh, you know. Planning is well underway. Have a good time now." She steps back.

"Posters huh?" Doc John chuckles, coughs, and wipes his mouth with a handkerchief.

"You're bleeding." Buster points.

"Shush!" Doc John uses his hands to quiet the air. "Shush. Just a touch of the influenza, nothing serious. Hold on while I fetch my keys." He withdraws and returns a moment later pushing his way out the front door with his hat and coat and his cane. "Second thought, I could use a drive."

Buster rides in the passenger side for the short trip down Main Street to the hardware store while the doctor inches them along like a big black snail. He appears focused and preoccupied all at once.

"Do you think the bandit has a loaded gun?" Buster asks.

"The scoundrel who's been robbing folks? I imagine."

"I mean he wouldn't need bullets. Just the sight of a gun gets people moving."

Doc John raises an eyebrow. "You're not planning anything foolish are you?"

"Course not. I was just thinking."

The boy's face is rough, more hardened physically in its expression than it was even a few months earlier, but there is a new level of interest the doctor recognizes. He glances out the window. "There's been a lot of speculation in *The Tillsonburg Observer*," he says. "One writer is turning out a weekly column."

"I bet the bandit would like that," says Buster.

A few minutes later he steps out of the car to go and fetch Jelly Bean, and Doc John creaks and moans his way out of the driver's side, calls to the boy and tosses the keys over the hood. "Catch," he says. "Can't very well impress the ladies without these."

Buster brushes past Donny who is head down, reading a comic book and carrying a package of licorice, one piece dangling from between his teeth like a long black tongue.

Donny raises his eyes. "Hi Buster. Whatcha doing?"

"Not much. You?"

"Heading to Ivan's. Wanna tag along?"

"Can't, I'm busy."

Just then Jelly Bean skips out onto the steps carrying an armload of posters. Her movements are nimble and airy. She smiles brightly at both boys, wearing an outfit Buster has never seen before—blue pedal pushers, a yellow halter top, matching sweater tied around her waist. Penny loafers. Her face is fresh and inviting until she notices Doc John, a chaperone, sitting in the back seat. "He's coming too?" She makes a weak attempt to wave at the doctor with her free hand. A poster slips from her arms and Buster bends down to pick it up.

"Gotta go," he tells Donny. "I'll see you around though."

"Yeah, see ya."

Buster takes the stack as Jelly Bean opens the passenger-side door of the car. She slides in, grazing her head on the roof, and he passes the posters to her and walks around the front of the car while Doc

John unrolls one. "These sure are fine, Judy. I didn't know you could draw."

"Not really, but thank you." She rubs her head. "I wanted to do a good job for Mother so she'll let me out of the Miss Tobacco competition. I used an ink pen and oil pastels. Do you like them Buster?" Buster cranes his neck to appreciate the poster and Doc John unrolls another, holds it out. All around the edges are small figures, dancing and laughing. Buster is impressed with the detail, with how she's captured their likenesses. He picks out his mother right away and reads the text.

Biggest birthday party ever! Smoke's 150th
Saturday September 12th, 1959
Clowns, Rides, Fireworks and much more!
Organized by the Order of the Eastern Star,
Violet Rebekah Lodges.
All proceeds to charity.

"Looks good to me," he says. He's getting out of town for the first time in too long and he has wheels.

"I drew you both. See?" Jelly Bean points to the next poster and Doc John holds the image up, adjusts his glasses with one hand. Buster turns to face the front again, this time with a heaviness setting deep in his bones. She's included him in one of her drawings all right but she's painted him with his scars. "The letters are hardest," Jelly Bean continues. "There's a lot of information to include. Mother thinks the full name of the Order is exotic and might attract foreigners."

"What foreigners does she think we're gonna see in Tillsonburg?" Buster scoffs. He slides the key in the ignition and starts the engine.

"You never know." Doc John drops his walking stick on the floor of the car. "We might run into that bandit you were asking about a few minutes ago. Or Alonzo Boyd. He's broken out of the Don Jail in Toronto twice already; maybe he's escaped again. The papers used to say he wandered these parts wearing cosmetics and a kerchief on his head. Passed himself off as a woman in public. That's mighty exotic if you ask me." Doc John smiles at Jelly Bean and waves a crooked finger at Buster as he accelerates. "Slow down, son. You're driving too fast."

Buster makes eye contact with the doctor in the rear-view mirror. Before the accident, he thought Doc John was little more than a cranky old goat—someone to make fun of with the other boys for his mannered speech and his mucky-muck walking stick. A throwback to another generation. But with the old man he'd discovered that contempt and judgment could be replaced by respect. He forgot about the usual distinctions settling people into their proper places in the village. He forgot that doctors and farmer's sons don't generally have much to say to one another. It wasn't his father bringing stories or sustenance after all. A marked dependence has developed between the two of them; a bond that no one else can share. It's the bond between the damned—one damned to suffer and the other to heal. "I'm only going thirty," Buster says as they veer onto Dover Street. Jelly Bean smiles nervously and spins back around, brushing Buster's hand with her own. She jerks away, reaches for the radio, switches it on and folds her hands in her lap like braided bread. She stares out the window and lightens some when the doctor begins to hum. "I've been thinking," Buster continues. "You never finished the one about the Collingwood Manor Massacre."

"Didn't I?" The doctor knows he didn't. He knows that in Smoke cars and clothes and hobbies may speak volumes about one's station in life but it's *conversation style*—implying things rather than explaining outright and taking pains never to brag—that's the great leveller. People here make a concerted effort not to place themselves above each other. If Jelly Bean Johnson enjoys painting pictures, she hides her paper and brushes and enjoys them when alone. If Walter knows more about operating a small business and about music than anyone for miles around, he makes a special effort not to show it. Individuality indicates uppityness. But if information is requested and you can talk the talk, you will be accepted. If you can tell a good story? *Well,* you can practically get away with murder. "You're right," Doc John says. "I guess I didn't. Let me see … Detroit was preparing for a national convention of the American Legion."

"Kind of like we're getting ready for the sesquicentennial?"

"Yes, Judy. It was like that, except booze had been ordered for cabarets and speakeasies around the city. You've got to understand, bootleggers were struggling to match demand. Wasn't like it is now with alcohol any time you like. As I've told Buster already, back then it was illegal, which meant the first law of human nature kicked in fast and furious and every man wanted to lay his hands on a bottle no matter what the price." Doc John leans forward on the seat and lowers his voice. "The Purples had more than a few who tried to get in on the action. The River Gang. The Legs Laman thugs. The Westside Mob. They were all interested in horse racing across the river, racketeering, gambling, keeping the unions in check, and of course rum-running. There were several independent operators too, and they caused as much trouble as anyone encroaching on territory where they didn't belong. Didn't want to mess with them, no sir. Just because they weren't part of an organized group didn't mean they weren't out for blood. If you so much as gave a sideways glance in the direction of one of those loners he might wrap you tight in plastic sheets and lock you in his car trunk so you'd wish an anaconda had you in its grip instead."

"Eeeuw." Jelly Bean makes a face as if she's tasted cod-liver oil and Buster smirks. He enjoys seeing her romantic notions fall away. Life has always been brutal and bloody and the gore of existence is precisely what he relates to now. If she wants to hang with him she might as well know it. He slows the car as they approach the bridge at Ball's Falls.

"It was a different place and time Judy. Prohibition drove men mad. They were willing to kill for a taste of the forbidden. Smelled like sewer water much of that rotgut did but it didn't matter so long as we got our share. Anyway, tempers were wearing thin as the

Purple Gang and rivals battled it out. It got so that one night the Purples would hijack a load coming over from Canada and the next night the River Gang would hijack it back. Federal agents were also cracking down."

"So there was a blow-out?"

"The Third Avenue Terrors, that's all. Three hoods from Chicago originally, who wouldn't respect established boundaries or follow orders. They started muscling in on other people's business and it didn't go over very well. The Italian mob was growing angrier by the day and Irish organizations wanted to take the trio for a ride, but it was the Purples who finally settled the score." He wags his finger at Buster. "Nothing good ever comes from being greedy."

"Which fellas were they?"

"Herman Paul, Joe Lebovitz and Izzy Sutker. I don't think I've told you about them yet. The Purples tolerated them so long as there were kickbacks. But the trio cut out on their own, and before anyone knew it they were hijacking from friends and enemies alike and double-crossing their partners."

"What year was it?"

"You're awfully stuck on details, son. You want to hear it or not?" The doctor sits back on the car seat and feels the sun warm his neck through the rear window. "They needed a cover for their real trading interests so they set up a handbook and hired Solly Levine to run it."

"I know him," says Buster. "He was the stool pigeon."

"That's right. He came from a good family though, with lots of money. But Solly had a taste for the rougher side of life, and unfortunately he had bad timing. At first everything was looking up for the trio. They still had profits coming in from all directions and Solly was covering their debts. But pretty soon Paul, Lebovitz and Sutker were overextended and couldn't manage. Several nasty gangs came after them, so they did the only thing they could do to generate extra cash fast and that was to buy booze from the Purples on credit. Hear: if there's one thing you never want to do besides double-dealing, it's buying on credit. What looks free now is sure to cost you plenty more later on."

Jelly Bean nods. "Did they get away with it?"

"Tried. They diluted their stock further than usual and undersold the market price. The trio was clever; got to give them that. They asked the Purple Gang directly for another favour, Raymond Bernstein in fact. Asked him to hold off collecting his share until after the legionnaires' convention. Bernstein said he'd be in touch."

"That doesn't sound good," says Buster.

"Bought them time but if you'd ever seen Ray Bernstein you'd know not to trust a single word that came out of his mouth. He was wiry, fish-eyed, and had a smile like an oil slick." Doc John smiles.

"Then what?"

"Then all hell broke loose. Gangster style, which was cool and unpredictable. Bernstein came up with a clever plan to trap the trio and eliminate competition. He told Solly he wanted to stop all the squabbling for once and for all and bring those other boys into business officially, make them his liquor agents. He invited them to what they used to call a peace conference. The trio relaxed, loosened their belts, slept a little sounder. But morning and a setup comes fast and soon it was September sixteenth."

"Hey," Jelly Bean points to her posters again. "That's almost the date of our sesquicentennial."

"Sure. The day of the massacre. Solly was working when he got a call that the meeting was scheduled for three that very afternoon. He was to bring the others to 1740 Collingwood. Apartment 211. He committed the information to memory, afraid of leaving a paper trail." Buster meets the doctor's alert eyes in the rear-view mirror, sees his spindly shoulders drop, and is struck by his deceptively ambiguous countenance.

"How do you know that?"

"Don't believe me? Check the papers. It all came out eventually."

"I believe you," says Jelly Bean.

"Thank you, Judy. I appreciate that. Fact is, when you owe you do what you're told so you're darn tooting Solly did exactly as instructed. The four of them, with Solly leading the way, arrived at the Collingwood address right on time. Unarmed too, as a gesture of good faith. Solly thought he was there to be a bridge, see. The middleman. So he was feeling pretty chuffed when Ray Bernstein met them in the lobby of the building and shook his hand. Ray smiled slippery and escorted them into the apartment where a 78 was playing and where Harry Fleisher, Irving Milberg and Harry Keywell were waiting. Now anybody with a brain the size of a pea would have known what was coming next. Fleisher and Milberg were bad news. Their records spanned a decade. Sure Keywell was baby-faced, but he was hard as a two-by-four on the inside. I guess it goes to show—when you're desperate the mind will play tricks 'cause those three hoodlums still thought they had a chance."

"Suckers."

"Hmm. Paul, Levine and Lebovitz sat next to each other on a couch and Izzy sat on the arm. One of the Purples yanked the needle across the record, making that terrible scratching sound. You know the one? And the room was suddenly quiet. Keywell passed around expensive cigars and the men exchanged a few words. It all seemed safe enough until Ray Bernstein announced that he was leaving to find his accountant. 'How the hell am I supposed to do business without my books!' he said, storming out. The trio and Solly sat nervously waiting for him to return."

"But he doesn't, right? He just lets the others do his work. One, two, three pop!"

"Pretty much. He was the mastermind so he wouldn't want to get his hands dirty. He descended to the street and waited in the car— a big black Chrysler. He started the engine and then leaned on the horn."

Buster presses the palm of his hand into the car horn, but doesn't cause it to sound. "That was the signal."

"Right. And before they ever knew what hit them, Fleisher pulled out his gun and fired at Joe. The bullet flew straight past Solly's right ear so that he could practically hear the end coming. At the same time Milberg and Keywell fired at Sutker and Paul. Within seconds the apartment was all sound, spark and fury, and Paul's back was full of holes. He was slumped face down on the hardwood floor in a widening pool of his own blood. Lebovitz was right behind him, trying hard to reach the bedroom for cover when he was hit. The stub of his cigar was stuck between his teeth. Izzy Sutker died on the floor in the bedroom with his boots touching a pretty floral-print area rug and his bullet-riddled forehead tucked under the bed."

"What about Solly Levine? Was he shot too?"

"No, but he expected to be. Stood there waiting on his execution while the Purples consulted briefly and then rushed him out the door, leaving only God and an apartment building full of confused and terrified tenants to babysit his three dead partners. The Purples and Solly clambered down the staircase and out to the getaway car. They screeched away, guns still smoking in Keywell and Milberg's pockets. After a few blocks Ray skidded over curbside and dumped Solly out. 'Remember who your *real* friends are,' he said. 'We'll be in touch.' Solly pulled himself together and ran back to the book.

"He fretted for hours after, nearly wet himself sitting in the window watching for Purples or the police. Bernstein never did come for him. It was part of Ray's plan all along to frame Solly. To Raymond Bernstein's way of thinking it was best to have a disposable man available in case an alibi was needed. But he didn't get the chance to use Solly because the police moved fast on the Collingwood shootings and Solly was eventually linked to the killing spree. Next thing he knew he was being called to testify against the Purple Gang."

"You can't rat out a mobster!"

"No you can't. But then the city was run by real criminals. Not the kind you two come across at the picture show, with their guns all exposed and their hats always tilted to one side as if they've got something they want everyone to know they're hiding." Doc John adjusts Buster's fedora so that it sits straight on his head. "No, not like that. Some gangs were illegal and others were on the up and up. The Detroit mobs might not have been as well known, say, as Capone's Chicago bunch or the New York crew, but they were clever, kept us all on our toes. And I'm sorry to say but the local police weren't much better. After the massacre the police brought Solly in for questioning and a good shellacking. They were willing to beat a confession out of him if it meant getting names." Jelly Bean wraps her arms around her body like a comfort blanket.

"He confessed?"

"Yeah. Shame about that. Confessions are like eating sweets dipped in double sugar, if you ask me. They never do any good. Besides, sometimes there's nothing a confession can do that a good story can't accomplish just as well. So, even though no amount of talking was going to improve Solly's situation, he squawked, told the police some cockamamie tale about the trio being kidnapped on their way to a secret meeting. Swore he hadn't come across anyone at the crime scene. Police ruled out the kidnapping line fast though—Solly wasn't a very good storyteller."

"Not like you," says Jelly Bean.

"Well." The doctor is flattered. He smiles at the girl. "Next thing you know the police ordered all Purples and affiliates rounded up. In less than forty-eight hours tips had come in from various parts."

"Rival gangs," spits Buster. "Taking advantage of the situation."

"Nasty business, all right. But that's how it was."

"Did they catch them?" Jelly Bean wants to know. "I hope they did."

"Sure, the police learned of Ray's hideout from an anonymous caller. Surrounded the place. The gang was quiet when they were brought into headquarters. Ray Bernstein's matinee idol grin had left him altogether. He looked pretty rattled on that day."

"You were there?" asks Buster. "What did he do?"

"It was all over the newspapers. Within two days the others were captured. There was a trial of course, and you know what? Bernstein always denied his part, up until the very end. No surprise there. But the *real* mystery was Solly Levine."

The doctor adjusts his vest and a piece of gauze pokes out the bottom end of his shirt. He appears smaller in the rear-view mirror, his face hard, and it occurs to Buster that he usually keeps his shirt buttoned to the top, even in warm weather like today, and yet his collar is loose, his shirtwaist untucked. He looks dishevelled. There *are* mysteries close at hand, Buster tells himself. Puzzles to be solved. At the least, a secret or two. "What do you mean?"

"First he was whisked off across the border by police, his name changed to protect his identity. Then from America he was placed on a boat to France for protection, but when he docked officials wouldn't accept him into the country. They sent him back, where he tried to snag a passport to Ireland. That didn't pan out either."

Buster's throat constricts, his mouth goes dry. An indefinable place inside him aches on Solly's behalf, wrings and twists with the lonely idea of a throwaway.

"So what did he do if no one wanted him?"

"He disappeared."

Buster swerves, slams his foot on the brake pedal and barely avoids a fox on the road. When he regains control of the car Doc John has fastened his vest and jacket.

"Better watch the road son." The old man pats his rib cage. "I've already been in one accident, you know."

In TILLSONBURG, Buster parks in front of the Royal Hotel. Doc John has errands of his own to attend and heads off down the street. Girls and women aren't allowed in beverage rooms so Buster alone carts the posters and his fishing bag with the tape into the hotel. Patrons are startled by his appearance and stare at his face as though a creature from a Hollywood B-movie is staggering around in their midst. One fellow's mouth hangs agape. Buster faces him directly and doesn't blink as he pulls the tape from his bag, unwinds a strip, cuts it with his teeth and sticks a poster up over the counter. Might as well give him a good long look, he thinks. He holds his breath to avoid inhaling cigarette and pipe smoke and returns to Jelly Bean. Together they walk down the street and around the corner into the library where they ask if there might be someone else who'd be willing to hang a poster on the premises. Next, they are directed to Albert Lum's restaurant.

The place is packed with afternoon patrons and clanging with the noise of plates and bowls and silverware. Albert stands behind the counter with his wife. A local fellow pulls a deck of cards from his breast pocket and another offers around a box of his best cigars. Strangers either ignore Buster altogether or make no effort to shave down their pity or curiosity. Once the doleful staring is over, as in Smoke, they simply carry on, unaffected. Several who know Tom McFiddie from auction or from his recent profile over the tobacco marketing board make an effort to be kind, reminding Buster to say hello to his father. Buster senses their discomfort by their overcompensation, by the way they speak in short, choppy sentences—deliberate, controlled—and face him head-on with their arms pressed tightly against their bodies like statues standing at attention. He's pretty sure he hears whispering. He and Jelly Bean hurry to the pool hall, and then the beauty parlour, where Buster receives the same reception.

Finally, they drop the remaining posters in the trunk of the car and wait for Doc John on the steps of the hotel where the Honeymooners, playing on the radio, carry outside. Buster points across the street to the dairy bar.

"That's the first place the bandit hit. I wonder if he's watching us now."

"Very funny, Buster. Don't tease."

Buster laughs. "Don't you want to know who it is?"

Jelly Bean shrugs, and then a moment later taps her feet, one and the other.

"Thanks for driving."

"Won't take us long to get to Simcoe, then home."

"Have you ever been to Her Majesty's Royal Chapel? It's the oldest Protestant church in Ontario. Maybe all of Canada. I'm not sure, I'll have to ask my dad next time we visit my grandparents. But it's where the Mohawk chief was buried."

"Cool." Buster pulls an orange from his fishing bag and peels it with his thumb and then with his teeth. He spits the rind out onto the ground. "That's how Brantford got its name, right? After Joseph Brant?"

"Yeah, how do you know?"

He speaks with a full mouth. "Everybody knows that."

Jelly Bean doesn't like his tone. It holds the same casual disdain that her mother's does whenever her grandparents are mentioned or when her father refers to being Mohawk. It's as if Buster is watching a Western movie at the Strand and commenting on a brightly coloured headdress or coveting a bow and arrow set, admiring what isn't his from a safe distance and yet feeling superior at the same time. "Not everybody. Indians know all about tobacco though," she says, as Buster passes her a pulpy section of fruit. "My dad says they grew it first."

Buster nods. His father has told him that, long before names like McFiddie or Rombout, tobacco was grown and traded and smoked by Indians.

When he isn't looking Jelly Bean examines his face at close range and sees that each patch of scarred tissue is a slight hue of red or pink or yellow. It appears that he changes with the seasons, like the fields or the leaves on the trees. Criss-crosses and overlapping flesh make for interesting patterns and while he chews the patterns come alive. "Wonder what Doc John's doing?" She taps her fingers on the sidewalk. "Hey, when we're done here I could come over to your place."

Buster sees that her ankles are exposed where the hem of her pedal pushers fits snugly against the shape of her calves. She has fine bones like a bird and her skin is tanned and smooth. He could sit here looking at her all day and all night. She'll have his vote for Miss Tobacco Queen if she enters the competition. But he can't go on accepting her kindness. He's been learning things about himself from spending time with her, not that he can put these things into words. He's been learning that after fire there is more than physical pain, there is the wrenching pain of disentitlement. Wanting what you can't ultimately have. A longing that continues despite all else. It's worse than never having wanted in the first place.

"Naw, I don't think so."

"Why not?"

"You'd get bored."

She takes a deep, mournful breath. "I'm kinda bored now Buster."

"Oh." Her comment makes him feel a responsibility he hasn't known in a long while. He scans the street for Doc John. "How about a story then?" It's the first thing that comes to mind. She huddles closer, hugging her knees, and he feels the warmth of her body against his own. "Let me see." He relaxes and slips into his other world, the one in which he is powerful and strong. The one where anything is possible. He will make something up and she won't know the difference. "Uh ... did you ever hear how my grandfather made himself famous during the Prohibition?"

"Nope." Jelly Bean shakes her head.

"Good. Okay. Well listen. His name was Milton McFiddie, but they called him Mick, and he ... he packed up and drove a rusty jalopy south to Windsor in the dead of winter. Pushed it onto the frozen river early in the morning. Crossed like that to bootleg."

"Did not."

"Did too. Lots of fellas did. Ask Doc John. They were desperate for a break. They did it and I'm telling you that my grandfather was one of the best." Buster tries to sound confident so she'll believe him. "His car had false floorboards and a second gas tank to hide the hooch, and he inched it across the river with all four doors open in case they had to jump out fast. Didn't do him much good though. He lost the jalopy and the other two men in it—the load being heavy. It cracked the ice and the rear went under. Gurgle, gurgle, gurgle ..." Buster gestures downward with his hands.

"Oh no."

"But it's okay, it's okay. *He* bobbed to the surface and tried to pull himself onto the ice. Each time the ice gave way and he splashed back under. Then when he was sure he was a goner, he saved himself by stepping on the hood of the car. Later, he told folks that he hadn't wanted to. That it was like stepping on the heads of the others and pushing them down."

"How dreadful. That's a dreadful thing to do."

"Yeah, well. Sometimes you have to take advantage of a bad situation."

Jelly Bean chews a fingernail. "I guess so. Then what?"

"He crawled onto his knees back to shore, shivering and half alive."

"*Wow.*" She can visualize the whole thing. "So you're *related* to a criminal?"

"Um, sure, you could say." Buster is inside the story now and sees how easily it has slid away from him. He's thrilled to have captured her attention but feels guilty; he'd never even met his grandfather. "And I suppose it could've just as easily been me crawling on the river that morning. Or me hollering and scrambling with *my* face pressed up against the windows for air."

Jelly Bean can't dodge this final graphic image. She squeezes up her own features.

"What a terrible way to die."

Buster shrugs. "There's probably worse."

She runs her tongue back and forth along her top row of teeth, expectantly.

"Have *you* broken any laws?"

"Me?"

"You can tell me," she prods. "I'm not saying that you have but *if* you have I promise I won't breathe a word. Cross my heart." She demonstrates with her fingers. Furtively he glances at her full chest, where she's drawn an invisible X. Before he has a chance to respond, Doc John makes his way around the corner carrying a small box of clarinet reeds.

"I'm afraid I'm not up for any more today," he says. "I'm sorry Judy. Buster can drive you to Simcoe another afternoon."

"Oh, all right." She is disappointed. "Gee, you do look awfully pale."

Buster jumps to his feet, notices the stiff, pained way that the doctor is advancing. "Where'd you go?"

"Had to see Doc Baker about this flu."

"He'll be fine," Alice reassures Buster when he drops the doctor off at home. "The heat most likely. He just needs a rest. Off you two go, and keep the car until you're done with it." She shoos Buster off the veranda and waves to Jelly Bean who is sitting in the front seat. "Oh and Buster. There's just been a meeting called for tonight at the church. What to do about the bandit. He struck again. Make sure your father knows."

"Yes, ma'am."

A moment later he pulls up in front of the hardware store.

"Here we are." He expects Jelly Bean to let herself out.

"Yup, here I am." But she doesn't move. She can't. The thought of that cross-eyed Barbara Ann Scott doll and her mother waiting with bleach and dye keeps her feet rooted to the car floor. She looks at him, really looks at him.

"Buster?"

"Yeah."

"Wanna tell more stories?"

AT THE FARM they walk around the house and Jelly Bean stops to admire Isabel's lily pond and garden. She rubs lemon thyme on her wrists and neck while Buster runs into the house to fetch his transistor radio. Then she follows him across the lawn to the root cellar where a tabby is asleep curled up on the trap door, purring. "This is where I used to hang out," Buster says, pushing the cat away and lifting the door. "Quick, before someone sees." He helps her down and she tears her pedal pushers on a nail sticking out of the wall.

It takes a moment for their eyes to adjust. The cellar is a small, square room with one wall of wooden shelves—a dozen Mason jars arranged like medicine bottles, though they'd only ever contained tomatoes, green beans, cherries, pears. There are dates written and faded on the wall above each shelf—1949, 1954, 1957—the years that his mother put up preserves. A stream of late-afternoon light fans in where the trap door is propped open with a stone. Sun filters down white and irreverent. It isn't much of a balm from the world above but it is quiet. From this muffled underground place his mother's charmed voice is a vague and distant dream and his father's brassy commands provoke no reaction. The smell is of raw dirt and old potato skins, a smell he never tires of. There's also a faint odour of sawdust and wood chips that, when stronger, used to cause his nose to tingle and sometimes made him sneeze. He ignores the hint of tobacco smoke. Here he is with Jelly Bean, between the stillness of the underground, like a premature grave, and the lively madness of the fields above. It's the last place he was before the accident. Being down here with her is like a starting gate, a shot at getting back into the game. Their figures loom large on one wall and creep up towards the ceiling.

"Look." Jelly Bean points. "Our shadows."

Buster sets the radio down and makes a peculiar figure with his hands. He casts the shape of a rabbit onto the wall. "Guess what this is?"

"It's a rabbit. That's easy, do another."

He changes the position of his fingers, thinks about how a shadow is just a projection onto a hard surface; it isn't there but people accept it as real.

"Dog," Jelly Bean says this time.

"No, try again."

"Cat?"

He drops his hands, moves to switch on the radio. Johnny Cash is playing.

"I know another game." Jelly Bean steps forward. "Close your eyes." Buster shakes his head so she pushes her plump lower lip out. "*C'mon,* close your eyes." This time he does as instructed, though he flinches when she reaches out and runs her fingertips across his cheek.

"What are you doing that for?"

"Trust me. It'll be fun."

He closes his eyes once more, simply to feel the velvet touch of her fingertips on his paper skin, to know a featherweight touch, not quite a tickle but less than a scratch. He is surprised that he can feel her. Desire resides in his flesh as well as in his mind after all. She smells of the garden and vaguely of his mother and of all things hopeful and steady. He permits himself to smell nothing except this, feel nothing but the heat from her palm near his mouth as she traces a thick, dense spine of mottled flesh all the way along his nose, follows his one good eyebrow and continues down the right cheekbone to where his scar knots and raises up like a railroad track. The tendons in his neck pull taut as if they are currents in a river that has never been explored. The cellar smells of salty, acrid sweat and determination. He balls his fists and the veins in his arms bulge out blue-black as if poisonous blue worms are coursing through his body, as if the fire is inside. Blue and hot and ready to explode.

There is little fresh air and his hair is sweaty beneath his hat, which gives off a musty odour. Of all the shades a flame can burn, he thinks, blue is by far the most dangerous. Of all the shades a flame can burn—red, orange, even mean old white—blue burns hottest. Buster is sure he is meant to know something few people ever learn; that Hell isn't red at all. No fire can scald like an unlived life. Hell is as blue as the hydrangea in his mother's garden he's no longer able to smell. A Chevy Bel Air that he can't afford. Hell is the sky and Jelly Bean Johnson's eyes, no end in sight. Yes, yes. Jelly Bean's true blue eyes. Hell, he knows, is right here on planet Earth. He tries not to think about what she must be seeing, tries not to flinch again or open his eyes and banish the sensation. He pretends he is someone else.

Jelly Bean runs her fingers across his cheek and under his chin.

"Where am I?"

"What?"

"Concentrate." She circles a patch of scar tissue. "Here's the post office...." She presses her finger to his bottom lip. "This is the bank." She underlines his lips, back and forth. "And here's Main Street.... Now where am I?" Buster squeezes his eyes even more tightly, imagines himself as Ray Bernstein, a real ladies' man. He focuses on the song playing in the background. *If they freed me from this prison, if that railroad train was mine, I bet I'd move it on a little farther down the line.* He concentrates on the invisible path she is drawing with her finger. His eyelids flutter.

"This is a stupid game."

"Just try. *Please*." She has him within reach and can't let go. His skin curves and overlaps beneath her hand, layers and texture and shades of pain. On his skin her pain too, on his skin transcendence. In this moment she wants nothing more than to be his girl, ride on the handlebars of his bicycle, go to a drive-in movie. She isn't worried that he's dangerous or weird looking. In fact, his ugliness could rub off and she wouldn't mind for hers is a mask of a different kind, but a mask nonetheless. Buster is grotesque, surreal, and yet it occurs to Jelly Bean now that beauty is not goodness, though the two are often equated. She imagines he has scars on his lungs the shape of home.

"The park," he guesses.

"Yes but *where* in the park?"

"Near the swimming pool." He sounds irritated, impatient. "Are you at the swimming pool?" Jelly Bean smiles and then does something without thinking, something she didn't intend to do; she leans in and kisses him on the corner of his mouth where her parents' hardware store sits. A taste as sweet as a lump of sugar explodes on her tongue. Buster blinks and pulls away fast, stands looking down as if a dumbwaiter has fallen from his chest to his knees. "Don't," he says, opening his eyes and half-expecting to see Mo Axler's daughter there, sealing his fate. He grabs Jelly Bean's wrist and holds it tightly away from the side of his head. "I said, don't!"

She drops her arm and shrinks back, tries to remember what he looked like before; that appears to be what he wants. What would anything look like without mutation? She doesn't know. She understands only how she's always felt; half in one world and half in another, neither this nor that. And to think that they share this feeling? It's irresistible. In this moment his features could be as pure and smooth as Devon cream but she couldn't want him any more. The farm sitting above them might be glimmering crisp and bright, cupping the sun beneath their chins like buttercups, but if all is predictable and flat, why bother? Jelly Bean takes Buster's scars in deeper. She'd rather see only this if it means she never has to look at the dull repetition of beauty again. "I don't want to stop, Buster," she finally whispers. "Let's not stop."

They stand in a silence marred only by the sound of their own weighty breath. The song comes to an end and he hears his name as she spoke it. *Buster* with a soft "B." *Buster* with a pleading tone. His scars aren't as obvious when his name is said out loud like that. His face is merely a smudge. He's a chameleon. A ruffian.

He is anybody she wants him to be.

LATER THAT EVENING Buster sits between his father and Hank in a pew at the United church on Palmer's Hill, staring at the back of Len Rombout's head. Len called the meeting after another break-in, this time in Springford. Most everyone has turned up. Lorraine Rombout with Ivan and Susan. Herb and Gladys Peacock. The Claxtons. Percy brought another primer, Frank Wadley, along. The Brysons are missing and so are the Grays. Is Doc John still sick? Buster is ill at ease without his fedora. "You're not wearing it into the church," his mother said as he and Hank stepped inside. So his father reached over, elbowing Hank in the process, and lifted the hat from his head. Now it rests in his father's lap as innocently as Buster did when he was a boy playing horse or tractor.

He admires the organ on stage, the austere stained glass windows to his left—a series depicting Jesus carrying his cross, being crucified, and finally rising again. Jelly Bean is squished between Hazel and Walter five pews ahead, also examining the windows. Buster can still feel her lips brushing against his own. He tries to see in the windows what she might. Bright colours. The face of Christ—pale and healthy, blue-eyed—apparently indestructible.

Jelly Bean cranes her neck and meets Buster's gaze. She hasn't stopped thinking about him since the cellar. She didn't expect him to be as tender as he was. She's seen him silent and angry. She's known him to dismiss people with a coarse joke or act the tease until feelings got hurt, but with her in the cellar he'd been respectful. He'd looked at her with an expression that said "I will prove myself to you" rather than the usual "I will make you mine." Alone, away from others, he'd been a little bit flattering and a whole lot of butterflies in the belly. And then there was the kiss. The kiss that joined them together against the rest of the world. She's played it over in her mind as if it's a moving picture show, and in each version she is more embarrassed by her brazen behaviour. As the meeting gets underway, her mother pinches her arm and she rights herself.

"All right, everyone." Len stands and faces the room. "Thanks go to Minister Duff for letting us meet here on short notice. You've all heard by now; there was another theft this morning. The Robertson place in Springford. Some of you may remember Vern Robertson from church years ago. He was born in Smoke."

"Was anyone hurt?" calls out a voice from the back pew.

"No. Just rattled. But Vern's gold watch was stolen. I'd say it's high time we started taking this bandit for the threat that he is."

"I hear he's been spotted," calls out another voice.

Everyone turns.

"You seen him, George?"

"No. I thought you did."

Eyes shift back to Len Rombout.

"I seen an odd-looking sort pass through town early this morning."

"That must've been him," says Percy.

"Now how do we know that?" Tom rises from his seat.

197

"You saying we don't know who belongs and who doesn't?" Len's face is red.

"I'm just saying we can't go tossing accusations around like insults. Tillsonburg was crawling the day he hit up the dairy bar, and we were all at the spring fling when he broke into Mrs. Bozek's. If the Robertsons didn't get a look at him then we can't be sure of anything."

"He's getting too close for comfort," says Len. "We can be sure of that. First Tillsonburg, then Zenda, and now Springford. We're sitting ducks."

"Listen," interrupts Hazel. "For all we know the bandit is from right here in Smoke."

There comes a collective gasp from the women in the church. Laura Claxton's eyes grow wide and glassy and Gladys Peacock covers her mouth. "Hazel Johnson, what on earth would make you say such a thing?" She scans the pews. "To think that any of my neighbours would—"

"Well it *could* be one of us." She rests her gaze on Buster momentarily. "It could be someone right before our very eyes."

"Is there something you're trying to confess, dear?"

"Don't be drippy, Walter. This is not the time or the place for your brand of humour." Hazel sits right on the edge of her pew and points at Gladys and Herb Peacock. "We must take action. It could be your place robbed next." Then she points at the minister's wife. "Or *yours*."

"Hazel is right," says Percy. "No disrespect Tom, but if it was your place ransacked I think you'd be singing a different tune. I want this fellow caught and I want him caught now."

"I wish I'd kept better track of foreigners stopping in at my place," says the owner of the dairy bar. "I've got a gun in the back now. Any more funny business and I won't be accountable for my actions."

"Jelly Bean can do up warning signs for those who want one," Hazel continues. "We could at least try and scare him off."

"I want one." Gladys raises her hand.

"So do I," says Len. "And what if we take turns patrolling Main Street?"

"Hold on now." Tom adopts a calmer tone. "I thought we were just meeting to talk. We sound like a bunch of vigilantes."

"Oh I suppose you'd rather set out a welcome mat just like you did with the marketing board," says Len. "Let in any outsider who wants in. Next thing, you'll be having that rotten thief over for dinner."

"Better him than you."

"All right gentlemen." Minister Duff gestures for them both to take a seat. "Remember where we are. This community has always been a peaceable one and look what's happening; we're turning on each other. Now, I suggest we let the law deal with it."

Hank glances sheepishly at Susan Rombout as his father sits, shaking with rage. Tom has been publicly humiliated and it's taking every bit of strength he has not to leap over the pew and grab Len by the neck. Buster faces his father, unable to think of a single thing to say to match the man's toppled, wooden expression or make up for such a halting. All at once he feels part of the community again; he isn't the only one with a cross to bear—he is every man, all of them. He's Hank without Susan. He's Walter and Percy and even his father. "My dad's a stand-up guy," he says, pushing onto his feet. "And I won't have folks saying otherwise."

"Sit down," says a voice from the side.

"Yeah, sit down," says Hank, pulling on his brother's sleeve.

"Not until Mr. Rombout takes it back."

"You're out of line, son. Let me handle this."

"But it's not fair what he said, Dad. If it wasn't for you this place would still be full of blow sand and tumbleweeds. You shouldn't let him get away—"

"Sit down!" Buster does as he's told this time and Tom folds his arms across his chest. "Now Percy I've known your family for years. I want this bandit caught as much as you do. Let's post a reward for information leading to his capture. I'll throw in a few hundred to start. That oughta get the ball rolling."

"Best idea I've heard so far." George pulls his wallet from his back pocket.

"Count me in too," says Walter.

Buster feels a migraine coming on. Embarrassment reddens his scarred face. He tried to stick up for his father like any loyal family member would do and his father still disapproves of him. He can't win. And then it hits him: There was a celebration in the streets the day of the dairy bar heist. The bandit could've been spotted by a number of people. Percy's mother was home when her place got robbed; she might have woken up. This Springford break-in took place when the family was eating breakfast together. The bandit doesn't want a sure thing, Buster thinks. He wants risk. And what would be his biggest risk yet? The sesqui-centennial! Buster can hardly sit still as a plan begins to take shape. His father's solid form presses against his side like a warm stone pillar and Buster thinks, Don't give up on me Dad. Don't you give up on me yet.

"I'll collect donations and pass them on to the sheriff by midweek," says Minister Duff. "If something unusual happens again this'll be a good incentive for folks to come forward. This hooligan has got to know we mean business." He opens his large black bible and motions the congregation to rise in singing the Lord's Prayer.

Tom is slow to his feet. He shakes out one leg and then the other, straightens his good pants. "Our father who art in heaven. Hallowed be thy name." He's rattled by Len's attack and Buster's display. His son took his side and he was ungrateful. He bows his head. "Thy Kingdom Come, thywillbedone, on earth as it is in heaven." He glances around surreptitiously. Just because he doesn't think God is housed within these four walls doesn't mean he thinks God isn't watching him at all. How many in his community agree with Len Rombout about the marketing board? How many are angry? "Lead us not into temptation but deliver us from evil, for thine is the Kingdomthepowerandtheglory. Foreverandever. Amen."

The prayer is recited as if by assembly line and this annoys Tom. Prayer is what you do, not what you say, he thinks. Prayer is a daily routine found in the fields, not a pious Sunday activity. It engages all of his senses. When he bends. Primes. When he waters and sows. He encourages life and devotes his own to it. Growing is arduous, fervent—his own passionate bonfire of belief—and judgment day doesn't come when Len Rombout or anyone else decides. It comes once a year at auction. It comes every morning in the form of his family's respect. And every night when he stands on the back patio, surveys the land and takes stock of what he's done with his own blood and sweat. Idleness is the only real sin. Idleness and vanity, and there's no time for standing around looking good.

"Dad?" Buster leans in, whispers. "Can I have my hat back now?"

Tom looks at the fedora, feels its worn material on his callused palm. He remembers how he felt the night of the accident. How disgust can come at you from underneath yourself, driven up by some visceral force. Fear too. Fear that says "There but for the grace of God go I." Of course Buster should have that surgery, he finds himself thinking. He'll do some figuring after harvest. If it had been Ivan Rombout or Donny Bryson who'd caused the fire Tom would have railed at the boys, demanded they be punished. He would have made amends, or at least shown Buster that he tried, on his behalf, to redress the injustice. But the accident was not their fault, it was no one's fault, so up to now he's done nothing. His hands are useless dry mitts against the softer felt of the hat. Anger lifts with his eyes.

"Here," he says, gently crowning Buster with the fedora.

~2~

Tom stands beside Buster in the middle of the field. Hank is fifty feet away, trying to fix the joint where the irrigation pipe meets the sprinkler pipe, and floundering. The sun beats down relentlessly as Tom tries to understand what's gone wrong. They were arranging the irrigation system when something burst on that last sprinkler— the water pressure built up in a weak spot and the pipe blew off. A large part of his crop is in danger of drowning. The water, from an underground stream, is fed through a combination of points in the ground, supplying a larger main pipe. The whole contraption, Tom thinks, looks like a wagon wheel with a pump attached. The vacuum created by the pump sucks the water up through the pumps to the sprinklers and, with a liquid pulse, beats it out over the crop. The sound is loud at close range. At night Tom hears it from his bed, a rhythmic *pth, pth, pth* lullaby followed closely by the quiet *hum* of the motor in the background. It's reassuring.

Tom doesn't sleep much at this time of the year. He checks on the sprinklers at two-hour intervals all night long except nights like the last when he was too damned tired to haul himself into the field. Instead he'd gone into Lizzie's room, stood beside her crib and listened at the window for her breathing and for the unbroken sound of heaven spitting on his crops for good luck. He reached out to touch Lizzie's damp amber curls. "Remember, whatever's good for the crop is good for you." Then he slipped out of the room as unobtrusively as he'd entered it, and back into bed beside his wife.

Now, he is impatient. "Hank for cryin' out loud, hurry up!" He twirls the wooden A-frame that he used earlier to measure across the field. He's thinking of the expanse of water pooling like a lake, barely twenty-three feet below them. Just this year an archaeological crew from the University of Western Ontario combed the property for arrowheads and told him that the body of fresh water sitting under his land was so pure it might as well have melted off an arctic glacier. This thought makes him feel worldly, though he had nothing to do with putting it there or discovering it. It also makes him agitated wondering what might happen if the vacuum somehow sucks that lake through the pipe and pours it out and over his tobacco. He calculates the cost of lost stalks—thirty-five acres at eight acres per field, two hundred and twenty-five feet wide, six hundred and ninety-five feet long. And that thing is delivering water at a rate of … six hundred gallons a minute? "Jesus Christ! Hank!" Tom turns to Buster. "Your brother's strong as an ox but sometimes he's as thick as one too. Hank! Shut off the pump, hurry it up!" Tom hands Buster a four-inch pipe. "Go see if this one fits any better, and tell him to get a move on." Buster jogs to where the pump is, shuts it off, and then hurries over to his brother.

"Dad says make it snappy."

"Dad can shove it!" Water spews up into Hank's face as it cuts out, soaking him. The cold liquid is a nice antidote to the hot sun. He forces the pipe down into the earth with both hands. It still won't stay in place. Now more than ever he wants to tell his father that he needs to go and work on the Walker farm. With money in his pocket he could approach Susan again without fearing she'll brush him off or make a joke of it.

"Here, try this one." Buster hands him the larger pipe.

"He's being a prick," says Hank replacing one pipe with the other. "I'm working like a dog. Anybody else'd be paid."

"What's it worth, you figure?"

"Be damned if I know," Hank says, without turning around. "Fifty a week at least. I should go work for George Walker. He asked me to, you know."

"He did?" Buster is surprised by this. If Hank leaves to work for another farmer, even in livestock, their father would feel he's been stabbed in the back. Buster also knows Hank prefers raising animals to growing tobacco. "What'd you say?"

"What do you think?" Hank fastens the larger pipe more easily, kicks it down into the earth with his boot heel and gives it a good stomp. "There. That should do the trick." He wipes his brow and waves to his father a few yards away. "Try it now!"

"It used to be I didn't think twice about being here," says Buster. "Before my accident. But you always wanted something else. You should go work for George."

"Dad'll flip."

"Yeah. He'll get over it though."

Why not leave? Hank thinks. He's got nothing to lose. He's the big brother of a freak now, which means that he might as well be the big brother of a track star or a rock 'n' roll legend. Any kind of celebrity. All of his misfortunes or ambitions, however small and petty by comparison, are irrelevant. Not even worth mentioning. It isn't fair. He is supposed to be first. First to drive. First to get a girl. Stronger, faster, superior. Now he's just average. No, worse than average, he is *the lucky one.* Hank knows that he should be grateful that the fire didn't happen to him, that he was down in the rumpus room watching television when it broke out, and most of the time he is, but sometimes, every so often, like now, when he feels his own demotion, he wishes it was him instead. "Thank Christ," he says as the sprinkler finally spits and rotates. He turns towards Buster. "If I had to stay out here any longer I might go ape."

"So ask Dad to cut you loose."

"Right." Hank shoves Buster. "That'd be like asking you to part with a bad mood."

"Maybe, but you get what you settle for."

They reach Tom, Hank dripping wet, and all three stand with their faces bent towards the sky watching as the last steel fountain rains down over the field like glass streamers. *Pth, pth, pth.* "Let's call it a day," says Tom after a few moments, and they start back in the direction of the house. Tom walks, flipping the A-frame, one wooden leg around to the other. They advance in three-foot increments. He is happy to finally have both sons at his side again.

"Dad?" Hank feels every muscle in his body go rigid.

"Mmm."

"It looks like the yield is gonna be good again this year. I was thinking maybe you could let me out of working harvest."

Tom stops, balances the A-frame up against one thigh while he pulls a package of Players from his breast pocket and lights a cigarette. "That what you thought." He resumes walking.

"That's right. Tobacco's not for me any more." Hank looks at Buster, tries to sound less definitive than he feels. "I might like to take my chances at something else."

Tom stops again, blows a puff of smoke so that it hangs before his lips, and takes aim with his tired dark eyes, first at one son and then at the other. "First off," he says. "Family's a team and you know it. I can use as many free hands as I can find. Second, your place is right here, with the rest of us. Jesus, Hank!" He takes another drag off his cigarette, spins the A-frame in the dirt and walks on.

Hank clenches his jaw. He's not going to be stuck rotating the bloody sprinklers for another season. Tobacco isn't going to eat up his days and swallow his dead-tired nights and leave him with nothing of his own. This year his hands won't contort into claws during sleep so that he wakes to find them stiff and sore from priming. He's not working like a derelict machine any more. "No it's not!" he says. "Just because you do it doesn't mean I have to."

Tom swings around, shaking with rage. "Do you two think I can manage here alone!?"

"All right," says Hank. "Fine. I'll stay through one more harvest. That'll leave you plenty of time to replace me."

"I can't replace you, Hank. This is *your* land, for Christsake! Yours and Buster's. The sooner you two get that through your thick skulls the better off we'll all be."

"Dad," Buster interrupts. "A man's gotta carve out his own way."

"What did you say?"

"Yeah, Doc John told me: if he doesn't know what he wants, he'll end up with a life meant for someone else."

Tom's arm shoots out to backhand Buster, but stops short. "Who do you think you're talking to?" Tom drops his arm. "What he *wants*? This is about what needs doing." He storms ahead and smoke from his cigarette feels like hot, stale breath on Buster's face. Buster watches a hawk circle over them in the distance. The bird's head is tucked into its feathery chest, eyes like darts pinned onto a target only it can detect. Buster's arms and legs are at once heavy bags of topsoil and weightless, as if they don't belong to him any more. He doesn't inhabit this ugly body. He wants to fly away, fly away, be anywhere and anyone else but here, this. He continues on beside his brother in silence until they reach the patio where Tom props the A-frame against the house and steps up inside without another word. Hank grabs Buster by the shoulder and holds him back.

"Nice going," he says. "What the hell were you thinking?"

"What do you mean?" Buster jerks his arm free. "I was trying to help you."

"With help like that I'll be stuck here forever. Say what you want to Dad about Doc John, but leave me out of it. You're not the only one around here with plans." Hank walks inside leaving Buster to sit on the steps alone.

Moments later the patio door opens and his mother emerges with a cigarette in her hand and Lizzie awkwardly propped on one hip. She sidles up beside him on the bottom step and settles the baby at her feet. Lizzie tugs on the trim of Isabel's dress.

"Your brother's just told me what happened."

"I don't want to talk about it."

"Brian, what I told Hank was—"

"I said I don't want to talk about it." He looks at her.

"All right. But your father's under a lot of strain these days."

"It was nothing. Just forget it."

Isabel takes a nervous drag off her cigarette, blows smoke to one side. She hates it when Tom loses his temper with the children. It doesn't happen often but the few times it has have left her jittery for days afterward. She'd be cooking in the kitchen, hear any little noise and jump. Those are the only times she ever refuses her husband's advances. "I'm sorry," she says, feeling partly to blame. "Your dad doesn't mean to be so harsh. He just gets frustrated. We all do." She pats Buster's thigh twice as if to punctuate the thought.

"Can we talk about something else for a change?"

Isabel's eyes fill with tears. She lifts Lizzie and passes her to Buster. Then she drops her cigarette on the steps, stands and squashes it with the toe of her shoe. "Fine. Don't keep your sister out long. I've got a bottle ready." She turns and disappears through the patio door.

Buster feels a pang of guilt. He remembers what Doc John said about being good to his mother. But he can't seem to do anything right; he wants to hurt someone at least as much as he's been hurt. Punish the world. He observes Lizzie for a moment. Steadies her in his lap and then pulls her closer. She tugs on his rubbery earlobe and coos. She smells of talcum powder and sleep. He plays pat-a-cake with her, and when she giggles and laughs the sound of unfettered happiness makes him even more sick of himself, of his weak attempts at bargaining on his brother's behalf, and of his own abiding sense of frustration. He looks at the old oak tree where his tree fort once was. It reminds him of Ivan and Donny, of marbles, Chinese checkers and childhood pacts.

He remembers moving through the woods in single file. Ivan, the tallest of the three, was last that day. Even then Ivan had a pronounced jawline and more muscle than other boys his age. He carried a big stick. Donny was in the middle, with a comic book stuffed into the back pocket of his blue jeans, and Buster led the way in his favourite cut-off overalls and rubber boots. He had messy curls that hung around his face like a soft halo. His skin, an even tan left over from the summer, was as smooth and golden as corn syrup. He remembers what it felt like to sparkle at the thought of undiscovered treasures. A coin, green with age. Smooth flat stones for skipping on the river. An old pair of glasses with the lenses busted out. He never knew what was coming next and this lent a fever of thrill to their expeditions.

"Shush," he said pausing and turning, one finger up before his lips. "Listen."

Nothing. Then a slow drag through the grass.

"There it is! I'll get it." He remembers hitting the ground, arms spread out in front as though he was flying. He reached blindly. "Got it." The green body in his hand was not slimy but smooth and velvety as a tobacco leaf on the stalk before it was primed. A solid, thick pencil. He tightened his grip as it wriggled to escape. He was up on both feet again, like a jack-in-the-box, with the others at his side. They stared at the creature, its sleek head, its eyes absolutely round and without lids or lashes. The snake flicked its pink tongue in protest, and as though resigned to captivity, went slack.

"What should we do with it?" Donny asked.

"Kill it," said Ivan.

"Naah, I've got a better idea. C'mon."

Again they were off, shooting through the woods like three bullets fired from a pellet gun. Twigs snapped beneath their sneakers and boots. Sunlight filtered through the tall trees, blinding them in spots. They reached the edge of the forest and came out onto a field. With the snake still in his hand, Buster darted in between the wide green leaves and drank in their tangy brine. It coated the back of his throat. It was the smell of his father and of his older brother. He knew it better than he knew himself. Tar from nicotine on the weed was gummy and rubbed off black on his bare arms and legs. He ignored this. When he reached the top of the property, where his house sat, he crept up to the rear patio. "Wait here," he whispered to the others. "I'll be right back."

He took the steps two at a time and slipped inside through an old wood-framed door. He found his mother's gingham apron looped over the back of a kitchen chair. The faint scent of her Evening in Paris washed over him. He lifted the material with his thumb and pointer finger, so as not to leave a stain, and carefully dropped the snake in the pocket. He replaced the apron and hurried outside once more, gently shutting the door behind him. "Quick," he said, motioning his friends towards a large tree. "Hide."

As they climbed he placed one rubber boot on the bottom rung, relying on the rules of three-point suspension that his father had taught him when they'd built the fort. He moved with confidence, one hand or one foot at a time, reducing his chances of losing his grip. The others followed closely doing the same, and when they were all up they faced one another ready for the secret handshake. Two firm downward motions with the right hand followed by a double-wink, the right eye and the left. It sealed their pact—friends for life. Each boy repeated this exchange until he greeted the other, and satisfied, they fell to the floor and pealed into laughter. Resting high above the adult world they were invincible.

A half an hour later, a shrill scream came from the direction of the house and they scrambled fast, sliding onto their bellies and slithering across the wood floor to their peepholes. There, in lookout position, they watched as a tall redhead in a red and white apron dashed from the house waving her arms and dancing around the backyard, shrieking. Buster remembers that his mother undid the apron and threw it to the ground and the snake slithered out of the pocket and off into the garden. She glanced around the yard and, relieved at finding the creature gone, began to cry. A moment later, she raised her head and peered over at the tree. Started towards it, faster, faster, with a wild look in her eyes. "I know you boys are up there!" she hollered, wiping her cheeks dry on the back of her hand. "Wait until I get my hands on you. I'll wring your little necks!" Buster flattened, pressing his ribs sharply against the plank floor. The boys were motionless and covered their mouths with their hands to keep themselves from releasing any sound. Seeing and hearing nothing, Isabel finally turned, grabbed up her apron and marched back inside the house.

"Whew, close call," Ivan said.

"Yeah." Donny sat up. "She really flipped." He pulled the comic book from his back pocket, began skimming pages. "For a minute I thought we were gonna get creamed."

"Nah, I knew we were safe." Buster found a blue marble in one corner, rolled it in his palm and tossed it over the wall. "Mom would never climb up here. Besides, look around." He stood then, and gestured with both arms to the tobacco spread out all around them, a rich green empire. "This is my kingdom. Nothing can get me here."

Lizzie begins to squirm in Buster's lap and he's ashamed of his behaviour towards his mother. She's always been an easy target, easier than his father. It's his life he can't stand now, not her. It's the fact that they've all moved on without him. The funny thing is though, hearing Hank say he really wants to leave the farm makes Buster reconsider whether he does. He's always been more interested in growing tobacco than his brother, and as much as he's withdrawn from it and the family since the accident, his has been a general withdrawal, a sweeping defensive reaction to everything he once knew and loved. But Hank never wanted to be a grower in the first place, or to have a future in tobacco. For a moment Buster feels ashamed of the way he's been acting towards his father too. Hank's request to leave has got to hurt, even if it's the right thing for him to do. He'd be betraying himself if he stayed forever. *What about me?* Buster thinks. *Who am I betraying?* He sticks his tongue out at Lizzie. She's young and all adventure ahead of her. She hasn't yet grown jaded about the future or been disappointed in other people. He wonders whether he'll eventually become one of her disappointments. He lifts her closer, whispers in her ear. "Naah, I'm going to impress you, Lizzie. I'm going to impress everyone because I'll be the one to catch the bandit. I might need a little help, that's all." Before he stands to carry her inside he lifts his mother's flattened cigarette to his nose and inhales. The smell of dried blood and stale nicotine cause him to gag.

Buster is pacing in the root cellar where it's as damp and dark as it was on the night of his accident. His flashlight is propped up in one corner and aimed at the ceiling. The radio is playing *Sixteen Tons* when there comes a loud knock at the trap door. The knock has a rhythm to it—two long followed by three short, two long again.

The old code.

"Come," Buster says, moving to switch off the radio.

Donny pulls the door back. A gush of fresh night air and moonlight flood the cellar. He squints and climbs in. "What's up?" He reaches into his jacket, under his rolled shirtsleeve, for a pack of Export A, taps it on his knee until one cigarette falls partway out. He brings it to his lips and fishes in his pants pocket for a light.

Buster's head pounds with a ferocious ache and he kicks an old apple crate across the floor and pulls another over to the centre of the room. "The bandit's going to rob the bank," he says as soon as Donny sits. "I'm sure of it."

Donny stares, dumbfounded. "It really *is* you." He moves to stand but Buster sticks out his arm, pushes him back down.

"Don't be a moron. I called you here 'cause I've got a plan and I can't do it alone. C'mon, hear me out. Our man seems to hit up some place every few months. I figure he lives on his take until it runs down. The big news around here all year has been the sesquicentennial, right? The whole village is going bananas with planning it. There'll be big crowds. A lot of money is going to change hands that day and I'm betting the bandit has figured that out. The bank would be a windfall. You remember us and the stores?"

"Yeah. So?" Donny digs one hand deep into his jeans pocket, trying to keep up. He rocks back on the crate. "What does our pocketing candy and magazines have to do with you robbing the bank?"

"I'm *not* robbing the bank. Aren't you listening? I have a better idea." He grins like a drunk on the steps of the Royal Hotel. "Remember how we felt before *we* pinched stuff? We'd be jumping out of our jeans with fear but that didn't stop us. The bandit's the same. He knows he might be caught; I mean he knows there's got to be a good chance he will, especially on a day that's crawling with people. *That's* the thrill, Don. Think about it: he held up that poor sucker at the dairy bar while a bunch of scouts rode through town. He went after Mrs. Bozek's jewellery while she was home. The Robertsons were eating breakfast when he broke in to their place. Those are daring heists, and they were well planned, but they're small peanuts compared with robbing the Bank of Commerce on the day of the sesquicentennial. Mr. Claxton installed new locks last year. You'd have to be a real fingersmith to get inside without anyone seeing."

"Let's suppose you're right. What? You just wave your gun in his face and he'll turn tail and run?"

"Worked with Ivan, didn't it."

Donny folds his arms. "I guess *you* don't remember that chump from Langton."

"McAuliffe. Yeah, I remember. He made off with twenty thousand."

"Got hanged too. Right in the Simcoe jailhouse. No thanks Buster."

"You've got it all wrong. See we wouldn't be stealing the money, we'd be getting it back. Think about it: for years to come people would talk about who it was that robbed the bank and who it was that saved the day. We'll be heroes. *The two of us.* A team again." There it is, all his cards out on the table. "The way I figure it, we'll be legends in our own time like Raymond Bernstein."

"Who?"

"Never mind. Look. I'm offering you the chance of a lifetime. This fella's probably been through a half-dozen rinky-dink towns in the region that we don't even know about. He's still around; I'm sure of it. And if he is he's thinking about the bank. I'm sick of folks gawking at me sideways. Let's nab him."

"You *are* off your rocker. That could be dangerous." Buster's plan is more like a fever, a bubbling, boiling determination that causes him to buzz like a beehive.

"You're a real square. I knew I shouldn't have asked you."

"Maybe you shouldn't have." A moment ago Donny was flattered thinking that Buster had come crawling back to him and now the possibility that he is Buster's second or even third choice dawns on him like an overcast sky. "Does anyone else know about this?"

"No. And they better not find out either. Blab and you'll be sorry."

"Don't blow a gasket." Donny takes another drag off his cigarette. "Ever since the accident you've been acting queer."

"You're just worried what your mommy will say."

"That's it. See you around." Donny stands and heads for the trap door. Then he turns with a stern expression on his face. "My mother left. You've got some nerve bringing that up."

"She did? I didn't know. I swear."

"She'll be back though."

"Yeah sure. Course …"

"Yeah."

"So what do you say?"

"I say you need to get your head checked."

"Listen. Herbert McAuliffe only got hanged because he shot two people. We won't hurt anybody. If it works we'll be helping. The town's posted a reward. Five hundred dollars."

Donny taps the toe of his boot, drops his cigarette and extinguishes it with his heel. He is standing where he'd been on that night when he and Ivan taunted Buster into drinking too much. "I can't think when I'm down here. It's hot and it stinks. Let's go up."

"Yes or no?"

Donny rubs his forehead. He wants to be a sport; he owes it to Buster, and with his dad on the sauce again they could really use some extra money. "Ivan might want in."

"This is *my* plan! Leave that yo-yo out of it."

"Okay, okay. Let's say for a minute I go along with this hare-brained idea. Then what?"

"Then we've got time to plan. We'll set up a lookout, just like we did in the old tree fort. We'll watch and wait and if we're lucky we'll catch him." Buster winks, which looks more like a strained facial tick. "So, do we have a deal?"

"Fifty-fifty?"

"Seventy-thirty."

"Find yourself another dupe."

"Okay, we split it even-steven."

Donny looks Buster in the eye and there behind two determined green peepers he finds a flicker of reason, a flicker of the friend he used to know. He extends his hand.

"All right. For old times' sake."

Two weeks later school has let out and Donny's Bel Air is parked in the McFiddie driveway. He smoothes his palm across the warm hood. "I want her to have straight pipes," he says.

Buster nods. "Without a muffler she'd be really loud and fierce sounding." He removes his fedora and pokes his head inside the driver's-side window, examines the two-tone interior and steering column. "I'm thinking I'll get an old Merc." He tilts his head towards the house to make sure no one's listening. "Once we collect the you-know-what."

Donny opens the driver's-side door. "I'll probably send some of my cut off to my mom and sister." He slides onto the seat. "Like to get the heads milled down though, maybe get a trick valve job. More horsepower. It'll cost a pretty penny, almost as much as I paid for her. C'mon, hop in."

Buster opens the passenger door. "Start by drilling the jets out. That'll let more gas into the carburetor."

"Good idea." Donny starts the engine and Buster fiddles with the radio until he finds Perry Como singing "Round and Round."

"Why didn't you go with your mom when she left?"

"I couldn't." Donny shifts into reverse, backs them out of the driveway. "Dad's worse than he used to be. What if he falls and hits his head? I empty bottles down the drain every morning and he doesn't notice. Someone had to stay."

"That's rough, Don."

"Yeah." Donny shifts into drive, pushes on the gas pedal and lays a strip. "But not right now. Right now we're free!"

They fly through Springford with Buster hanging halfway out of the car, hooting and hollering to no one in particular. He waves with his hat in his hand, wondering if the bandit can see him, and lets the noonday sun beat down on his face. They turn north onto

Highway 19 and Donny floors it until they reach Ingersoll. There, he takes them across to Highway 59 and then south to Norwich, where he squeals to a stop in the empty school parking lot. The school that once looked so ominous to Buster is now a gentle giant. "This is the life," he says, fixing his hat on his head. "Go anywhere you want, do whatever you want." He lets himself out of the car and walks around to sit on its hood.

"Watch you don't scratch her," says Donny. He joins Buster and they stretch their legs out and stare up into the cloudless summer sky.

"School's never looked so good," says Buster.

"Yeah," Donny laughs.

"I don't expect I'll be coming back to it."

"Why not? No one talks about you any more."

"They don't?"

"Naah. You're old hat." Donny glances at the fedora. "I mean—"

"Don't worry about it. Here," Buster removes his hat, passes it to Donny who flips it over, reads the label. He twirls it on his pointer finger. "You know what today is?"

"Saturday."

"My birthday, you dope. I'm sixteen today." Buster runs his hand through his wind-swept hair. "My mom's making a chocolate cake. Come for supper if you want. Last year I was in bed recovering. Don't even remember it. But no matter, as of midnight last night I can officially get my licence."

ON THEIR WAY BACK through Smoke they notice Walter standing outside the hardware store in his overalls, examining the building. "Slow down," says Buster, searching for Jelly Bean through the store window. "Pull over."

"Hello boys." Walter approaches the car. "I was thinking I'd fix the place up a bit, for the sesquicentennial. What do you think?"

"Can't hurt," Buster says, stepping out of the car. "What did you have in mind?"

Walter points to the facade. "See all the peeling?"

"Uh-huh."

"It's been five years since I last painted."

"A new coat would clean it right up."

"Judy says to go with white again. What do you think?"

"Sounds good. Is she around?"

"She's running errands. Banking and such." Walter faces the boy. "Buster, I don't suppose you'd be willing to give me a hand with the painting? If you're not needed elsewhere, that is."

"Right now? Uh, I guess I'm not. Let me just talk to Don." He walks over to the car, leans in Donny's window and speaks over the music. "Mr. Johnson needs us to help paint."

"Are you pulling my leg?"

"Just for a couple of hours. He's a friend of my dad's. C'mon."

"No way. You go ahead if you want. I'm on vacation." Donny shifts the Bel Air into reverse and Buster steps away from it. "I'll swing by later, see if you're still here." Donny sounds the horn and waves as he drives off.

"Well I don't like it one bit, Walter," whispers Hazel moments later when she notices Buster outside, mixing a can of primer with a stick. "I don't care if it is a help. Haven't you heard a word I've said?"

"It'd be hard not to, dear." Walter rifles under the counter for his paint gloves.

"He could be the bandit. He could be the very one we're after and now you've got him out front for the whole world to see."

"That's right. I do." Walter grabs his gloves, stuffs them into the pocket of his overalls, lifts the ladder and slips out the door with it. "All set, Buster." He leans the ladder up against the wall. "You've already got a screwdriver to pry up the lids. Your brushes are right there, small one's for trim. I found you a pair of my gloves. Might be a bit big. If you need more paint just let me know, but two gallons of each should more than do it. Try and keep a path clear for customers. Whatever you don't get done, not to worry. I'll finish tomorrow. You've painted outdoors before, I take it?"

"Yes sir."

"All right then. Let's show this village what an industrious young man you are."

"DON'T FALL." Jelly Bean looks up at Buster on the top rung of the ladder with a gallon of primer in one hand and a paintbrush in the other. He sets the brush across the rim of the paint can and takes a careful step down.

"Here I am, at your service." He tips his hat, smudging white paint on it, and she smiles broadly.

"Nice job so far." She walks around the ladder and leans up against a part of the wall that hasn't been painted.

"Your dad said you were at the bank. Does that mean you're carrying a knife today?"

She flashes him the knife. The sun catches the metal and blinds him momentarily.

"Cool."

"Mind if I hang out awhile?"

"It's your store." Buster steps up, lifts the brush and makes a long, fluid vertical stroke.

"You should really be painting the other way." Jelly Bean shows him what she means with a sweeping gesture. "Go with the panels."

"This isn't a masterpiece."

"I know." She moves to the end of the porch, where she sees people crossing the street. Gladys Peacock passes before the store with a large bag of groceries.

"Well what's this I see?" She stops. "Hello Jelly Bean. Hello Buster."

"Hi Mrs. Peacock," they double.

"Buster, it does my heart good to see community improvements like this."

"Mr. Johnson just needed a hand and—"

"Never mind false modesty." She shifts the weight of her grocery bag onto the other hip. "Lovely job. Bye now."

Jelly Bean giggles and then sees her mother standing in the doorway wiping her brow on the back of her arm.

"Judy, are you distracting Buster from his work?"

"Mrs. Peacock was by, that's all."

Hazel bustles around to have a better look at the facade. "That is much better already, Buster." She waves her hand. "All right, Jelly Bean. Inside with you."

AFTER THE HARDWARE STORE has been given a new face, after it closes and Donny has driven Buster home, the bandit crouches in the dark behind the bank. He cannot be seen from either Main Street or from the apartment above. He works fast surveying the property, measuring the window with his eyes and examining the rear door handle. He could jimmy it but that would make too much noise. He crawls between the red brick wall and the bushes and dirties his clothes. He doesn't care. His only concern is for what lies inside—stacks of crisp bills, coins to weigh in his pockets like freedom. His mouth waters and he stands. A light comes on in the window upstairs and he immediately flattens against the wall, the windowsill digging into his kidneys. He holds his breath. After a moment the room above goes dark again, and Mr. Claxton, the banker, moves off and the stranger slips away. He'll wait for another day when the stakes are high and he can really test his mettle. He will wait for the sesquicentennial.

Doc John sits on the edge of his bed in his robe and black knee socks. The double box spring and mattress is firm beneath him. He holds his arms in proper concert formation, back erect, feet flat on the hardwood floor. He supports the weight of the clarinet with his right thumb, and all seventeen keys, which he's finished polishing with a cottony cloth, feel smooth to the touch. The cloth lies beside him on the bedspread. Only a small lamp illuminates the room, though his eyes are closed. He is inspired to practise.

His bottom lip is rolled over his bottom row of teeth and the mouthpiece of the clarinet rests there, his lips sealed around it so that no air can escape—a good embouchure reserves all precious breath for the instrument. His lip is raw from much practising lately, as if a fine piece of sandpaper has been pulled tightly over top of a balloon. On the outside of his lip, in the shallow valley above his chin, there is a sensitive red patch. Playing is all about breath control, moisture and vibration. There are holes to release his breath, pads to hold it in and shape it. But it is a tremor which makes the music come to life. Alice enters the room and he stops to acknowledge her, holds his posture and opens his eyes.

"No, go on," she says. "I like to hear you." She watches his hands, and even in their arthritic, gnarled state finds them to be agreeable. His healing hands. Soft and capable and almost feminine. Yes, she loves him for his hands and his good Christian heart, always helpful in a pinch.

Doc John shifts position to face her now, one wiry leg dangling over the side of the bed. He flexes his diaphragm as Alice slips from her blue housecoat, spreads it across the back of a chair and sits on her side of the bed in her old nightgown. She kicks off her slippers, right foot and left, stretches across the bed to find John's pillow, and props both it and hers behind her back. When she reaches into the small drawer of her bedside stand for an emery board he notices how her small breasts fall together to one side, and how her pouch of a belly slopes, pressing through the worn material of her night-gown like a soft blue moon. Her salt-and-pepper hair hangs shoulder length and sweeps partway across her face as though a net has been cast out to catch him. He licks the clarinet reed without thinking. Doesn't feel tired any more. "This one's just for you," he says, the mouthpiece between his teeth. Alice fluffs the pillows, settles herself comfortably with her legs stretched out so that her feet are down at the bottom of the bed beside her husband. She begins to file her fingernails. "I think you'll know it," the doctor adds. He gives her feet a squeeze. Her toes are freezing and he covers them with the polishing cloth and resumes the song from the beginning. Pain pools in his knuckles while he plays. His fingers are stiff. Inflamed. He is aware of how quickly his playing has deteriorated over the past months.

When he joined the Smoke Brass and Woodwind Pipe Band, years ago, he thought he'd prefer the trombone or the trumpet, but Walter had given him a quick introduction to the woodwinds and he soon came to realize that it was clarinet that spoke to him especially. This instrument is not boastful or showy—indeed there are few good solos written for clarinet. No, it's an instrument that sounds best when accompanied—bassoon, flute, strings—though they haven't any strings in the local band. He enjoys the way it makes him feel to hold its heavy, twenty-six-inch-long rosewood body in both hands, and let loose his fingers and everything he cannot otherwise express. He loves the taste of the reed on his tongue, especially a new reed, and speaking foreign words like *crescendo* and *staccato* reminds him of medicine, of the Latin terms his father had once forced him to memorize. Clarinet suits his hands—any larger and he'd have trouble with the cramped positioning. Even with arthritis he can manage regular rehearsals and with enough effort his clarinet can be made to sound sad, joyful, mysterious all in one breath.

Every instrument, Walter has told the band on more than one occasion, reflects its player. And John has thought about what of him comes through the long body of his clarinet. Tact. Practised and controlled formality. It's a humbling sound, but the best thing about playing it is belonging, having a defined and valued place in the band, with every player working towards the same goal. Tonight he wants to release all his pent-up anxiety, to arc and bow, negotiate with the past and calm his implacable stomach. And yet when he blows hard the instrument squeaks in protest and reminds him of his place and of how music, like life itself, responds best to a powerful but gentle touch. His wife's emery board scrapes accompaniment as he finishes up the composition with a dramatic trill, blowing gradually stronger and making the final notes more potent.

"That was lovely John." Alice sets aside what she is doing. "It gave me gooseflesh."

He carefully places his clarinet on the chair and moves to lie beside her, his head resting on her abdomen. Her stomach grumbles and he feels her cool flesh beneath the thin material. "You know what I do with my clarinet when *she's* cold?"

Alice makes a motion to rise, to scuttle under the covers, but he presses his fingers into the plump flesh of her hips to hold her still. He thinks of the way the pads of his fingers feel when he presses them into the silver rings on his clarinet, how the metal leaves round circles imprinted, like octopus tentacles. Alice runs her hand through his hair. "I can't imagine."

He lifts his face, regards his wife in a way that he hasn't in months. She has so few wrinkles, even for a woman ten years her junior. He reaches up and removes his glasses, sets them on the bedside stand. Before she knows what he's doing, he's eased her nightgown up and over her hips and is rubbing his head into her belly, blowing on her bare skin and making a rude, flatulent sound. She laughs artlessly and tries to push him away but his lips tickle and she only laughs harder.

He's always taken great pride in offering Alice pleasure—never demanding it. He's learned to touch her radiant and red. Learned to give her what she wants under covers, in the dark, and the secret to feeling good about it is to never ask anything in return. You can live a long time, a beautifully long time, being as singular in purpose as a stone.

Early on in their marriage Alice modestly questioned the one-sidedness of their intimate relationship, but over time even an interrogation that goes unanswered eventually ceases to exist. Now he crawls on top of her, pressing his weight into her body, and she receives him. He smiles and kisses her on the neck. She turns her face, feels the emery board digging into her side and her husband's warm, wet mouth tracing all the way from below one earlobe to the crevice of her collarbone. She shivers when she hears him whisper *"Tremolo."* He reaches over to pull the chain on the small lamp, folding the two of them into darkness.

In the moonlight Alice sees only the bright white nickel silver of the clarinet keys as they gleam like stars beside the bed. Every surface of the room is cast in a silver glow and she can't help but think of their twenty-fifth anniversary, only a few months off now. She sighs and conjures the melody as her husband's twisted but agile fingers play along her body, circling her shoulders, down her rib cage and across her stomach. She bites her lip. His hands have always been her undoing, her Judas, for they betray her weakness every time. His hands are able to heal and to play as if they belong to a charmed soul and sometimes, like now, they fly across her skin convincing her that she and John are as endless as the great good sky itself.

The song he played for her was slow and sultry. Despairing. Broken-hearted, Alice thinks, the way she would feel being severed from him. But mercifully he changed the pitch and the tempo and it became lighter, fast, like his speech pattern when he's telling one of his silly stories. Yes, that song sounded like one of John's yarns and knowing that he can communicate as effectively *without* words strikes Alice as precious and ironic, and above all, divine. She feels desire inside like a buttery thickness. Her breath catches in the back of her throat when his arm reaches under and around her waist, holding her in place. His body cleaves to her softer form, begging entrance. He parts her legs. The silver, shadowy room spins into wider and wider concentric circles until Alice's stomach drops and her mouth waters and she feels John above her, coaxing. Then he is undressing as he's always done, throwing off his housecoat and falling onto her again, the straps of his jockstrap on his backside familiar. When she reaches around to grab them, the tensor bandages beneath his cotton undershirt rub up against her nakedness. His socks scratch her feet. The spicy smell of his aftershave fills her senses. Her own wispy breath rises and falls, then falls and falls and falls....

John's tongue circles her nipples as if he is tonguing the reed of his clarinet. Then he kisses her on the lips as though for the first time. Or the last. Alice tastes the woody reed and her blood quickens. She won't admit it by daylight or lamplight, not even by the sterling glow of the moon, for it surely is blasphemous, but lying with him in this way she is certain, every time, it's the closest she's ever come to knowing God.

He grips her tightly, one hand down between her legs, fingers blustery with promise. Slowly, he guides himself inside. *"Forte,"* she hears him say while he rocks them both. Then *"Piano. Pianissimo."*

Soft, soft soft.

AFTER, THE DOCTOR TRIES to sleep but finds himself rattled and fretting. He lies in bed listening to the radio tucked under his pillow, to the muffled voice playing like a contained and frantic whisper. *Midnight. One more night without sleepin'. Watchin' till mornin' comes creepin'. Green door, what's that secret you're keeping?* He flips over, switches on the bedside lamp and thinks about medical discoveries made year after year to revolutionize the way the world understands and functions. Insulin. Vaccines for polio, measles, mumps. The average human lifespan seems to be increasing. Will there come a time when death can be delayed indefinitely? Averted? When a man can sidestep his own ending? Doc John wants to be reborn like those believers the televangelists baptize, or roll away like the tide and slip seamlessly from rivers to lakes to oceans and farther, to be the first line of a new story, a different story. Begin again. Science teaches that there is variety in nature. Anomalies, mutations. Sometimes it's these exceptions to the rules, he knows, that lead to a whole new discovery, or a cure. He believes in endless possibility and surprise discovery for he's practically invented the very ground that has carried him forward.

Even after all these years he looks to what he knows of research and the newest experiments for comfort, not Alice's big black book or even her diminutive frame laying next to him in bed. She is goodness and faith and superstition. He is a man of science. Should he once more broach the subject of all that is coiled up inside him like a spring?

"Settle down," Alice whispers. "It's been a long day, John. I'm bushed."

"I can't. I'm not ready."

"Pardon?"

"I'm not ready to go."

"But I thought we agreed. You need to start holding office for half days."

"I don't mean work."

Alice rolls over, faces him in the thick moonlight. "What then?"

"I'm not feeling any better," he admits.

"You're just run down. Doing too much. I've been saying it for months. For one thing, you shouldn't be on the road any more. Your eyes aren't good enough." She reaches for his hand under the bedspread and accidentally touches the spot where the lining of his stomach, and the tissue beneath, have deteriorated. He flinches. He's seen inside many bodies, inside where blood and tissue and bone erode, and it makes faith harder to hold on to in the face of his own mortality. He clutches his abdomen. We all begin inside, he thinks, and then it's alone the rest of the way. And alone after we're dried up completely, shut down, cold, immaterial once more. We rot and cave, we stink with the foulness of life long gone. That's all. Despite himself he is sick with the flavour of a frightful ending; punctuated time. Death, sick, sick death.

"It's coming soon," he whispers into the night. "It's coming fast." He searches Alice's face through the waning darkness and finds the gentle curve of its silhouette. A reverse cameo, the outline of his life. He imagines her body beneath him as it was only moments before, pressing and straining. He sees them dancing in the kitchen by the dim yellow of the stove light as they have on many nights, and he gives her a reassuring cuddle under the sheets. Alice, younger and more optimistic, doesn't yet understand that aging is a magnifying glass held up against time, reminding him that he is not infinite. He can change, effect much change, but transformation is only as good as his last breath. Yes, Alice has always denied what she hasn't wanted to admit out loud and he understands this; her refusal to talk about their situation is sacrosanct. Her panacea his permission. He's relied on the generosity of her spirit to smooth suspicions and mask evidence and she has always delivered but now he must be even more certain, vigilant. "When it's my time I want you to take me away from here," he says. "I want to be cremated."

"John, don't talk like that! I won't listen."

"Please." He moves to her. "You have to do it." His voice is trembling and weak. He hates that he's asking anything directly yet what choice is there? He has been his own fragile creation; not every doctor is, of course, but he is and now that the long empty silence is coming, he knows he must find a way to face it with her future in mind. He must think of what life will be like for Alice, after. He doesn't want to leave. He doesn't want to be that—dead. Discovered. But, if he is to go first it must be clearly planned, otherwise they will find him and he will cease to be himself in too many ways, unbearable. And, it will be Alice held to task. He slips closer beneath the covers, warms his feet on hers.

Alice stiffens. "You're not making any sense." The wind picks up outside the window. She senses a storm coming on. "We'll talk in the morning when your head's clear."

"I want what's easiest for you, that's all."

"What's easiest is silence!" she snaps. And more softly, "There's nowhere I'd rather be. You should know that by now. We're not going anywhere. Please. Settle down to sleep with me." She closes her eyes.

After a moment the faithful sound of Alice's shallow breathing, low and solid, fills the room. The doctor feels the heat of her mouth against his shoulder, smells the mint flavour of her tooth-paste and a trace of their lovemaking perfuming the sheets. But Alice is not asleep. Her mind is awash in panic, a blinking, shutter-speed panic. She knows what it is he's dreading; she is dreading it also, but still cannot compel herself to confront it head-on. Knowing something in private and making it public by sharing it are two different things. It's hard for her to examine her marriage closely after all this time for in doing so she is made to once more examine herself. Alice knows John inside and out, knows him, no doubting it. But who is she? What woman would have stayed with him? Has she too slid along the slippery slope towards sin?

She won't think about these things. There is simply no point summing up life's accomplishments and failures, just for the sake of it. False comfort is a figure gleaned from all the minuscule bits of information that most people think account for a life. Her John, of all people, should know better. She should know better. If it's got to do with living it's all been immeasurable, imperfect. Blessed. Let people think what they want, Alice tells herself. A man shouldn't turn himself inside-out for what-ifs, and neither should I. Doubt can shake and rattle the whole house. A couple needs a strong foundation. Every family needs some stone.

Doc John reaches under his pillow to silence the radio, closes his eyes to soothe his restless soul. He's been taking in more sunshine and avoiding large, greasy meals and sugar but it's the anxiety that is grinding him down. After he is gone he won't be around to defend himself or to explain. *Mend*. This, above all else, is a chilling thought.

"Alice? You still awake?"

"Mmm."

"I have provided well, haven't I?"

"You know you have."

"Been faithful to my vows."

"I should hope so!"

"Then promise me, no burial. Bury me after if you like. I need you to give me your word. There are things that money and the most impeccable reputation cannot buy. You must know it as well as I." Alice drapes her arm across his midriff and pulls herself on top of his chest. Steels herself against a long overdue conversation, a conversation she's never been sure she wanted to finish. She hears thunder in the distance. Sees a flash of electric blue cut across the ceiling. It never strikes twice, she thinks. It never strikes twice in the same place.

"Shush." She lifts her finger to his lips. She won't have him destroying all that they've built together. But what is the point of loving if it's all about parts and nothing about the whole? The *real* story. The point is their relationship, she tells herself. The point is that it works. She doesn't need to go digging around, looking for trouble. What they share is as truthful as it ever gets between two people. Imagine if everyone decided to reveal their most private confessions. There would no longer be men or women, husbands and wives; only people with nothing left to lose. Is there no virtue in silence any more? Can they not share a real marriage without cutting themselves open so crudely? Of course they can. They already have.

"It's the past," Doc John presses. "It's been chasing and when something chases long enough it usually catches up."

Alice sinks lower under the covers. "I'm not listening any more."

"Please dear." It breaks his heart to have to put it into words.

"I can't stand this one more minute."

And then he can't. He isn't sure why but all at once her resigned tone and the chilly rib of space parting them on the bed tells him in terms he has not understood before: she would rather live in the pale dusk of wilful ignorance for as long as they have left before she'd live without him in the exposed dawn ahead. Telling isn't worth it. It never has been. Making her admit it out loud would only be selfish and mean. "No, you're right," he says. "You're right. Let's not talk about it any more."

"Good."

"Alice?" He reaches for her hand and finds her ring finger, rolls her wedding band between his thumb and forefinger, his heart wringing dry like a sponge. Even after all these years she is beauty and openness. A true believer when he has many doubts. He married her for the same reason any man freely marries: to be recorded, to have *been there,* with someone, written into history. "I've always loved you," he whispers. "You know that." And in an instant that old, raw silence is back again, worn but comforting as a moth-eaten sweater.

"All right." She rolls off of him, relieved. Defeated and yet relieved. "If it'll bring an end to this nonsense, I'll see to it. I promise. No burial, but I never want this subject raised again." Every muscle in her jaw slackens, as if all the words that have ever needed speaking are finally gone and there's no longer a reason to clench. She'll do it. She'll keep him.

"Yes," he says, sinking into the mattress with a lighter heart. "Of course. Thank you." His eyes fall shut like lead curtains.

Alice stares through the darkness at the ceiling with a thickness in her abdomen she's not felt in years. A pit as hard and unrelenting as a child never to be conceived. This secret they share is a barbed wire fence that sometimes, for brief periods, holds them apart, holds her apart from herself too, and lately makes her feel unworthy.

But the threat of death causes an even sharper division, a plume of smoke spiralling up and away, dispersing into the atmosphere. Mingling. Infecting, and possibly leaving her alone. It is no longer the time for revealing, for excavating old lives, if ever there was such a time. That time is long gone. Death is all around, Alice feels tonight. All corners of the house, every story untold. Lurking, hovering.

She will instead focus on what *is* known. Her husband is a good man. No matter what. A good man like George Walker who tends his sloppy hogs with the vital creed of a mad scientist or Tom McFiddie who tends his crop the same way. Yes, Alice reasons, farmers and growers and healers are all in the passionate business of chemistry and biology, of sustaining life and creating new strains. Tom McFiddie cures, she thinks as she drifts off. John cures. Aren't all men doctors, really? Looking to cure and yet helpless in the end.

MATURATION

On the first of August in 1959, harvest begins. It's wet out in the fields—a thin dew coats the tobacco as Buster trudges off at six o'clock in the morning. The plants have all matured and been topped, pinkish-red and white blooms broken off. The sun teases the horizon and he stands shivering, does up his rubber suit and waits for the others. A tobacco worm crawls up his sleeve and suctions on like a toilet plunger. He shakes his arm, plucks it off and flings it hard at the ground. The meaty green slime bursts on impact, like a water balloon.

His father has already demonstrated how the brand-new priming machine works, and being the youngest, Buster knows without being told again that he is to drive. He's glad of it, because though it isn't apparent at this early hour, tobacco's sticky gum mixes in with the sandy soil and wet leaves and makes for a particularly harsh brand of sandpaper that easily turns a primer's hands sore by noon. When the other fellows join him a few minutes later he steps onto the priming machine and takes his seat, six inches off the muddy ground. Two men sit on either side—Percy, his dad's best primer, Hank, Bob and Donny Bryson. Bob is either drunk or hungover, Buster can't tell which, though the smell of booze fuming off the man's body suggests both.

"Where do you want me?" Donny is none too happy being stuck working with his father. He's expected to pick up the slack and he knows that whatever money he makes is sure to be swallowed down by Bob and pissed out just as fast.

"Right there." Buster points. "Hop on."

The machine is lightweight, made of a thin metal and looks like an insect—a daddy-long-legs. Buster enjoys its sleek, wily appearance. He drives them between the stalks and each man reaches out and picks two or three of the sand leaves. Next run-through and they'll move up to seconds and up to thirds and up, up, up as the plant ripens, eventually stripping the stalks to mere skeletons and leaving the field full of scrawny green stems, naked as chicken bones.

Sitting low to the ground, brushing through the short, thick stems and pulling off the wide leaves causes the plants to snap back and slap them in their faces. It's a cheeky smack across the mug that they learn to anticipate, Buster sees, but that cannot be prevented. From where he's perched Bob is being punished hardest, though Donny is getting it too. Under the hard sun Donny's black hair shines like hot coal.

There are strong smells in the field, faintly skunky and restorative. Buster breathes them in and before he knows it he's off, drifting through his old life on a melancholy wave of newly primed tobacco. The memories should be comforting but they aren't. They fill him with a jumpy nostalgia, one that pulls him backwards, ripping him from his present situation and relieving him of the burden his life has become only to callously hurl him fast-forward again and land him smack-dab in the middle of here and now. He is skittish while he drives; can't shake the distance between who he used to be and who he has become. This restlessness will stay with him all day.

The same sinking sensation has been lodged in his rib cage when he wakes each morning dreaming of unmarked skin and average concerns, dreaming that he is whole and handsome only to realize yet again that the accident *has* happened, that the fire has actually burned him and his face has been destroyed. Driving, he shifts his posture and allows himself to be lost in sleepy indulgences where he's like everyone else, even better, where he is untouchable. He sees himself tromping through back alleys instead of trudging through the mud. Plotting to overthrow a rival instead of wondering how to get along with his buddies. He plans the capture of the local bandit in detail, thinks how proud his father will be and what others will say when he and Donny turn the thief over to authorities. He imagines collecting his share of the reward money, buying a car and finally skipping town. He may be leading a priming gang through another hot and heavy day but he is also someplace else, building a new future. He escapes Smoke and everything it represents, easily escapes, to a neat hideaway with an unknown address. He sits atop that primer as though he's sitting next to Ray Bernstein or Solly Levine. He is ready. He is driving. He stares straight ahead and he is there....

At ten o'clock Isabel sends treats of banana bread and chocolate chip cookies out into the field with Tom. He passes the sweets around and sifts through what has been primed, lifting a couple of leaves from the pile in one of the canvas baskets. He inspects both sides.

"Not bad." He looks pleased. "Over a foot 'round."

"Yeah, over a foot," doubles Hank.

To Buster the leaves are as wide as the tires on Donny's Bel Air.

"How's the new machine, boys?"

"A hell of a lot easier than priming on foot," says Percy, lighting a cigarette. His hands have blackened and gone sticky from the tar.

"Good." Tom reaches onto his tractor for a jug of water and passes it to Percy. "In a few years these contraptions'll be commonplace. My curer's working out too. He's stoking now. The leaves are soft but he's bringing 'em into case just fine."

After a few minutes standing there talking but not really talking, smoking, stretching and quenching their thirst—and Bob's isn't nearly quenched enough—they all climb back into position, adjust their caps and hats. Buster watches his father empty the baskets onto the boat hooked to his tractor and drive off in the direction of the table gang. He starts them back to working.

The humidity is thick and his legs are soon numb from sitting—one foot falls asleep. The smells of the field eventually prove stronger than any fantasy he can concoct and reality seeps in, one leaf at a time, leaches under his dirty fingernails, coats his hair. Soon visions of bootlegging and even of capturing the bandit and redemption float away and Buster is overcome by row after endless green row. He can think of little else except right here, this verdant marshy place. The soil all around is a living, breathing entity sapping him of all that is good, all that might be good again, reminding him of his one big mistake like an infected, dirty wound that just won't heal. The repetition of priming is endless and so, like the women who are standing side by side at the tying table handing leaves, the men gossip in order to stave off the monotony. They don't call it gossip though; they just say they're shootin' the shit.

"Your father know about Rombout's petition?" Percy asks Hank. Without breaking priming rhythm Hank responds, "What petition?"

"To oust your father from the parade. Says he's got twelve signatures so far."

"Never happen. Dad's president of the Growers Association."

"Might," says Percy. "Folks don't like hearing about quotas."

"Don't like petitions either."

"No need to sneak behind backs to make the point," says Bob. "Must be on account of Susan's condition. It's making him crazy."

Hank's face turns ashen. "What say?"

"Didn't you hear?" Bob leans in. "She's got herself knocked up."

Buster spins around to meet his brother's eyes and Hank is looking as humiliated as a wet cat so he knows it isn't Hank's fault.

"Whose is it?"

"Dunno," says Bob. "Hazel told me when I went in for batteries yesterday. She says it's a French boy most like, but Susan's not telling. Donny, you used to be over at their place a lot. You know anything?" Donny fidgets with his gummy black hands and shrugs.

"She's as stupid as a cow and deserves what she gets!" Hank spits. His throat is dry. Caked. He can barely swallow. He wants badly to hit someone hard—Susan most of all—and just as fast he is plunged so deeply and completely into despair that he can barely make out the leaves he is priming. They continue working in silence though

Hank sits on the primer staring at the wall of tobacco moving past to his right, letting it *slap slap slap* hard against his face, and thinking that Susan, *his* Susan, is having someone else's baby.

AT NOON THEY BREAK for dinner and by then they've picked under half a kiln. Not good enough. Hank is off the primer, storming through the field away from the others. Percy is furious with Bob for plodding more than usual. Bob has given two tugs instead of the necessary one to snap the leaves from their stems and he's slowed them by an hour or more. Percy avoids Bob's bloodshot eyes for fear that he'll slug him and embarrass Donny who has primed twice as fast to atone for his shiftless father.

"I told you my dad's got a real problem," Donny whispers to Buster as they hurry in.

"Makes it our problem too. At this rate we'll be stuck working to friggin' six o'clock. He knows we can't quit until the kiln's full."

"Yeah, all he does now is sleep and drink. I don't think he even paid our rent last month."

"Hang tight, Don. We'll have that reward money soon enough."

The blood-scent of roast beef and fried steak reaches them as they close in on the farmhouse. Buster notices that the kiln door is open, ready for the hanger. Percy climbs up the ladder and stands in the opening. Bob begins to pass the tobacco up slowly, stick by stick. Percy moves them into place as fast as he can. Later, at the end of the day when the kiln is full, he'll seal it so the curer can yellow them, dry them green to gold. It's a near perfect system as long as everyone pulls his weight. All of this will continue until the stalks in the fields are completely bald, every kiln full and the leaves hung as they are ready, turned from bold green to dark brown to a bright, expensive yellow. Or until an early frost closes them down— whichever comes first. Buster trudges over to the tap where the table gang are in line to wash up. His mother has left them a bar of soap and cream hand cleanser to wash off the tar. He unzips his rubber suit all the way down the front and an invisible wave of steam rolls off his skin. Funny, he thinks, watching his brother ahead of him splashing cold water on his ordinary face. Funny how "kiln" is always pronounced "kill."

Isabel is in the kitchen moving hurriedly between the stove and counter, flipping steaks and then checking on boiled potatoes, corn and peas. She lays the meat on a platter that, when full, she passes to Jelly Bean. "First batch is done Judy." She moves to the sink to rinse her hands. She is weary but can't afford to stop working long enough to think about it. If she pauses to sit, she is sure she won't rise again.

Lizzie, in her playpen, begins to cry and lifts her short arms, and Isabel speaks to the child as she removes the roast beef from the oven. "Lizzie. Don't fuss. I'll be right there with a bottle." She gestures to Jelly Bean, who stands wearing an old red and white gingham apron tied around her thin waist, stirring a pan of gravy. Jelly Bean accidentally splatters grease on herself.

"Oh darn," she pouts, looking down. "I'm sorry; I'll clean that for you right away."

"Don't be silly, Judy. A little dirt never hurt anyone."

WHEN JELLY BEAN SETS the potatoes and gravy, corn on the cob, peas and meat down in the centre of the table a flurry of muscled arms reach out like prize fighters'.

"Plenty of rain this year," says Percy. "Looks like a good yield."

"Too soon to predict." Bob slips a flask of vodka from his back pocket for a quick swig while Jelly Bean has her back to him and Isabel is safely out of the room. The vodka is odourless and calms his trembling hands. "Depends what happens at auction."

Buster spoons potatoes from a large bowl onto his plate and pushes them around with a fork. The dirty fedora hides his over-heated face. His skin is unusually discoloured because of the humidity, the shine on his face inevitable no matter how many times he wipes it with a bandana. The brim of his hat isn't wide enough to protect from the sun so the tip of his nose, lips and chin are already smarting. Jelly Bean passes so closely by the table that he feels her long blond ponytail swing into his back.

"Hi Buster."

"Hey," he mumbles through a mouthful. He doesn't look up or reveal any special fondness for her, though he watches her from the corner of his eye.

"Seems you've got a fan," says Bob, after she moves off outside to join the table gang who have each brought their own lunch.

"That ankle biter?" Hank scarfs down his steak. "She's a little twerp." His square jaw is a snake's. Distendable. Limitless.

Buster wants to defend Jelly Bean, it would be the honourable thing to do, but Hank is obviously feeling pretty clutched. Hank isn't himself. Buster pours gravy over his roast beef and half of his plate and watches his brother chew and glower at Susan who is eating her lunch alone under the oak tree. Hank's been acting strange for a while, now that Buster stops to think about it. Ever since he told their father that he wants to leave the farm. Hank usually darts around the property like he can't wait to get the work over with, but lately he's been yawning all the time. Now the sight of him in a defeated state makes Buster want to once more tell Hank to forget about Susan, tell him to give her the old heave-ho. There will be other girls and the seasons pass, days roll on. You can get used to just about anything, with enough time.

Percy reaches for the biggest cob on the plate, shakes salt over it. "Gonna ask her out?"

"Not my type," says Hank, assuming the question is meant for him.

Percy clears his throat. "Buster?"

"Me?" They don't know about Ivan's New Year's bash. They don't know that he took Jelly Bean out for a drive or that he's already kissed her. "Naw, nowhere to go."

"Drive-in at Courtland," says Bob, a faint slur to his words. "Donny and Ivan went every weekend last summer, didn't ya?"

"A couple of times."

"She's quick as a whip," says Percy.

"Yeah," Bob agrees. "I seen her count change at the hardware store."

Buster shifts in his seat as the clouds move in temporarily, leaving a dreary, overcast sky looking back through the glass door. He doesn't want to share Jelly Bean with anyone, least of all this bunch of sorry slobs. They don't know her the way he does.

"Jelly Bean's an artist," he finally says.

"An art-eest," says Bob, winking at Percy. "You don't say?"

"Yeah, if you want to know. She paints people the way they are." It gave him a clear, cool satisfaction saying it.

"Who does?" Isabel appears carrying two large pitchers of lemonade from the refrigerator to the table. Bob hides his flask out of sight.

"Jelly Bean," says Bob. "Buster's sweet on her."

Isabel and the men wait for Buster's reaction and when there is none Isabel sets the pitchers down and moves off again, an exaggerated wiggle.

Buster glares at Bob, the loudmouth ingrate. He's collecting pay for doing less than his share. How dare Bob comment on Jelly Bean. How dare Bob eyeball his mother that way. As if Bob can hold a candle to Tom McFiddie. Buster feels defensive of his father and for the first time in a long while protective of his mother. Bob's a drunk. A sponge soaking up whatever he can. Can't hold down a regular gig. Can't even keep a wife. "Hey Mr. Bryson?" he asks. "When did you say your wife was coming back?"

Donny kicks Buster under the table and Bob takes another, longer swig from his flask. He stands without speaking and teeters off to relieve himself in the downstairs washroom. "I told you he's dead weight," mutters Donny. "You don't have to rub it in."

Buster couldn't help himself. He lowers his eyes. "Sorry, Don." Then he stuffs the remainder of his dinner into his mouth, wipes his sticky hands on his pant legs and skulks off to sit on the ground a few yards away from the table gang with his back up against the half-full kiln, licking his fingers clean of the gravy. He won't bother with dessert. God how he hates the fellas razzing him about Jelly Bean, especially in front of his brother. She is his, a secret more secret than the plan to catch the bandit, for even she cannot be told. He'd like to tell her. He'd like to be near her all the time, but he also needs to be where she can't see him, where he can confidently imagine her off painting a barn or another dead bird, something plain and common. And wanting him in return.

He once dreamt of touching girls any way he pleased, any girl he wanted. He felt entitled. He belonged and so he hadn't known to hunger for belonging. Same with Donny and Ivan and Hank, Buster thinks. Those fellas have nothing to worry about; they always find another and another opportunity, even if it's only the opportunity to screw things up. Hank was born with a horseshoe up his ass. Buster recognizes it because in many ways he used to be Hank, younger sure, but Hank all the same. He laughed without noticing the sound that air made pushing through his nasal passages. He teased others mercilessly without concern for what it was like to be on the receiving end. Now he knows he is hungry, starving—a brassy gut-love hunger that is beyond the physical and builds to a pressure point inside a person, replacing fear and rage and even loneliness with a rumbling well of dry-mouth desire.

Jelly Bean Johnson.

From under his hat he watches her eating her lunch, and all he can think is how the heat from her fingertips traced an illicit script over his face. All he can feel is the terrible need to be read.

He turns and stares out at his father's field, squinting a dark inky glare, but the tobacco sways like a sea of emerald. It appears to be talking to him, saying *Here I am, where I've always been. Waiting for you.* He uses his grower's eyes—eyes with years of practice—to distinguish different patterns in the field. First, a dark shape rises like a cloud, rounding and circling. Then the wind pushes harder through the plants, drawing sandy snakes and tunnels up and away. He stands to make a serious inspection. To other folks it might all look the same—a single moving mass of green. Even boring. The work itself is that, boring, though never the tobacco. For the first time in a year Buster accepts its subtle changes, how the shiniest of leaves catch the light in the sky and reflect it back in a million bubbly mirrors. How green isn't only green, but a grudging forest or a resentful lime, some parts drier than others. When the wind blows he even thinks he can smell the DDT his father sprays as pesticide. Taste it the way Tom showed him to do when mixing for the proper amount. Tom sticks his finger in the water barrel and touches it to the tip of his tongue. When his tongue tingles he knows to stop.

There it is rolling out to meet the horizon, a prickling, fuming boneyard. His old stamping ground. Home. Buster looks at his boots, his arms outstretched. He opens and closes his hands. He's here inside it again—solid, strong. Healthy—if not handsome. He scans the property and finds his father's old horse, Darlene, beside the stripping barn drinking from a bucket. Will his father ever understand the heartsore that being burned is, or that Doc John's stories and all they represent are just as important now as family ever was, for they make the quiet violence of this small-town existence concrete? Real. They make sense of malicious gossip, petty turf wars and rifts in friendship. And, if all goes according to plan, the stories will have provided the inspiration to return him to his rightful place at the centre of it all. Who is his father when he isn't in the fields, Buster wonders. When he's alone? Is he afraid of anything? Is he ever afraid of himself?

Buster remembers his father fishing with him at Long Point, how he took him and Hank and Donny to watch smelt run on Erie shores. He taught them to sit patiently for hours, to show no fear of bumblebees and so avoid being stung. But it has been through the suckering and the seeding and the priming, through every season, that his father has proven himself. Buster leans back. The kiln is warm and he welcomes it, even in the heat of harvest. I can't stay thinking what a raw deal I've been dealt forever, he thinks. Any burden will only be carried for so long before it drops.

Jelly Bean stands, removes Isabel's apron and sits once more with it folded across her lap. Her turquoise halter top fits tightly over her chest. The straps of her brassiere don't align with the straps on her halter and have slid down one shoulder. Buster has seen the way some of the other boys watch her, as if hers is a body housing infinite possibilities for all of them. The sting of a sharp metal wire tightens around his gut and he hoofs a rock with the toe of his boot. Thinking about Jelly Bean with someone else is unbearable, cuts into him in a thousand invisible ways.

Hank emerges from the kitchen full of rich, fatty flavours. He stretches and makes his way down the patio steps, towards Susan who is sitting by the stripping barn, drinking a glass of lemonade. Hank's stride is determined. He is going to get to the bottom of things for once and for all. Hank is definitely finished with games. In front of Susan he is animated, waving his arms about his head, shouting as she tries to *shush* him and drag him around to the side of the barn, out of view.

Buster wipes the dirt from his jeans and walks over to the barn to spy on them. When he is close enough to see and to hear the argument, whatever has transpired is already winding down. Susan is crying, wringing her hands. "I can't tell you!" she hollers. "I just can't!" Hank storms off into the field and both Susan and Buster watch him withdraw. Once it's clear that Hank is not about to turn around, Susan bends over and vomits. She straightens again, wipes her mouth and eyes with the backs of her hands, and returns to the others who are meeting up at the tying table. Percy, Bob and Donny head into the field and Buster turns to catch up to them. He waves at Jelly Bean as he goes. It's true that she wants to produce beauty, he thinks. She could probably make a diamond of a lump of coal. She doesn't avoid life the way he does. She runs at it, makes it brighter, bolder. She wants beauty by her own design. Besides catching the bandit what does he want?

Another kiss that opens possibility.

Skin as smooth as the ribbon on his fedora.

He wants change.

THE HANDERS LIFT THE TABLE, move it around to the other side of the kiln and begin the process of handing and tying all over again. They work fast. This year tobacco is also being tied by Tom's hired man Simon Vandemaele, who strings it expertly onto long sticks. He stands beside his wooden horse at the side of the table before a thirty-inch-long slat of wood, the stick, suspended on another wooden horse. Tying is highly skilled and Tom trusts only Simon and Isabel to do it properly. This is a point of pride for Simon, who is wearing brown leather wristbands. Isabel sometimes tapes her wrists, though she hasn't today. Each time Simon receives a hand— stems first—he ties it onto one side of the stick, wraps the string around the next hand and flips that one over to the other side. All day he ties and flips. Ties and flips. It requires a keen eye, agile, quick fingers and sturdy wrists.

Gladys Peacock, Susan and Simon began at six-thirty in the morning, shortly after the primers made their way into the field. Isabel and Jelly Bean have now joined them for a stint. They all stand in their plastic aprons and rubber boots, growing hotter by the minute under the heavy afternoon rays. Isabel ties a blue kerchief around her thick red mop. "It's like passing a baton," she explains to Jelly Bean. "When you're good you don't have to look."

Simon nods. "You'll get so your fingers know how many feel right." He flexes one hand, opening it and wiggling long, bony fingers. Thick blue veins push out through the skin. The widest part of his fingers are their flat, rounded tips, as if they've been pressed with an iron. He is a tall gangly man from top to bottom, with a long neck and narrow torso. Jelly Bean thinks he looks something like the salamanders the local boys used to collect by the pond. She glances at her own small hands.

"The idea is to space leaves evenly in the kiln," Isabel adds. "Like clothes in a closet. Any not tied or hung properly fall to the bottom and are wasted. Watch how we do it."

Gladys passes to Simon alternating in an unblinking rhythm, and Susan passes to Isabel without breaking stride. There is an unselfconscious musicality and skill in their interlocking gestures, an enviable pace to the handing and tying and handing and tying, so that Jelly Bean wants to take her turn but is sure she'll fumble and drop something. When that slat is full—the tobacco tied on by the stems—it looks to her like a hula skirt made of leaves.

"Let's pick up the pace," says Simon. He knots the string twice around the finished stick and breaks it with callused fingers while Isabel prepares another stick and motions to Susan, the hander at the front of the wooden horse, to pick up the full stick and lay it in the pile next to the kiln. Each time Susan does this she layers the stick of leaves in a pattern so the pile won't fall over.

Susan is sullen, her eyes obviously red from crying and lack of sleep. Only two nights before her mother had informed her father of her embarrassing condition. Len called Susan a whore and slapped her across the face. He ordered her mother to telephone their relatives in Leamington and arrange to have Susan sent by train immediately, before she drew any further attention to the family. Susan would be forced to give birth and then relinquish the child.

She waited until her parents stopped arguing and turned out their bedside lamps before slipping out of the house. She didn't know where she would go but there had to be somewhere. She wandered alone in the dark, through the fields and down the hill, and hurried along the side of Main Street. She was blind with grief. Did she want this baby? Could she love it? Would people ever let her live it down? The only person she could think to ask for help was Hank McFiddie, but she was certain that he'd reject her now too. She was better off to steer clear of all boys, anyway. Homegrown or otherwise. When Susan saw Isabel driving past in the red truck that Hank had taken her out in, she lay her head in her hands and began to sob. Isabel stopped, ordered the girl into the truck. Now Isabel has persuaded Tom to allow Susan to work through harvest in exchange for room and board.

The older women at the tying table take charge of the conversation and lead it in a most detailed and salacious direction. Simon throws in the occasional "Hmm" or "Right, I heard that," but it's Isabel and Gladys who shock Jelly Bean with the level of gossip permitted. She is horrified to discover things she's never known about her neighbours; whose wife turned up at church with a black eye, who has been taken to the cooler in Woodstock for getting into a drunken brawl. Who is philandering and shouldn't be. She feels a bit guilty with her ear to the wall, eavesdropping and looking in at their lives. She is aware of Susan beside her and that something about the girl looks and sounds different today, blunted. It's also clear to Jelly Bean that Gladys Peacock has a bee in her bonnet.

"You girls hear what's going on with town council?"

"They've posted a reward for capturing the bandit," says Jelly Bean.

"And the petition. You hear about that?"

Susan fights back nausea. The last thing she needs is to be reminded of her family. "Dad's pretty determined." She doesn't look up.

"Do you hand on your father's farm too?" Jelly Bean asks.

Susan raises her eyes. "Why are you asking?"

"Just curious."

"Find my life exciting do you?"

"What's got into you?" Jelly Bean whispers. "Usually you're so full of advice."

The other women and Simon pretend they haven't heard this and Susan says nothing in response, even when Gladys and Isabel exchange knowing glances.

"How are you feeling, Susan? Any queasiness?"

"No, just fine thank you Mrs. Peacock."

"I've rarely had morning sickness myself. Maybe you'll be lucky too, dear."

Jelly Bean's mouth falls open. She meets Susan's eyes but neither girl speaks. Susan has always appeared invincible, impenetrable. She's teased Jelly Bean about her own uncontrollable lapses. To think that Susan's body could betray her in a public way, that she could make a mistake, means that anyone can. Jelly Bean's shoulders drop, her face softens. A clean, transparent loosening happens inside of her and spreads like a cool stream of water. She's not only got the hang of handing to Isabel but she's actually pretty good at it. By four o'clock when Isabel removes her kerchief and announces that it's time for her to check on Lizzie and finish preparing supper, Jelly Bean's fingers are moving fast and sure for the first time in her life.

Walter is in the hardware store when Len Rombout pokes his head in the door. "My petition's been passed around," Len gloats. "Looks as though Barbara Ann Scott will be leading the parade after all."

"I didn't see any petition," says Walter.

"Let Hazel know, will ya?" Len turns and is gone.

That evening Walter phones Tom. He hates to be the one to do it but he'd prefer Tom hear it from a friend. "If that's how folks feel," Tom snaps into the receiver. "Then I guess that's the way it'll be." He grumbles a few more words to Walter, it isn't Walter's fault after all, and he hangs up. He stands in the middle of the kitchen, stunned.

Buster and Lizzie are asleep and Hank has snuck down to the rumpus room, found Susan there and persuaded her to take a ride with him in his father's truck. They are parked by the river. Isabel moves in behind her husband, wraps her arms around his gut and licks his sweaty neck. He tastes of salt and a briny tang. Her belly, flatter than it has been in months, presses into his rear. She fishes in his pants pocket for a Zippo and dallies there a moment longer than is necessary. "It's not folks," she says, having guessed the conversation from one end. "It's just Len." She reaches around behind to the counter where she left an open package of cigarettes, lights one, inhales deeply and turns to blow the smoke down the back of Tom's neck, under his collar. "His nose is out of joint because we took Susan in."

"If it's not one damned thing it's another. It's always something with him. Well he can shove it. See if that bastard ever gets so much as a hello from me again!"

"You don't mean that," Isabel soothes. "You're a better man than that."

A better man. No. Tom doesn't think so any more. Their livelihoods depend on tobacco, and the marketing board getting government support is a good idea but instead of making things better for the community it's become a great glass ceiling shattering down on him. He's been fighting someone or something all year because of it. He collapses his weight against Isabel's and is unspeakably tired.

"You know what's worse? The boys."

"Thomas."

"No, Hank's miserable here; I can see that. And I can't talk to Buster any more without it turning into a fight. I've tried. I'm through fighting, Isabel. In fact, Hazel can bring in someone else to lead the parade. Len can produce and sell as much as he wants, goddamnit. I'm washing my hands of it all." He meets her eyes. "We can manage the costs of that surgery too. Tell Doc John if his offer to go with Buster still stands, we'll take it."

The farm and everything it represents is Tom's right hand, his left hand, his entire sense of himself carried in both and Isabel knows it. The fact that someone has taken such a public swing at his reputation leaves her husband feeling as if he's holding air. "Len's all piss and vinegar," she says. "Everyone knows that. It'll pass. As for Buster, he's been angry with both of us, not only you. This is not about you." She means it when she says it, and hopes he is listening. It's time she ushered in a reconciliation. She blows smoke rings into the air and rubs up against him like any one of the farm cats rubbing ankles to be let into the house. "Lizzie adores you," she says. "So does Hank, whether he wants to be a grower or not. So do I. And this surgery is the right decision. You'll see, it'll all work through in time. Buster's coming around. He's just stubborn. A lot like his father." She presses her cigarette to his lips, nibbles on his earlobe and watches as he sucks hard, his cheeks hollowing.

Tom exhales in a narrow stream of hot, grey mist.

Smoke. Some say the place gets its name because of the tobacco, but perhaps it's because its bravest men never really leave, they evolve into something larger than themselves, into elusive mists and visible fogs that rest high above the village. Doc John never gave a second thought to it; he's only ever wanted to call it home.

On the morning of the sesquicentennial he wakes with a start as he has on many mornings since the day he and Alice were married. Perspiring. Ready to bolt. He's been dreaming again, the same dream in which he's lying on the Ambassador Bridge under a warm blanket when someone—he doesn't know who—rips the covers from his body and leaves him naked and exposed. In the dream people drive up, gather, point and laugh; a few are ready to take up arms. When he wakes, relieved that Alice is already downstairs, he feels himself begin to shrink as though even with rising he might still disappear. He tries to push away the feeling that soon his life will be unwrapped like a long-forgotten present. The first thing he does is dress.

For most being bound would not feel like any kind of salvation. Alice occasionally curses those tight-fitting girdles she wears, but for him the bandages offer protection from prying eyes, and the gift of a life he's struggled against all odds to maintain. Some men tighten a necktie in much the same fashion and feel stronger for it. Some men step into work boots, lace them and fall into line as they are meant to. He is held together like this, with gauze and pins and in a precarious manner, always under the threat of exposure. It has been so many years that he no longer thinks much while he dresses; he simply dresses.

The bindings flatten his chest. He winds them tightly around his torso, covering himself from the bottom of his rib cage to well up under his arms. He pulls them as tightly as can be tolerated while

249

leaving his lungs free to breathe. After all these years, the muscles in his chest no longer resist and a flabby layer of flesh pushes against the gauze. He winds the bandages six or eight times before fastening them off. Then on goes his undershirt and the neatly pressed dress shirt, followed by his vest. Curious, the order to which a man habituates himself; alter that order and the house might come tumbling down. Once his feet are into clean socks and his toes are no longer cold on the drafty floor, he fastens the gear. He learned to craft it from cloth and finely treated deerskin, soft as a newborn. Read about it once in a medical book. He still adores the faint odour of old, sweaty leather and the feel of a tight grip eating into his thighs.

The straps are brown. The member itself is dust and bone coloured. He sewed it tightly with horsehair, by hand. He's made several over the years though this last one is the most durable. He's watched Alice mending to discern how she manages a tight stitch and so, in a way, the thing has her handiwork all over it. In the beginning it had felt artificial. Fake even. But once he discovered how to pack it into his pants so that its discreet bulge was authentic and once he learned to use it in bed so that his wife was satisfied, to lift it before urination and to dress before she rose, it became a second skin. Without it he feels naked, the victim of an amputation. He wears it while he sleeps. He rarely removes it except briefly each morning to wash it or himself, and even then its absence is replaced by a phantom limb. Without the harness he isn't the man he wants to be, though he doesn't wear it because he thinks it makes him a different person, a better person. He doesn't wear it to change the world. He wears it, he knows, so the world won't change him.

As a physician he remains hard-pressed to define the sexes or the space between or beyond them—define human—to anyone's satisfaction. Before the accoutrements of hair and clothes and shoes that he adopted, there was that small brave knowing, *knowing* that the blood pumping through his veins was on a course all its own. He'd once thought himself a monster, a reversal of nature, a perverse wretch. Sure he had. *What am I?* he'd asked in his quietest moments. *Who am I?* He'd felt as guilty and confined as that girl in the Mo Axler story. He long thought of himself as wrong and kept it under wraps through his younger years when his father's textbooks all confirmed it, until holding on in silence rotted straight through his core like a worm desecrating an apple. Mind body. Body mind. He still doesn't understand which governs though he is sure they must match. Week after week, year after year that original plot goes on stuttering in his brain like one of Walter Johnson's records stuck on the player. *Man man man.* But a human being could exist somewhere between male and female, couldn't they? Or be neither? Or both? What if there are others straddling this equator called sex. Do they move through the world with an ever-widening sense that there is no cure for ambiguity, that to carry on with any measure of peace and safety they have to choose? I am a doctor, he tells himself whenever the question of definitions returns. A husband. The man I always wanted to be. Once he'd decided there was no turning back.

He'd left home and started over. Since then he has taken the trouble of wearing a coat and tie, always the height of fashion, pressed trousers and lifts in his shoes. He maintains carefully barbered and oiled hair with which he never plays. He won't cross his legs at the knee or allow himself to appear animated. His gestures are large. He shaves his face daily. He dresses left and this affects the hang of his trousers. He cleans the gear with saddle soap and water, and before it begins to smell, replaces it using the same measurements. Alice is accustomed to the feeling of straps on his body. When they make love it's always dark. He flirted with suits and ties in private, when he was younger. Studied others for years. And what he found was that in matters of recognition, costuming and confidence were just about everything. Yes he's discovered since leaving Detroit that if he dresses as the other men full-time, behaves as others do and does so with his head held high, he gets by. It's as if his skin somehow stretches into maleness and it's that stretch, that sense of entitlement, which shows most convincingly to the world.

In the earliest days of his marriage when his time of the month came around and there was the worry that Alice might detect blood dotting his underclothes in the laundry hamper, he explained about the hemorrhoids he suffered time to time. Then the change came and that stage brought relief; an end to any lingering biological reminders of an underground existence and where he'd been, adding a wirier sprig of whiskers to his chin, further lowering his voice and squaring off his jawline. Passing requires luck, keen observation and vigilance, and accommodating expectations so that eventually he cut the feminine from his daily routine as if it were a slow-spreading disease.

He is no woman. Not now and not even when he was living in Michigan. His skin isn't soft as a woman's, except for his face and hands, which he's taken care to keep manicured—a physician must have sensitive hands. Everywhere else has always been tough and dry and that's as he prefers it. For years he's stared into the faces of the wounded, treated colds, allergies, cancer, tobacco poisoning, treated those who have problems with sugar and nerves, and they've all looked back at him with relief and security. He does his job better than most, has rarely missed a day, never forgets an appointment or rushes a patient out of the office. He even treats those who have no money to pay. He believes it's his debt to do so, the cost of freedom and deserting his family. He's practised medicine without allowing himself, even once, the luxurious instinct to recoil. He's cut into diseased flesh, read up on new medications, punctured skin with needles, tended burns. It's penance, he knows, as much as it is pride.

His decrepit face, once smoother, reveals nothing any more except borrowed time. And each of the four chambers of his heart beats its own message; beats privacy, secrecy, beats sacrifice. Fear. His stomach is inflamed and ravaged by an excess of acid. Still, there have seldom, if ever, been funny looks or even raised eyebrows. Occasionally a new patient, one from a neighbouring town or village, will stare a bit long, think that she's glimpsed something not quite right. And recently Buster has become suspicious. But these moments are easily shaken off and forgotten, and until this morning not even Alice, who's held his hand each day and accompanied him on this walk across an invisible threshold, could know for certain that the past will be revealed in the end. His hair, yellowing and thinned out in patches, is relaxing to the touch like fine cornsilk. Loose flesh hangs off his arms like balloons filled with wet sand. Brown patches of speckled skin decorate his hands and face more than they should at his age. All bodies transform, he knows. Young to old. Thin to fat. Some soon, some late, sometimes transforming full revolutions. They belong to no one; not the families they are born into, not those who offer love or assistance, not even the communities they inhabit. He hopes for a place far ahead, far, far into the future, where one day bodies might become maps of possible return, where a body like his might be an individual right and not a public outrage. Perhaps in Smoke? Michigan? But not yet. He lives as everyone does, rooted to a specific time and place, and that circumstance makes him a wanted man.

And yet, there is a growing field to treat such conditions. Endocrinology boasts of hormone therapies, radical surgeries. If he were young today, he wonders, would *he* seek such treatments? If he could erase all traces of this transfer would he do it? He had once wanted nothing more than to be released from the tomb that concealed him, and he would have risked infection, scarring, life itself, to do so. He would have travelled the earth seeking willing surgeons, bribed them if necessary. But now, in his latter days, he has the luxury of seeing the limitations of remedies like conformity. There must be a purpose to me as I am, he thinks. I exist.

And what female qualities, if any, he dares to think, still lurk in the chemistry of my brain and blood, under my skin? Do these qualities make me a more nurturing physician? A better doctor? What if my bedside manner has been tempered by a dulcet touch in a way that Elgin Baker's, for example, has not? Should I really eradicate that? Perhaps I am something else altogether, he thinks. A category not yet named. We all become something else, even as the sun sets, and again when it rises. We become something else on the way to something else again. Only a fool and the dead don't change.

Doc John knows better than to ever voice these thoughts out loud or to lose himself inside Utopian fantasies for he's heard of boys not unlike him strung up like mutton in back alleys or on fence posts. He's doctored all kinds from all kinds of places—he's even doctored himself. There is no point any more in imagining life as anything other than what it is. Confounding. Messy. Flawed. There is no proof, no good science, in conjecture. But oh, the stories, the marvellous tales he's embellished from what he witnessed and overheard long ago, now those *are* worth imagining. They tell everything the real world is not yet able to hear, and why not? Curing and fixing and recovery is not all there's been to his life. There was a world before. Back-room deals and business conducted under the table. There was love and death and guns and there was a girl once. There were many things and many people but with Alice he has known pleasure so bright it turns ugliness to beauty and justifies existence like no stamp on a birth certificate ever could.

Changing sex is no disappearing act; it's a love letter to the self.

It rains in the early morning—skies like mud, and then a quick drizzle that peters out. By breakfast the September sun is poking through the clouds, the clouds are moving off like defeated opponents and Smoke is lit once more like the blessing that it is. Alice serves a late breakfast of burnt toast and orange marmalade and answers two phone calls—one from a man in Zenda looking for a doctor to treat his cataracts and the second from Doc Baker in Tillsonburg.

"John, Elgin Baker on the phone."

"Tell him I'm on my way out. Band rehearsal's in twenty minutes."

"He wants to speak with you directly. Says it's important."

The doctor rises, disgruntled, and walks down the hall to the phone. He clears his throat, picks up the heavy black receiver. "John here. You can? Right. I'll let folks know then. You coming today? Right, right. We'll see you." He hangs up and returns to finish his breakfast.

"What was that about?"

"He'll start taking referrals as of Monday. Got a nephew fresh out of school to help."

"Then it's finally resolved." Alice moves towards her husband, sits on his lap and reaches her arms around his neck. "Good. You'll have more time for other things." She leans in and kisses him on the lips. It's a long, dry kiss, almost chaste in its delivery but not quite.

"I've got a few ideas already," he says.

"I can tell that you do," Alice grins. "But they'll have to wait." She stands, straightens her dress. "I'm due at the church. We're putting the final touches on the banner over there and we'll have to carry the cake down to the park."

"I'd better go too." He feels his abdomen sear. "Meet you back here for dessert?"

"Oh, John. I just told you. We'll be having cake."

He winks. "Nothing at all wrong with my hearing, dear."

For months his colour hasn't been good. He explained to Alice that it was a lingering cold, then influenza, and refused to have himself checked by another physician. He said he could care for himself as well as anyone could. After several weeks without sound sleep, Alice told him to see Elgin Baker in Tillsonburg or not to bother coming home. She'd not been thinking clearly for if she had she would've admitted how dangerous such a simple visit could be. He went to appease her, but spoke only of passing on some new patients. So, they'd gone on and on together, a merry-go-round of comforting routine the same as always.

He didn't need to tell her what was happening to him physically; she didn't demand to know. The pain in his abdomen hasn't been easy to hide, though he has tried, and his face has aged significantly. In fact this morning he noticed it has lost its sense of humour entirely and sunken in on itself. He hasn't told a story in weeks, and this, more than any physical sign, alerts him to what must be done. So he stashed money in Alice's drawer for Buster, along with the name and address of a surgeon at the Hospital for Sick Children in Toronto. And he started writing Alice one last letter. Left it unfolded. Later—after—when she comes to discover it, she may wish that she had known in advance. He doesn't want her to. It wasn't planned this way but he must disappear and no one will be the wiser. His only wish now is that when his time does come he will be judged more for what he made of himself than for what he did not.

ALICE FINISHES WASHING their breakfast dishes, changes her clothes and walks around the corner and up Palmer's Hill to the United church with a flirtatious step. She's been looking forward to this celebration for a year. The Women's Institute has put together historical displays of the region and the Violet Rebekahs will have their own float in the parade. Hazel is late, so Alice sits alone in the church basement on the piano stool and finishes decorating the banner. She sews two long ribbons to either end and rolls it up; it will be easier to cart down the hill folded under her arm. She removes the large square cake from the church refrigerator and waits. After twenty minutes Hazel still hasn't turned up and it's getting on, so Alice gathers what is needed and carries everything by herself.

JELLY BEAN FINDS WHAT SHE NEEDS right where she hid it, in the hall closet on the top shelf beside two bags of yarn, a set of knitting needles and a bottle of white glue. Then she locks herself in the washroom.

The first streak is the hardest, as if she's painting over her old self. She stands a second or two with the dye brush poised, smells the clean, mean sound of colour mixing, and watches in the mirror as the blondest strands darken to mysterious feathers. After that it's easy. *Stroke, stroke, stroke,* until her bangs are brown, almost black, and she's coloured around the ears, on top and at the back. For someone dyeing her hair for the first time she thinks she's done a fair job, but her forehead and ears are stained in spots. It doesn't matter; each streak banishes the sense she's had of being at odds with herself. Beauty is uncommon, she thinks while she covers the blond. Beauty is remarkable. She paints away the rest, getting as close to the scalp as she can, matching her roots. A head of fine, unnaturally white curls colours over and vanishes like a total eclipse of the sun.

The Miss Tobacco Queen contestants line up at Main and Dover in their tiaras and pink and black chest banners. Each of the service clubs has decorated a float. Several local boys in period costumes saddle up restless ponies and Simon Vandemaele balances atop a penny farthing. Visitors park, honking horns and waving to one another through open car windows. There is a cool fall breeze and the pavement is still wet from the early-morning rain but the sky is clear. The smell of cotton candy and roasted walnuts filters through the village centre.

Buster is ready. He is dressed in full formal attire—the fedora of course, but also his tie, suit pants, suspenders, shirt and vest. He found a proper holster for his gun by taking up part of Hank's old Davy Crockett costume. It's riding low around his waist like a leather horseshoe offering good luck. It's how he imagines Solly Levine wore his under his coat on the day he disappeared. There are coloured lights on both sides of Main Street, banners and streamers, and several flags—the provincial and the Union Jack, some made especially to celebrate the sesquicentennial. Store windows are frames for antiques and collectables. The streets are lined with vintage cars. Buster flattens on the ground beside the bank, hidden by a thicket of bushes. This is an excellent spot from which to observe both ends of Main Street. The bank is closed. He and Donny have been positioned here since dawn.

"Okay, let's go over things one more time. When we find him, let's say jimmying the lock or breaking a window at the back, I'll approach head-on. 'Stick 'em up!' I'll shout, and when you hear me what do you do?"

"That's my cue to jump him."

"Good."

"But what if he shoots me?"

"Don't worry; I'll have your back. And even if he's a big fella, pound for pound the two of us can take him." Buster swats a fly. "Remember; we have the element of surprise on our side. This chump hasn't got a prayer."

"I hope you're right, Buster."

"I am. Today's the day. It's gotta be."

"That's what you keep saying."

Buster cups the fly in his hands.

"Trust me, our man's gonna make his move today. I can feel it."

DOC JOHN CREEPS DOWN into the park and finds the others already arranged in proper formation—horns together, tuba at the back, woodwinds up front. Walter is polishing his French horn with an old cheesecloth, Bob admires his distorted reflection in his trumpet—and they're all waiting on Tom. Percy Bozek stands a few feet away puffing on his bagpipes and making them whine like a cat in heat. There are twenty-five men who form the Smoke Brass and Woodwind Pipe Band, all members of the Oddfellows or Kiwanis clubs. "I'm slow today," says the doctor when he reaches the bottom of the hill. He sets his clarinet case on an empty chair, glances at the sheet music tucked under silver clips in the music stand.

"You're not the last," says Walter. "I rang Tom about the petition. I expect he's none too happy." Walter gestures in the direction of Len and Ivan Rombout who are hollering back and forth to each other a few yards away. They are busy erecting a large tent. It was used before—on Dominion Days and for fall fairs—and now it will be used for the sesquicentennial.

Tom has no intention of being run out of his own village by anyone, least of all by Len Rombout. As soon as he and Hank finish loading up the back of his truck with chairs and folding tables from the town hall he'll catch up to the band. They will crowd together in one corner of the tent when it's up. The swimming pool, which has already been cleaned, will attract children who will splash nearby and do handstands in the water, and the band will blow and drum and mewl off-key through several old favourites and a few new tunes.

"Let's start," Walter says. There are nods and much scrambling to adjust the height of music stands and flip through sheet music. Walter releases the spit valve on his instrument and Doc John unbuckles his clarinet case. He uses a weight cloth, pulls the weight through the longest section and tugs the cloth after it. When he looks down the barrel of the joint to inspect, he sees a shiny, smooth, dry finish inside the black tube. He lifts his clarinet to his lips, resting most of its weight on his right thumb where a slight groove has formed over time. When he gives the first hard blow he feels a space break open inside, a scrappy tear coming from some-where deep, immediately followed by a wet wave of nausea. He ignores it and blows harder the second time, pulling back to execute greater control over airflow as he tries to hit the upper-register notes. His instrument squeaks instead of sings while the others play on at the proper tempo. He can't maintain pace. He stops, counts another bar by tapping his right foot and joins in once more.

This time when he blows he cannot relax his diaphragm; he is tense, his lips tight, and the music comes out sounding stiff and tentative. Not music at all, merely disconnected notes. He blows harder, too loudly, and his abdomen feels as though it's ripping wide open. He grows light-headed but makes his fingers go through the motions of playing so that the others won't notice. A moment later a gnawing fire eats into his belly and a current of fear runs through him. A tart woody taste coats his tongue. His mouth fills with a warm liquid and blood, as brown as rust, drips from the bottom of his clarinet out onto the earth below. He swipes the ground with his foot to cover the tiny speckles dotting at his feet. When the burning and the bleeding don't stop, he swallows and it becomes harder to breathe, to think. He stands, careful to maintain his balance, shuffles his belongings, disassembles the clarinet and packs it up. Walter waves the others to stop. "Something the matter, Doc?"

"No. Keep playing. Forgot to do something for Alice that's all. See you boys later." He hurries across the short patch of grass and up the small hill again, as fast as he can manage, which means that he relies more on his cane than he's ever needed to before, and stops at the cenotaph to catch his breath. Leaning against the engraved plaque he drops his clarinet case, the pain in his stomach so severe that he doubles over. The case doesn't open and he doesn't bother to try to pick it up, but instead kicks it into the brush where it won't be found until the following spring when Hank and Susan stumble upon it as they walk with Susan's daughter, Jenny, through the woods.

Several strangers from out of town scurry down into the park chattering, oblivious. The doctor moves the same as he always has, deliberately, but this time he is holding on to his stomach with one hand and advancing without the comfort of music. As more people pass him on the wooden steps, no one guesses where he's going. No one guesses where he's been.

THE SHADOW OF A FIGURE appears beside the bank.

"There he is!" Buster is propped up on his elbows, ready to pounce.

Donny stiffens and then Doc John emerges from around the corner. "Oh, nice call." Donny rolls onto his back and stares up at the clear blue sky. "Let me know when you see something real."

"Ah nuts. I was sure we had him." In the distance the band is playing. Buster notices the doctor's pale face, his pained walk. "Wait here. I'll be right back."

"Where are you going? Hey! I'm not doing this alone."

Buster jogs across Main Street. "Everything all right, Doc? You don't look so good."

"Just need to lie down for a bit."

"But you'll miss the parade."

Doc John clasps his ribs and Buster reaches to steady him, sees that his teeth are stained pink with fresh blood. They walk, the old man leaning on him for support. "Just need to catch my breath," he says. "Just need a rest."

When they reach his driveway Doc John hunts in his breast pocket for car keys.

"You can't drive," says Buster. "There's no way."

"Leave me be. I'm all right."

"I'll run back and find Mrs. Gray."

"No," Doc John coughs, spitting up more blood. "No point in worrying Alice. I can cart myself over to Doc Baker's. You go on about your business now Buster." He opens the Oldsmobile's heavy black door and collapses onto the front seat, pulling one leg and the other inside, and shutting the door. He reaches across and locks the passenger side. "Don't fuss over me, you sound just like a woman!" Then he waves dismissively. "I'll be seeing you, son." He starts the engine and is gone, a dry wake of dust spilling out behind him.

Buster runs as fast as he can up Main Street and stops in front of the hardware store where he finds Donny's car parked. He opens the driver's-side door but there are no keys in the ignition. Jelly Bean emerges onto the front steps.

"What's the matter?"

"It's Doc John. He's sick. I've gotta get Donny." He faces her a moment. "What's wrong with your hair?"

"Nothing's wrong with my hair." Jelly Bean is at his heels, following up Main Street. "If you don't like it too bad. Guess I won't be Miss Tobacco Queen after all."

"I like it. I'm just saying." Buster points beside the bank. "Over here."

Jelly Bean reaches for his hand.

"You really don't mind it?"

He turns to face her and this time cocks his head to one side.

"It's just different."

"I NEED YOUR CAR," says Buster. "Quick, Doc John's in trouble."

"Forget it." Donny stands. He stares at Jelly Bean. "I'm the only one who drives it."

"Fine. You drive."

"But my mom's bringing my sister for the parade. It should be starting soon."

"Then hand over the keys, Don. This is the last time I'm going to ask nice."

Donny swats the air. "I'll be right back. This wasn't part of our plan though." He marches off towards the car just as Ivan is getting ready to test a firecracker he stole from a pile on the back of Walter Johnson's truck. Ivan stands in the woods near the entrance to the park, lights one end, hears it sizzle alive and tosses it up into the air, over the river.

Jelly Bean steps in front of Buster, her breath hot on his face.

"Take me with you."

"Out of my way."

"C'mon, let me help."

He ducks around her. She blocks him.

"Are you flipped? There's no time for goofing around."

"Don't you at least want to kiss me? The real me." She moves closer. Her firm breasts press up against his bony chest. He stares at her straight dark hair and her blue eyes, which appear bigger now. "I know you want to." She closes her eyes and lifts her face, and he can't help but lean down, closer, closer. He kisses her briskly—to once more feel his skin alive, seamless, and it's in this split second that he knows he needs her.

"Okay," he says, taking her by the hand and running with her up the road as a firecracker explodes nearby. "Let's find Doc John."

While the two of them hurry towards Donny's car, Hazel discovers an unopened telegram from the United States that has slipped between the candy jar and the cash register on the counter. It's dated yesterday. Walter must have forgotten about it. Hazel rushes to open it. "Not coming," the note reads. "Sincere apology. Barbara Ann Scott." Hazel tosses the paper across the counter and storms out of the store, and as she goes she knocks over the doll. It merely teeters at first, ever so slightly off balance, but then it tips completely over the edge and tumbles straight down to the floor where it lands headfirst. The doll's face cracks open, splits in two parts. Both eyeballs come loose, roll to different areas on the floor and stop, pupils upright. Eyes finally uncrossed.

BUSTER SLIDES INTO THE PASSENGER SIDE of Donny's car after Jelly Bean. "Quick," he says. "Try the Wolftrack. Hurry, Don. Drive!"

Donny turns the key in the ignition and shifts the car backwards, taking it flat out along Main Street. The village looks older. Burnished. The street buzzes with chatter. Drummers at the front of the parade practise—*thrum, thrum, thrum*—their thunderous beat matching his pulse. He drives south on Dover, passing only one vehicle. Then his car's tires lose traction on the dirt road, but he doesn't slow down. And just as they reach the curve at Ball's Falls he swerves to avoid hitting something. "Shit!" He slams on the brakes, skidding the Bel Air to an abrupt stop like a powder-blue bolt of lightning.

"It's Doc John!" Jelly Bean points to a black car with its front end crashed into the bridge. Plumes of grey and white smoke from the engine flood up towards the sky like souls escaping. The doctor is slumped over the steering wheel, his head bowed, blood painting his forehead.

Buster cranks the handle and flies out of the car and over to the old man as fast as he can. "Are you all right?" He opens the driver's-side door.

The doctor turns his head and looks at the boy through shattered lenses. Then he slumps forward as a searing pain, relentless now, twists and strangles his body.

"Here." Buster helps him gingerly from the Olds, rolls him onto his back on the ground. "Your car's a wreck, totally creamed." He kneels and pulls the collar of Doc John's shirt away from his neck so that he might more easily breathe.

"Ulcers," Doc John says. Rivulets of blood drip out the corners of his mouth, seeping between his teeth. "I ... I ..."

"He can't breathe," says Donny, panicking. "He must be bleeding inside."

"Go get help. Don't just stand there. Go!"

"I'm staying here with you," says Jelly Bean.

The doctor motions to her with his hand.

"No Judy," he chokes. "Please. Go with Donny."

Donny and Jelly Bean dash back to the car and once more tear out of sight, leaving a brown cloud of dust in their wake. By the time they skid to a stop in front of the bank minutes before noon the drummers are synchronized and all five Miss Tobacco Queen finalists are atop the flatbeds waving to the excited crowd, blowing meaningless airborne kisses.

In an open space, where families picnic on the grass, Alice is busy organizing the younger children into pairs for a three-legged race. Later this evening (and this is what she is most looking forward to), there will be an interdenominational church service held in the park. The United church choir will sing and John will play with the band.

Hazel reaches Alice in a panic. "The parade's about to begin and Barbara Ann has cancelled. What shall I do?"

"Oh, I knew something like this was bound to happen. Go and find Tom."

Hazel nods and darts off again.

Celebrations are otherwise getting off to a good start, with Mr. Kichler supervising a baseball tournament and children squealing and splashing about in the pool. The pool floor has recently been painted turquoise and in the shallow end the image of a giant orange octopus appears to move beneath the surface of water. Sun pours down over top of the tallest trees and lights the children's glistening hair and arms and legs with beads of wet glass. Gail and Doreen Manning take turns aiming softballs at the target on the dunking tank by the river and try to soak George Walker. Isabel carries Lizzie on her hip, walking and bouncing the child on a picnic cloth. Already another child has taken root, unannounced, inside Isabel's belly.

Len Rombout confiscated the rest of the missing firecrackers after Ivan set one off. Now Ivan is idle, standing beside his sister. When he thinks no one is watching he reaches over and pinches Susan on the rear, snickering to himself. Susan swivels. There is a hurricane in her eyes. "Don't you ever touch me again!" she spits. "You've done enough already!" But someone *has* been watching and hears the exchange. Hank looks at Ivan, who is grinning loosely—a corrupt engine. Hank's stomach turns. He begins to shake, a graceless, lovesick figure in the middle of something he does not understand. He forces himself to meet Susan's eyes and in them he finds shame enough for two. She looks away, as though slapped across the face, and her bones seem to settle with the saddest of resignations. She usually has a tongue so sharp it could cut wood but she does not speak. Is anyone listening? Where is everyone when Susan Rombout needs to be heard? Hank grows feral. Every dullness in him sharpens. Every softness and impulse to nurture or tend shifts to stone. Susan has been hurt and Ivan has made the trespass. Before Hank recognizes that it is loyalty that has risen up inside he charges and is on top of Ivan, *pounding, pounding,* fist after fist. "Rotten son of a bitch!" He yells as he pummels the boy. "You're gonna get it!"

"Get off me! Get the hell off me!"

"How do you like it?" Hank bashes Ivan's nose in, feels the bone break under his knuckles. "Not such a big man now, are you?"

"He's gonna kill me. Susan, tell him to let go!"

Susan steps away without uttering a sound. She smiles at her twin brother, on his back, powerless. She will pretend, as she has for years, that nothing out of the ordinary is taking place.

WALTER IS CONDUCTING THE BAND when Jelly Bean comes running and screaming, waving her hands in the air like fly swatters.

"Dad! Dad!"

One by one the band members set their instruments down. They stare at her long, dark hair.

"What's all the racket?"

"We need help." She's out of breath and regards Donny with urgent eyes.

"Yeah," says Donny. "There's been an accident."

Hazel pushes through the crowd with Tom at her side. "What's going on here? Judy Beatrice Johnson, what on earth have you done to your hair?!"

Alice races over to see what the commotion is all about, and Hank and Ivan, who is hunched over holding his bloody nose, follow closely. Susan hustles to stand at Hank's side. She takes his bruised, swollen hand in her own.

"Buster was with us," Jelly Bean says, ignoring her mother's question. "He thought something was wrong with Doc John."

"John? Is something the matter with John?" Alice grabs hard on the girl's arm. "Is he all right, Judy? Where is he?"

"With Buster. Out at Ball's Falls. C'mon."

Alice feels her stomach tighten into a hard commandment. *Thou shall not bear false witness.* She follows the others to the car, her feet as heavy as mud. She doesn't need to be shown anything to understand. It has happened; time has finally run out and she knows intuitively, the way she's always known, the way she knows her bible—bone to bone, blood to blood. One psalm, one verse— one unconditional love. Heaven help us now, she thinks. She scratches her right palm and begins to weep.

BUSTER UNBUTTONS THE DOCTOR'S VEST and starts on his shirt, but Doc John reaches up and pushes his hands away. The smell of gasoline is overpowering. The doctor turns his head and beside him a puddle is forming. He lifts and drops himself onto the warm liquid and then he raises his right arm, holds it an inch from his body. "Son, in my pocket." His voice gurgles and fades, as exposed as soggy parchment.

Buster searches in the old man's trouser pockets, retrieves his wallet and a matchbox.

"Here you go."

"Fire," says the doctor, barely audible.

"What?" Buster leans down, presses his ear to Doc John's mouth. He smells sour, like battery acid.

"Fire."

"You're not making any sense, Doc. Don't worry. You're gonna be all right. Hang on. They'll be back any minute and we'll drive you to the hospital in no time."

Doc John coughs up a big gob of brown and red mucus. Spits it out. It dribbles down the side of his face. His eyes film over like stained glass in the rain. He lifts his head and the tendons in his neck strain. "No, hear … listen … when I'm gone."

"You're not going anywhere. You're too cagey for that. You're Solly Levine, right?"

The doctor clutches Buster's wrist, leaving red welts. He searches the boy's scars. The whole world is mapped on his face. "Yes. Yes. But the others … they mustn't know."

"On my honour," says Buster. "I swear. Jeez, I knew it! I knew you were Solly. At first I thought Raymond Bernstein, but that was too obvious. Tell me how you managed it. I figure you stole papers. Changed your name, that's easy enough. How you kept up the charade this long, that's what I really want to know." Buster removes his hat and places it on Doc John's head. "Here. You're cold, boss."

"Son?"

"Yeah."

"You've got to help me." The doctor reaches for his wallet, opens it and drops its contents, including all of his personal identification, at his side.

Buster is certain that the old man is delirious now. He looks around for help. None is coming. "Just relax," he says, trying to hide the fear in his voice. "Cool it." The doctor's eyelids quiver uncontrollably. "Hey? Hey! Hang on. Don't you die on me!"

"Everything dies," whispers the old man. "Dying is easy." He releases the boy's wrist and allows his head to fall back into the dirt. Buster's voice is a distant drone. An impossible breeze blows, as soothing as a woman's caress, as real as it was on the day he met Alice all those years ago.

It was the day after he'd walked across the Ambassador Bridge. The countryside sped past in a green and brown blur as the train approached the station. Fields were crawling with workers and cows and every few miles he found a fruit or corn stand on the roadside in the distance. So different it was from the world he knew back home. Irreproachable and keen.

"I'm Alice Armstrong," the young woman said when she sat across from him. "These are my two aunts. We're on our way to Port Dover for a show at the Paradise."

"I'm a fan of the theatre too," he answered. "Good to meet you." He rose to accept their hands. "I'm Dr. John Gray." The words fell from his tongue more than rolled that first time and he immediately wondered, If you borrow something, how long before it must be returned?

Beyond his window a small glassy lake stretched miles into the distance, blue and white reflected from above until it met on the green horizon and the difference between sky and land was hard to tell. John didn't look like a man with no place to go when he turned back to face Alice. "It's peaceful."

"Oh it's not much," she said, as they pulled out of the station. "But it is home."

"Got to be from somewhere."

"Yes, I suppose that's true. Though I'm afraid Smoke's most exciting when you're coming and going. Just try and stay put your whole life." She smiled like the sun splitting open. Warm alabaster cheeks. Healing eyes.

"I might take you up on that dare," he said. "I might just do that very thing."

The gas tank on the Olds is nearly empty, the doctor's jacket, shirt and pants soaked in blood and gasoline. He hears the petrol *slosh, slosh* onto the ground, inhales the metallic odour of it, feels it settle on his lips like sweet berry wine. Buster watches trembling as blood drains from the doctor's fingertips like thermometers losing their mercury. He bends over and rests his ear to the old man's chest, his own wound fervid with pain. "Hang *on!*" He glances over his shoulder frantically and tries to pull the doctor's shirt open, release the bandages.

"No," whispers the old man. "Stop."

"Let me help," insists Buster. "You'll breathe better."

"Leave it." The doctor uses all of his remaining strength to resist.

"Keep your eyes open," Buster pleads. "C'mon, look at me." He shakes the doctor hard but he is fading. His lips are blue, almost purple. He is pigment, weight, limbs, cells and muscles, organs clunkering away like twin pistons in a race to the finish. Buster shakes harder the second time, opens the doctor's shirt, lifts his undershirt and tugs at the tight strips of gauze. He lies still, breathing shallowly as the boy struggles to unwrap him. A few of the blood-soaked bandages are loose, sagging away from his body, and the flesh beneath bulges out between the strips of gauze, stained brown. Buster lifts himself onto his knees, ready to pump the old man's chest. Tears fall like incomplete thoughts and pool in the hollow of the doctor's collarbone. Then he stops, recoils onto his boot heels, dizzy. What the hell? The doctor's chest is covered in red welts from the tight binding. Buster tugs off another bandage and sees two wrinkled, aged hills of flesh, as pale as milk, with darker centres. Breasts!? And gradually, as though placing a familiar face, his own skin shrivels and crawls away, disgusted. "Jesus!" He jerks back violently, reaches for his pistol with his free hand and waves it.

"What are you gonna do, shoot me?"

"Shut up!" Buster rocks back and forth. "Jesus Christ. For once shut your trap while I think." Saliva fills his mouth and the back of his throat closes. A hollow gesture anyway, reaching for the gun, for what is there to protect against? He drops his hand and the gun falls to the ground. His head pounds machine-gun fire. What is he looking at? Who is Doc John? He stumbles backwards, every conversation they've had tearing through his skull in fiery flashes—Detroit, Fingers Fontana, Raymond Bernstein. Solly Levine. He searches for a clear explanation. How can this be? Was *everything* a lie? The trees all around rustle like blank pages.

"It's just me," whispers the doctor. "You know me."

"No I don't. I don't know anything. You're a freak. A fraud!"

Doc John gives a weak laugh. "Me, a fraud?" He coughs up more blood. "C'mon now."

"This is impossible." Buster can hardly make himself look at the doctor, and when he does, he cannot pry his eyes from the old man's chest. "Who would … how … *why?*"

The doctor is shivering now. Desperate. "Well, haven't you wanted to look like somebody else?"

"Sure but what does that—"

"If there was a way." The doctor forces every word. "If there was a way to make your outside … match your inside again. Would you do it?"

"Course."

The doctor wheezes. "Me too."

Buster takes a deep breath and another peek at his friend lying upon the dusty side of the road. The motionless, half-naked body is not a man's, but what is it? It reminds him of tobacco after it's been topped—a clever weed manipulated into a whole new figure. Doc John has been a traveller in that traitorous home called skin. He has gone unseen though not invisible. What do you do when one of your own turns out to be a stranger? What about when that stranger is you? Buster glances over his shoulder and still no one is coming.

"You won't tell will you, son?"

Buster shakes his head. "But what do I do? I don't know what to do."

The doctor chokes on blood and bile. He smells smoke and gasoline and wet clothes, inhales deeply. "Help me finish it. You're the only one who can." Then, he closes his eyes and is still.

"No!" Buster hollers. "No please!" He falls to his knees, scrambles to replace the gauze strips. "See, it's okay. I'll cover you. No one will know." He curtains the doctor with his wet, bloody shirt. "We'll pretend this never happened. I didn't see a thing. Just don't go." But the doctor is already gone, across that last border, and Buster stares at his wrinkled face and weeps.

After a few moments he lifts his head, still feeling the doctor's tight and determined grip. He wipes his nose on his sleeve, thoughts scrambling. Soon the others will arrive. They will ask questions. Make judgments, and erase, erase, erase the doctor's life. They will see only ugliness and deceit, and want irrefutable facts. He mustn't allow it. He owes the doctor that much at least. Facts are dull dreary things, Buster thinks, dead things. He leans over the old man's body one final time to listen for a heartbeat and finding none, stands and clasps the matchbox tightly in his fist. The outside is nothing but kindling. The outside is all luck and chance and mad shadow tricks. Then, with fingertips cold and blue as if dipped in fresh ink, he slides the box open, lifts out one stick, shuts his eyes and strikes the match. It lights on the first try.

The quick, raspy sound of the match tip being dragged across the side of the oblong box is followed by the bright flicker of fire and all at once Buster spins backwards to the night of his accident. He trembles, that uncontrollable shaking again, only this time he doesn't refuse it. His throat closes as the scent of sulphur suffuses the air.

He opens one watery eye.

I made it.

And then the other eye.

I'm alive.

The lit match burns between his fingers. The doctor's lifeless form lies at his feet. He takes a deep breath and then he lets go.

He runs. He runs as far from the fire as he can and falls to the ground, scraping both knees through his good pants. He collapses in the middle of the road and turns to watch with unblinking eyes as the flicker of reds and oranges and blues snap in the breeze like clean sheets hung out to dry. A wave of heat rushes over him even from that good distance, and his throat is instantly parched, his skin tight. He covers his head as the car explodes, one small explosion and another larger, taking everything he thought he knew up into the sky with it and hurling it back down to earth. Glass shatters like diamonds and sharp rain. Pieces of debris fall like shrapnel. Chrome plate. Leather from the car seats, bits of tire and plastic, felt from the lining of his fedora, it all flies up and tumbles onto the dirt road, mixing with the stench of gasoline, oil, gauze and flesh burning. The searing heat dries his tears before they have a chance to fall.

He peers across to where the conflagration rages and out beyond it, squinting into the distance through the dense metallic fog as Donny's Chevy Bel Air races towards him, a faint blue flash against the bright green fields. The car is carrying Jelly Bean and Alice and closely behind follow a string of trucks. His father and mother with Lizzie. Walter and Hazel. Hank and Susan with George Walker. Len and Ivan Rombout. The parade of Miss Tobacco Queen contestants. Fire crackles and hisses and flames shoot off the Oldsmobile and blaze higher. A fine steel dust lines the inside of Buster's mouth and tastes of spoiled powdered milk. In this moment he realizes we are all confined first to our physical selves. Though not for good. Not forever. He reaches up with one hand and feels for the scars on his face. His skin is like wet twine, an engraved plaque. A badge of honour. His skin is the tobacco winding up from his father's fields like arms desperate to be received. Yes it's a hideous garment, because bodies are nothing if not read like books. He can see that now. But that is not all, and the rest he will just have to make up as he goes along.

Seconds later Tom shifts his Dodge into the highest gear and accelerates past Donny and the others, leaving them in his dusty wake. He slams on the brakes, skids his truck to a noisy stop, and is out of the cab before Isabel has time to gather Lizzie in her blanket, before any of the others have even parked. Tom's fear of losing Buster is unmistakable now, primal—a father who might not reach his son in time. He runs to Buster and tries to look him squarely in the eyes. "I'm here," he says, catching his breath. "I'm here now." Buster stares wordlessly through the thick wall of smoke, trying to make out Doc John's car, and Tom follows his son's gaze. His eyes sting. He places a rough hand on Buster's shoulder.

There is smoke everywhere, white, black, grey, curling and snaking up over the land. And there will be smoke long after this fire has burned down and the charred remnants have been cleared away. For Buster there will always be a twisting foggy mist in the sky, gold in the sunlight, silvery blue under the moon. It will be here when he has his next adventure and the next. Shrouding the village. Protecting. Calling them all home. Dark plumes converge overhead like a heavy, dead cloud, and with Doc John's last story guarded safely inside he steps out from under its shadow.

Meanwhile

A lean figure slips like a garter snake from the rear window of the
Bank of Commerce. He lifts a potato sack full of crisp twenty-dollar
bills from the ground where he dropped it, rises and saunters
blithely out onto the sidewalk and through the crowd without
attracting attention. He pulled it off. Easier than he thought. He
advances along Main Street, passes the greengrocer and the hardware store and the throngs eating cotton candy and ice cream. He
continues, without a backward glance, two miles west where he
crosses a newly primed tobacco field. A radio, accidentally left on
inside the farmhouse, plays loudly and a popular song by The
Platters drifts out. As the stranger disappears into the woods
behind the McFiddies' property, he slows to the pace of the ballad,
smiles triumphantly and sings it to the sky.

~~~

Note to Readers

I did a great deal of research preceding the actual writing of *Smoke*, and this included county records as well as books and newspapers of the period. Among these various sources was *South of Sodom*, a history of South Norwich by The South Norwich Historical Society, which included this intriguing aside: "Dr. James Barry, Inspector-General of Hospitals in Upper and Lower Canada, had been found to be a woman as he/she was laid out for burial."

Acknowledgments

This book was written with the support of the City of Toronto, through the Toronto Arts Council and the Ontario Arts Council's Writers' Reserve Program. St. Peter's Colony and the Saskatchewan Writers' Guild provided time and space to write, and Shelley Sopher helped to make that time bearable. I am grateful to everyone at Westwood Creative Artists, especially my agent, Hilary McMahon, for her never-ending enthusiasm and risk-taking. Also, I thank my publisher, David Davidar, at Penguin Canada, my patient and meticulous editor, Barbara Berson, and the entire Penguin team. The following people must be acknowledged for their assistance: Susan Charlotte Blanton, Erin Clarke, Sally Cooper, Mary Lou Crichton, George Davis, Mike Hicks, Maureen Hynes, Ruth and David Jackson, Alex Latoche, William Lenares, Judy Livingstone at the Delhi Museum and Cultural Board, John Miller, Andrea Németh, Isaac and Gretel Meyer-Odell, Shannon Olliffe, Kathleen and Pat Olmstead and The Ladies Bridge Group of Walkerton. Dr. Judith Perry. Linda Dawn, Joanne, Joyce, Marion, Hugh, Dorothy, and Sara Pettigrew. Laura Pettigrew D'Addario. Denise Phelps. Trish Salah for her course, Articulating Differences, Ron Smith, and Ralph Vuylsteke. A special thank you to Lee Pierssens for allowing this city girl to poke about on the family farm. Finally, I am indebted to the village of Otterville and surrounding region, for early and lasting inspiration.

❧

Sources

Numerous bibliographical sources were consulted. The following were most influential: Patrick Califia's *Sex Changes; Canadian Tobacco Grower Magazine,* May 1958 issue; C.H. Gervais's *The Rumrunners: A Prohibition Scrapbook;* Judith Halberstam's *Female Masculinity;* Paul R. Kavieff's *The Purple Gang: Organized Crime in Detroit, 1910–1945* and *The Violent Years: Prohibition and the Detroit Mobs;* Joanne Meyerowitz's *How Sex Changed;* Carl Morgan's *Birth of a City;* The South Norwich Historical Society's *South of Sodom; Springford Tweedsmuir History, Villages and Farms* by The Springford Women's Institute; Lyal Tait's *The Leaf of the Petuns: Tobacco in Canada;* and Diane Wood Middlebrook's *Suits Me: The Double Life of Billy Tipton.*